MW00882589

Fox Hunt

a novel

C.F. Forest

Stone x Stone
Publishing House

To the bravest I have ever known for loving me.

"Here is the difference between Dante, Milton, and me. They wrote about hell and never saw the place. I wrote about Chicago after looking the town over for years and years."

- Carl Sandburg

FOX

HUNT

_____   _____   ____   __ __:::

_____   _____   __   ___   ____   ___   _____   ____   ____   ____,

_   ____   ____   __   ___   _____   ___   ____   _____,

_   _____   _____,

1) pg 47 line 11 word 7
2) pg 127 line 30 word 9
3) pg 61 line 5 word 4
4) pg 6 line 11 word 7
5) pg 5 line 4 word 9
6) pg 126 line 30 word 10
7) pg 1 line 1 word 5
8) pg 4 line 20 word 4
9) pg 6 line 2 word 5
10) pg 99 line 1 word 2
11) pg 27 line 8 word 2
12) pg 41 line 5 word 2
13) pg 61 line 5 word 4
14) pg 39 line 2 word 3
15) pg 5 line 27 word 5
16) pg 42 line 11 word 5
17) pg 3 line 20 word 7
18) pg 2 line 6 word 9
19) pg 140 line 1 word 4
20) pg 7 line 30 word 8
21) pg 17 line 4 word 9
22) pg 80 line 14 word 2
23) pg 30 line 3 word 1
24) pg 145 line 2 word 12
25) pg 34 line 8 word 5
26) pg 45 line 13 word 5

Clue: He awoke every   day   to November 5th. He awoke to destroy
      keys.

CHAPTER ONE

No stars overhead to pretend to read.

Timber beams, not wispy clouds, above with brick to the sides. Men had walked these steps to a day's work nearly a century ago. Would they recoil at the click of my heels with each step? Did I defile the spirit of honest work done? Maybe they would have gawked. Maybe not even at me. I found myself doe-eyed at the gentleman on my arm.

God could've spoken to me, and I wouldn't have heard. The man struck the senses when dressed in formal wear. Black tie was the only option for the night, and Owen Lyon had a tuxedo molded to him. Paired with an alarmingly, albeit rehearsed, smile that invited danger and undress. He was solid to my touch. His proffered arm as my rail. He himself was my invitation in.

The gala location was clever. A nondescript, four-story brick building that blended in with the modesty of the industrial neighborhood. The interior recently converted. The intent to draw the visitor back to the industrial might of early 20th-century Chicago. Function over beauty for this one. But it lacked the trademarks of the horrid working conditions common to the time. Who was I not to romanticize the past, though? Authenticity at any cost.

Tonight was a celebration of "Discovered Art." Hosted by the Chicago Guild of Saint Luke. That was the name on the tip of culturally hip tongues throughout the city. It'd been explained to me that on this night, "The Guild" would heavily focus on unconventional sources of art. Proletariat, not bourgeois.

A pleasant young woman met us at the top of the stairs. She was young, at most twenty-one or twenty-two. Cute in an odd manner. She'd taken abstract to a permanent state of dress. Her gown was a collage of other gowns sewn together. It created a maelstrom of color on a strapless cut to bear her soft shoulders and still smooth skin. Her unhappiness with her assignment for the night was apparent in her defiant tone. Careful not to push the envelope too far, though. Eager to stay within the good graces of the benefactors. It was easier to climb when a hand reached down to pull you up. I knew from experience. Let youth have its well-tamed adventures.

Owen retrieved the invitation from his breast pocket and handed it over. A slight smile politely accompanied the motion.

"Mr. Lyon and…?" The girl's words dripped from her mouth as she fixated on him and his shine. For all her attempts to capture an edge, she'd been reduced to a fawning teenager struggling with a surge of hormones and attraction.

"Winona. Winona Winthrop." The severity and sternness of my response finally caused the girl to peel her gaze off Owen. Realization dawned on her as a slight blush appeared, and she refocused on the task at hand. Apparently, I wasn't alone in my assessment. Ever the British gentlemen, Owen hadn't even taken care to notice. His eyes fixated on me. I tried not to blush. I guess feeling like a teenager again wasn't so bad after all.

"Of course. Please do come in. The exhibit is designed to be an escalating experience of visual stimulation and thought-provoking exhibits where you will move in accordance with the guided posts."

Of course it was.

The large steel doors ahead appeared as if somebody had pulled them from furnaces the size of a bungalow. An inscription read "ALEA IACTA EST."

He mistook my reading for hesitation and leaned over.

"'The die is cast.' It is reported to be what Caesar stated when he crossed the Rubicon River. He departed as Governor of Gaul and marched a legion on Rome. Knowing the penalty of the action to be death, Caesar understood it to be a point of no return. It was a gamble played out like a throw of a die. He marched anyway, and the world still remembers the name."

"I preferred when you told me of Alexander and the knot." Men felt important when they told you things. Even things you already knew.

We walked through the doors as if they were grand gates. Standing before the room, I knew I'd come to drink in the painted treasures and create tension. My dress was low-cut with a slit cut high. My intentions bare and clear. I imagined Joan of Arc at Orleans. Concrete for a battlefield. Gowns for armor. Time to cross the Rubicon.

An hour slipped by, and I stood unscathed. I fought off yawns in the place of battle fury. A redeeming repetition kept me sharp. They all wanted to know how Owen Lyons and I had met.

A shared cab ride by chance. A rendezvous the next day at the Art Institute. A free walk that felt like an escape to a place where the magical and abstract seemed token. A lunar month later, this gorgeous man had made the most unexpected move. He placed a simple page of a book in my hand. The page ripped from the spine, the words redacted, leaving a trail to follow. A soft reciting, barely audible to those gathered around of what remained on the page, read:

"Don't know where you're going for one instant, for sparkling moonlight explodes when you smile to the howling darkness."

Hearts clutched. Eyes softened. Honestly, Owen's quip had been a Molotov cocktail to my heart. Language destined to be our beautiful highway to travel. Sentimental hack job, but it was authentic. To the crowd gathered here, authenticity was an elusive intoxicant. The night's theme may have been outsiders, but the guests were blueblood insiders.

A loop through the museum floor revealed that a natural order had asserted itself. First, the lords and ladies of high art held the purse atop the perch. Then, a notch below, the artists orbited around them to provide a handheld explanation of what they were looking at. Then came the bureaucrats – lawyers, academics, and bankers who graciously provided cover. Lastly, the politicians lent a veil of public concern. Each fiefdom had the requisite boxes checked.

A hand brought me back to reality as he found the small of my back and gently guided me forward. A gentleman who was in charge and directed the tour without hesitation. A girl's dream, but I couldn't help but wonder when the nightmare would come.

A new group of them to meet. Do I curtsey? Do I offer my hand? Fuck. How can I still stumble on etiquette?

Round and round the introductions went. Polite smiles. Hidden fangs. I took them in. They didn't hesitate to talk of ventures and deeds.

"Do you have any holiday tips for us?" The one named Amber turned to me. She was older than me. Fit for her age, though. A woman who cared. Her nails were recently done. Her red gown looked natural. The rest continued to chatter, but here Amber and her friend had turned into me. Were they taking a litmus test? Had they already sensed my idea of a family vacation was the crossing of a state border? Not the cross of an international one.

"I'm not sure I'm your best guide. I haven't taken a memorable one in a moment."

"What a pity," Amber said. "We've debated. Interlaken or Nice. Are you familiar?"

"The Mountains. A beach—" I said what I knew.

"Yes, darling, those are apt descriptions." Amber cast her eyes to her friend in amusement.

"—Neither," I finished.

"Neither?"

"You heard right. I prefer the woods. Deep. Dark. Mysterious. The beaches of Nice or the views of Interlaken? Beautiful. Like a post-card. But I'm not too fond of the obvious. I want to be lured in. In-vited in by the prospect of the unseen that watches. A proper forest is enchanting, even here in the heartland." They'd come to play an exotic card. I stripped them of their uniqueness and made their zenith a commercial. Beauty dimmed when bought.

"You do not prefer the obvious beauty?" She looked from me to Owen, who engaged with a soft man. "Darling, I think that close to home, you are more like us than you'd like to believe."

Fair point. I'd underestimated Amber. A veteran of the circuit. Sharp through years of pleasant conversational combat.

"Do you read, Winona?" I was surprised by the question. The soft man who had engaged Owen spoke to me now. Stephen, his name. The whole collection of them turned to face me. I was open season. I felt the beginning of movement from Owen to intercede on my behalf. My hand stayed on him with a light touch.

"Let's start with Tolkien."

"Fantasy?" Stephen's attire of a casual blazer molded around weak, downturned shoulders hiding a hastily buttoned Oxford should've made his occupation obvious. The need to prey on the per-ceived weak drove the point home—a professor. An overdramatic survey of the group followed the word.

"Fantasy born of a need to escape. A man who took his own personal tragedy and created worlds. You would need to have experienced life to understand, though. How deep the need can hit in your bones. You can't relate if you hide all your life in lectures."

His eyes came back sharp now. "I hope you'll forgive me, Winona. I seemed to have misjudged you. A modern Amelia Earhart to regale with tales of adventure."

"I'm afraid not. I would not want to keep you up at night."

"Did you get a bad tip as a waitress? Get a paper cut filing documents? Do not worry. Undoubtedly a level of trauma we can bear to hear. Where does our heroine gather her contact with risk? You have judged me correctly as a member of the academics, but we still need to place your profession for the context of this exchange," he said arrogantly.

"Murder," I quipped.

"Excuse me?"

"I'm a detective. Homicide detective. Murder is my business, Stephen." I delivered the line flat.

He was momentarily caught off guard. The surprise was evident on his face and the others. I caught a genuine smile from Owen momentarily.

"Ah. You're a police officer." He found his counter and didn't need to say more. He counted the label alone as a smear, conjuring an instant connection to a Gestapo force.

"Yet I still do not burn books."

"You might want to start with your copies of Tolkien and the like. It does not enrich an adult's life to keep the habits and genres of children."

"Would you prefer to burn the books or me? I might catch a chill at the stake, Stephen." A sly, playful smile to disarm the tension and a trace of the neck to push him over. "I hope I'm one fantasy worth keeping." Stephen's face blushed. What was more predictable, my weapon of choice or his fall for it? Elementary use of sexuality, but I didn't care.

Oh, but with one look over, it was clear I had tugged the tail a bit too hard. What a surprise—sculpted but not pliable. The others enjoyed the joust, though.

"Don't be so taken aback by Stephen." The voice carried from behind. I turned to a blonde with her hair pinned up, framing her natural, symmetrical beauty and accented by a blue teardrop pendant necklace adorned with stones. Here, class had been established, but not to be thought of as a burden. The light blue gown was stunning in fit and style. The result a timeless elegance that would look natural topped with a crown. It took more than God's gifts to accomplish the presence that had spoken. Gabrielle Jardin. Heir to a pharmaceutical fortune. A socialite you could not ignore.

Where I stood, my breasts felt smaller, my form emaciated, and I was acutely aware of the movement of my body as if I was skeletal—a lightbulb before the sun. The man with her engaged Owen at the same time. An odd pair they made. Barely a shadow in her presence. I doubt I would've even seen him if not for his conversation with Owen. He was outfitted in a loose-fitting tuxedo and carried a lackadaisical posture. The man's fingers laced together as he spoke to Owen.

"Stephen was harmless." I attempted to meet her on even ground.

"First name basis already? Comfortable here very quickly."

"Comfortable everywhere. Although which here do you refer to?"

"Among the Chicago Guild of Saint Luke, of course."

With that, the men turned their attention to us and made introductions. Guillaume, the strange man, introduced himself as Gabrielle's twin brother as though it was a title in and of itself. Then he drifted off in thought. Gabrielle let her stare linger like I was an animal at auction. "You are the femme fatale detective that is the talk of the night? I've been dying to meet you." The appraisal quick and efficient.

"What a way to frame it. I'm Winona."

"Gabrielle. But call me Gabi." She offered her hand. How natural she was at this.

Overcoming a slight smile, Gabrielle focused back in on the fight. "Owen Lyon is quite a catch; I'm not sure anyone has been able to sit him down for this long. Those Old Harrovians run wild in the blood, but you are pretty in your own way."

"I've already made an Eaton boy blush. Figured it's time I set myself to a true challenge." A girl from Bridgeport did her research before letting a man into her life. Of course, it didn't hurt that the neighborhood bartender hailed from Liverpool and was more than happy to tutor me on the intricate social life of British society.

"No need to ruin a perfect night with talk of that other place!" Owen interjected. His face finally relaxed to show more emotion, and talk of boarding school commenced–British, the States. I found myself a true outsider.

As they conversed, my mind wondered if there'd been a physical history between the two. Owen rambled on unabated in relative comfort, but his gaze didn't isolate on the woman. Possibly a deep fake on his part. His eyes and smile found me, though.

I caught myself in an attempt to pull her twin into conversation. I wanted the bitch to watch. A sliver of me wished for Owen to watch, but I found no footing. Guillaume provided no ability for a solid back-and-forth. He met my inquiries with one-sentence responses that lacked in the reciprocal. Reality went to one twin and creativity to the other, apparently.

I stood ready to throw in the evening glove when the strange man spoke unprompted: "Curiosity and imagination spring much greatness."

As I began to engage him, Gabrielle cut in quickly. His spontaneous line had finally caused her to break from Owen. "Guillaume has always been cursed with a soft heart and strange fascinations."

"When you walk down the street slaying dragons, it can be entertaining," I said, surprising myself with how quickly I came to his defense. Before I knew it, I'd pushed another boulder down the hill. "You'd be surprised what you can find beyond the estate's walls, Gabrielle. I've shown so much to Owen. You wouldn't believe how he has taken to life with a little more creativity. He positively howls for more." Let your imagination run with that, bitch. Peace had quickly arrived and quickly gone.

And with one disappointed look from Owen, I knew I'd again crossed the line. He fumbled to an excuse about how we "must see the next exhibit" and ushered us away down the walkway. One last look at Gabrielle Jardin. She stood and smiled as she and Guillaume conversed with rapt attention on a hanging tapestry. Owen followed my vision and looked back but didn't give her open dress backside that framed her heavenly assets more than a momentary glance in goodbye. Men would march to their doom behind that silhouette, but the consummate gentleman remained in control here. Why did I want him to lust after her, even if only for a split second? The competition? The rage that comes with jealousy? He could be too stiff in all the wrong ways.

"Thank you for playing nice," Owen relented.

"You think that was nice?"

"For you, yes," he followed with a genuine smile. Not the well-rehearsed handshake of a smile he would use to melt a room. Instead, the smile of a man who genuinely seemed to be present in the moment with me.

And with that, the warmth of hope settled deep in the bones. His way of making me feel less like a stranger in an unfamiliar land lent me the hope that he was more than a starlit sky to gaze upon. That he would roll through with thunder and lightning too. Determination to experience the power of his emotions unleashed reverberated deep inside me. But, in the meantime, I didn't have to look to the sky to believe I read the stars.

"Owen, do you know where the name Chicago Guild of Saint Luke comes from?"

"I had the same question. I am happy you asked. The 'Guild of Saint Luke' was a guild for artists, sculptors, painters, and lovers of exhibit in European cities during the Renaissance. Seats of power that regulated and controlled the art economy. You can draw your natural conclusion."

"Power."

"Precisely."

The tour continued. His body never wavered in direction or indecision. Exhibit after exhibit, his education showed value. He could've been conjuring it all up, but each step brought us to where the night needed to crescendo. A deep nook in the wall stood recessed in near absolute darkness. Like any decent officer at heart, I scanned ahead for the potential home of danger. I was to be the danger, though.

I took firm control of both Owen's lapels and pulled him into the recessed carve out. The breadth of his natural size in shoulders and chest swallowed my entire body. My back hit the wall, and the momentum of the pull landed Owen's body hard-pressed against my own. His chest rose and fell against mine. Both hearts worked furiously. There wasn't a sliver of light between us. Time suspended as our eyes connected. Our lips mere millimeters apart. I brought him this far and simply needed him to lean in. I could handle the rest. Instead, he paused and cupped my face. With a whisper, he tried to be ice to fire. He didn't realize he stood already on the tracks and the train was coming.

"Let's see how blueblood truly flows." Burn the entire fucking house down with a match if you have to.

My knee slid along his inseam, and I felt his body betray his words. His blood flowed precisely how I wanted. In that moment, his perfect granite cracked. Owen finally blinked and lowered his gaze. It was all his.

"Not now, dear." And with that, he offered his hand to guide me as if we were on the street and I were too delicate to walk through a puddle. I wanted to jump in the puddles. Would he ever understand that? Or was his world so consumed by rails and guidelines that I was seeking the impossible?

I smoothed my dress. We exited the escape. Painted smiles back on our faces. How hollow it all was. Polite greetings enveloped us as the now caught-up stragglers welcomed us back to the fold. The floating islands of conversation were interchangeable. The dresses were different, but the passion was always absent wherever we went. I can't die slowly.

"I'm going to freshen up. Continue on, and I'll catch up with you." I needed to get out of here.

The service door beckoned. I looked back and admired what I was walking out on. Dear Lord, even the light molds around the man. If only he would stroll in the dark for a bit.

Bare hallways and flights of concrete steps. Quick steps to freedom. Or was it an escape? Fleeing? Each lens different.

The stairway gave way to the street. The city sidewalk quieter. Just west of the loop we were, but industry, not people, reigned here. Green St. gave way to Randolph St. Vagrant eyes still leered from alcoves and processing loading docks. The Chicago Guild of Saint Luke was a star unannounced tonight. Red dress and white-gloved doe walking like she was lost in an open field. I must look like easy prey.

A damsel in distress was in trouble because she was stuck in place—time to get moving. I extended a leg and hand into the air. Luck struck. The wait was short. A yellow carriage fresh from the expressway. The driver as eager to move the wheels as I was.

"Where to, my lady?" Asked the driver in a playful tone.

It was time to trade bowties for neck tattoos.

"The Ossuary. Fullerton and Ashland, monsieur."

---- -------- ----

The plastic lining creaked with any movement I made. Cigarette smoke permeated the fabric, but the windows were clear. I watched the pavement pass beneath us. People used to endure unspeakable hardship over multiple days to travel mile by mile, and here I was, running away from the appetizers, slightly annoyed by the residue of cigarettes. Pathetic.

West of the Loop gave way to neighborhoods. Men on payphones the only constant. Street by street we rolled, and the regular flow of the city became more abundant.

I counted streetlights. Witnessed the peaks and valleys of prosperity. Pristine flowerboxes to overflowing trashcans and back. Finally close. I'd left, and that was that. Camelot had no use for me. I would never be his wife, anyhow.

"We have arrived, mademoiselle."

"Merci beaucoup, mon hero."

I fumbled through my purse and realized the bills would smudge my white gloves. The driver noted the hesitation and insisted he took the most feasible route. $3.25 due. $5 given. Keep the change, please.

One step out, and I was on my own. I inhaled the free air and took in the unremarkable building standing squat. Another brick building. Two stories, a single block glass window wrapped in rolled steel, with a sign advertising Pabst Blue Ribbon above the door. No drawbridge here. Enter at your own risk. I marched in without hesitation.

The lighting was terrible. The walls were pinned with flyers advertising concerts. Music obnoxiously fast and loud. The place was benighted. It was an assault on the senses. A constant undercurrent of violence lingered. Nature couldn't just be seen in a forest. Cinderella had indeed left the ball. Little Red Riding Hood now needed to make it to Grandma's house.

The bar beckoned as that house. The tables were socially crowded. People kept to their own. No one willing yet to take the title of Gavrilo Princip. Give it time and drinks. Actual Molotov cocktails.

I walked slowly to embrace the heel status. The benefits of working around men never ended. I endured the turned heads and slight grins from men and women alike. The bar had stayed the same, scarred and beaten with nearly every other stool off-kilter. The crowd grew tired of gawking and returned to brooding. My elbow rested on the bar, chin in hand, and fingers tap, tap, tapped the bar. I was already old news.

What did a girl have to do to get service, though? Fine, he can win this time. Stubbornness was in the bones. I waited and watched him serve three customers and engage them in conversation and give recommendations after each one—a ringmaster who never tired of his trade.

"JOHNNY BONES!"

The barkeep with the pompadour, clinging black shirt, and Levi's finally broke down with an about-face. Theatrics in the walk itself. Toothpick moved from left to right, and hands smoothed the sides of the ducktail into form. He was a caricature, but it worked for him.

"Hello, love. Long time between getting lost."

I launched myself over the bar and threw my arms around his neck. I took in his embrace and thanked the Lord that the stool supported the movement. His emaciated physique surprised me again with its solid composition. You would've expected him to crumple or snap like a twig with a slight breeze.

Perhaps that was how he earned his nickname. No one knew his Christian name.

I knew he had stepped in so many years ago when I needed him. A smoke break and a flag down of a patrol car. The men who stepped out in uniform did the rest. A night where a predator became prey.

"My guardian angel. How are you, Winnie?"

"Decent, I suppose, Johnny." He watched my fingers tracing the nicks and crevices of the bar. What an odd infatuation he had. People took an interest in the small gestures if they genuinely paid attention.

"You've been climbing ladders again. Where have you been playing debutante?

"I won't bore you with the details. The hands of that clock have done more work than the hands in the room I was in. People who live soft die soft, ain't that right, Johnny?" My voice was always soft with him. I could feel his lifetime of hardship. I never wanted to add to it.

"That's right, love," he said with a raspy laugh and deep cough. "But don't be stealing my lines. Took all that I have to come up with so little."

"You're the wealthiest man I know."

"Alright. A man can only take so much pumping. What can I get you?"

"The usual, please."

"Water, lemon, and ice it is, love." Prompt delivery and then off to quiet the Visigoths.

The corner of the bar was my refuge. You could trace your own constellations and still have a full vantage of the place. For a carnival of humanity, the herd mentality was staggering. Leather studded jackets and ripped jeans could be a polo and dockers here. Everything was relative.

But what do we have here at the end of the bar? A man of stern disposition with a severe focus on the backstop shelves. He spared glances for nothing and no one, let alone me. Socially isolated and content. What secret did he know?

Is my hair still together? A quick adjustment and peek down to ensure the assets were still in prime positioning.

He captured my full attention, and I couldn't even get a glance? Still nothing. He seemed to move in slow motion in comparison to the surroundings. Easy on the eyes with his dark hair in shambles, jawline cut from stone, and a plain white t-shirt. He was not majestic or powerfully built like Owen, but he was svelte and seemed to cast a large shadow. With every movement, his disciplined muscles rippled.

He'd do. Thoughts accompanied by a jostle of ice. Johnny wouldn't miss the quarter left behind. I'd make a note to pay him back a few times over.

My slide off the stool in a dress proved more difficult than I imagined, lest I advertise to the entire bar. Now the crowd parted when I walked. People naturally melted away in my path. It felt preordained. Primal desires to well up with each step. Biology was hitting full stride tonight.

Once I was within meters of him, he snapped his head around. His eyes bore into me. His crystal blues instantly stopped the click-clack of my heels and gave my breathing a pause. Again. Stoicism personified who he was.

The back foot just wouldn't do for me tonight. I flipped the quarter into the air. He caught it and slammed the coin down with his hand, trapping it to the bar. Barely a smile grazed his lips as I closed the gap. The air was electrified, the eye contact unwavering. I placed my heel at the foot of his stool, conveniently causing him to sit a bit wider. I leaned in.

"Heads, I turn around. Tails, I sit right here."

He lifted his hand from the bar. Two pairs of eyes moved to see what fate decided. Heads. Before I could parlay the lost situation, he turned the coin over to tails. His hand gripped me by the backside and pulled me in. He staked his claim.

"You're a wild one."

"Wild ones never die."

A man who desired and took. Finally.

CHAPTER TWO

Owen hadn't answered my calls for a week. Why? The same short inquiry rattled in my head like a pinball with the power of a wrecking ball. The ride was why, wasn't it? Was it worth it? In the moment, yes. But another dead end. What had he thought when I left? What had he thought of the messages left on his answering machine? People had proper self-destructive tendencies in relationships, but I sowed salt in the soil. I wanted to burst through to a spiritual plane to batter my physical self.

I needed to atone. The man who flipped the quarter had taken me to sanctified ground. A graveyard. A small, abandoned chapel. The walk on the dark side masked the disrespect and shame I felt now. With the night's memories, I closed my eyes to fight any tears that might materialize.

I imagined myself back home, staring out at a storm rolling in from the front porch. I recalled the feel of the wooden planks beneath my bare feet and the slow chorus of nature's power building that broke the world's sleep—all to be ripped away and replaced in my early adolescence by a move to the city.

A city stuck in a parochial past. You could live the vast majority of your life in a neighborhood, and you would still be an outsider. You arrived in fifth grade and were constantly reminded that you weren't from here. That designation was a birthright, and the feudalism that followed tinged their blood. Citizens were seen more as serfs tethered to a series of city blocks. Spend one's youth defending the border blocks, meet a neighborhood girl, buy a house a few blocks from your parents, grave plot preplanned. Tip your hat to the political machinations of the establishment, and you might even covet a few additional scraps. The age of barons never left Chicago.

--- ---- -------

Recognition of my name being called on the detective floor prompted me to open my eyes and let the fluorescent lights torture me for my sins. I nearly knocked the coffee from my desk. Thirty-two watts to burn you and a cheap faux leather office chair for a stake slowly killed your spirit but left your body relatively untouched. Welcome to 20th-century purgatory without the guide.

The detective floor was arranged loosely as a cluster of desks facing one another. Each one stacked with folders, loose papers, and permanent marker scribbled files. In one corner, men grumbled and pored over the documents, but the majority here were still in love with the job. They coalesced around a lifetime of working-class experience—one of the last authentic vestiges of adventure available to the willing.

The world had become safe. The country had been fully expanded. The world was mapped, but it was still uncertainly wild in the corners of a concrete jungle. Order in the city achieved by a brutal combination of intellect and willed physicality. Often the latter more than the former. I contemplated how little on the detective floor had changed compared to the outside. The bones of the building dated to the turn of the century, and its inhabitants could be taken back to the time of construction and not miss a beat. They had no idea how lucky they were.

I stared down the route to the sergeant's summons. Sergeant Hartes, a man of advancing years, waited patiently. Competent in his role. The consensus on the floor only lukewarm. They hesitated to embrace him, and I never knew why.

"You caught one, Winnie," he barked over the desk. My eyes raised from the framed family photographs on the desk. A wife and three children to cling to like a buoy. His priorities were always straight, and that deserved respect. A roll call of divorcées could take all night, after all. Maybe that is another reason he caught so much flack. Detectives came in for assignments and saw a happy man with constant reminders of a still-together family to dote on. It had to eat at them. They could let work turn into their true home and purpose. He shattered that mirage.

"I asked you not to call me that."

"I know. Why do you think I do, Winthrop?" The slight smile that accompanied wasn't malicious or arrogant—he simply tried to jostle me like the other men on the floor. Not every aspect of equality I thanked the heavens for sharing. He couldn't have known, anyway.

"Do you still read?"

This fucking question.

"I do." My mind shot out of the starting gate to get ahead of where the lane ended. His eyes remained locked in. Yes, I had carried a book with me for as long as I can remember. The instant escape, the ability to feel—books had given me solace. Not to mention, the ability to pass the time. No one ever told you how much waiting was involved in detective work. The mechanics of the department moved at a glacial pace in response to being needed. Maybe he was half a jackass and simply continuing to get under my skin ever so gently by going after a clear love of mine. He didn't seem like the type, though.

Steadily, he leaned forward with his elbows resting on the desk and his hands held in suspended animation. All playfulness vanished from his expression as he looked for words.

"Do you want me to show you how a library works?" I quipped. The attempt to break the tension ignored.

"You caught a body."

"Okay. What do we have?"

"Hyde Park University. Preliminary information related an open throat. But, a cryptic note," he continued his newfound stoicism.

"A note?"

"That's all I have. The officers mentioned it, and the rest is your job. They are holding the scene with the callout witness. Hansen is going with you."

"The taxman? Wonderful. If a leg needs to be broken, then we're set."

"Nick made sergeant. You're floating right now, so you take who is available."

I wrapped my head around the development. Nick had been a solid partner. Solid in that we both stayed away and allowed the other to work. Griffin Hansen had time on the job but was late to detective. Having spent two decades working on plain clothes teams, he'd developed a reputation in a land of reputations. He moved deliberately. It was said that others did the catching when an offender ran, but Hansen ensured the running tax was paid.

"Lay off it. You might be surprised." I hated being read so easily. He had started with a bite but slowly let a smile creep across his face as he finished and reclined to the squeak of the chair. I'd been gripping the chair handles myself. An imprint of sweat left slickly behind.

I momentarily returned to my desk. In truth, the week hadn't left me yet. Normal people met one another, fell in love, and raised families, but had to endure a workday they despised. A cosmic joke, how inverted it was for me. Blessed by work but perpetually loathing any foundation of love. Time to see how blessed at the scene I had been.

-- --- ----

"Call me Finn. Griffin makes me sound like a vestige of a children's book." He said it without breaking the view over the steering wheel. We continued our way to the scene. It had beaten his previous high count of three words strung together. Loquacious this one. Without asking, he'd opted to drive. You could catch the street still singing to him. His eyes momentarily glanced at porches of abandoned buildings and into cars that passed. He still felt the pulse of it all. At least he had the instincts to go along with his rumored heavy hands.

"I can handle that, Finn."

A smirk for acknowledgment. I knew his reputation but wondered what he'd heard about me. It was a near monopoly of men on the job. Be friendly, and it's an invitation. Be removed, and you're a queen of ice. His nearly a dozen words on the drive had yet to give me much of an idea into his constructed view of me. That would be bound to change. Murders were a box, and both of us were in it now.

The boulevard system was a series of garden medians, significant in width, that wound through the city and connected parks. We traveled it right to the University. At the turn of the century, the greystones that dotted along the boulevards were the social corridors of the well-off. Now the buildings were boarded up, trash strewn, and stood in various states of urban decay. Adult males pretended to converse aimlessly as they stood along the fence lines. Peddlers of poison stood eager to spread the joy to dope sick customers. Venture inside these once-grand residences to see a nail driven through white marble that's a century old, and you would gasp. Let the people collapse in on themselves, but the treasure? Save the treasure.

The campus opened as we approached the lake—a flower to bloom out of the surrounding desert of violence. A marked car parked outside a gothic building of large cut rectangular stone. Ivy climbed the façade, and gargoyles ominously loomed at the peaks. One of several structures that created a uniform design, imposing a collective template reaching through time.

Once Finn parked the car, he pulled out a cigarette as we sat. I tugged on my jacket sleeves and idly looked out the window. Anyone else and I would have shot out an objection and asked for courtesy distance when smoking, but I kept fidgeting. Maybe he needed the drag. When you don't know a man's story, you tend to fill it yourself. From the dark recesses, I had already painted a Greek tragedy for his story. A cigarette might be his only current reprieve. Why deprive a man of an escape? I had my vices, after all. It would justify the timid nature that had overtaken me with the familiar smell. The torrid memories that accompanied.

"Does it bother you?" He asked as he dragged the cigarette down, and it faintly faded a bit more.

"No, it's fine. My dad used to smoke."

"Let me know if you change your mind."

I'll let you know if my courage returns, I thought.

---   --------

The officers holding the scene were young. The key tell sign was their equipment—not worn down yet. They held the exterior yellow crime scene tape under a gated archway with a keystone engraved with Latin leading to the campus common. An attempt of casualness betrayed by the tenseness of their muscles as they stood. Young and fit, the officer on the right's forearm rippled as he gripped his belt in front of the holster. He felt the hate from the neighborhood and struggled to process it. He was black, but to the student body, he was the police—a heathen amongst intellectuals. Go deep into Englewood or Garfield Park, and you felt the hate, but there you were as common of a sight as a blade of grass. There, you were a passing annoyance who could potentially upend a day. Here, in the heart of academia that groomed world leaders and thinkers, you were the scorn of the earth. The hate was palpable and lingering. To be detested from the students' island of relative safety struck differently. Workers of the world unite rallies, but from ten thousand feet. Read the signs, kid. It was etched on the faces that passed. It had been on Stephen, the professor.

"Our sergeant, the paper car, and evidence technicians are inside. The scene is through that side door and down the hall. The office is about three doors in, but you'll see them. Not much space."

We gave a nod and quick thanks.

The red tape marked the interior crime scene. Where money was made. Finn lifted the tape and let me take the first steps through the barrier. The evidence technician's camera bloomed with overpowered bright flashes. Its presence made you feel like you were walking a red carpet in 1950s Hollywood. The camera looked to be from the same era.

The evidence technician neared completion of the scene photographs and processing. A heavyset sergeant stood and tapped the wooden handle of his revolver with his index finger on his right hand and patted down his thick mustache with his left. Likely a sunset or two from retirement. The dreams danced clearly in his mind. We were the kids to him.

"How are you? What do we have?" I started with the softballs.

"You have a white male victim, thirty-eight years old. Peter Hickey. He's a political science professor here at the University. Currently seated in an office chair with a deep laceration across the throat. Damn near ear to ear."

"The call mentioned something about a note?"

He flashed a grin. "Aye, yes. A note attached to his lapels. I'll leave it to you professionals to discern anything else from that particular detail." He looked over and past me. Then, with a snap, the good sergeant turned his attention. "Good to see you, Finn."

Finn stepped forward and shook the sergeant's hand, meeting the grin.

"Sounds like you miss your old job. Your pension won't, though."

The sergeant laughed and shook his head. Once again, I was an outsider. Even here. The men continued catching up on small talk, and the chatter faded into the background. I continued alone to the office. Where the body was.

The office wall held a framed sign complete with a wooden handle attached for protest purposes. The message called for an end to apartheid. Another wall of shelves covered with thick books and small framed photographs. Upon closer inspection, the photographs contained large groups of what appeared to be students gathered around our victim. The photograph backdrops ranged from lush greens on cliffs to St. Petersburg Square. Plenty of photo documentation to commemorate involvement in protests against Vietnam.

Expanding out, the office was moderately large for a professor in a building confined by the space of being built nearly a century ago. It had enough room for a small sitting area, furnished with a table and two chairs. The chairs looked exceptionally stiff and didn't appear to be inviting a long chat by a fire. A game of chess set on the table seemed to be in mid-play. A large wooden desk dominated the other side of the room. Papers strewn about gave the impression of a chaotic workspace. A Rolodex prominently rested atop several stacked books. Behind the desk sat our victim. He hadn't moved since I walked in. How rude of him.

He was positioned upright in an oversized office chair that seemed unnecessarily plush. The wood handles were ornate in detail with gold inlaid. Moreso a throne than a chair. Blood streamed down the victim's chest to stain his button-down. Armani button down, I should clarify—a professor with expensive taste. The paper clipped to his lapels. Held on with just a paper clip. The blood gathered and dried behind it.

"Right to work?" I nearly startled at Finn's voice bearing in from a few feet over my shoulder. He moved quietly for a large man. "There was no sign of forced entry. The door and frame are much too old to have hidden any damage. Makes you think the offender was known." He had a sharp mind for a brute too. I nodded in agreement. Instinct told me it was competition, but it was not, I reminded myself.

Finn closed the gap on the victim. He began to examine the wounds. Leaned in on the note. I stopped by the desk. I drifted a paper aside with the end of my pen. Finn heard my sudden inhale and turned. He then noted what I had uncovered in the sea of papers. Three Polaroids. The same three people in each.

In the first picture, two men stood behind a woman in a chair. The men were in suits. The woman in a shimmering cocktail dress. The men wore masks that looked to be animals, covering three-quarters of their faces. I leaned in. One man in an off-white mask seemed to resemble a canine. Touches of turquoise, yellow, and red were painted upon it, with feathers affixed behind the ears. The second man wore a mask of black and grey with more aggressive canine features. Markings of white and red adorned it. The woman's face remained bare. She was young. Her smile made her look happy.

In the second picture, the positioning was the same with one distinct difference: the man in the black mask now held a large blade to the woman's throat. Her head tilted slightly up towards him. A fainter smile this time. A smile that reached for trust.

The third picture. I did not look away. The woman's head dipped. The man in the off-white mask gripped a handful of the woman's hair.

She had stayed in place. Blood or red liquid ran down the front of her dress. The black-masked man held a dripping knife at his side.

"Do you think it's real?" Finn broke my concentration. He had given my mind an escape, though. The possibility it was a staged act hadn't initially occurred to me. The girl's trusting smile seemed too real. Too hard to fake.

"I don't know."

Finn gestured to our victim. The note. I examined it closer now. I took it in. Typewriter written, formatted harshly. A small fox that looked to be produced by a rubber stamp ran along the side of the paper. A marriage of a game of hangman and a book. I reviewed it.

____ _____ ____ ___...

____ _____ __ ___ ____ ___ _____ ____ ____ ____.

_ ____ ____ __ ___ _____ ___ ____ _____.

_ _____ _____.

1) pg 47 line 11 word 7
2) pg 127 line 30 word 9
3) pg 61 line 5 word 4
4) pg 6 line 11 word 7
5) pg 5 line 4 word 9
6) pg 126 line 30 word 10
7) pg 1 line 1 word 5
8) pg 4 line 20 word 4
9) pg 6 line 2 word 5
10) pg 99 line 1 word 2
11) pg 27 line 8 word 2

12) pg 41 line 5 word 2
13) pg 61 line 5 word 4
14) pg 39 line 2 word 3
15) pg 5 line 27 word 5
16) pg 42 line 11 word 5
17) pg 3 line 20 word 7
18) pg 2 line 6 word 9
19) pg 140 line 1 word 4
20) pg 7 line 30 word 8
21) pg 17 line 4 word 9
22) pg 80 line 14 word 2
23) pg 30 line 3 word 1
24) pg 145 line 2 word 12
25) pg 34 line 8 word 5
26) pg 45 line 13 word 5

Clue: He awoke every day to November 5th. He awoke to destroy keys.

I reviewed it again. And again. Strange way to cipher.

"He awoke every day to November 5th. He awoke to destroy keys." I found myself repeating.

"The plot thickens." Finn looked over, and I followed his gaze. The off-white mask stood affixed on an intricate display stand. It was on a higher shelf. Easily missed at eye level. I looked closer, and it became clear. A coyote mask.

The rest of the room became the focus—no black mask to report. Instead, a fine leather carry-on with an open zipper sat next to the table where chess had been played. Inside sat bundles of cash.

"Who would carry out the murder but leave the cash?" I asked without expecting a reply.

---- ---- ----

We settled into what looked like a seldom-used cafeteria. The floor reverberated with the sound of our steps. We passed vending machine after vending machine, ready to dispatch sugar in all its forms.

The janitor stayed standing as we settled into the cheap chairs. After our insistence, he finally sat down. We introduced ourselves to the unfortunate man who had discovered the victim. Gavin Halfpenny. The surname he gave us matched the embroidery over his breast pocket.

"You're a custodian here?"

"Yes, ma'am. Paychecks say the University name and all."

"How long have you worked here?"

"Four, maybe five years now. I work the graveyard shift usually."

"Night to morning can be rough. The body's clock never quite adjusts. Any chance of being able to work a better shift in the near future?"

"It's by choice for me. I prefer the moon to the sun."

The attempt to relate via a shared sympathy for work conditions hadn't landed. Still, he'd been decently receptive, if not overly enthused, to speak. Maybe the product of a past arrest. Who knows. Who cares. We needed to know how he found the victim, what he saw, what he heard. He probably needed the job.

"Solid recognition, Halfpenny. You know which god in the Pantheon to worship. For what brought us here, can you walk us through your shift?"

He flinched slightly, kept his eyes downcast, and moved to cross his arms in front of his torso.

"Apologies, all this has me startled, and I've always been told to be careful around sirens."

"You could have a pound of blows on you all packaged up, and I wouldn't care. I'm here on what happened in office 018, and that's all. So don't worry about anything else." He needed to know any habit he had didn't bother me.

"Fair, Detective. Well, I'm a man of routine, to be honest. I was on schedule. I start work in the offices. That way, I can work through cleaning and removing the waste in each room without worrying about the corridor. I can circle back on the corridor with a mop for this wing before the sun rises usually."

"And take me to office 018. Where were you before?"

"Well, I had just finished taking the collected trash to the dumpster. You see, this wing has a ramp with a long slight incline. By the end of the shift, when I'm tired, I'm thankful it's here. It makes for a much easier push. Limits the chance of it all rolling away. Enough trash can feel like a boulder." He paused and held his stare at the ground before a slight chuckle was produced.

"Something come to mind?"

"No, ma'am, it's just that here I am talking to two detectives after finding a dead man, and I'm yarning on about a dumpster."

"You can stop with the 'ma'am' too. I'm younger than you, and I've had a hell of a week. No need to make me feel even more withered."

"Alright, Detective. I finished and headed down the line here. At 018, I knocked and opened the door and saw him sitting in the chair with the blood and everything."

"You knocked?"

"I always knock at 018. He kept odd hours. It wasn't unusual for him to be there working till the sun came up."

"How far did you make it into the room?"

"Maybe a few steps before I realized it all. I shouted, 'He dead!' I went scrambling for help or a phone."

"You realized he was dead quickly."

He snapped his eyes up with alarming speed to meet mine. His hair hung over his forehead, disheveled, but he radiated intensity despite the mess. "I was in the Corps. Served, ma'am. I know when a man is dead."

"0311 myself." Finn leaned forward as he spoke. What he said put noticeable ease back into Halfpenny. A handshake cemented the moment and moved me to the stands of the arena. Again.

"Where did you go after you got out?" Finn took the reins now. Moved to build trust.

"Phoenix, but the business there can be rough, so I left and bounced around a bit. Made my way here. Large enough city to get lost when you don't know anyone."

"Can't say I blame you for working graveyard. I used to prefer it too," Finn continued. "About what time did you knock and walk in?" Maybe he'd sensed my frustration and tension. He worked it back the way I wanted.

"Maybe six? I ran to the receptionist desk and used the phone damn right away, so when the call came in, it can't be more than a few more minutes from when I walked in."

Time to force my way back in. "You mentioned it wasn't unusual for him to be working through the night. Did he keep company? Can't imagine his office hours took place that early or that late."

"All due respect, ma'am, I don't wish to speak ill of the dead, but it looked like office hours on more than a few occasions. I still have offices and rooms to clean. Do you mind if I get on with it? I tend to keep a low profile with the bosses and don't want that to change."

"No problem. A couple of last items before you go on your way. Did you get a clear look at anything in the room?"

"I didn't see much of anything except the body and blood."

"Take my card. We'll follow up, but if anything else strikes you, call this number, and we'll be notified."

He rose and walked out the door. Trash didn't stop for murders. Working folk did not have the luxury of mourning each sad encounter. Finn and I sat silently in the chairs that would be returned to a stackable position when this was all done. I ran the photographs through my head again. The note too. A literary quagmire.

Finn grated his hand over his unshaven face and blurted out, "He's a killer, but not a murderer."

"The janitor?"

"Yea. It becomes obvious when you talk to guys who went. He killed and came home, but not the same. I'm sorry, Winona. I shouldn't have jumped in like that when you were controlling the conversation. It's just I thought when he knew I'd been there too, he'd relax a bit more. He didn't. He carried the tension in his shoulders the entire time like the shadows still moved. I know plenty of guys like that. Guys who survived in Vietnam. They came home and sought out silence. Wanted nights to be left alone. You heard him—he recoiled when talking about Phoenix. Have you been? It's sunny with beautiful, happy people. He acted as if it were Siberia. That man is happy shoveling shit as long as he is left alone."

"Nah, haven't been, but I hear it's a time." I settled back in the chair with a grin and met his eyes level before he bellowed out a laugh. It made me happy to hear him laugh. I hated myself for worrying he was about to slip into a veteran's coma on me. "I was thinking on the note…."

"Yea?"

"It doesn't sit right with me. It seems an excessive memento to include alongside whatever those photographs were."

"It could all be misdirection, complete coincidence, or the keystone. Overly theatric, but what we do have is the late-night office hours. Either way, we need to notify the next of kin and talk about the cash."

CHAPTER THREE

The Professor's residence was nestled on a one-way street off Jackson Blvd just east of Ashland Ave. The border of Little Italy in the city. An idyllic canopy of trees arched over the sidewalk. Each brownstone looked back to the turn of the century, most framed by a wrought iron gate. A dense city dwelling placated with suburban uniformity. The freedom to live wildly within the city while coloring inside the domestic lines.

The steps to the front door were quite peaceful. I may have been too harsh in my immediate assessment. Finn didn't seem to care one way or the other about the block. He hadn't revealed an opinion even when I probed.

The University had passed along the Professor's emergency contact as his wife, Miriam Hickey. She welcomed us graciously. Her reaction varied when it came to the notification. A steely internalized grief or a complete breakdown accompanied by shrieks and wailing. You became callused to the situation, or so you told yourself. The exception was when children were involved. In those cases, you simply asked for strength to make it through each minute as they never did.

I was surprised by Miriam's youth. Only a little younger than me, mid-to-late twenties. She wore a pretty air, if not overpowering. Interesting soulmate for the middle-aged, intellectually cloistered man I'd developed in my mind upon view of his work sphere. She took the news hard. Her legs gave way, and she folded into a greeting chair in the foyer. Recovered, she now sat at the kitchen table with us. Brown eyes stared out the window. The black Labrador she called Yo-Yo stayed nestled into her legs. Dogs knew emotion better than us.

"I haven't had a cigarette in four years. We'd been trying for a baby, and everything that could tip the scales in our favor, we agreed to. Thought it would be good energy to put out and show the universe we were serious. That *I* was serious." Her situation sounded familiar. Friends were going through the same. When you're a teenager, you fret about taking all precautions, thinking it is one slip away, but grown women tracked lunar cycles. Anything to improve the odds of becoming a mother.

The cigarette continued to burn down as it clung to the groove in the clay ashtray. We sat in silence. Gave her time before questions. It would hit her harder in the future. The rush of emotion and cocoon of family that would envelop her would provide a protective coating for the immediate and through the pomp and funeral. Then, when normal routine returned to all the others' lives, she would feel the absence of light.

It would happen on a Tuesday when you run into a room to update your mom on a minuscule life detail. And the realization that she would never be there again crashed into you. That is when your soul bled. My time to bleed was over. Time to talk.

"I'm sorry if this seems forward, but I was hoping we could work through a few questions to get a better understanding."

"It's alright, Detective. Anything to help."

"When did you see him last?"

"Five days ago. I just returned from Napa last night. He wasn't home, but I called his office, and he said he would be home late. Told me not to wait up. He could work through until the sun came up on occasion. So, I didn't think anything of it."

"Napa with friends?"

"Yes, well family, actually. My family. My cousins."

"Beautiful trip. When did you speak to him on the phone?"

"10 PM? It was my usual time to turn in when he was gone."

Her emotion read genuine. Her eyes were still wet. She pulled her legs into her chest in an attempt to self-soothe.

"Did he keep late hours for work often?"

"His class schedule would change by the semester. Occasionally, he would have a night class, but he would become just so engrossed in his work." Her eyes momentarily broke the view of the outside window and darted to the floor. A slight rose-red flush in her cheeks developed before it all disappeared back to the shell of the woman she was before we knocked on her door. Perhaps a quick memory of a time when she had kept late-night office hours with him. "He was such a compassionate man. His life's work was to bring awareness to the inhumanity humans were capable of across the globe. His lens was permanently focused on inequality and how to help raise the voices of the forgotten movements. It's why I fell in love with him during his lectures."

"You were a student of his?" I asked, sounding more surprised than I intended. I felt Finn stir too.

Another slight blush, and she cleared her throat. A detail rarely let out in polite conversation?

"I was, but we only began seeing each other after I left the University. It was a chance run in at a rally downtown at the Thompson Center to end Apartheid."

A solid spin and believable story, but I bet this house that his work office was familiar territory during her time as a student. She was quick.

"Detective Hansen and I both understand what it means to be taken away by passionate work."

Did I oversell the relatability? Her heartbreak seemed real. How would that change as more details eventually came out to her? The details that would come from the Polaroids.

"Were there any recent late nights? Any of these thoughts he mentioned that stuck out to you?"

"I don't know. I mean, yes." She paused herself before a dismissive gesture swept across her face. "It wasn't anything of great note. Just something that came across to me as creepy, and he seemed quite obsessive over it."

"What was it?"

"It was a letter in the mail. Well, less of a letter and more of a pair of notes."

"Do you still have it?" Again, I failed to keep an even demeanor. I felt my body stiffen and had no doubt it was noticeable even to the grieving eye.

"It should still be on his desk. He received it a few weeks back and, at first, was amused by it. A challenge. His friends loved to best one another. As time passed, though, if I even mentioned it, he would become irate and change the subject. It looks like it was written on a typewriter—"

"A typewriter?"

"Yes, a typewriter, but a relic. Everything was stamped directly on the page in the way they used to. I liked it for that reason. I thought maybe he would end up having a friend I might like."

I breathed deeply and leaned back against the wooden chair to allow her to dial down the perceived aggression in posture. But, unfortunately, Finn completely missed the change and locked onto Miriam.

"Miriam, can you take us to where this letter is?"

"Of course. It is most likely on his desk if I can find it under the mess."

"I hate to make requests that sound like orders in your own home, but please just show us to it without touching it."

Miriam led us out of the kitchen and down a hall. The path to the home office was lined with framed newspapers as if they were family mementos. Not wedding photos or extended family, but news documentation of events and political upheaval. Topics ranged from the Belgian Congo to Mao's victory in China. I didn't even like watching the nightly news report, yet here they bathed in the misery on the walk to what should be a sanctuary. It created a frost in the home. The lack of small family artifacts disturbed me. I hated homes devoid of love. Mama always covered the walls with memories. Our own places to look into and hide. Full of love.

The Professor's desk at home mirrored his desk at the University. Papers were strewn about, stacks of files cluttered along the edge of walls. Underneath the paper, though, was a beautiful oak slab desk with delicate lines traced into the edges. The legs of the desk were curved in before flaring out when finally touching the floor. Where they connected at the desk whittled down to resemble perfect spheres. The contradicting geometry was aesthetically pleasing.

Miriam remained off to the side as if she could enter no further. Her left arm crossed her waist, and the other shot up with her hand open and ring finger tracing her jawline. The result was a subservient pose that appeared to freeze her still. She retreated to the shadows and murmured, pointing to the far corner of the desk. I followed her gaze and saw an envelope sat atop the pile. Finn came to the realization about the same time as me, and we rounded the desk from opposite sides. Made out to the victim by name and address. The return address placed squarely in the bounds of the University grounds. Finn slipped on a pair of thin rubber gloves while extending a pair over.

The gloves battled the sweat that had appeared on my hands in the last few seconds. He picked it up along the edge and turned it about to find the fox stamp running along the back border. No words were exchanged. He traced his finger down, and underneath was a non-distinct sheet of completely white paper with a message that married hangman and a book typed out. The exact same.

"We need an evidence technician. Now." It was all I could squeak out as we stared at the table.

— ———— ————

The car proved to be a surprising sanctuary after the evidence technician had worked the envelope for ridge impressions and photographed it before collecting it. Inside the envelope was a small rectangular white business card etched with the same typewriter font:

Solve today or wither away.
Invite R.R. No mask needed.

A rubber-stamped fox for a signature.

The Polaroids flooded back. The brutality captured. Who had she been? Please be theater. Did this "R.R." wear the other mask? The cipher and the card. The game being played here. It was all conceivably connected.

"Want to grab a coffee?" Finn's carefree inquiry brought me back to the physical world. I raised my cup and shook it to show I was still working through the first order.

"That's alright. I need some. You can tag along. We can start to hash out what the fuck we have on our hands."

"Where do you start?"

"I start small. Did you catch the return address on the envelope?"

"I wrote it down, the University of Hyde Park grounds."

"Saw the same thing I did, then. I want us to get the observations out and clear. Downtown will have heard about the particularities of all this by the time we are back. Let's grind down on what details we can and break the rock into manageable pieces. I don't feel like being caught in an avalanche of stone. We will see what comes back on the prints from the envelope."

"They took her prints under the guise of elimination prints, right?"

"Yea. He played it smooth," Finn reassured me.

"The fox as a totem. Clever. They think very highly of themselves. A certain level of arrogance to accompany the note. Are you thinking it's a straight domestic case?"

"Maybe. She seemed genuine, but that can be easily faked. The note and the like are periphery. Let's charge at anything physical. Pull call logs. Check her alibi. Check banks for the money. It would make sense to stage it to look like a quasi-robbery gone wrong if it were a domestic. Throw the scent off."

He was right to keep our feet on the ground. I already had run down the path of the fantastic, chasing the unusual with my mind obsessing over the cipher in my own head. "Do not incriminate the interesting or insane for the curiosity they had found," my mother used to shuffle around the house and whisper to me. Understand my mother was a glutton for creativity. The spoken tales of fantasy buttressed by colored lanterns to project on the wall. It was best to give the mind an image and let the words be heard to shape what you saw. She considered most visual mediums to be cheap impersonations compared to the power of the mind. Other parents stressed grammar and mathematics to mold their children for success while we were taught of spirits and fables. Despite all the light, she interjected that I chose to live in people's nightmares. I wondered how disappointed she would be in me.

-- --- ---------

The car kept moving, and we kept breaking rock right into coffee. Finn's choice of diner was ripe with nostalgia. Situated off the corner of Canal and Roosevelt, it was complete with a flickering neon sign, dim interior lighting, and a checkerboard-trimmed counter. Open twenty-four hours a day. The patrons and staff all looked to have been coming for decades. Progress in the culinary arts or coffee appeared to die at the door. Men sat on stools hunched over with white cups of black coffee. The pie on display seemed stale, but the waitress knew her audience. I saw her dote on a man seated at the corner of the counter who seemed to be in a kind of hurt that can elicit physical pain from just an observation. The kind of self-loathing misery that seemed like a blackhole personified. It would prompt most people to turn away, but she juggled a pot of coffee and placed her free hand on the square of his back. She said a charm or two that caused him to raise his head and laugh briefly. Not ninety seconds later, she pivoted to clip the back of a patron's head as she walked by and took umbrage to comment, but if you looked closely, both smiled in the aftermath. Emotional intelligence in spades. Difficult to quantify, but rare and valuable. She was a hidden treasure stuck here pouring coffee.

The cup's clink on the saucer returned me to the present task. The width of the booth seemed to be below standard. Personal space would be in short supply with a man of regular proportions, let alone Finn's boxy frame. His hands nearly engulfed the entire coffee cup as he set it down. His hands were weathered but deft in handling. He treated the cheaply made and mass-produced cup as if it were an inherited set of Belleek China.

"Respect."

"Excuse me?" My head snapped up, level with his. He caught me off guard.

"Your face is all twisted up in attempting to comprehend why I hold a slight bit of reverence for the things I use here. It's out of respect. It may not seem like much, but Sue, the waitress you were ogling earlier—"

"Excuse me?"

"Don't worry. I don't think you're her type. But as I was saying, she treats everyone in this place like it is their home. Doesn't matter how fine the door they open for you is. You have a duty to treat what they offer you with respect as it may be all they have to offer."

"Thanks, Dad. Next time I will wipe my shoes when we walk in." Jesus. I wasn't going to start smashing plates on the ground.

"In Mount Greenwood, we wipe shoes. Do you have to wipe heels?"

"They should be clean before I break them off in your—." Deep breath.

Finn smiled slightly and reached across the table for a packet of sugar, shaking it lightly and clearly amused with himself for having raised my hackles with the lesson in propriety. The undercurrent of contrast out in the open. The working-class Irish fortress of a neighborhood that was Mount Greenwood. For generations bred the ranks of the fire department and police department. No easy victims there. Come to pillage and you were likely to end up a victim yourself. My Gold Coast condo, minuscule and aged as it was, positioned north of downtown in the heart of the nightlife led to this.

---   ----   -----

We wore down the practical and traditional of the case. There'd been no forced entry to the office. We called to put in the request for the office phone records, which should provide some level of clarity on frequent visitors and Miriam's tale. I chewed over the possibility of an extramarital affair with these late-night office hours. It was the unsaid up to this point that gave me pause. The abstract. The Polaroids. The mask.

They were pieces to build an investigation on sand. The practical was the proper way to go. To work the physical evidence and build leads through interviews of the people in the victim's life. Layer it all together and sift. Pull on the strings and see what unraveled. The theatrics of it all was an alluring component that screamed precision, intelligence, and, yes, a deep well of creativity. It had to be addressed eventually. But we needed a base first.

Finn stayed content with his coffee for my bout of introspective thought. He was solid in presence which betrayed his violent reputation. He had been logical and reasoned in recounting our findings and potential next steps to the investigation.

Sue returned to the booth edge and stood for a moment. Upon closer inspection, I could see her face was deeply lined and bore the signs of hardship. More tired and beat up than I'd realized. The uniform hung less on her, and she stuck her hip out in a caricature fashion, allowing her to rest the arm holding the coffee pot. Her deep-set brown eyes were fond of Finn as they traveled over the table, taking inventory.

"Dessert to pair with the coffee?"

"I'm good, Sue, but thanks."

"And you, darling? A slice of chocolate cream pie, perhaps?"

"I'm more of a butterscotch girl than chocolate, Sue."

"Oh, you are unique. It's not just an aura, then."

With that, I smiled as she left and continued in her rotation. She was a treasure.

CHAPTER FOUR

We returned to the office, and the good Sergeant Hartes took the briefing well. We spun the dots to be connected. Painted a complicated picture that may have a simple solution. We had enough progress, in theory, to act as red meat. He knew the truth. We would need time here. No forty-eight-hour cliché mystery to unpack and solve tightly. Nor a gangland slaying that would remain unsolved till the end of days. Hartes would send what we spun up the chain. A good sergeant he was.

— —————— ——————

Upon my return home, my condo felt dimmer than usual. The same magazines addressed to only me collected on the stand at the entrance. No voicemails waited patiently for me to press play from the machine next to them. No English accent had dropped a "How are you?" to replay. Over and over. The small belief that another soul might actually care for you was extinguished. Even the slight strike of flint can be nurtured into a fire that consumed all. Not even a spark faded tonight. I couldn't curl any closer into my own self this night. The darkness that was loneliness consumed all of me instead. I had turned out the lights myself. Self-destruction amplified without a vice. A match in the darkness was worth burned fingers, but here I was, unable to dilute the mind. They did not tell you that part when you don't drink. Or partake in drug cocktails.

I looked at the balcony and dreamt of the infamous Evelyn McHale. How beautiful that had been. A girl can dream all the way down.

I hated the broad categorization of the label for suicidal tendencies. The medical and psychological professional class failed to see it as more than an escape. I had been young when the slavish obsession with the mystery of death began to unfurl. Less interested in the physical manifestation of death in corpses and ghoulish endeavors like some suburban goth kid who sought rebellion. The spiritual unknown floated at the end of my fingertips. The incomprehensible finality of the ceasing of self-awareness pitted against everlasting expansive paradise or damnation. All that hung in the balance was forever. Each scenario was unable to be truly comprehended by the mind. We examined a grain of sand and thought we understood the desert. The great joke was that only those who walked through the door actually knew. Taking it a step further, if it was by their own hand, the door could be damnation. The reality was it could be nothingness, but still. The stakes were too large for that cast of the die. The true Rubicon. The answer would come.

I found the cheat in the rules, though. A profession where danger was the duty. Where time could be usurped by circumstance. The culturally aristocratic thought that we took up the profession to oppress and harm. Barbarians who sought blood each shift. I would love to see them mull over the fact that I took the job to answer a question. To die.

Nights like this made me wonder even more. Nights when I was worn down. Nights there were no stars. I wanted an answer. It wouldn't even be bleak. You wouldn't know. Or so I told myself as I struck a match. Extinguished match. Struck match. Extinguished match.

It took all I had to roll over from the back of the couch. The fabric was in style but uncomfortable. The pillows the same. These were my life choices. I made my way to the desk in slow, somber steps. The one bedroom apartment forced the collaboration of living space. The desk sat outside the entrance to the semi-open kitchen. My real estate agent had told me it was all the rage. I would sit and write a letter to whoever would find me.

The letters would be my apologies for the trauma of discovery. Word followed by word to dispel the notion that I had acted out of a fragile or troubled space. Write that it was rooted in faith married to the scientific pursuit. The step of faith into the unknown to answer the question science could not. The letter handwritten to ensure a personalized bow to place on top.

The sudden buzz of the refrigerator's motor broke my concentration and led me to scribble on the note. Modernity interrupted my whisper from death.

I glanced up and saw the calendar hung squarely and neatly on the fridge. Held up by a magnet in the shape of Montana. Dakota had sent it to me when she first trekked West to Big Sky country. Now, my own sister wouldn't even entertain my call.

Why did I even own a calendar? I had no particular dates to track, no annual anniversaries or birthdays to note with a doodle. Blank square after blank square for each day. To taunt me in unending similarity. The galas and dates had sufficed to pretend I had a life worth living. I had tracked each eagerly on the calendar at one point. Suitors lined up in an attempt to whisk me behind society's velvet rope. The courtships had been overwhelming at the start, but each disappointed.

It all revealed to be an arms race of luxury and vapid interests.

I was the ornament brought from the outside. Used to define them as different before they drifted off to marry one of their class. Then Owen came along. More than a tryst. Easy on the eyes, but his mind worked like a beautiful symphony. A whisper in my ear in a crowded room. I was both protected and fulfilled.

And what did I do? Ran away. Chased the only kind of love I knew. The cheap, instant intoxication of being physically desired. The more time that separated me from my action, the more I hated myself for it. The heart I had drawn on the calendar date for the Guild night stabbed like a knife in me.

Dates were important. I would need to date the letter. Who knew the timeframe until discovery? Well, now I had written November 5th when I started.

"He awoke every day to November 5th. He awoke to destroy keys."

November 5th. What was so special about that day? Personal tragedy? Triumph? What made it a steppingstone on the trail to murder? The theatrics of the Polaroids. Please be theatrics, please. A cosplay of murder. An elaborate night of mystery staged for the amusement of guests.

Tonight wouldn't do. I was too tired for rewrites, and Lord knows I couldn't go out on a scribble. The letter went with me to the balcony. The matchbook I'd swiped from the boneyard too. Johnny had asked why I always needed a match when I didn't smoke. I told him he should only worry the day I asked for a fiddle. The match struck solid and burned bright. I touched it to the corner of the paper and watched the fire consume. The decorative pottery kiln to serve as its final resting place. Wide enough in opening to swallow the burning paper as it dropped from my hand. Enough air flow to allow the fire to breathe until it died. With the fire snuffed out, I tilted the kiln to level the mound of ashes inside. Fresh and old. Let it all blend together. I thought of how my bloodline would've gathered around fire at various points for survival in the night. Hopeful to survive one more. I hoped they couldn't see me.

CHAPTER FIVE

The city slept, but that was because it also worked. The uniform could vary from single-breasted with pinstripes to Carhartt caked with dust, but the people I passed on the sidewalk in the morning were deliberate in pace and purpose. The spine of this city in full display. I enjoyed my observations while perched with my coffee. I never understood the point of jolting yourself awake and just putting your head down and traveling in isolation to where you were needed. Instead, sit in public and take in what is around you. Acknowledge that everyone has their own struggles. Strangers passed and provided fodder for the imagination.

They hurried about without realizing they were now involved in the story being thought out. The man with the briefcase went from being an innocuous accountant who reconciled the financials to a reluctant man who'd been pulled into a game of espionage. His briefcase contained trade secrets to be delivered to the Soviets. Waiting at the crosswalk, his foot tapped to release the nervous energy. No doubt sweat beading on his forehead. Or the pretty slender woman in red with the white heels who passed by and turned back if just for a moment to look at where she had come from with a slight sigh. No doubt a mistress wishing she was the wife. A man taken, but one who made her heart beat. A rare thing, for she had spent a lifetime with the view of romance as a ladder and men all too willing to obey for a chance at her company. Tables turned, and desperate to win.

Projection and imagination. I liked it here. A quiet café on Schiller Street. They did not treat their customers like cattle. They arranged the tables with just enough distance to make you strain to hear a table over. It created an environment where you only picked up pieces and quips before losing the conversation in the cacophony of the place. The patrons here conversed about vacations and family schedules. They didn't have a mystery to obsess over. It was refreshing. I could sit and pretend to be one of them. I envied the mundane and trivial.

Still, I wanted a girlfriend across the table. To tell me not to worry and that it was a good idea to leave Owen a message on his answering machine this morning before I trekked out. That he would hear my voice on the machine and probably smile that genuine smile of his. I would tell her the message was light in tone but hinted in the apologetic. We would strategize over his possible responses before I promised to follow up as soon as I heard back. Instead, I turned back to dial into the strangers who surrounded me. You had to take the company you could.

A sip of my coffee quickly reminded me how the twenty-something with the doe eyes for me stood behind the counter today. He was always generous with the pour when I was here. Cute, but young. Still had a bit to learn.

The ring from the cup stained the notebook page. My notes were scattered anyhow. A script that looped and looked like it had been written with my right hand.

Awoke.

November 5th.

Destroy.

Keys.

R.R., who are you?

A clever cipher. The second man in the photo. I imagine the good Mr. Hickey and maybe R.R. had been pulled into it. A challenge carried and delivered. Who or what had he gotten involved with? His wife denied knowing any meaning behind November 5th. She seemed to be entirely in the dark on the letter. Finn had set out to confirm her alibi of travel. She mentioned he had been curiously amused at first but subsequently enraged as time passed. The mere mention of it a provocation. What it said seemed to have wounded him deeply. A matter of the heart or a matter of the head? A man's ego was a gentle thing. Again, here I was, clinging to the most abstract part of the investigation. Finn had been right—the practical and mundane would solve this.

Speaking of, I had to meet Finn and Hartes at the top of the hour, which left me thirty minutes to fight traffic. Wonderful.

———   ————————   ————

"The nest is stirred up on your case, Winthrop." Hartes had been pacing back and forth in his office when Finn and I walked in. He still hadn't sat down. Instead, he chose to stand in front of the desk. He leaned back in an attempt to will a message of relaxation. Still, a disheveled tie hung loose, and sweat had seeped in to stain the shirt.

"I understa—"

"No, you don't, Winona. The ground itself might as well have fucking opened up beneath us. The phone calls are from up and down the chain of command, including downtown. Every boss who has taken a free cup of coffee called to pick at the edges." I could count on one hand the number of times Hartes let loose with a curse. He might as well have been at the steps of a guillotine.

"John, we get it. We saw the house. We saw the pedigree," Finn said to interject in an even manner. I turned to realize he had stayed in a casual seated position while I had, at some point, straightened my posture as though I wasn't malleable in the slightest. Deep breath out. I had internalized Hartes' waves of anxiety and needed to level myself. Finn's eyes were as constant as his voice.

Hartes took note of Finn's resolve and allowed himself to exhale. He rubbed his face as though he needed to wake up.

"You're right. You're right…you both know what is happening here and have a handle on it. We've all had heater cases, and the noise is noise. I let it get to me. Between us, the follow-up from downtown was strange, though. The calls were short and probed where we were and what we had so far. Not a lot of concern for your victim. He doesn't strike me as being the primary cause of concern here, and I don't know why. Where are we?"

"We're following up with the University today. We will interview some of the surrounding staff who knew him." I attempted to keep my voice disinterested to force an even keel. "We'll compare it to what the wife said and get a better understanding of our victim. See if anyone can give us something to chew on. Someone wanted him dead but wanted it to carry a message. That's my sense." So why did I feel like I was hovering over a precipice?

Finn chimed in, "I confirmed the wife was in Napa with family for an extended period of time. Multiple alibis that place her thousands of miles away."

"All blood. Family," I inserted. Finn turned and regarded me. Hartes ingested and approved of the immediate next steps with a slight nod. We took it as a direction to leave immediately.

Finn followed me out, and we were halfway across the floor when he gave a slight whistle. A signal for a dog to stop. He looked more weathered today. His shoulders hunched forward, and his face had a tinge of melancholy.

"Under the weather, Finn?" I asked as he stood in quiet embarrassment of my betrayal of partnership in front of a supervisor.

"Nah, I'm fine. Look here. We have to keep this tighter than usual. It's hard to get John riled up. I've tried for over twenty years to get under his skin and break the God-loving veneer he has, but it was failure after failure. He is spooked right now. I trust him, but for now, let's feed the chain selectively. Only concrete items."

"You'll have to teach me how to be selective from your experience."

He seemed to brighten up, and a slight smile creased his face. You had to redirect people at times. Memories were the perfect vehicle. The rearview mirror was rose-colored. We set out.

--- ---- -------

The ride back to the University was mostly silent. An occasional murmur or complaint about the condition of the roads or other drivers was the extent of the communication between us. The temporary smile I had pulled from him vanished by the time the tires rolled. I wasn't in the mood either.

The first time we came to the University, I'd been solely focused on my anticipation of the body and scene. Being so close to death's work constrained my vision like a child who walked into a party. The sensation dissolved quickly and became mechanical in repetition when confronted by the body itself. What death left seemed to strip away all the allure. It was anti-climactic, as if I would only be satisfied with the grim reaper able to field questions on scene. Anticipation beat reality at many points in life.

This iteration of the drive allowed me to soak in the area a bit more. The demarcation line of the neighborhood couldn't have been more apparent. The immediate area surrounding the University nestled in a patch of radical chic. Professors and university bureaucrats had anchored the neighborhood upon the white flight from the city in the sixties and seventies. Prairie School architecture dominated, and public spaces were kept free of debris. Violent crime remained generally low, by comparison, but property crime remained high. Extend out mere blocks, and you encountered a wasteland. Why steal from a neighbor when you can steal from a professor who won't sign complaints?

Hyde Park University and its inhabitants hated the police to a degree that they would cut off their nose to spite their face. It was almost difficult to wrap my head around. The students and professors were veterans of protest. That's why I'd been less than surprised at Hickey's office at home and work. As they'd tell you, they were self-appointed guardians of the underrepresented and mistreated. Quick with a sign and a march. Soft hands to cry. To carry the burden of the working class. Odd how out of place they would feel in any true union hall. Any place where there was cheap beer on tap and men whose hands were cracked and broken from years spent exposed to the elements.

The temperature was more controlled in a lecture hall. The lectern acted as a steady support to preach to the impressionable like-minded. Theory was debated, taxed their minds, and kept their bodies soft.

Universities shaped the staff and, in turn, the students. The administration threw the ideological branded rock, and the ripples reverberated throughout campus. Even when the rock sank, the ripples continued outward. Maybe the brutal murder of a co-worker would soften the approach to the police investigation.

Sneer as they would, they knew they were protected by those they claimed to hate. The netherworld over the border would consume them in an instant without us. Pristine lawns, though. I realized how hard my jaw clenched. Surprised Finn didn't make a comment.

We sat patiently to find out. We parked and made the walk under gargoyles again.

First to meet with us was Sandra, the General Secretary of the Humanities Department, where our victim fell under in the organizational chart. Sandra quietly walked in and took her seat. She dressed frumpy and wore her hair in a messy bun. She carried extra weight but nothing out of proportion for the average woman in her mid-forties.

"Hi, Sandra. I'm Detective Winthrop, and this is Detective Hansen. We are assigned to handle the investigation. First, thanks for sitting with us. The administration relayed to us that you could perhaps help us gain a bit of an understanding of Mr. Hickey and his schedule."

I heard myself and wanted to wince. I sounded like an automation giving directions at an amusement park. She cleared her throat, and her light eyes tracked my pen rising and falling as it tapped my notepad. Time moved slowly in an interview. You wanted to register reactions and subtle movements. Tells to be noted that people were not even aware they were making. I might've misplayed the woman-to-woman angle here. Finn had suggested taking point, but I argued that she'd been answering to a majority of male professors for their whims, and resentment could've built with time.

"I'm more than happy to help. We're all still in a bit of shock at what happened. The whole University has been talking about it. However I can assist, please let me know."

"You work as a secretary for the Humanities Department?"

"That's right, in a way. I prefer the term 'coordinator', but beggars can't be choosers, as my mom would say." She let out a small laugh to herself. "I work with the professors here to help them logistically with travels for conferences and presentations, procurement of supplies, and to shepherd them through the University bureaucracy. I always like to say that I keep their feet moving on the ground while they're busy with their heads in the clouds."

"Essentially, they'd be lost without you," I said with a soft smile and allowed my shoulders to relax forward to a less austere position. "Couldn't even tie their own shoes, I bet."

The corners of her mouth upturned slightly. I wasn't being facetious. Women like Sandra truly kept the gears moving in the machine. The professors and orators may have produced the research and railed away, but I doubt a single one of them would've been able to navigate the mundane tasks associated with the backend. She relaxed.

"I really want to help. I've been here for nineteen years. This feels like my second home. To have such an evil act done here makes my skin crawl."

"Were you working the day of the incident?"

"I had been, yes. I usually clear out by 4 PM when I can. I like to get home quickly on days I can. We're empty nesters now, so my husband likes to try and surprise me with small gifts. It frustrates him when I am waiting at home for him, and he can't be waiting for me. It's just a little game we play with one another, but we both can't stop." A slight blush appeared on her cheeks. Her eyes brightened when she mentioned her husband. Decades together, perhaps, and still acting like two teenagers desperate to see each other. I hope she appreciated how rare that was.

"You sound like a smitten teenager." I smiled widely as I said it to mask any jealousy. "Now you mentioned leaving when you can?"

"Yes, but that night I had to work late. I think I left around 10 PM. I was scheduling a last-minute flight and stay for Professor Harrington to San Francisco. So, it was complete chaos dropped off at my doorstep. I don't work late most nights, but there are still nights like this one where I stay almost as late as Professor Hickey would. They've really gotten in the habit of expecting me to swoop in and save the day."

"10 PM sounds about right to your memory?"

"10 PM, and the Professor was still locked away in his office. He even shooed me away when I popped my head in to say goodnight."

"Did Mr. Hickey usually work late?"

"Oh, yes. Quite often. He was a dreamer, even by the standards here. He would stop by my desk and tell me all about some injustice here or there. It might be here in the city or on another continent, but he was just full of passion about it all. It was like his own family had been harmed. Honestly, I'm not one to follow the news, so I couldn't contribute much to the conversation. I would just let him go on like a train on the tracks and feel the wind of him speaking."

"I know the feeling." I gave a slight head tilt in Finn's direction. Sandra had a small laugh for it. We were connecting. Finn grunted, and we both turned to him. He knew he didn't stand on solid ground to fight for his half. He simply raised a hand and nodded in agreement. Sandra seemed to enjoy the small victory.

"That's the truth. Professor Hickey really took it all so personally, it seemed."

"Was there anything recently he'd taken personally? Anything local he might have railed about?" I asked to push the conversation forward towards what we were here to truly ask.

"Not particularly. He just had been in a sour mood lately. I'm not sure why, but he would barely say hello. I'm not one to gossip, but I had chalked it up to trouble at home."

"Trouble at home? Why do you say that?"

"Just a feeling. Men usually carry the anger throughout the day. They think they keep it buried, but the things that hit deep can't be hidden. Usually, that is related to a woman…especially a wife." She paused. Almost as if she had been about to say something else but caught herself and switched course.

"You're right, Sandra. Men are dreadfully sensitive." I couldn't help but turn and grin at Finn again. Another grunt. "Nothing else comes to mind, though? Nothing specific? No notes or mail?"

"Mail? I know nothing about mail, but I don't handle that. Each has a box labeled for them that the mailman delivers directly to. If I helped them get their mail, then I would be taking their trash out next."

"One more thing. Do you recognize this girl?" Sandra seemed eager at this suggestion. She perked up and leaned forward. The cropped copy of the photograph slid across the table. It was the girl's face from the first photograph. The one with the smile. The copy wasn't perfect, but it provided a clear enough image. The anticipation and excitement on Sandra's face immediately deflated upon viewing. Her shoulders returned to a slight slouch.

"No. I'm sorry I don't. She doesn't look familiar. Do you think she is involved?"

"We're not sure. It's just something we were curious about. You know, you should title yourself as 'gatekeeper'. My aunt worked at Arthur Anderson downtown for years, and her stories about the parties would make a sailor blush, Sandra," I said. "Thanks for your time and take my card. Let me know if anything else comes to mind."

She took it and seemed to hold onto it with care. Sandra had been the last person to see the Professor alive. The rest of the University staff swore they were out the door shortly after 5PM. Not a single one had lingered. Notable that the only forthcoming employee had been the lowest on the chart. I guess values and justice diminished the closer it was to home and the higher you climbed. At least they provided us the office phone records without much fuss.

CHAPTER SIX

I would've preferred to read bathroom stall graffiti to the sifting of phone numbers in the call log. But the wife's story stayed true to it. There were calls to and from Napa in the immediate days before the murder. Otherwise a call each night at 7 PM for the three nights that preceded. Three different numbers. All under thirty seconds. At a minimum, it gave us an excuse to stand and drive.

We stood at the first address: 122 N LaSalle St. A suit occupied the payphone. I much preferred the conversations I created to reality. The phone was placed in the shadow of City Hall. Pedestrian traffic remained high. The phone sat adjacent to a twenty-four hour convenience store. The clerk was unable to control himself when we asked him about the use of the phone outside. Said we might as well ask him to walk on the moon. He wanted to know what we would do about the bums he deals with nightly. The store was his world. Beyond the door, chime gave no bearing.

"The two key is missing." The empty suit turned to us.

"Excuse me, sir?" I met him at eye level. A short man in a game of power.

"The two key on the phone is missing. You're police, right? Can't you make a notification? "

"Sure, sir. We'll get right on that."

"A city that works." He sneered and left. I felt terrible for whoever's life involved a lay with him. Banker or lawyer. Always bad in bed.

We approached the phone, and beyond the missing key, the phone was remarkably unremarkable. The casing was relatively clean and unblemished. Having a seat outside of City Hall had its benefits, apparently.

"Anything?" Finn asked.

"Nothing. It's a high-traffic area. I'm sure the phone gets regular use." Nothing but a decent escape and fresh air.

4442 N Western Ave next. Here the phone sat alone at a sidewalk intersection across from the park. Not much else. And in poorer condition than its kin outside City Hall. The poor cousin, perhaps.

"Beautiful," Finn remarked as we approached.

The recognition hit. We both stopped at the same moment. The phone, beaten and nicked, had a part of it torn away. The four and seven keys gone. The fuck is going on?

"We need an evidence technician. I don't care how many people have used this." It was the only action I could think to take. The canvas for cameras around the area was negative. The evidence technician balked at lifting any prints. We swam up current with payphone keys as our only raft.

The last address brought us to 915 N Orleans St. A third phone. This porridge was just right. Neither too damaged nor too clean. Its only substantial blemish being one missing key. The five key ripped away.

2475.

Two. Four. Seven. Five.

The fuck is going on?

—— ——— ————

Anubis would stand in the Egyptian afterlife and weigh your heart on a scale against a feather. If the heart was heavier than the feather, it meant a life of ill will. The soul would not pass to the afterlife, and the heart would be fed to a demon. Wiped from existence.

The textbook memory was triggered by a set of scales sitting atop a filing cabinet against the wall near my desk. Balanced on each side with a single wooden children's block. One block scribbled with permanent marker read "denied," and the other read "approved." The block for "denied" was slightly larger and heavier, keeping the scales at a permanent tilt. The State's Attorney's Office made the decision on whether charges were approved or denied before you even called a case in. The supervisors had to keep morale up in the fair and honorable Cook County.

There were lists after lists of other phone numbers to be pored over. I had myself a date with the yellow book. I'd once gone on a dinner date with a special agent from the FBI that had been more riveting. The month before, the Professor made calls like a teenage girl from her room. Most of the calls beyond a week leading up to the murder were to and from home, but we denoted a few to follow up on. No other pay phones. The rest appeared ordinary.

Two. Four. Seven. Five.

"Think it was ransom in a way?" Finn abruptly asked, taking my thoughts of numbers and affairs a step in another direction. "The pictures are found; he was pressed for money, or they tell the wife. Why the cipher, though? A ransom shakedown should be fairly straightforward. You want the money delivered. Not a mystery."

Ransom was an honest motive. Straightforward. Compelling. Understandable and explainable. Money meant a paper trail, but we just had the letter. "Maybe they only knew to send it to his house and were afraid the wife would open it. Maybe they wanted to hide their message in case she did. If she had opened it, then the entire thing would've been up in flames. Or it's all a game."

"Maybe. Sandra and the janitor hinted at the youthful taste. We can press it more on the follow-up. We have to follow up with the janitor and show him a picture of the girl. The scene acted out in the Polaroids has all the markings of a highly sexualized power game. Maybe a repressed fantasy finally acted out. Guilt buried in him that is now going to be exposed."

A scene. It'd been a scene depicted in the Polaroids. An intricate act. A secret game played out. Mask removed after the final click with a thank you and a smile. The cut of the suits spoke of a fine tailor. The fit was custom to each man.

It felt like a victory discovering that no homicide records on file matched her. Or missing person files. No body found in a garage or alley with a throat slashed open. We'd contacted the other detective areas for both identified and unidentified matches. The congruent County Sheriff's offices all received a picture of her face, and no one had anything of note. Finn was right. It had been a game, and someone played for keeps.

"People kill in that situation. They usually are not the ones killed."

"Maybe something went wrong, or he wouldn't pay."

"Maybe."

"It would help if we knew what the letter said. It would help if the letter, R.R., or the 2-4-7-5 made any sense."

November 5th seemed to drag behind me like stones. And now the phone keys. These stones wouldn't determine my innocence as if I were a witch. Only my competence as a detective. A telephone cord as my rope.

"Shall we play a game?" I whispered.

--- --------

27th and Lowe. Half Italian grocery store and half restaurant. The seating was tight, but few uniforms. When you knew a spot, you had to guard it. Whether that was for surveillance on a dope spot or a place that gave you half off your meal. Uniforms would burn up either. But there were no secrets when you worked a murder with someone. I suggested it, and Finn had nodded in approval. He knew it to be a sincere olive branch extended in reciprocity to his own secret garden for a meal.

We broke bread and ordered. The place felt alive. Grandparents surrounded by family at a table. Young neighborhood adults coming of age who looked to navigate the semblance of an actual relationship beyond the back of a car. It seemed cute in all the right ways.

Reminiscing jarred my long, buried emotions of innocence. When you were very young, you had a vision of life unfolding. Everything in front of you had a shine. Being back in the neighborhood brought a little bit back. I could see myself as the girl with the dirty blonde hair next to us on the date. Barely over eighteen and fully developed. It made her feel like the world would bend a knee to her. It probably would, based on her measurements, but the boy across the table was bright with a smile that locked onto her face as she talked. No posturing. People were happy with who sat across from them. It strongly contrasted with the jaded social posture I'd become accustomed to.

"You're from around here, aren't you?" he asked as he handled a book of matches stamped with the restaurant name and logo. He must have nabbed it when we came in from the hostess stand. Something we had in common. Now he must've noticed my pleasant gaze had wandered around.

"35th and Sangamon, but let's pretend I'm from east of Halsted Street. I don't want you to be asked to leave."

"Don't worry. I've been kicked out of nicer. Solid neighborhood."

"You're a northsider, right?"

"St. Florian's." He recognized my lack of recognition. "I thought I was speaking your south side language. Parish for zip codes."

"You forget. I moved here as a kid; consequently, I hadn't been baptized here."

"Close enough, Winona."

It was a welcomed change of pace from how this conversation usually went with natives. Any desire I had to be combative ebbed away. It was a small gesture if you were anywhere else, but here it was the moving of a collective mindset that resembled a tectonic plate. He registered the dip in my shoulders from the simple acknowledgment that I belonged. I embraced being an outlier, but it still could wound.

Finn stopped studying the matchbook and raised his eyes to meet mine. He laughed to himself and leaned back in his chair, folding his arms across his chest. I leaned forward with my elbows on the table to close the gap he'd created.

"Your neighborhood has stirred my long-buried memories. I had my first kiss after a night at Sox Park. Odd how you associate places and events. You're young, but the fondness for recollecting will eventually come for you. It does for most, anyhow. I wouldn't take it away from anyone. It softens the blows of age." He smiled as he talked.

Here we were both stuck in the past. Another reason I could love this neighborhood. The secret of Bridgeport is that it allowed memories to live on because so little changed. The buildings and houses barely altered from Finn's days of chasing girls to now. The stagnation and lack of progress appeared to bend time and place you in your youth. The rest of the city was torn down and built up, but Bridgeport protected itself and the time that passed through.

"You know, I don't know much about you," Finn continued.

"Is that right? The way the department gossips, I find that hard to believe."

"Think you're the center of conversation wherever you go?"

I couldn't help but blush like a child called out by a teacher for their arrogance.

"Only when I'm at a table of two. What is the worst thing you heard about me?" I defaulted to the only thing I knew. Hitting back.

Finn took his time taking a drink and casually looking for the waiter. No doubt eager for the meal to be served now.

"That you were from Bridgeport, that you had your hackles up, and that you go out on a limb for a hype bartender."

He left out that I was prone to climb the social ladder and that I was easy on the eyes. Glad he left out the former. It shouldn't bother me that he left out the latter.

"You have two of three right. I'm too pretty to have hackles," I said as I ripped a bite of bread in the least feminine way I could muster. I smiled broadly with a mouthful and chomped like I had once seen a hippopotamus eat a watermelon.

"What's the story with the bartender?"

"He's a friend. He suffers from substance abuse problems. I can't turn my back on him because of it. Have you ever been close to someone who's an addict?"

"Luckily, no."

"Lucky is right. It's like the devil's claws are half in them, trying to own their soul. He has a problem, and I don't see a reason not to help him when I can. Is it so different from vouching for someone brought in drunk behind the wheel? Honestly. No one would blink an eye at that, but I make a call for Johnny Bones, and I'm a bleeding heart being taken advantage of. I meant it when I said you were lucky. I've already had to bury someone I was close to over it. I'm not losing him too. He's kind and freethinking. No matter how insignificant he may seem to you, the world needs him."

"Who?"

"Who, what?"

"Who did you have to bury?"

A deep pause settled into the conversation, and I couldn't meet his eyes anymore. I couldn't meet the eyes of anything except the floor. My turn for memories to flood back. The type of memories that shattered a rebuilt soul.

"Drew. My kin. My cousin. We were close. He was a refuge for me growing up. Always looked out for me and stepped in when anything got out of hand. His family is why we moved here. He suffered because of it too. He'd take the blow to give me time to escape. Never had time for his own problems, though. He always looked out for others. He was an electrician and got hurt on a job site. The physical pain from the injury ate away at him, so he found a way out of it. Never stopped working, though." I had to pause to wipe a tear that welled in the corner of my eyes. "That's what he always told me when I would worry and hover over him. He wasn't a hype. After more than two or three sentences conversing with him, you knew he was bright. Didn't look the part at all. The girls chased him wherever he went. You would've sworn he could've played Tarzan in a movie. He had settled down and beaten it. He was set to be married. His fiancée stayed by him through it all. He'd won, but then he slipped. He slipped back and it killed him. One bad batch born from a moment of weakness, and it all collapsed."

I didn't hear what Finn said in response. The grief that still blew a hole in my heart was overwhelmed with the anger of what came next.

"The real insult came after, though. He lived in La Grange. The police department out there fucked up everything. The most effort they could muster was to call an ambulance. They didn't know what happened but went ahead and assumed an overdose. They didn't hold the scene. Didn't process anything for who might've been over. Who might've delivered the drugs. They didn't care. It was a bad batch, and who knew how many others were going to get it because they were too fucking lazy to do the basics. His father went into the station a few days later and was told no one was available. 'The detectives would reach out to him if they had the time' is what they said. Not even a fucking notification. We knew what it was, but you still do your fucking job. I saw Drew in Johnny Bones, and I said not again. Not someone I know. Not again." I had to stop myself. I looked to the young couple to allow for the beginning of a smile to hit.

"Memories are an odd thing, Finn. Drew is carried in my memory but will be lost to time. We spend our lives being taught that the memories of the world are held in heartless works and inconsequential papers that are debated over and glorified. At the University, they have built a shrine to it. What is that compared to a small letter of love between two souls? The quiet whispers between cousins hiding? Time will never register it. A lecture will never be done on it, but it's the true memory of the world. The bind of why we should live."

Finn continued to turn the matchbook around in his hand, pausing to gently open the lid and trace the tops of each of the matches.

"The thing about matches is the purpose. Take a single match you have there in the book in your hands. That lone match can accomplish so much. It could burn away the Earth with no regret. Or it can be the necessity of life. The fire to cook. The fire to stay warm. The utility of the tool is in the hands of the user. Love isn't so dissimilar. The whispered letter you speak of can cut both ways…but I am sorry, Winona. I truly meant I was lucky. Family can be everything in a situation like that. And Johnny Bones is lucky to have you."

The grief that turned red-hot anger became instantly cold and removed. The wetness in my eyes dried as the memories continued. He had been right that love can cut both ways. It can cut deep to the point of no return.

"The wake. The last time I saw him."

"Your cousin?"

"My dad. He has his own set of issues along the same line, and we were at the wake. He had been standing there alone and out of place. Racked by a sense of duty, I felt I had to chaperone the man. We were waiting in the back, making appropriate conversation over the collection of photographs that traced the young life. The immediate family attempted to compose themselves. They were to bury their eldest son, and we pretended to smile over photographs of family events that he missed. We watched the procession line be greeted in front of the casket, and my precious father turned to me and said, 'That could have been me.' If that doesn't tell you everything about a man…I told him I wished it had been. I excused myself and let the years pass without ever looking back."

I sat in an arctic desert of emotion. Not even a spark would survive inside me.

"La Grange. Another town, but still Cook County. The suburban police departments are all political. Things can be done incorrectly, and no one would know. People don't like to draw attention to their plights," Finn finally had spoken again. Having held Finn hostage to my box of emotions in public, he chose a practical method of escape. Such a brutally honest conversation could survive only so long. It was a fire running wild, sucking in oxygen.

Cook County. Chicago resided inside of it but was essentially severed off from the rest of it when things came to law enforcement and politics. The king ruled here, and the crumbs that fell in the outlands were left to the various lords and ladies of political power. The law enforcement agencies operated entirely independently of the department. It could be a shock how little information was shared. The city, and by extension, the police department, had walled itself off in arrogance.

The arrogance struck each of us in the department too. The department engrained a culture of superiority. We knew how to police. We knew how to handle chaos with a club. As if by osmosis, we had let it seep into us, unaware of the blind spot it produced. The glaring oversteps ran me over.

"Finn, we haven't checked with the County for the girl. We skipped right from the city and town limits to over the county line."

"God damnit." And with that, Finn threw his napkin.

CHAPTER SEVEN

Helen Waterloo. Female. White. Light brown hair framed a face of youthful beauty. She had hailed from Wilmington, IL. Found in the Cook County Forest preserve by a hiker off a trail one morning three months ago. Cause of death determined to be a self-inflicted laceration across the throat. The file surmised she'd cut her own throat. A suicide where she cut her own throat? With the body found in County Forest Preserve land, the case had fallen under the Cook County Sherriff's office. By extension, their investigators. Not detectives but investigators. A patronage job. A position that was but one crumb the political machine sprinkled out to be divided up.

The investigators who had handled the investigation were unavailable to speak due to the hour of the night. Apparently, the County was a Monday-to-Friday, nine-to-five operation. Their office had an investigator who handled inquiries on the overnight shift. He faxed the investigative file, including a photograph of Helen Waterloo from the crime scene. The same dress. The same eyes but shut permanently. Her hair entangled with leaves and general brush. Her driver's license photograph from the Secretary of State had also been included. It was her. It had been a blow to my own heart. Young, impressionable, perhaps even vulnerable.

A revisit to our copies of the Polaroids. The girl in the cocktail dress looked different now. Her nervous energy apparent in the first photo as she sat on the edge of the chair. Her body drawn forward to create space between her back and the two men who stood behind the chair. Her shoulders drawn in, knees tightly held together, and her heels pushed wide. A confident smile. A natural smile. A smile that blinded. Adorned in a delicate dress. A long way from Wilmington, I would wager.

The second picture. Where Helen twisted in the chair. Head tilted towards the black wolf mask. That's what it was. A wolf. Her body pulled slightly back from the knife, but the smile nervous. It reached for reassurance.

The third Polaroid. Her mouth agape. Reality set in.

It was the moment between the second and third Polaroid I lived in. The moment of fear. How her instinct in the moments that led up had been right. Trapped, had she wished for a guardian to come? A callout to who can help. Like in the stories. Like they helped me. The savior in the nick of time. But no one came. No one saved her. I thought back to my own moment of need. They had come for me, but Helen's need had been unanswered. Her life ended in fear. I hated myself for being saved. She needed help. She deserved help.

Even in death, she hadn't received help. A suicide classification? The case file included the M.E. report. The Medical Examiner saw a body in a dress in the woods that died from a powerful laceration across the throat and determined it to be self-inflicted by a girl who weighed no more than 105 pounds. The fuck? I still took the review better than Finn. He hadn't spoken, only paced back and forth, cutting a line into the floor.

I needed the night. The moon. I walked out a side door into the quiet of the dark sky. The job was death. You worked homicide, then you worked from the graveyard back. It calloused your soul. The work usually involved combustible elements. A domestic that had simmered for years before exploding into tragedy. Gangland violence that revolved around narcotics and cash. Passion was understandable. Greed was understandable.

The murder of Helen Waterloo had been nothing of the sort. This looked to be sport. A wolf and coyote playing with prey. The build on the coyote matched Hickey. The mask matched. The suit matched. How much more did I need? We had to go to Miriam. Had to have her look at the photographs. Let her confirm. Let her life crumble in. Let her be thankful she did not have children with the man. Take herself and fold into a new life. Burn his memory.

I took a deep breath of the crisp air and reminded myself that Professor Hickey was our body. Still, Helen was ours now too. Unofficially. Let Hickey be the cover for her. The investigation into the Professor's death would unravel the fate of Helen Waterloo. Whoever murdered Hickey knew more.

It was as if the moon had empathized with my logic. She hid, half herself. As if she wanted to turn away from it all but couldn't. A jewel in the darkness that I wanted to break apart. The fixation had been broken with a slight cough by Finn. He must have walked softly to get beside me.

"I've been inside thinking as you muse on the pavement to no one. Remember when Hartes said this was catching heat from everywhere? It struck me odd that I haven't read anything about it. Don't recall a thing about Helen in the paper, either. I asked Niamh. She works sex crimes. She hadn't ever heard of a Helen Waterloo. You should understand she pushed harder than anyone for victims' rights in domestics and the like. She is going to speak with her contacts on the street. Ask around about the masks. Something is not right."

"This is off. We're going to Wilmington. Going to her family. I want to talk to them first. Before the water gets contaminated when we talk to the County side," I paused. "A homicide, and we have to avoid other coppers. That's fucked."

"Murder."

"I said that."

"You said homicide. Don't use euphemisms. It sanitizes what happened. Remember what you saw…we're going in the deep end, Winona. Be ready to drown."

He had no idea how ready I stood to die. Now though, I needed more time for Helen. What happened to her had become the most pressing question.

---- ---- ----

The fluorescent lighting of the high-rise garage proved to be a poor replacement for the moon. I had almost missed the elevator ding for the 11th floor. I sat in darkness in my condo, staring at the answering machine. The nightly routine had been interrupted. Finally, the machine had something to say. Owen had returned my call. He wanted to go to lunch. He didn't sound distant. He actually gave a damn. I sat on the ground next to the answering machine and replayed the message on a loop. My knees were pulled into my chest, and my back rested against the wall. I couldn't stop the smile. I turned away from no one to hide it. Not being discarded proved to have meaning for me. My heart pumped with each thought that passed through my mind. It was only lunch, but an invitation meant a chance. Life bloomed again.

- ---- ----

The next morning's call with Owen pulled my heartstrings even more.

The banter had been light but heavy in flirtation. He was open for an early lunch, and I now stood before the mirror, faced with deciding what to wear. The lingerie in the corner of the closet beckoned to me. I had wanted to don a lace corset with stockings. Sit him in a chair and bring him back into the orbit of my boudoir. Force him to wait. Tease the man and draw out his deep-rooted masculinity until it overpowered his sensibilities. Unlock his cage. I was all wrong to ambush him. I thought the sudden strike would catch him off guard and let nature take the reins. It was a sloppy thought to take an approach reliant on a lack of impulse control. The man oozed control. He would weather a storm without breaking decorum. It wasn't an obstacle. It was to be utilized. Sit him down and let his control be on full display. Let him feel me against him. Show him his hands were welcome. Let the control carry me to bed. Lace didn't work for lunch, though. A tight black top with a slightly revealing neckline and jeans that fit well would do the trick. Time to win.

Forty-three minutes later and he was across from me. He got up to greet me, and the eye contact didn't break. He leaned forward with that genuine smile. The space diminished, and the time drew out as we both appeared to simply enjoy the view. I forced my legs to be crossed and stopped myself from tracing my lips. I had to be a good girl, but not the good girl I wanted to be for him.

"I am happy you called, Winona, and happy you could make time on such short notice."

I'd forgotten how natural he felt in an environment such as this. The dining was fine, and the help was attentive. He moved through it all like it was as easy as breathing. His shirt fit well and accentuated his defined upper body. I tried to suppress a blush.

"You know I have very few friends, Owen," I confessed. No point in lying. I leaned forward, pushing my breasts forward and together. No point in being shy. The bluntness seemed to take him back a bit.

"I thought maybe you had made a new one."

Ice swept over my fire. There had been a flash of unrestraint in his face for a moment. I sat up straight and attempted to relax my back against the chair while my heart stretched, threatening to thump out of my chest. Owen was never this direct. Never this bold in inquiry. He hadn't waded into the waters but instead taken us over the edge into the deep end.

Seeing my hesitation, he continued, "You're a beautiful woman, and I can't imagine you have not been swept away. I should have called you first."

The trademark softness returned to his cadence. The Ossuary might as well have been Auckland to him. Blood returned feeling to my fingers. His intentions were good. The support structure within me had cracked a bit. I'd fallen into what had doomed me before. I'd planned to play on base emotion. Most men buckled easily. They would be led accordingly, but never Owen. I framed it as he wouldn't leave his cage when it was me who simply raged against mine. He showed his appreciation for me in the small nudges when we were together—when we stopped at a shop or when I fabricated extravagant stories as we walked through the Art Institute. In those tender interactions, I felt him naturally bind to me. The genuine smile never left.

I pulled my shoulders into myself, and the vixen demeanor faded out of me as I reached across the table and placed my hand in his. It was a marvelous feeling how well my hand fit into his. It flooded my mind with the feeling of completeness when I lay against him, hearing the steady beat of his heart. Nestled into the nook under his arm. Felt his physical prowess taking hold of me.

I started, "I shouldn't have left you at the Guild event…."

"It was dry, anyhow. I can't say I blame you. A slow death with that company."

"Still, I should've taken you with me. Dragged you out."

"You did drag me somewhere, dear," he laughed while saying. His eyes glanced to the side momentarily.

"Don't remind me. I really blew the doors off of the woman of mystery motive I had built, didn't I?"

"You still have the cloak of mystery. You're a detective, after all. I cannot figure you out, Winona."

"I won't be any help there. I can't figure myself out."

"I thought about you constantly. Thought about how it felt to be around you. Even if I was just in the wake you created, I never felt as natural as I do with you." His hand clenched firmly on mine. I wanted to melt. No walls to break through. No small gestures to interrupt. Decorum be damned. He had been open and forthcoming. He had pulled me into his corner and pinned me against the wall in his own way. He hadn't needed a seductress to entice him but a Valkyrie to guide him.

"I've been knee-deep with work, anyhow. I can't say I've been checked into my personal life, but I'm glad you called." His gate had been opened. I needed to take the steps through. Instead, I hesitated and fell back on work. Paralyzed by emotional fear. Stuck in an emotional purgatory, afraid to make the leap. Heaven or hell awaited. Either would be better than this complacent desert. My eyes dipped to the table, but Owen's hand held steady.

"What's happened with work?" He was to pull me forward step by step.

"The usual." No. I won't continue to close off. I can connect to the man. I can talk to the man. Even if I just start by cracking the door. "I doubt you will find it interesting. Murder and intrigue. Masks and November 5th."

"I fear your 4th of July has replaced my November 5th after all my ti—"

"What do you mean?" My blood stilled, and my eyes sharply focused on him.

"November 5th...it's Guy Fawkes Day. The English holiday? Bonfire Night, if you will. That is what you are referencing? I did not mean to interrupt. I'll be honest I did not know how you were going to tie work to England, but I appreciated the effort, Winona." His eyes had narrowed. He registered the sudden wave of attentiveness that had overcome me. The vixen was dead. The tender hand was stone. He had no experience with who he conversed now.

"I'm not following you, Owen. But please, what IS November 5th?!" I had been paralyzed by anticipation. I regained focus by massaging my index finger against the serrated blade on the table. The physical world returned through touch. Forever my ace to play. Pain was a companion to lust after as much as pleasure.

"Winona. It's a national holiday in England. It revolves around the Gunpowder Plot." Seeing the statue before him, he sighed and continued, "The attempted assassination of King James I in the 17th century. Catholic revolutionaries led by Guy Fawkes planted gunpowder to kill the King, his family, and Parliament. We celebrate its unraveling on November 5th."

He awoke every day to November 5th. He awoke to destroy keys. It repeated in my head. The cipher could be the keystone. How was the Professor tied to Helen? Why was Helen murdered?

"What do you mean celebrate?" The blade wanted to break skin. I know that pain of sensation. It was used to distract from the present. Ever since my mother passed, I used touch, pleasure, and pain to escape the recesses of my mind. Wondering where she went. If she was waiting for me. Watching over me. God had taken the wrong parent.

"Fireworks, bonfires, and general festivities. As I was saying, it's much like your July 4th. But, Winona, I don't understand how Guy Fawkes Day relates to your work?"

Mama loved fireworks. Always had. The true sign of celebration, she said.

"Owen, I have to go. I am so sorry." I licked my finger to numb it and hastily stood. The physical world was a more convenient place to reside.

Owen sat at the table without a look of surprise, and a crack formed in the foundation of my heart.

—— ——— —————————

Helen Waterloo's family had already received the notification. No doubt contrite investigators from the Cook County Sheriff's office had tapped lightly as a family's world crumbled. Told them that their daughter had taken her own life. They were left to grieve with so many unanswered questions. Left to wonder what missteps they had made. Now we were coming to cast doubt on all of that. To move the earth from below the walls they had built to deal with what happened. I already hated myself for it. I would rather have delivered the news fresh with a knock than what we were about to do.

The map put the town of Wilmington off Route 53. A seventy-odd mile drive that so far had the feature highlight of taking us past the old Joliet Prison. A prison that pre-dated the Civil War and appeared accordingly. It had been antiquated at the turn of the century. The tales of haunted cells even made their way to the city. Guards having a drink, inmates after a light sentence—they all spoke of wandering souls the devil had yet to collect. For even he avoided the place. Purgatory built in stone.

"Have you ever had to go inside the prison?" Finn looked over from the steering wheel. His shirt had been ironed. Hair combed neatly. He wore a sport coat too. It was evident he'd woken up early today and cared for himself. An appropriate evaluation of the task at hand. Physical appearance was a barometer for the severity of how you measured a situation. People spoke of how you looked at your wedding and in a casket. Meanwhile, I chased a boy.

"Can't say I have. Can't say I want to."

"Avoid it. If just for sanitary reasons. Not to mention the staff. It's a hellscape."

"Speaking of familiarity, have you heard of Guy Fawkes?"

"Can't say I have. Can't yet say if I want to."

"Sharp dressed with a sense of humor. I'm going to have to keep the women of this town off you lest I have to break the news to your wife."

"Don't think you have to worry too much about that." I saw his hands tighten on the steering wheel with his response. Tight enough to hear the leather wrap strain.

"Guy Fawkes, though. It doesn't ring a bell?"

"Nope. Is this going somewhere, or were you that put off by the prison?"

"November 5th, Finn. It's Guy Fawkes Day in England."

He turned to regard me while keeping the car on the straight and narrow between the lines. Slightly more interested than usual when he talked to me.

"It's related to an attempted assassination of an English King by Catholic Revolutionaries that failed."

"How does it fit into the cipher? Where is this coming from?"

"I haven't worked that part out yet. I might have mentioned that as we passed the multitude of fields over the last hour to break up the conversation. As for where this came from, I found it from something handsome."

"He awoke every day to November 5th. He awoke to destroy keys." Finn let it linger after he said it. It still refused to become stale. "It may be more in line with the revolution than the papacy. The emphasis on destruction and the universal sentiment was that the Professor was a professional agitator. A bit of a revolutionary in his own right." Finn had made quick connections with the information.

"A revolutionary comrade from the comfort of office hours," I quipped. Finn simply grunted in reply. I continued, "Fair point, though. We have a string to pull on now."

The drive continued in near silence. The route's near conclusion was signaled by a Route 53-themed memorabilia shop and diner flanked by a gas station. The stark line between native and out-of-towner was evident even out here. I had to remind myself that we were the former more than the latter. Parochialism was not just for the city. The small community we entered could fashion itself as a fortress, especially with regard to a tragedy. Maybe I should cover up a bit.

The Waterloo residence was nestled on a street off Route 102. A small one-story house that most likely contained two bedrooms and one bathroom. No sidewalks. The road met the yard and continued to the front porch. An American flag hung down the porch beam. It felt like the people here had given the country more than it had taken. Small towns were like that. We parked out front. Finn had called to ease the introduction, so they were expecting us. He wiped his hands on his pants and stared out the window.

"You alright?" I asked.

"Sorry, yea. Feels different for some reason, you know?"

"I do."

With that mutual acknowledgment, we exited the car in unison and approached the house. As Finn reached to knock on the screen door's frame, the interior door suddenly creaked open. A small, wiry woman stood and peaked out. Leda Waterloo. Her features placed her in her early forties, but her body language placed her much older. Defeat aged an individual. She had been pretty once, and not just in the small town way where the boys had chased her in high school. No, she was a ruin, a once majestic place that had been abandoned. You could see the beauty but had to peel away the neglect.

"Are you the detective who called?"

"Yes, ma'am." If Finn had been wearing a hat, he would've doffed it.

"Come in."

Her voice was monotone, and she moved weakly. Her body, although small in stature, did not strike as frail as she moved. Finn made the entrance, and I followed suit. The walk in brought us past a wall of Helen's youth. Sports teams, class picture days, family vacations. A home full of love. The same little girl grew up across the span of photos, but the smile was transcendent in the time between. Finn didn't glance at a single one.

We continued down the hallway and ended up in the kitchen. Seated at the kitchen table was a man with a lit cigarette in an ashtray before him. He had long hair that was pulled back into a ponytail. He had most likely never stepped inside a gym, but he was taut with the muscle shaped by work. His hand reached out to knock the ashes from the cigarette. I noticed his knuckles were awash in old scars. A brutishly handsome man to whom a woman could gravitate. Where the mother had been defeated, the father sat shoulders back and chin high. His eyes were fierce, and he tracked our arrival in the kitchen. He gestured for us to join him and his wife in the empty seats around the table.

"Coffee?" Mrs. Waterloo asked.

"I'm good. Thanks though," Finn replied quickly and solemnly.

"Me too."

She set herself to work anyway. Moving through cabinets and taking out the requisite items.

"I'm Jim, Helen's father." The declaration as close to a greeting as we had encountered to date. All the while, Mrs. Waterloo continued her mission for the phantom coffee. Finn hesitated under the weight of it all. When Finn had phoned before, he relayed that we had an update related to their daughter. Here we were, about to tell them their daughter didn't give her life away. It was taken.

"Thanks, Jim. Thanks for seeing us," I had to start small. "I first have to ask you about the days surrounding September 30th. Would you be able to account for the night?"

"September 30th? I was in the middle of nowhere Tennessee. I drive trucks for a living."

"And I worked a double at the diner," her mother added, "I'm a waitress at the Launching Pad. It's the diner at the entrance to town. I work doubles when James is on the road. It helps to be busy. I thought you were here for our daughter. They found her on June 29th."

"We'll get to that, ma'am, I promise," I said, still unsure how I wanted to frame the macro view. They had been solid and unquestioning, but it would need to be verified. "As you know, we did come here to talk about Helen."

The mere mention of Helen's name caused Jim's head to dip low. His chin fell to his chest, and his shoulders rolled in. The strength I had observed in him vanished in a second. The silence was broken by a quiet sob. The way he had greeted us was apparently every bit of strength he had pooled together. Mrs. Waterloo turned and placed her hand on his back and caressed him softly for a moment. Her expression not changing. Her well was apparently too empty to join. She finally took her chair beside his and met our eyes. They were empty.

"I'm sorry, it's just that she was my baby girl," Jim muttered in an attempt to recompose himself. His bones were physically intact, but the man was broken.

"It's okay, honey." Mrs. Waterloo leaned in and returned her hand to the middle of his back. She returned her focus to us. A flash of hatred had panned across her eyes. "What made you finally meet with us? The secretary tired of passing along the notes that I had called?"

"Ma'am, there might be a slight bit of—"

"Don't you dare walk into our home with contempt for us. You didn't even care to meet with us. You moved us like cattle to where we identified her body. One phone call and a man in uniform to tell us our only child had killed herself? Not an answer beyond that. I've called the Sheriff's office damn near daily, and not a single returned call. We just wanted to know! And then you show up at our doorstep. Do you want to know what her last words to me were? 'Save yourself, Mama. Get out of this town.' I'm haunted every night by those words! My baby is gone, and you couldn't even return a phone call?!" The fire had emerged explosively in her eyes. Set to consume all in her field of vision but burned out in a blaze as she wilted, exhausted. It was Jim's turn to comfort her as she leaned into his shoulder and hid her face.

"Mr. and Mrs. Waterloo, I want you to know that we are not with the Sherriff's Department. We are detectives from the Chicago Police Department. While the incident occurred adjacent to the city limits, the location technically is under the jurisdiction of the Office of Cook County. Being a forest preserve made it the prerogative of the County's Investigators. Hence the Sherriff's," I said. "We don't have any functional connection to the Sherriff's Office. It's an entirely separate entity."

Finn stepped in, "I know this all sounds like bureaucratic garbage, but it cuts to the heart of the issue of why we are here today."

"You're not with the Sherriff's? Why are you here then?" Mrs. Waterloo moved right to the point.

Finn hesitated. I didn't. "We don't believe Helen committed suicide. We believe she was murdered." She had been a direct woman. It would've been arrogant to treat her with any less of a response. Two mouths fell slightly open. Mrs. Waterloo grabbed her husband's forearm.

"MURDERED?!" Jim said, barely able to stay seated. He began to rise, but his legs gave way, and he fell awkwardly back into the chair's wood-slatted back.

"I knew it. I knew it, James. I knew it," she said as she became viscerally aware of the present. Tears from a replenished well filled the woman's eyes. In short order, she was sobbing.

"Yes…We've come across some evidence that leads us to strongly hold that belief. We may ask you some questions that don't seem relevant, but please bear with us," I interjected.

"I knew something was off, James! Helen, James, our baby girl! Someone took her!"

Jim reached over and pulled his wife into a tighter embrace. She appeared to dissolve into him.

"My entire body has been on pins since they told us! Not just the despair, but I just knew it was wrong. My dreams. She came to me. Do you remember? Do you remember? She came to me crying in my dreams. I couldn't hear her! She was trying to tell me! She couldn't rest until we knew."

"I remember, darling. I remember. I remember." His back had straightened, and his appearance solidified as he held his wife.

"If you don't mind, it may be more constructive for us to work in that direction."

I told them as much of the truth as I could. Finn sat still. They told us more about Helen's life. Her life around the months her body had been discovered. Her mother, once hollow, had flung herself from purgatory to fresh pain. She was ripped open with the knowledge that her daughter had been taken. The father took that knowledge in. His eyes steeled with the realization. Hate would slowly weld back together the broken man. Perhaps the thought that his only daughter's final screams had been a call to him for help, and he had not been there for her.

Finn and I left with a promise to return. We had shaken the foundation of the Waterloos, and they would need time now. We drove a few blocks to a McDonald's next to a large home improvement store to decompress. Finn's call.

"What did you think of them?" Finn asked me over his tray of French fries and a Coke.

"I was a little surprised. Nothing religious in the house. I thought they'd be devout out here. Thought we'd show up, and they would've talked about the strength of Jesus or something. Small town and all. They didn't seem overly concerned if their daughter had gone anywhere after her death," I said without any self-vetting. The letter had nestled religion into the back of my mind. I had been too honest. "You?"

"You realize we just set their healing back to square one, don't you? They might have to grapple with the fact she was taken first before they process the afterlife. Jesus, Winona."

"I'll be sure to lie better next time, Finn." He was right, and I knew it. "You're also avoiding answering what you thought of them."

"They made me reflect a bit. And for a different reason than you think. I don't have kids. Always wanted them, but…well, things get interesting there." He stopped and looked at the ceiling as if trying to look to the sky. He returned with a deep drink of the Coke. "I'm just not sure I could understand a wound that won't heal like we just delivered. I sat there and watched them, tried to put myself in their place, but can't unless you have your own kids. It happens every time I talk to parents on one of these." Brutal honesty apparently had been contagious at the Golden Arches.

"It gets easier with time." Time to lie again.

"They didn't know much about her love life. Might be the small town dogma peeking through. Parents with their heads in the sand and all."

"Most girls Helen's age don't run home to talk to their parents about dating. Trust me. Unless it was serious, they wouldn't have known much," I said.

"Still, her mom mentioned that she had talked about a guy. What was it she said?"

"Said 'Helen talked about a guy.' Notes come in handy."

"It sounded casual. She didn't have much more to offer. Just that Helen talked about seeing a guy in passing. Paired with your logic, it probably was more. Could have been testing the water with her mom to see a reaction. Maybe he was her way to stop from backsliding into town. They said she left at 19, and those last words to her mom screamed of someone desperate not to come back here. I'm still trying to figure out why. I rather like it here."

I cracked and stole a fry. The windows were adorned with purple and white and a message of "GO COUGARS!" This place would undoubtedly be hit with an early wave of families, mothers, and fathers with young sons who tossed a football into the air and daughters waving pom-poms. Next to follow would be the gaggles of teenagers with nothing to do. Nights to revolve around the big game, waiting on friends to gather as various work shifts ended. Sit atop the hard plastic tables in the diner and talk big. Sketch out their dreams and plans to escape town. Youth was full of possibility and potential. The idea of a conventional life illustrated by Norman Rockwell probably appalled them. They didn't know they could stray too far from the picturesque orbit. Be left to drift endlessly into oblivion. In truth, maybe they were just happy it was their friends working this shift and not them.

Even kids in the big city dreamed of movement. To be young and able to dream.

CHAPTER EIGHT

I was thirteen when Oligoastrocytoma, brain cancer, finally took Mama. She had held out for eighty-seven days beyond the doctor's expectation. The people in her world knew her as a dreamer, first and foremost. Her imagination formed a garden of high-hedged walls around her. Within those walls were the most fantastic of thoughts. It made people think she was soft. She was anything but. They saw her head in a book but never knew it to be the escape from the fight she had endured. She never stepped back from a challenge, no matter how grueling or hopeless.

It made me think about why she ended up with my father. I imagine she saw a man in the cold and thought she could bring him in. Where the world had failed, she would succeed. He would have his temporary moments of breakthrough with her that vindicated the thought. A small gift or memento. A mention of a memory, and she would be enthralled to fan the flames. It was always too brief, as he would retreat to a distance and emotionally torture her. He would be gone for days. Over the course of those days, he would taunt her with his freshly extinguished cigarette butts on her windowsills.

A year before the diagnosis, I had been hiding in the hallway to the kitchen when she was assailing him after he'd returned from a five-day hiatus. She'd been tired and angry and was beating on his walls. The emotion in her voice was desperate for recognition and understanding. He sat and absorbed it all without a flinch or turn away. Plea after plea, and still he sat. Then without a trace of emotion, he spoke, "Luna, you have no idea what I'm capable of." I felt the cold overtake me in the same way it affected her. He stood and walked out of the kitchen. Barely registered my presence in the dark recess. Her body had been frozen still, but her eyes tracked his exit. I stepped out into the light, and she saw me. She rushed forward to embrace me. Her touch allowed my heart to pump again, and she held me tight before leading me to sit at the table with her. I sat silent while she reached out and held my hand. She had not soothed away the event, did not ask for me to bury it. Did not distract me from it.

Instead, Mama talked to me about The Lord of the Rings. Reminded me of the high drama and anticipation I had felt as we read the series. The first installments in our private members-only book club. She often liked to take me to faraway places, and I had anticipated the gesture. This night was different, though. She told me of how J.R.R. Tolkien had experienced the intensity of the Battle of the Somme in the First World War. Surrounded by horror, he responded with fantastical thoughts and began to create. The seed of epic fantasy had been planted in blood-soaked soil. Even the legends we worshiped had suffered terribly and required an escape. In one stroke, she had allowed me to grieve the burgeoning recognition of who my father was while giving me the tools to build a bridge to cope.

When the cancer struck, it ate away at her beautiful mind. She faded physically and mentally before our eyes. In her moments of clarity, she clung to strength through my sister and me, imparting the fantasies again and again. Tales of Maeve, the fairy queen of Connacht, the story of Rapunzel, and many more. Ample worlds and spaces narrated to us from her bed. Places to retreat to planted deeply in us. When she was gone, we were to be left alone with him. She knew the clock ticked.

When the clock finally hit twelve, and she succumbed to it all, there were no trumpets or grand gestures to mark it. Mama faded into a hospital bed with the cacophony of medical equipment beeps, and speaker calls as the only sounds. A woman who had lived countless lifetimes across the realms exited only this one. Her spirit was bound to travel, and I was desperate to know where she would go next. Who was to greet her and take praise of her kind nature? To salve the wounds inflicted upon her and carry her to her former strength. Civilizations differed, but the afterlife persisted. I wanted to believe that. I did not know, though.

With my feet on the tiled hospital floor, I swore to protect my little sister above all else. To bear the burden as Mama had. To be the knight in the valiant last stand. I knew the reality of what was to come. Provide food and keep the house moving when he would disappear. Mama had taught me that that was just as worthy as any stand to echo in history. The tribulations of the common man and woman were the stones on which time had been built, but the histories recorded only the powerful. A fraction of the truth.

Mama's fight, her stand, had been our whole world. When we lost her, the gates fell.

I blinked amid the memories, and Route 53 came back into view. Our return to the city. McDonald's was a distant memory, but the conversation lingered in my mind. A young girl's love life was to be a tangled mess. Her understanding of love would not have fully evolved. From the confusion of lust with love. The eager desire to believe what the boy told you to the dawning realization of sex as power. You could expect the command of a room with the right amount of cleavage and a smile. The master of a look that brought a man along. To understand what you did when you opened your legs to him. He would think he had climbed the mountain, but he had simply been allowed to walk forward. There was a difference.

The power could intoxicate. She might be counted lucky to have avoided the ever-disappointing future that presented itself when you wanted passion. When you wanted imagination to accompany the bold movement that intertwined bodies. Eventually, the physical became a cheap exchange of currency between like-minded partners. Both their needs satisfied. Check the box to find each other suitably attractive to proceed in the process. Humoring themselves that this was freedom. I wonder how Finn's love life had played out. I looked over, and he simply continued to mind the steering wheel.

The Route passed beneath tire. A slow return to the life we knew. Farms and fields gave way to dense clusters of suburbia. Pickup trucks became scarce in lieu of wagons and sedans. Slowly, things became more sanitized up until two miles outside the city. Then we reached Beirut on the Lake. Refuse strewn roads and a motley mix and match of vehicles. No clear identity of the community. Here everyone felt like they were in it for themselves. Here the barbarism made you alone in a throng of people. How different it was to the farmland. Even suburbia had community. Chicago, a series of fights. A fight for life on the south and west sides. A fight for status on the northside. Deadly in the combatants' minds.

We ran through everything we had. Organized our notes and updated manila folders. We wrote the truth, but none of it felt real. Finn was hung up on the money left behind. I was hung up on the letter and R.R. Both of us weren't sure what to think about the payphones. The next step scheduled.

--- ---- -----

Once through my front door, the order of business was to water the plants. It felt good to be needed. With no pets in the building, you had to take the fulfillment where you could. Succulents, moth orchids, hanging pathos. My unit was a garden that needed to be tended. Lest I die prematurely, and they take over. My own dystopian nature reclaiming civilization. Flowers to burst through linoleum, roots to crack asphalt, and vines to climb streetlights. Nature always took back. Again, I sat imprisoned in my imagination. Images of being found naked, alone, and exposed in bed, victim to causes unknown. Being found on the kitchen floor, victim to the granite on a fall. The "how" shouldn't concern me, but in my vanity, it did. Evelyn McHale had set the bar high. Impossible to best, but a girl could hope for some dignity when discovered. Perhaps Owen would find me. The officers who responded might know me. I did not want to look back from an answer to realize I had been left as a punchline on the work floor. Let them remember me as the cipher they could never understand. Was that too much to ask? If I was going to die before solving the Fox's cipher, then the responding officers could live without understanding me. A fair trade when you're single. Death is such an ornate event, after all. The arrogance of it all dawned on me, and I couldn't help but laugh at myself. I would expect every flower to be thrown for me in a curtain call.

Flowers.

We signal the surrender of life with the laying of the flowers. Bring nature's beauty to the tomb. Where the tradition started was lost to time, but I like to imagine it was born of a beautiful grief long ago. In my own place, I had accidentally laid my own flowers. To be honest, I was as comfortable here in my unit as I would be in burial. Occasionally, I would climb into my bed and lay still. Feel the presence of the plants and imagine myself already beneath a dolmen with either an answer or endless nothingness.

Tonight, I had no such time for the theatrics. I was simply tired. I felt like a corpse of emotion and needed a rebirth. Sleep with a wish to dream. When you slept, you were a god without even knowing it. You created subconsciously. I truly felt for insomniacs, but for now, I needed to take the first step toward becoming a god. Finn and I were to meet with the Sherriff's investigators in the morning, and I needed to be able to feel.

Finn was waiting for me. I arrived on time, and still, he had waited. He sat in his chair, slightly disheveled, with eyes still a bit red. The customary white shirt wrinkled and held together by a horrendous striped tie that I would prefer to bury in a backyard. I'd voiced my opinion, and he'd been terse in greeting. I'd accepted that we each coped in different manners. I hovered around him most of the morning, watching as time slowly melted before us. The anticipation of our meeting grated on my skin.

Sergeant Hartes had been briefed. He chewed over the revelation of Helen Waterloo. He'd turned away at our finish. Issued us a series of warnings. The Professor was our case. Keep it civil at the meeting. I noted that he hadn't called us off. Simply reminded us of boundaries. Message received.

We were to go to them in their offices at the county building located at 26th St and California Ave. Be civil. The investigators were the first link in the chain to Helen. She had been dressed for a night out on the town. Instead of returning home, had been found in a Cook County Forest Preserve with her fucking throat cut open. Suicide. The concluded notion felt like a knife to my gut. They'd moved right along. Patronage hacks. My blazer hung open as I sat on the edge of the desk with my shoulders slumped. In truth, I hadn't said much to Finn after the initial gestures. Maybe he picked up on the clues to be quiet, not vice versa. The other detectives on the floor cut a wide berth around us. They knew nothing but to stay away.

"Time to drive," Finn finally said. He stood slowly but surely. He didn't wait for me. It forced me to chase after him.

Time to be quiet. Investigators Mark Romano and Charlie Escamilla sat before us, thoroughly unamused for the first ten minutes of the conversation. They had yet to catch on to the Trojan Horse. We had started innocuously with questions from ten thousand feet. Charlie Escamilla had barely looked up from admiring his slice of pecan coffee cake to register my words. Mark Romano had slightly changed his demeanor from the moment he looked at me and licked his lips. Each was detestable in their own ways without the knowledge of Helen. The opening move a feint of ignorance. We told them the meeting was a response from the community. That they were concerned about rising suicide rates amongst the youth. After all, it was always political season here, so the command staff wanted to say we were looking into it. An overreaction that prompted homicide detectives on the shelf to look into cases. They had us penciled in as stooges, and now we were quiet after our lame questioning and review of Helen's file with these two.

"You have about the jist of it. An overdramatic bitch made a mess in the woods," Mark Romano snapped after raising his eyes from my chest.

I heard Finn's hands tighten on the arms of the chair. The wood was ready to splinter.

Mark Romano continued, "Lovesick. That is what her mom said. Probably saved the world a bit of trouble. Too many mouths to feed in a trailer park town like that."

Finn's temple beat furiously.

"It was all open and shut pretty quickly. Don't have to be Sherlock Holmes to see she wanted an exit and found it." Charlie Escamilla just kept picking at the crumbled chunks of cinnamon as he spoke. I found that I struggled to maintain a steady breath. A clear of my throat was the only acknowledgment before my turn to emerge from the wooden horse.

"I'm no Sherlock Holmes," I said as they laughed, "but how many girls barely over a hundred pounds have the strength to cut their own throat to that degree? The laceration had been deep. Impressive power for a lovesick bitch who just wants to end it. Violent way to do it, too, wouldn't you say?"

Charlie Escamilla suddenly lost interest in his pastry, and Mark Romano didn't care to imagine how he wanted me anymore. Greeks were in the streets of Troy and ready to burn it to the ground. I had their attention. Good.

"Hand to God. Impressive work, gentlemen," I let the words fall out of my mouth. They shuffled uncomfortably in their seats.

"Didn't come just to dance, did you? Ask what you want straight out. I don't need to be wiping up Mark's drool any longer than I have to," Charlie Escamilla snarled in place.

"Hey! She isn't even…wait, what the hell are you here for anyways?" Mark Romano chimed in less enthusiastically. Apparently only half-aroused now.

I leaned forward with all the façade of kindness thrown from my face and only the hate I felt for them visible. "I want to know how you found a nymph in the woods. Attired in a cocktail dress that didn't have a tear. Not a scratch on her arms or legs from the walk through the trees. Found deep in the forest, but she must have done quite the dance, right?"

"She—"

"Didn't catch onto one branch. The girl's dress barely covered her, and she didn't have a nick. Well, except for the fact that her throat was opened. Must have left her heels behind. I know she grew up poor, but you would think shoes were a staple for a night out. Not to mention what a walk through those woods without shoes would do to her feet. Pictures are a damn treasure."

The color had drained from their faces. Mark Romano's mouth was a quarter open, caught in an apparent dumb stupor. Charlie Escamilla was the sharper of the two and had zeroed in with a quarter of a smirk. Finn was out of my periphery, but I could feel him. Evolutionary biology trained us to sense danger. It sat next to me.

Time to burn, baby. "Couldn't have been that the body was wrapped, carried, and dumped in the woods?"

"It wasn't even our call to make. We get directions to lighten the caseload, and you fucking expect us to go against the grain?" Mark Romano shot out. "The people who make decisions—"

"We're done here is what we're saying," Charlie Escamilla cut in and raised his hand to motion towards the door.

"For the record, fuck you." I stood. Time to go. Mark Romano mirrored my rise while Charlie Escamilla stayed in his seat. The path toward the door filled me with mixed feelings of disgust and victory. They had revealed enough truth. Power was at play here. Strings were pulled in the genesis with Helen and our dear Professor being involved. We might have pulled on a tiger's tail instead. Worth it to be eaten for, though.

These stooges wouldn't tell us anymore, and I couldn't help but feel that Mark Romano had started to get off when I snapped to tell him off. He had returned to leering with a slightly heavier breathing pattern. I needed to be gone. He was still behind me on the way to the door, with Finn's heavy footsteps trailing close.

"Let me do you a favor. Honestly, who was she? She was nobody. Nobody cared about her. Why the fuck do yo—"

Mark Romano's last effort to flex power to me as a perverted, saving grace flirt cut short. I felt the power that took Mark Romano to the wall pass by me. I turned back to see Finn had taken the man by the throat. Pinned him like prey. In a move of desperation, I saw

Mark Romano's hand go for the handle of his service revolver. Apparently, Finn had anticipated the move. His free hand smothered the grip. I barely registered the primal nature of the confrontation before quickly taking in the fact that Charlie Escamilla was frozen in fear in his chair. The guttural attempts for breath by Mark Romano were the only sound in the room.

"I've killed men for less," Finn whispered soft and cold. The entire scene before me finally developed in my mind.

"FINN! FINN!" I might as well have been screaming into a void. "GRIFFIN HANSEN!" Nothing. "JESUS FUCKING CHRIST, FINN! LET HIM GO!"

And just as quickly as he had captured, he let free. Mark Romano collapsed to the ground in a desperate search for breath. A coughing frenzy and bewildered eyes. The room was still again.

Finn turned to lock eyes with me. The man was filled with not rage but purpose. "Let's go," he casually said and made his way through the door.

I turned back, "Does R.R. mean anything to you boys?"

Heads shook no.

No one followed in our wake.

CHAPTER NINE

"Water with lemon, please."

My order had solicited a brief smile from the bartender. A bar in midday. The only place that would be dark. Near empty.

Finn still unsettled me. To him, it was as if he had simply asked for a mint on the way out of the investigator's office. Attempted murder was a footnote to his day.

"I'll take a Coke with light ice," Finn had followed my order. Surprised me again. The cliché expectation of a heavy pour and a cigarette to appear. Clichés were for unimaginative minds, though. I should have done better. The silence lingered, and my imagination terrified me. Finn's capability morphed and evolved in my thoughts. My hands trembled slightly while he simply sat quietly next to me. His elbows propped up on the bar casually. Maybe it wasn't the silence that terrified me. I needed him to know. I needed to connect with him. It was time to cross our interpersonal Rubicon.

"I know it was you that night."

Finn turned his head around. A small glimmer of life returned to his eyes.

"What's that?" his only response.

"I know you were the one who carried me all those years ago. The alley adjacent to The Ossuary. You picked me up as I lay helpless. Gently carried me back to your patrol car."

Finn returned his cast forward and tipped his chin down. "That's the job."

"You didn't have to care so much. I remember feeling as though you were taking on my pain. It felt like you carried me, an unknown girl, like your own family. That night I stood on the precipice of death. He had pinned me. I thought I was going to die. But, with you, I felt safe and protected. I never said it, but thank you. For taking me to shelter. A dumb, young girl who thought she was invincible. I was about to find out how wrong I had been. He was going to rape me, and you stopped him."

"I didn't stop him." Finn's grip on his short glass of Coke tightened.

"Yes, you did. You broug—"

"No, I didn't. I carried you. Bill saved you."

The slivers of the night rotated in my mind. The animal had climbed off of me when he saw the uniforms. I had been helpless and held down to the alley pavement. The half step back with raised hands. His fucking line, "She wanted me to surprise her in the alley." The light had dimmed as Finn came into focus above me. He hovered into my view, and we made eye contact. He must have seen the pure terror in my eyes. Next, I felt the weight of his coat come around me. Solid arms to levitate me. I turned into him and did not say a word. Only a silent thank you to St. Michael in my mind. Those were my memories. They had been replayed one-dimensionally in my head countless times.

"You may say I carried you like we were family, but Bill reacted like you were his own." Finn had leveled his gaze. Clearly, he held himself together in the moment. His own reel of the night playing in his mind.

The attack had been two years before I came on the job. It took a few years, but I had run into him while working in uniform. I instantly recognized him. He barely gave me a passing glance. As I matured in the job, I grew to resent him for having to carry me. I was my own savior, and the recollection of needing such help felt like a festering weakness. It's what had consumed the memory. Caused the story in my mind to fold around the actions of Finn. I had forgotten his partner. I had forgotten the gargled screams that pierced the nighttime alley air as Finn carried me to safety.

"How have I not remembered him?" I whispered.

"It's hard to remember someone you saw once."

"I remembered you," a tinge of guilt followed my words. "What unit does he work in? At this point, my thank you to him is longer overdue than yours." The blossoming of the other man became more vivid in my mind as we sat.

Finn simply sat.

"Finn, what unit? I owe the guy. If I have walked by him and don't know it, I will die of embarrassment."

"Bill Yenot. We were partners. He always did the work. So that night didn't surprise me. He had two daughters himself. You should've seen what that son of a bitch looked like after," Finn chuckled to himself. A faint smile flashed across his face, but water traced his eyes.

Past tense. No. Please, no.

"Finn—"

"It's too late for that. Nine months later…." The water was falling now, not just from Finn's eyes, as the recognition that I had been right struck deep into my spiritual plane. A man I never knew. A man I would never know. He had exacted vengeance on my behalf. In a world where my own father did not look after me, Bill Yenot had taken up my cause in a moment. I reached out and laid my hands over Finn's.

His hands trembled now.

"What happened?" I asked.

"He didn't give his life. It was taken. Nine months from the alley and a day before his birthday. Murdered. Not killed but murdered."

"Finn…"

Finn continued, "It was his way. He's the one that saw you in that alley. He is the reason we stopped the car. He saw it, Winona, I didn't. I missed it. Then nine months later, he saw what I missed again. In on the chase in his way. A fucking stolen van where the guy bailed. Bill had followed on foot while I was supposed to whip the car around the block to where he would've flushed the guy out. He never came out. I heard the shot and thought Bill had gotten one off himself. Until he didn't respond to my shouts. The motherfucker had gotten a round off. An inch above his vest, he was struck."

"Finn, I'm so sorry." For someone who obsesses over death, I never had the right words to greet it.

"Proverbs 28:1— 'The wicked flee when no one pursues, but the righteous are bold as a lion.' He died a policeman's death. I thought about him today. He would have reacted the same way I did for Romano's remark." Now a half cry and half laugh from Finn.

I need a drink. A real drink.

"That's all I could think about when I had him against the wall. How resolute Bill had been. He had two daughters. They were four and eighteen months old when he was killed. He would have seen them in the pictures of Helen and wanted to kill any man involved. He would have thought of his girls. I watched those girls grow up. They may not be blood, but I'll be damned if they're not family." I really need a drink. Drop by drop, tears were pounding the bar top as Finn continued, "I thought of them when we discovered the truth about Helen. When we sat there with her mother. Thought back on Bill's girls. How life could've been so different for them if their mom had given in to the grief. She has gotten out of bed every morning and taken care of those girls. Places herself last and thanks God for them every day. I saw in Helen's mother the pain of a loss that made her a ghost. Her only child taken. We may never be able to give her a reason to get out of bed, but we're going to give her what we can." He turned and met my eyes in firm determination. "By any means."

I realized my hand had been slowly caressing his in an effort to comfort him. I had traced the battle scars that told the experience of his hands. "We do that by solving the picture. We solve the picture by solving the Professor's murder," I choked out. "The Cook County investigators hid behind a bureaucratic wall. Well, until you tried to cave it in. They are pawns in the game, but they still let us learn. They said it wasn't even their call to make. They exposed a crack. Rungs on a ladder to climb."

I replenished the lost tears with lemon water.

Finn whispered, "Fidelis ad mortem."

"Et postea," I responded. And in my mind, I bent a knee and swore to whoever listened that I would visit Bill Yenot and say thank you. With flowers. Faithful beyond death.

---- -------- ----

The rest of the day, we worked to extinguish the fire Finn had started with the investigators. An endless challenge to the reported sequence of events that had occurred. Phone calls and favors called in. It had been settled by closing time. The compromise being we were not allowed back to their office. I was exhausted.

--- ---- -------

"I needed to hear your voice." It was late. It was sad. It was true. I needed to hear Owen. He was home and had picked up for me.

"Is everything okay, Winona?"

I was curled in my own bedroom chair with my legs pulled up into me. Stitched comfort that felt like sitting on stone when you were alone, but it felt like velvet now.

"We're not a losing game, Owen. I want you to know that."

CHAPTER TEN

We spent hours on the phone. Life stories and all their details. We traversed it all. The consequences of a late night were evident in the morning. I looked like a mess on the walk into work. I could never quite nail getting dressed after a long night. The other detectives on the floor probably thought I was hungover after a night out. I didn't care. I had a companion who would pick up the phone when I called. To be human was to want to be loved.

I sat and looked around. The detective floor stirred in the chaos that passed for normal. Phones rang, people shuffled, guys bitched. Finn sat at the far end. Away from the noise. Far away from where he usually sat. He had company. Seated on his desk was a pixie of a detective, visible only from the back. I started to make my way over. Her slight build and short black hair gave her away. Niamh was one of my favorites, even from a distance. She had aged graciously and maintained a kind heart. Trafficked in sex crime cases which made her even more impressive. The cranberry known to carry a sprig of shamrocks encased and preserved in a small square meant for a young boy's trading card. A love for tokens and trinkets. A quick way to endear oneself to me. I closed in, and she gave a slight smile over her shoulder before she slid off the desk and made her exit. I caught her Irish accent saying goodbye to Finn.

Finn watched her walk away with a smile. "She was just telling me that everyone in Kerry carries a knife."

"What?"

"Kerry. It's her home county in Ireland. I didn't get the joke either but can't complain when she stuck around to say it."

Apparently, I wasn't the only one who had been making deeper connections. The previous day necessitated an outstretched hand indeed. "Women are magic, Finn. What can I tell you?"

"I think I could understand magic sooner."

He hadn't been wrong. The duty had been mine to steer back to work.

"Professor Hickey. We have to square that. We need to go to the wife. Make no mistake. I am glad he is dead. His murder is the path to Helen, though."

Finn nodded.

-- --- ----

The Hickey residence had changed. A light of femininity had broken through. It was brighter, and the décor less confrontational. The former Mrs. Hickey had set out vases with flowers at the entryway, and it felt like an invitation. The hallways less antagonistic without the political literature and photographs she had removed. Perhaps she finally had the freedom to do so. Seated in the kitchen, we watched her. Light on her feet for a wife in black. Death hits everyone differently. Still.

"Would you like something to drink?" Mariam asked while Yo-Yo the dog loyally rubbed along her legs.

Finn and I both refused in unison. The interview had been conversational to this point. She hadn't contacted us about the investigation. Hadn't followed up with a phone call. Even now, she hadn't dug into the matter. Perhaps she was just at peace. Perhaps.

"We wanted to talk to you about your husband. Some of the more personal details," I said.

"Okay. I'll answer what I can."

"Did you feel a change in him recently?"

She slightly shifted and moved to cross her arms, gripping herself. A cold air descended in the room. She projected herself as weaker. Drawn to the unpleasant. Reluctant. The woman dropped her hands back and met my eyes straight on.

"I did. It was intuition."

"How so?" I continued. Intuition was a woman's game, and hopefully, Finn understood that I had placed him on the sidelines with good cause. The ballet that commenced was delicate.

"Call it a feeling. Call it her name."

"Name?"

"Yes. A woman's name. You understand how unnerving it can be. He was my husband, but there was a separate circle. It was only recently I could connect a name to it. Only since he received that damned cipher in the mail. It was as though he stopped being cautious. He talked openly and loudly on the phone from that office. He practically barricaded himself in. He never quite understood how thin a door is when a woman wanted to listen. Men are like that. Projecting power through force and forgetting how far it carries."

Awoke. November 5th. Destroyed keys.

Who was R.R.?

"What do you mean a separate circle? And what name?"

"Daphne. Oh, he was never talking to her directly, but there were plenty of references to her on the phone. It was difficult to understand. Like they were talking about a game you didn't know the rules to. I had a feeling she belonged to his little club. The Chicago Guild of Saint Luke."

The presses stopped in my mind. The Professor? The Guild? I kept level and hoped neither Finn nor Miriam noted my temporary alarm. She was talking. I had a feeling that wine was playing a part in the loose lips today. Thanks, Amphictyonies. Without raising a conflict of interest, I could not probe into the Guild now. I had to file it away. Reluctantly.

"They never understand that when we are in the dark, we fill in the blanks. Make the rules out to be what hurts us the most," I said. Half to relate and half to remind myself.

"Right? Just tell us. Maybe that's why so many women turn to women when they leave their men."

Maybe I had gone too far. I could feel Finn's eyebrows raise.

"Perhaps. Had you met a Daphne before? Or heard of her?"

"Never. It came out of nowhere—the cipher, his obsession, and poring over books. It all started so happily. He seemed to think of it as a test. Then one day, he turned dark, and it never left him. The calls increased, and Daphne was a point of concern."

November 5th. Guy Fawkes.

"Did anything else change when he went dark?"

"Outside of barricading himself in his office here or at work?"

"Did any other components of your relationship change beyond the emotional withdrawal? For example, physically, did he change?"

"Are you asking me if he fucked me differently?"

Finn's shift caused the chair to creak.

"That's the more direct line of questioning, Mariam."

"Yes. Yes, he did." If she had her red wine in front of her, it would've been drained.

"He became more timid when he turned dark. It was like he was scared. From the time I was a student, he took control. He never wavered in the taking. I had to draw a line sometimes when he would go too far. But then he went dark and went from lion to lamb."

From when she was a student? That was a slip. Confirmed the disputed fact, though.

"Intuition take you anywhere with it?"

"Right to this Daphne. Maybe she had clipped him, and he was worried now. But I had no proof. It all happened before I could confront him."

Confront him. She seemed to have registered the words to herself after she said them.

"Can I ask you something on the same track? Do the use of masks mean anything to you?"

"Masks?" Confusion her primary emotion now.

"Yes, part of any facet of your life before then?"

The implication was obvious. How far did dress up go? I liked it so far. Memories flooded, and I could feel the faint blush in my cheeks and the heat.

"No. No, I can't say they were. He always did take me to a masquerade ball every year, but they were just half-faced coverings. Nothing too elaborate."

"And the coyote mask in his office?"

"The white one? I chalked that monstrosity to his collection of items from different cultures."

She seemed to be telling the truth. She didn't stress it or place too much emphasis. Her voice seemed clear in truth regarding the mask.

"Thanks, Mariam. We will be in touch. The investigation is moving along. Don't hesitate to contact me if you have any questions."

"Thank you, Winona." Her hand held mine a split second too long.

"Oh, one more thing. R.R.? Does that mean anything to you?"

"No, sorry again. It all seems like a foreign language to me sometimes." Her eyes now lingered.

Finn fumbled a goodbye and was ready for the door by the time I'd taken two steps.

--- --------

The Guild stayed on my mind. I needed to distract myself.

"Daphne?"

I could barely hear Finn over the V8 engine in need of love that was our chariot. The exit of the Hickey's neighborhood was as sublimely pretty as the entrance. I admitted to myself the hint of jealousy I had for such a pristine residential row.

"First time we've come across the name. Maybe she is related to Donald?"

"Winona—"

"I know, I know. We can't joke. Humor is dead. I wonder who got that job."

"What was your read on her?"

"Either the sun finally rose for her, or she killed the S.O.B."

"The sun rose?" Finn's turn to be confused.

"We either saw her experiencing a renewed sense of freedom and growth that comes from breaking the grips of a domineering, abusive relationship that feels like the warmth of the sun rising new to you or…." God, I knew that feeling. Most women did.

"The cut was deep across the neck. Hard to imagine a woman making that kind of wound."

"Don't underestimate us, Finn. We don't always have to get our hands dirty to get the job done." From the time we start to blossom, we learn the power we possess. A single look can drive a man to walk off a cliff willingly. It was a small jump to having one commit murder. "And she seemed to be outside whatever game is being played here. We, women, don't like being on the outside. Especially when it comes to our husband's sex life."

Finn acknowledged the wisdom with a sigh. We continued to drive. Traffic was bad. My thoughts worse.

The R504 Kolyma Highway in the Soviet Union. My penchant for history collided with the odd. Hundreds of thousands of political prisoners and forced laborers put to work in stretches of the most inhospitable terrain on earth. They would die. They would fall into their work, but the work would not stop. They simply became part of the fabric of the road. "The Road of Bones" it became known as. To die and to suffer the indignity of not even being worth a pause in the work was a nightmare. I dreamt of funeral pyres and monuments, and these poor souls were simply a weakened element to the chemical compound that formed the road. Even those you toiled beside didn't care to stop. Death could be of no consequence, but it was still human nature to pause. Even in battle, a man could pause after killing an enemy. Not for the progress of the state, though. When you are paralyzed about what happens when your heart stops, you could always cling to how your body would be treated and left behind. You could cling to the comfort of ritual with small gestures or large pomp. These men were denied even that. Dead men I wasn't jealous of for a change.

We hit a large pothole in the road. I looked over to Finn. My disapproval of his driving evident.

---- ---- ----

Throughout the workday, we attempted to make more concrete connections. Tomorrow afternoon we were to go to the University library. The listed return address from the envelope. The only concrete next step we had.

The physical evidence was limited to a smattering of fingerprints and photographs of the scene. No comparison to run against. The investigation would be defined by the connections of the people involved. Finn reiterated it throughout the rest of the day. Human connections of the participants were the pieces we had. I dreamt of the letter and note. It had to be the keystone, but Finn had been right. It would be useless without a stroke of genius to solve.

Maybe I'd spent the day fighting the importance of human interaction out of nerves. In our late-night call, Owen had invited me to another event tonight. I didn't want to jinx it. I didn't want to drown in my own happiness at his ask. I feared I would have come home to a blinking light on my machine. A message of retraction. An excuse as to why he could no longer attend. Or worse, if I had imagined the whole ordeal.

I hadn't, though. I had already played the message. Again and again. Owen had instead called to confirm. He truly hadn't given up on me. On us.

— ———— ————

Heaven could wait. I did not have glass slippers. Still a shame. Everything else, though, had fallen into place quickly. A cocktail dress that tiptoed along the ever-so-fine line. My hair cooperated. Even a cab was driving down the street when I made my exit. At Owen's door again. I gave a stiff knock. Waiting just enough seconds to admit to myself that I wanted him again. And again. Tonight was to be about us. Not work. I would walk the bridge between the Professor and the Guild another night. I couldn't afford a third strike with him. The door opened.

"…Hi again." I thought I'd still have a few more moments to dream about us. But, instead, he had caught me flatfooted and biting my lip.

"Hello, darling. You look amazing."

I watched as his eyes devoured me, and I wanted to reach out to feel if his heart beat like thunder. Instead, I settled on a proffered hand which he quickly obliged to take. I would not make the same mistake a third time. I used it to pull him out to the hallway.

"If I went in, we wouldn't come out."

"Fair point," he said with a slight, all-knowing smile. Then, with tension tightly confined, we made our way down to the lobby. Another cab waited. I needed to focus. We could be going to hell, and I would welcome the ride.

It was more château than a residence. The door was painted an ostentatious purple that contrasted remarkably against the stone block façade of the house. Oil lamps affixed above the door provided a soft light. The foyer gave way to marble flooring. A kind gentleman took my purse. I attempted to keep my eyes level and not be drawn to drink in the fine detail of it all. The structural components exquisitely classic, but the décor strikingly modern. A continuation of the clash. The woman did have a taste for duels.

We made it three strides in before Gabrielle Jardin came into view. She made her way down the hallway, but her eyes were focused on me. Not Owen. A graceful walk managed in an off-green gown and opera gloves. A smile the entire way. We stood ready to receive her. The dress accentuated the features of her body. Even my eyes were drawn in. I consciously moved my gaze to the marble tile floor. A pawn stuck on a square. The queen moved down an open row or rank. It did not matter.

"Hello, my dear," she said, accompanied by la bise. Her hands ever so slightly touched my shoulder. A quick greeting to Owen. Warm but not salacious.

She looped her arm through mine and promptly guided us further.

"Beautiful place you have here, Gabrielle."

"Thank you, Winona. It is the family's, but I am given free rein. You can probably tell. My twin thinks it is too much, but he is too subtle. Guy has no love for bold thinking."

"Fortune favors the bold." Owen quietly laughed at my remark before cutting it short as our eyes turned to him. Each guided step felt like a solidification of my invitation. Our feet clicked with each one. I became hyper-focused on the noise my heels made. I glanced down to ensure I was not scuffing or marking in any way.

"The floor is marble. Don't worry. You won't damage anything. Walk free, Winona." Gabrielle was more perceptive than most. I could not have looked down for more than a quarter second. "Do you like marble?"

"I prefer walking on grass." Maybe a too-honest answer. No. Owen did not know. She could not know. "I love your door."

"The neighbors hate it. All the families that refuse to adapt. They never change. They called their friends at the preservation societies. It did not work, as you can see." A sharp smile now crossed her face as if she were the proud architect of a less-than-noble deed.

"Burn the bureaucracy."

"Exactly!" She tightened her grip on my arm now. "I did not know you were such a natural rebel. Grass-walking and with a slightly gypsy hue. You are different. That is what Owen said when I first asked about his mystery girl. He said you were different."

I turned to find his attention stoically focused forward. If I was not mistaken, his features had a slight red hue. I wanted to burst at the compliment and jump into his arms. To radiate a smile down on him.

"Is that so?" I asked while keeping my eyes on him.

We arrived at the sitting room and stopped. A half dozen people seated and standing. Conversing halted as we arrived. More chatter drifted from an adjoining room. I wanted to stop and stare at them all. Take in the dress and jewelry. The suits.

A gloved finger lightly traced my ribs to bring my attention to heel.

"The men here are much less interesting than the women, Winona. I swear it."

"I certainly hope so."

Owen was suddenly pulled away by a gentleman. Left with Gabrielle, I followed her path of sight. She nodded to a man close to us. A man of reasonable attractiveness. Bland, but projecting enough confidence to make a woman curious. A fine cut of the suit. Average height and weight, but enough nature to him.

"His name is Noah. Attended Northwestern. A banker, but none of that is the most interesting part of the biography." She waited for my inquiring smile before continuing, "He cannot finish."

"Finish? Oh."

"A friend of mine, a beautiful woman, had a crush on him. She did whatever it would take, but nothing." She laughed and gave a gentle wave as he finally turned and realized we were looking his way. He locked onto the both of us, and I couldn't help but laugh too. How vain it was for him to pretend to desire us like this. Why would a baker make bread if you couldn't eat it? Men were strange in their obsession with projecting. We closed the gap with poor Noah and made the requisite introductions.

"Noah, this here is Winona."

"My pleasure." Noah extended to receive my hand. I obliged and let his eyes linger.

"I've heard a lot about you, Noah. Gabrielle recalled that you were a Wildcat."

He perked up at the mention of his accomplishment. "Indeed. Class of '86."

Strange that a person could define themselves by their high school accomplishments. With the right help, your seventeen-year-old self's resume lifts the velvet rope to prestigious universities. Graduate and subsequently work a job you hate. Your Alma Mater the perfect way to quantify your academic achievement but not your happiness.

"Did you enjoy your time in Evanston?" I politely asked, ignoring all my other thoughts.

"Of course. It is a challenging academic environment for a young man, but the results are evident. You can sharpen your skills when set against such peers."

"Were you a gladiator or student, Noah?" I couldn't help but ask. This spectacle of self-importance was ridiculous.

"Do show us your scars, Noah!" Gabrielle chimed in with a downward tilt of her head and a sexually enticing smile. This one played with her prey.

He blushed deeply at the direct confrontation of female attention that had suddenly avalanched him.

"Scars are only skin deep, ladies." Clever boy, as Gabrielle and I found ourselves suddenly deflected. I took a longer look at the man.

"Your suit. I haven't seen one like it. Where did you get it?" I asked as I reached out to feel the lapel. I prayed to an assortment of gods that Owen wasn't watching.

"It's from Milan. Custom tailor. Are you looking for a recommendation?"

"No. I prefer English against my body." I let my eyes drift to Owen across the room and held them to make it perfectly clear I'd been marked. Willingly marked. My eyes shifted back to the task at hand. "How long have you been involved with the Guild?"

"Barely longer than you. I only moved to Chicago from New York about a month ago. I needed to plug back into the cultural scene. Luckily I had some mutual connections with Gabrielle here, and voilà. The door opened."

Here a month, and Gabrielle already knew his secrets.

His self-confidence punctuated the rest of the conversation. He nary asked a question to Gabrielle or me. Thankfully Gabrielle plotted the escape with a deft comment about our need to round toward the "stallions." It was not immediately clear if he took to the insult. He only had taken to his drink after we departed. You could buy an education, but not biology. Or a personality.

Next, a fair-haired, unaccompanied woman in her late forties standing a little off admiring the books on the shelves. We steered in her direction, and Gabrielle leaned in. "Charlotte. High-value partner at Sille and Ward law firms. Three children. All sacrificed at the altar of her career. Marriage too. Pays her ex-husband thirty thousand a month in alimony." My heart skipped a beat. "Nice woman, though. Honestly kind for a lawyer. I wonder if she deems it all worth it when she comes alone to these events?"

The woman was small in stature and seemed unconcerned about any of the happenings around her. She addressed us without turning.

"Hello, Gabrielle."

"Hello, Charlotte. Plotting to steal a book?"

"None of your non-fiction, Gabi." She still had yet to look at us.

"May I introduce Winona Winthrop, Charlotte. She came here with Owen Lyons."

The woman finally turned and regarded me. Although small in stature, she had a significant presence even by my standards.

"Pleasant to meet you. Less demure than I would have antici-pated." She turned back without another comment to her examining of the books. A signal that she had decided the conversation had ended. Gabrielle leaned in and, with a slight flick of her head, signaled the need to move.

"You see how her soft skills have served her in her personal life now?" Gabrielle said once we were out of earshot. I could only nod along.

I looked around and found Owen. He must have seen my eyes. He broke free of his conversation and made his way toward us. Gabrielle talked to me about a couple on the horizon. Owen cut in and asked to borrow me.

"Everything okay, darling?"

I would be honest with him. "Gabrielle has me off-kilter. I imag-ined her differently from after our first meeting. Tonight she has been pleasant in a way, even if she walks me through everyone's dark secrets. What does she have filed away for you?"

"Of course she is." He had closed the gap between us. "Power is currency in this crowd. You can build it yourself or take it from someone else with their secrets. Come on, Detective. I expected you to arrive at that conclusion on your lonesome. How else does the Chicago Guild of Saint Luke live up to your imagination?"

"I expected more heraldry."

He leaned back with a laugh I didn't expect him to have. "Castles with candles. Tapestries and banners hung from stone cold walls."

"A girl can dream, Owen." The pageantry of the Middle Ages had been a perfect bridge between my mother's imagination and my love of history. She would sit with me and talk of heroes and heroines in resplendent armor. The trials and tribulations. Romanticized history served a purpose.

"I'll have to take you to the castles when we go to England."

My head couldn't help but run wild with thoughts of dark hallways and cold stones beneath my feet. Dreams indeed.

Owen smiled as he saw my mind work. Reality came back with the realization that a member of the wait staff fast approached. I wanted to pull each of them aside to let them know I was a visitor. That I, too, was in steerage class. Instead, the waitress felt my eyes concentrated on her and quickly approached like I had beckoned her with a whistle.

"Would you like a drink, ma'am?"

Ma'am? "Water and heavy ice with lemon. Please."

She nodded and made her escape from me.

"Water with lemon and ice? You can unfurl the sail a bit more than that, my dear." My original shepherd returned, grasping a martini. Gabrielle regarded me. Her look bordered on pure curiosity. Not a challenger as I once had been. Not a potential ally as I hoped to become. Rather a foreign entity. Because I passed on poison.

"I am okay to drift in water."

She continued to look me over. I scanned the room in the silence that lingered and took note that everyone had a drink. I wanted to explain myself. Even if I disliked her, I wanted to tell a story. It was a small thing to make me so self-conscious of being an outsider not just here but everywhere. I did not belong here. That was evident from birth. But they had a link to everyone else in the city. They drank. The city drank. Instead, I stood waiting on my water and ice. Another way I was alone.

"More surprises from you, Winona."

The waitress returned my request, and I took to it like a man in a desert. Gabrielle's interest in my order appeared to have passed. She resumed scanning the room, coming to a distinctive halt a couple dozen steps away. I wanted to avoid them. I wanted to avoid Gabrielle, but she would not let me.

"The Adfields," she said succinctly with a trace of disdain. She appeared to have made progress on the martini as I had retreated. Her eyes were locked on them. I wanted to move mine off hers but could not. She was a sight to behold in her natural state.

The couple was modest in physical features. He wore slacks with an Oxford rolled to the elbow. She had a dress that was simply pleasant. They were not drawing attention to themselves, and it piqued my curiosity. I had envisioned more from a couple that Gabrielle perceived to be competition. A duel contested by great houses that were to mirror one another. I wondered how the Adfields deftly handled the overwhelming brawn of the Jardin beauty.

"Careful with these two," Gabrielle whispered as we approached. Her body was tense. It was still difficult to imagine these two striking such a potent mixture of fear and vitriol. They turned to greet us in a natural and swift motion. The gentleman extended his hand immediately for a handshake. Introduced himself to be Nicholas. The woman smiled and introduced herself as Anna. Pleasantries were exchanged with Gabrielle. The conversation continued. They were not tense or reluctant to engage.

"Winona, you must be bored listening to all of us drone on. I bet you have stories for days," Nicholas spoke and leaned back on the frame of the door to the next room.

"I hate to disappoint. Mundane days and nights after a while. Exotic is a point of reference. From my perspective, you are all a complete change of pace."

"Smart point." Nicholas held the gaze for a second too long. Anna took notice.

"Owen Lyon. You two make a beautiful couple." A flash came to Anna's eyes as she said it. An oh-so-subtle tap back to Nicholas more than an uncontrolled slip of lust. The moves in this game were small and concise.

Instead of work, I spoke of gypsy magic. Spiritual planes. My sister, Dakota, the mystic. Everything Mama had taught me. Everything but work. The Adfields listened to my musings of fake darkness and intrigue. I even touched on Merlin. It had been the spiritual talk that bound their attention to me. A realm they could not purchase. Their eyes hungered for stories from every civilization. From every continent. They bought what I sold. It made me feel warm to be accepted, even simply in conversation.

Gabrielle stood silently by the entire time without interruption. At the end of the conversation, the Adfields had reluctantly allowed Gabrielle to lead me away. I replayed it all back in my mind. The truth I knew. I was perceived as Gabrielle's piece on the board. They needed to know me. Oh, they thought I was interesting. They thought I was different. To wrest control, they need to start by knowing me. Kind talking and kind exits. They needed the invitation of an open door to return. It was not much different from being courted by men. Except the prize was very different.

Gabrielle and I made a few strides towards the barren fireplace when she turned to me, "Did you know more about them than you let on?"

"No, why?"

"Just the point you made on education. Nicholas is the head administrator at the Roman School. Their fortune is hotel money. Her family. They married young, and he needed to stay occupied by their direction. He chose gatekeeper. Shrewd maneuver."

A clever maneuver. The Roman School was the preeminent prep school in the city. A fortress that families battled for entry into. Tuition on par with a university's. It was prestige, achievement, and scandal. Overdoses and sexual abuse by teachers were the cleanest rumors to make clear of the fortress. Nicholas positioned himself not only as a wealthy man in marriage but as an important man to what mattered most to this community. Prestige followed by children. You would appear to be slaving away as an obscure bureaucrat to help mold young minds, but in reality, you made yourself unassailable. Make a move against him in the greater game, and he locks the door to your children's future. I looked back and imagined daggers under the simple clothes.

Gabrielle sipped, and the party continued as we paused. I wanted a fire. A hearth to gather round. A place to collect and tell stories. Instead, I stared into nothing in the opening. These people did not have stories or authentic experiences. They were biographies. Not memoirs.

"Would you like another?" The waitress caught me mid-stare. She had asked me gently.

"Please. Thank you."

Gabrielle shook her glass to indicate she would take another and rolled her eyes as the young woman left.

"Who is next?" I asked. She looked over at her brother and his date. I felt for the girl after the look she received. Her brother had responded with an exaggerated roll of his eyes. They would not be next. The emotion was playful but with an undercurrent.

We were to skip her family. Gabrielle cast over at a man and woman in their middle thirties who would be next on our circuit. She sat with legs crossed in a highbacked chair as he stood next to the arm. Her dress had a high slit that she was making no effort to conceal. He made no effort to look away. Even from a distance, the energy between them appeared to be charged.

"The woman is a judge." She felt the breeze of my head snap towards her. "Don't worry. She is in family court. Maria Sulli. Went to Pepperdine. The man is Donald Malter. Finance, but he reaps without sowing. All handled by other members of the family."

More bureaucrats. I looked again and saw the same sexual energy. I guess paper pushers did more than missionary.

"They are...?"

"Both divorced. Both have an eye for younger companionship. They fuck each other when it is convenient. That is what I can make of it, anyway."

Fucking when it's convenient. Finally, something I can relate to here. We closed the steps towards the two of them. They paid our approach no heed. We were practically on top of them before they turned. The lust between the two of them had not simmered in our company. The judge and financier each had a devouring look for Gabrielle. I noticed her shoulders round back slightly. She pushed her breasts forward even as she greeted them lightly. She stood as a girl parading in front of boys. Deliberate and purposeful and enjoying the taunt. I found myself shrinking back a bit and caught my arms moving forward to cross and hide my own chest. When they finally took note of me, they settled in. The fire did not rage as it had for Gabrielle, but both lingered. These two were insatiable.

Over the following minutes, they commented on my dress, my drink, and my man. Everything that gave them worth in their own lives. They eventually talked about art. The self-appointed vanguard of the Guild. Avant-garde art. The works you would not expect.

"Anyway, we are most proud of our backing for the mail art exhibit last year."

Mail art?

"Mail art?" They both lit up to my inquiry. I might as well hit a switch.

"Yes, mail art," she finally said. "It can be the transfer of small pieces of art via the post. Or it can be the envelope itself that is the canvas. The drawing, painting, or scribbling directly on the envelope is the artwork itself. Then carried forward to destinations known or unknown. Mail art is the free exchange of art for the sake of art. It can be solicited or random. It subverts the sphere of commercial art. Nicholas and I brought it to light here in Chicago with an open gallery collection."

Stay level. "How did you gather it? I can't imagine either of you sifting at the local post office for pretty envelopes."

"We put out advertisements and requests in various art publications that travel the globe. We set up a return P.O. box and sifted through it all. The artists were throwing darts, never knowing how they hit. We did have a friend in the post office investigations section. Oh, what is his name again? He was such a help."

"Kevin Flans."

"Yes. Yes, Kevin. Not quite sure he understood the concept, but he was happy with the results on his end. His daughter was given a healthy scholarship along with advanced placement. Smart girl, but we all need a little quid pro quo. Wouldn't you agree, Winona?"

"Gatekeepers be damned," I exclaimed with a slightly hoisted water. They clinked with exuberance, and Gabrielle smiled. She thought her pet had done a trick quite well. I looked over to see Owen casually laughing in conversation. I wanted him next to me. To feel his presence and to orbit in the same space.

The conversation ended abruptly as Guillaume and his date edged closer. The judge and her lover made an excuse to leave.

Gabrielle squared off her shoulders to face her twin.

"What is the drink?" she asked casually but pointedly to Guillaume as if to leave the date out.

"Vodka is the only part I listened to when they made their sell."

"Predictable."

"It's my silver bullet, sis." He smiled and took a deep sip as he registered Gabrielle's annoyance. I occupied the mirror space of the date's framework of the conversation.

I gently ran my finger along the date's wrist to her tennis bracelet. "How beautiful. You wear it naturally."

The woman had not pulled back at my touch. Almost as if she had been expecting it. She tucked a strand of hair behind her ear and smiled in response. I realized the other conversation had muted itself. Both sets of eyes had turned to us. Instead of making a move, sometimes you had to flip the board.

"I'm Scarlett." Finally, the date had a name.

"Winona."

"Shall we, Guy?" Scarlett took her man by the hand and led him away from his blood just like that. He followed with no hesitation.

"That fucking social-climbing broodmare," Gabrielle quipped as she watched them stalk off. "My brother has a particular taste. Anyways, Winona, I'm impressed on short notice. What do you think of them all?"

"More variance than I had expected, to be honest. I expected many clones of you. But a heavier element of radical chic here." Maybe honesty would work.

"You think so?" Gabrielle had been taken aback by the assessment.

"A desire for it, at least. A romanticized outlaw fashion stays en vogue. People met me and were desperate to tell me they were in the trenches of emerging culture."

"Sharp girl you are. *Finally*, I can see the reason Owen has kept you around."

Ouch, bitch. I quelled the rise of a woman's revenge. I could have paraded my triumphs over her. A single glance and nod to bring him to heel next to me. Show her how deeply my claws would dig into his back tonight. But no. "It's usually not my mind." Well, maybe, no. No one respected a doormat, after all.

"Why water anyway?"

The sudden change in conversation visibly startled me. Gabrielle was a predator for information. The vulnerable parts of a person would be used as leverage. I would not allow her mine. Would not allow her to whisper about me for this. Let her tell people I was a slut who fucked for money.

"Nectar of life," I said. "Plus, I have work later. I cannot function like some of the others with a drink in me."

"Responsible. That is a nice change of pace from the usual company I keep."

I nodded, and the moment passed. The night passed. We continued to move between the people for a second round. Owen joined us, and the conversations maintained a level of admiration for our thoughts. I wanted to nail Owen's hand to the small of my back. I would not take a step away. No self-sabotage.

I didn't want to admit it, but I had gained a better understanding of the Professor from meeting more of the Guild. Even through the wicked and warped lens that Gabrielle wrought. Work never strayed too far, being honest with myself. Despite my attempts.

CHAPTER ELEVEN

R.R. November 5th. Awoke. Destroy keys. Daphne.

It all tied together somehow. Owen had been a godsend after the Guild for more than one reason. He had pointed out November 5th, after all. Of celebration and bonfires. A string to pull on alongside the return address for the note. I had shaken off the rust of the morning and kissed him goodbye while he still lay in bed.

--   ---   ---------

Later that day, Finn and I stood tucked inside the entrance to the University library. Sweeping gothic stone arches that framed stained glass windows. Rows of books neatly organized. Tables occupied by students. They all looked like virgins. The only way I would have found my way into a library like this at their age was for the flat surfaces. So why did I lie to myself?

The entire place flowed around a small woman. A plain woman. Ms. Eberhart, the librarian. Cloaked in modesty. A shawl wrapped around her shoulders. She was annoyed at our approach and surprisingly stayed annoyed after I had announced our office to be the detectives in the murder of the Professor. A hermit cloistered in her tower. The mention of the murdered co-worker barely a ripple on her pond. Odd, if not for the disdainful looks she had for us. The looks she had for the students. She preferred cats, not humans, I bet.

We had asked her about mail. Not her department, she said. Inquired about typewriters. Directed us to University procurement or basement storage that had not been opened in years. Books were her trade. Talk of books had cracked her door. The Gunpowder Plot. The Professor also had been interested in the subject, apparently. Had dogged her to be his guide. She had been well-versed when we asked her to do the same.

An hour with the woman and my own blood pumped slower. Is this what happens to women who age alone? Do they become a black-hole to intrigue and joy? Finn had been respectful, but even he had shown signs of frustration. The woman was dry. The woman hated me.

I had cross-checked a copy of the note against many a book. Page, line, and word. Failure.

"There are thousands of books here, Detective. Plenty more are brought in and moved out every month. So, your task at hand seems to be a fool's errand. I told him the same when he dragged that paper around."

"I'm afraid you're right. We at least had each other's company."

She turned with the natural grace of a gargoyle to take me in.

"If there is anything I or this library can be of assistance to you in the investigation of that man's murder, please do let me know."

That man? Odd way to reference a murdered co-worker.

"I appreciate that, Ms. Eberhart. Did you know Professor Hickey?"

"I knew Mr. Hickey only from a distance."

"How far of a distance?"

"Not far enough for me."

The sudden surprise on her face betrayed her stoic demeanor. The mind's words occasionally slipped by to be spoken. She quickly caught herself and pursed her lips, bringing her shoulders back.

"What I mean to say, Detective, is that the Professor and I were ideological adversaries in a way. We occupied opposing viewpoints on the role of academia. We both could find an idea detestable, but our responses differed greatly. He believed in the censorship of ideas. He would rail at faculty meetings. Scream that open debate forum would give platforms to fascists and dangerous ideologues. It's the notion that you defeat the idea you fight by silencing it. Burn the book as opposed to debate it. It's my thought that you let the lunatics you oppose talk for the world to hear. Give them enough rope and they'll hang themselves, as they say. When you ban an idea is when you drive it deep into the ground and make it alluring. Perspective is lost by many in the passions of the day."

I did not think the woman had this much speech in her, but it appeared I wasn't the only one not to shed a tear for the dear Professor's passing. Finn ran his hand over the stubble of his face and took in the woman before him.

"Sunshine is the best disinfectant, as they say," I replied. She had passion and a point. The fractures and fissures of the University were more complex than I had initially realized.

She paid my words no heed. I heard her breath exhale. Her entire being softened as she pulled the ledger cradled in her arms tightly to her chest. I followed her gaze and found the matchstick. The janitor. Halfpenny was making a round through the library. Emptying the trash cans in a quiet and steady manner. Nary a student's head lifted as he moved around them, performing the menial tasks set forth to the custodial class. He worked America's own Road of Bones. Embarrassment hit me as I realized I hadn't noticed him either. Ms. Eberhart had, though. It seemed she longed for something besides books to lay with. She was a woman, after all. She longed not to age alone. Maybe she was where she was supposed to be. A nymph hid among the trees of the forest to protect all within, and she hid here among the paper born of trees to continue the watch.

"Oh, and Ms. Eberhart, does R.R. mean anything to you?"

"R.R.? It does not, Detective Winthrop."

November 5th.

Awoke.

Destroy Keys.

Daphne.

We navigated our way from the University. As we drove through the surrounding ghetto, a small smile inadvertently crept across my face. Maybe Ms. Eberhart was onto something.

"What is the smile about? The only news I took away was that books rotate in and out of that place. We could sit there forever and never touch the right key."

"I know, but for now, I am focusing on the good we encountered."

"The good?"

"Did you see her at the end? She saw the janitor and looked like a schoolgirl. First love can strike at any age, Finn. That's the good."

"First love. First regrets. Age doesn't discriminate."

With that, we settled into the drive with our thoughts.

--- ---- -----

He had been gone for three days. Making lunch for a younger sister and getting her to school on time made me different from the other fifteen-year-olds in the neighborhood. He had returned by the end of school on the fourth day. In his mind, he had never left. Nothing to justify. He didn't possess the ability to be contrite or the shame that would require him to explain himself. He just went on as if nothing had happened. How do you rebel when there are no rules already? How do you beat on the walls put up to protect your adolescence by those who love you when there are no walls? You bring the trouble to the front door.

His name was Jack. Not John, but Jack. He claimed his parents didn't have the wherewithal to understand it wasn't a proper name. Set the tone for his life, he said. He was nineteen and worked at the local auto body shop. I had called him by dinner on the fourth day. He arrived in a 1987 Buick GNX. My father registered it through the front window. No harsh greeting. No demand for a curfew or questions about why an adult was picking up his fifteen-year-old daughter. Barely any eye contact.

Like most men in the process of becoming one, Jack sought to impress with a cocktail of bravado and bravery. In addition to an actual cocktail built with a foundation laid from vodka poured from a cheap glass bottle. Time warped the memory where I could tell myself it was all to be a Molotov cocktail to my dear father's heart, but the truth was I had been impressed. Jack was sweet and, under it all, a good heart beat. I knew it to be true when I was the catalyst to danger, and the concern crept up in him. I sat in jean shorts and a low cut tank on the window while he drove through the outlying roads of Illinois beyond the city. Even at fifteen, I knew how to lean forward to ensure my demand for more speed was met. The engine worked, and I welcomed it all. The liquor acted as gasoline to the fire of my true desire. Speed ran its course, though. Brinksmanship the policy. The wind called. I had climbed half out the passenger window. Jack reached over but not to caress. He had tried to pull me back in the car while masking it with a playful air of flirting. His eyes betrayed him, and there was real concern in them. It was all so foreign to me that it made me drunker with the power of control. It was me moving the chess pieces on the board now. I dodged his pull to safety with a laugh and a challenge to his manhood. He had taken the bait, and the GNX lived up to the billing. With the wind in my hair and death on my mind, I looked back into the car to see how tense he was. A man at war with himself over what to do, and I had started it. I loved it. In the spirit of victory, I launched one of the empty glass bottles into the passing night to watch it connect with a road sign.

From the darkness, the lights exploded along with sirens. Sheriffs. Shit. They had been okay with speeding—it was a way of letting off steam in these parts. They had been fine with me out a window. Daredevil behavior was apparently as common as speeding. To vandalize the County's property? That cost money, and the people out here paid taxes for a reason. To their credit, the Sherriff deputies politely related they didn't realize I was so young. Neither had Jack, but that fell on deaf ears. Jack was booked, and I was taken home. Even the Sherriff's attempt to appeal to my sensibilities on the ride home showed more care and intervention than anything from my father.

I never saw Jack again. I hope he found a nice girl who didn't push him too far. He was rare in his own way.

—   ——————   ——————

"Anything of note collected from the evidence technician's processing of the scene?"

"Need a suspect first, Winona. Same as before."

Fuck you too. The doldrums of an investigation are what no one talked about. The space far enough out where the scene became sanitized in your memories. The processing by the family less fresh. Then it stalled, and a new one landed in your lap.

Not now, though. The murder of the Professor was still fresh. Due to the murder of Helen, we could not leave it behind. We did not want to leave it behind.

"I suspect the librarian with the candlestick." I had wanted him to laugh. Get a glimpse of how he seemed around Niamh. Nothing romantic, but rather how a family would wish happiness on each other. The warmth she had instantly brought to the surface with her mere presence around him had been so endearing. People deserved to feel like that. "The librarian, though. She was not a fan of the Professor. She talked about his death like a minor note to a day's events."

"Let's look into it then," Finn replied. No hint of disagreement or attempt to dissuade. He still sat comfortably.

"She did seem to have her eyes cast on the janitor. Might need your down-to-earth, common man charm next time."

"Give up on humor. You are decently better at being a detective."

We knew little. The County was told to make Helen hush. Papers too. For Hickey, the wife presented a practical route. Jealousy? Infidelity? He had fucked her as a student. I severely doubt she was the first or last. The stretch lead, the librarian. The motive unknown, but the result appeared desired. My unspoken connection, the Guild.

Our house was being built on sand. Two men murdered a young girl. Butchered her like a hog and wanted the memory preserved. Their deed witnessed. We had to come to know one of them as best we could, but the other a complete mystery. Over the top of it all, the letter stamped with a fox that walked to taunt.

Payphone calls with keys taken.

November 5th.

The letter had even neutered him to a degree if what the wife had said was to be believed. Neutered a man who had built his life around ensuring to be entrenched among the nobles. Even a marriage to cement it. Again, I had returned to the letter.

I needed to think on the Professor. I hated it, but I could understand an outsider. You know you don't belong. You wait for the rug to be pulled out from under you. To be exposed as a common peasant. Replaceable. That's what we are. You had to constantly provide to guarantee your worth. Prove your value to the circle. To be an outsider was to show up in your finest and realize it was barely worth making into a curtain to them. You were never natural. They had been to the tailor since birth and wore it accordingly.

"Finn…"

He returned into focus from his rapt attention focused on the radio carrying the game.

"The other man in the picture with Helen. He isn't just power. He's old power. The clothes never lie. How they wear them, never lie. It can't be taught. Why would they want a middling university professor around? What could he offer these people? What did he have access to? A replenishing group of young women who would cycle in and out of the University year after year. Like the books in the library. He groomed girls, Finn. That was his part in all this."

"Groomed?"

"He might as well have been a pimp. They need a doorman. Hickey was eager to climb the ladder. He married her, didn't he? He didn't choose the prettiest student but the one with the best pedigree. Here he is with the man in the wolf mask. You fear exile after being taken in. I don't know why Helen. I don't know where she fits in yet." Helen. Poor Helen, who always wanted something bigger. Something better.

"That's one hell of a theory sketched to the edges."

"It's motive. The Professor lorded the photographs to maintain his position, and it eventually caught up with him."

"Up for ice cream? I know a place on Montrose and Ravenswood."

"Always, Finn."

---- -------- ----

The glass window was adorned with crossed ice cream cones beneath a single scoop. A clever take on the Jolly Roger to fly. Inside, the ice cream shop bristled with activity. A gaggle of kids ogled at the menu and debated amongst themselves while parents attempted to keep the herd in line. The teenagers behind the counter reminded me of Helen's hometown. They were in good spirits, and a slight air of flirting between a few of them permeated their movements. It felt good to be in the neighborhoods. People were more normal. To surround yourself with normal was paramount. I would need to remember to come back here and sit by myself to listen in on the innocent conversations.

The kid with the scooper called us forward. Vanilla with graham crackers and chocolate chips topped with caramel. It was second nature at this point to order it. No order followed mine, and I glanced over and was stunned. Finn was paralyzed by options, apparently. He stood there like a child, his eyes darting back and forth amongst the array of possibilities before him.

"Finn, order something!"

"I will! I will! This can be overwhelming."

Overwhelming? This man had walked point on patrols in the jungles of Vietnam, and here he was, looking like he had to write a thesis on what ice cream he wanted. Men. The minutes passed, and I just stared at the man I thought was a rock. Finally, he decided on vanilla with Oreos and fudge.

We took a two-person table by the side window.

"I think you're on to a motive."

"Cash as a distraction."

Finn nodded along with the assessment as he enjoyed his selection. It was odd what people could agree on. Ice cream had to be near the top.

"Near the end with my mom, ice cream was a regular occurrence. It made us feel like regular kids and not like we were racing the clock for memories. It really was the best. She was the best."

Mama, can you hear me?

"Who knew dessert could turn sentimental?" I finished with a genuine laugh and a slight swell of water in my eyes.

"Parents always seem to know just what to do. Even under the most difficult of circumstances," Finn said deftly.

The table of kids next to us continued on a rampage through the frozen treats. Finn and I both smiled and watched. Happiness could be contagious, after all.

"Why don't you ask Niamh out for some ice cream? You could even comb your hair to be presentable."

"Take Niamh out? Winona, I'm spoken for."

The ugly truth hung between us, but I didn't have the heart to speak it. It was an open secret that Finn's wife had left him. He had come home one day to find boxes and barely a note. It had been months. It hadn't been the first time she had pulled the Houdini. I hated her without even knowing her.

"I don't think she would say no, though." I could approach the line but not cross it.

"I really made a poor decision."

"Oh?" Had I gotten through to him?

"This damn Oreo. They crushed the pieces too much. Might as well be dust and crumbs. Just remnants of Oreos in here. I can't find a large chunk worth eating."

Jesus. Men. Fine.

"Well, you already ate three-quarters of it, so it can't be that bad."

"Even a thirsty man would drink water from a puddle, Winona."

"And I'm the delicate flower of detectives?"

"What can I say? My stomach is a graveyard of wants."

I could only stare as he simply looked disappointingly into his cup while holding his spoon. Men were merely large boys. But this one had protected me, and another had exacted revenge for me. I needed to place flowers, but I would watch this one sulk over ice cream for now.

We returned to the cluster of papers that buried our desks and sat with the regret of excess.

"You know, your talk had me thinking," Finn said. "It wasn't even the most unique piece in the picture."

The thought of the Polaroids was always a flood of emotions. What did Helen feel in the moments leading to her death? What had they told her to make her so compliant? A moment in a game to capture before she was ushered to cocktails. A ritual step to a better invitation. I dreamt of death, and she dreamt of a better life. Why didn't God exchange us?

Finn continued, "The masks. I know we ran nowhere at the University with them, but maybe that wasn't the place to look. You pointed the arrow with the sexualized component. Masks like those aren't disposable, no matter how much money you have. I would bet on them being a reoccurring feature. An outgrowth of personality. Carefully selected and adorned. Status in their own right. People who hid liked to hide."

"Fair point." Truly. Theatrics were a symptom of gluttony. To kill had not been enough. They wanted to play a part. They were as safe as in a play, though. They made sure to pick the weak and vulnerable. Could not risk going off script. "Where do you think we start?"

"I don't know, but I think I know someone who might." His face cracked from the rock bluff hardness that came over him whenever he talked of Helen's murderers to a softer, gentler layer that I only saw him display when around one other. These were not masks, though. Finn was a man of absolute feeling and could simply move between the raw emotion. There was no safety where he went.

"I'm sure Niamh would just prefer a couple scoops of ice cream, Finn."

"She won't be back till tomorrow."

"Know her schedule, do we?"

He shot up straight and looked away, adjusting his blazer and grumbling under his breath. I bit the top of my pen and smiled. I would pour gasoline on the fire in him. A flint spark to become a forest fire. Love was living. Living was love.

CHAPTER TWELVE

My condo was dark but organized. As though it were from the pages of a decor magazine. The writeup to fawn over accented walls or hip end tables. Visitors said the same. They meant it as a compliment. It felt like a stab. They spoke, and I heard that it looked as though no one lived here. That a ghost simply walked through it on occasion. I didn't even live enough to make a mess in my own place. I was working on making heavier steps in my own life, though. I was allowing Owen in. The pursuit. I had burned it down, but this time I would rebuild. I wouldn't exile myself from the realm of living.

Romeo had taught the world that banishment was worse than death. To walk the earth separated from your love was to endure the torture of hope. The hope of reconnection that was never to be. A swift execution brought answers, but exile brought a living death devoid of understanding. I was a coward to fear it above all else while watching Finn live it. He endured it every day, staring down a love that would not, or could not, be pursued.

I looked over the catalog page that I called home and laughed at the tameness. Dakota probably found herself sitting on an overturned wood crate in a yard in Montana. The wild surrounded her. Surrounded her in spirit. In temperament. In desire.

A desperate read of the night sky for omens. Forever her habit since she was sixteen. Forever guided from above, she said. Absolute trust and faith in the unseen. Her confidence in it all on one end. My uncertainty the fulcrum. At the other end, in opposition to her, sat our father. I had not heard from her in years. I had failed her, and she had run to where people could still be lost. Headed West. The last word from her had been a postcard from Missoula for me. Unsigned, but I knew. The girl believed what she sold. She felt the spirits in her bones, she would say. I wanted her here. I wanted the company. I could ask about Helen. Ask her if she felt Helen around me. If Helen had crossed over.

It was a sad state of affairs to crave such a level of affirmation. Helen was in the ground. That we knew. That and nothing more. Dakota could charge fools for ramblings, but me? Sorry, sister. Time for bed.

--- ---- -------

Mama? Are you there?! She had brushed my brow. The clock had moved to 2:43 AM. I sat up in bed. I desperately called out again. I needed to remember the dream. I tried to scoop water with one hand. Had she visited me? Or was it wishful thinking? Probably a trick of the mind with Dakota on mine. Sleep beckoned me back, and the night drifted back to dark.

-- --- ----

Niamh's expression softened as we approached her desk in the morning. I smiled like a child. It took everything I had not to glance up at

Finn to read his every crinkle and crease.

"Well, this is a pleasant surprise on a first day back," she said while sitting back in her chair.

"Thought I saw you walking around yesterday from a distance. Didn't realize you were coming off your weekend. How was it?" Finn had opted to play it semi-distant. Not as if his mind had a clock that counted down when he'd see her next.

"Fascinating. Late nights, fast cars, Russian roulette in the back of a restaurant," Niamh said with a slight smile of her own. "All the company I crave."

"The restaurant have good service?"

"You wouldn't hate it there. I can give you a tour."

"You can get ice cream after!" I blurted out. Fuck. They both regarded me. I had trespassed on a private moment. Their private world pierced by my inability to contain my own thoughts.

"Anyhow, the case we have now, Niamh, has an interesting layer. A component you might be able to help with." Finn had returned to the business on hand. I owed him.

"Is that so?"

"I was hoping some of your…well…contacts…might have come across any clients with a peculiar taste in ornamentation."

"Finn, if you want me to ask hookers a question, you must be a little more straightforward. Time is money for them, and I don't like to waste theirs."

Direct. I really liked her.

"Masks, Niamh. Can you ask around about ornate masks? Clients who would wear them. A white coyote. A black wolf. I'm not talking about the type for Halloween or a cheap pullover. I'm talking intricately carved and finely crafted. The kind that looks to cost."

"Expensive and needlessly theatrical? I have someone you could talk to. She has a love-hate relationship with me. I am not on her good side at the moment, but with this lovely by your side, I doubt she will hesitate to play question and answer. Her name is Zelda. She runs a house of domination over off Grand Ave just past Racine. Nondescript building. Black door."

"Thanks, Niamh," Finn said. He tapped her desk with his fist twice. He bit his lower lip. He no doubt sought to recapture the tension of the moment I had ruined. I turned to make my escape in no mood to further smother the mood. I failed and Finn followed. Silence lingered. Five footfalls and we were prompted to turn back.

"I like mint chocolate chip, for the record, Finn."

I wasn't the only one who blushed.

--- --------

Black had been an understatement. The door had been a midnight black. The reception area had been barely more. A few couches, a coffee table with Reader's Digests, and a receptionist dressed for clerical work. Calls needed to be answered, and appointments made by the sound of it.

Zelda was paged to the front. Finn and I both appeared to be taken aback by the subdued nature so far. I had conjured up a far different scene in my imagination. A walk through the door to another world, not the mirror of a dentist's waiting area.

The door to the back opened, and a woman stood. A statue of a woman. Tone, firm, with long black hair that had been pulled back into a tight French braid. She wore a black trench coat that ran down just past her hips. The stocking-clad legs were exposed, complete with black heels. Her breasts were prominent and clearly visible in the opening of the coat. I would guess a corset and garter belt framed the body underneath. She was pretty but stern. Quasi-masculine. She had titled herself a dominatrix, and her posture left no room to doubt it.

We introduced ourselves. She had been polite in our reception. She beckoned us to follow her through where she'd come from. Down a casual office hallway to a heavy leather plush door that had to be opened with an oversized silver key topped with a pink ribbon. Beyond the door, the hallway was lit low. Red danced with black.

"Not much farther, Detectives. My personal office is in the very back."

She continued like a lion on the plains. The farther we went, the clearer the territory was hers. Doors had been opened. A quick passing look inside gave way to what I had imagined. Bondage furniture built to hold. Benches complete with restraints. A stockade. I had not realized the breadth of handcuffs available in the world. Or whips.

We continued on, and even I couldn't help but feel drawn to the power a bit. No stranger to pleasure by way of submission, my mind drifted. Imagination was a terrible thing to waste. After a few more turns in the labyrinth, we arrived at an unassuming door that was near seamless with the wall. Zelda reached down and, from her pocket, produced a key of ordinary renown. A well-lit office lay beyond. More manager-like than dominatrix. Neatly organized across the desk were papers and ledger books. She took her seat and beckoned us to the two chairs before her. An office plant in the corner and a calendar on the wall completed the plainness of it all.

"This is my business. I run it as a professional. Don't look so surprised by my office."

I blushed slightly. I didn't even want to turn to see Finn's reaction.

"We know, Zelda. You know what we do, after all. The pleasure you sell to people does not interest, or bother, us." Finn surprised me with a soft tone.

"Niamh mentioned you were murder police."

"That's right." Finn kept his tone smooth. "We are here because you might be able to help us."

"I'm not sure how I could help the murder police." The heavy mascara around her eyes made me wonder if Owen would like the same on me.

"We will get there. We just thought you might have a better look inside the proclivities of society than we do, Zelda," Finn said.

After all my time taking the lead, I stayed on the sidelines here. On paper, sex should have been my realm and place of comfort. Instead, I sat.

"Men—and women—come here for release. It's fantasy. People carry terrible burdens day to day, and here they don't have to be in control. Don't have to be in charge. They submit. The proclivities of the clients I consort with are private. Without that, I would have built my house on sand."

"I fear you misunderstand our line of inquiry. We aren't interested in anyone specifically but rather in concepts. Larger picture, if you will."

"Surprisingly light touch for one with such heavily scarred hands. I can see why Niamh cares for you. Clear in her voice."

"I appreciate your assessment, but that line of inquiry, Zelda, is my private thought. I know you can respect that."

"Humble too. I hope Niamh realizes what is in front of her. I see many a men, and barely one interests me. They prescribe their own sexual fantasies that are more caricatures than reality. It clouds them. You, though, you are genuine. It's endearing. Rare. If only you were a little easier on the eyes."

Finn barked out a laugh. "I can't have it all now, can I?"

Zelda laughed with him. Not at him. Her focus had shifted. I felt myself being devoured. "No, but you...you are a beauty so sharp it makes me want to bleed."

I tried not to wilt. I tried to settle myself.

"What do you know about wolves, Zelda? Coyotes?"

Her eyes snapped away from me and back to Finn.

"Wolves?" Her voice overstressed to be neutral. She was good, but the overcompensation was a comet in the sky if you lived among liars. "Not much. You might have better luck at a zoo." Her eyes remained on Finn and didn't even drift towards me now.

"A wolf and a coyote that walk upright, Zelda."

"I don't follow, Detective."

"Masks, Zelda. I want to ask you about masks. Men who hide behind them. A black and red wolf mask. An off-white coyote mask. Either could be confused for a traditional Native American ceremonial mask. The kind that looks like you can't just buy them at a store."

He seemed to have unnerved her. A slight roll of her shoulders showed a dismissal of persona. The woman behind the whips and leather now sat before us.

"Plenty of people like to hide while they are here. Plenty of people come through here, but some jobs…I can't."

My movements mirrored Finn's forward. The crack in façade deepened and exposed a living, breathing woman here who had more to say.

"Do you look after the girls who work for you, Zelda?" I asked.

"Of course. They come to this profession because here they are in charge. Here they dictate and are in control. That doesn't mean that they haven't been on the other side in the past. Most have, in fact. I would never allow anything to happen to them."

"So do we. Even when they have been brutally murdered, we still look after them. We carry their burden in this life even if they leave it."

Zelda appraised me with a different look in her eyes. Attempting to find sincerity in my words. Not just an ornament.

"Your girls escaped, Zelda. This one didn't. They took her. Took what she had been, what she was, and what she could ever be." My words appeared to strike hard. More than her business sense.

"Masks…I don't know much. I can't say much. You can't say much."

We let silence linger as she prepared to share with us. You knew when they would. When the threshold had been crossed. Finally, she exhaled.

"It wasn't your garden variety party. They called and requested us off-site. Paid incredibly well to bypass identification confirmation. We usually photocopy I.D. cards. They even provided transportation. Top shelf the entire way. I talked to the three girls who were going with me, and they agreed. Money talks, and this money shouted."

"What about the party?" Finn brought the level questions back into the fold.

"The masks. The entire party was in intricate masks. A few that resembled animals. There were dozens of people. Men and women. The first thing we noticed was how well-dressed they were. Gowns and suits for most of the guests. Younger women were walking around in fine lingerie. We were brought to perform. Nothing completely out of the ordinary. The scantily clad girls were pawed at by nearly everyone as if they were party favors. The scene devolved into the expected debauchery. Our instructions had been strictly defined. Roam the party after a demonstration. Assist and guide. Put people at ease in exploration. Complete requests as we saw fit. Make someone feel powerful or powerless. Read the person or couple and go with it. Easy money." She stopped and turned to her calendar briefly before returning to us.

"Then I realized Simone wasn't around. I asked the other girls, and no one seemed to know where she had gone. They are my responsibility. I started working my way through the party. I must have burst into half a dozen rooms full of sex before I came to an unremarkable door slightly open. Her shoe outside. I slipped in. A man with his back to me. His head tilted down, and he had been so focused on what lay before him. Simone was on the ground. She had already started to bruise around the side of her face. I saw terror in her eyes as they connected with mine. He finally had flinched in recognition that they were no longer alone, but I had moved quickly."

In a fluid motion of her arm, Zelda produced a three-inch blade hidden beneath the leather bracer about her wrist. "I came up behind him, held it to the opening for his eye in the mask, and asked how he liked his vision. He didn't even breathe heavily. That still terrifies me. I know brutal men. I know dangerous men. Ones who truly are comfortable with violence that you avoid. Simone scurried out, and I backed out. He barely turned his head. He was almost amused by it all."

"Who hired you, Zelda, for the party? Where was it?" Finn had lost the softness of voice.

"I don't know. Honestly. It was arranged through a series of phone calls. Wall after wall. The cash came up front, and we were happy. The place had been drafty. Cold. Like an old factory that had been converted. I can't even say a location as they picked us up and drove us there."

"What else do you remember? Names? Faces? Anything?"

"His name? No. He was just some guy…they kept everything generic. The wolf said something when I was backing away with the blade. He said, 'You would give Daphne a run.' It gave me a chill the way he said it. I could feel him smirk beneath the mask."

Daphne.

Finn produced a cropped copy of the photograph of our wolves.

"Look familiar?"

"Yes. Yes. Yes, that's the mask!" The excitement struck first, then visibly ebbed away as realization dawned.

Finn returned the photograph to his interior coat pocket and continued to pepper her with logistical questions, all of which were dead ends. I believed she wanted to help but could only do so much. The woman in black said the event had been twelve to fourteen months past. Hopes were subsequently dashed for any additional detail to cling to.

I interrupted, "Do you remember a mention of R.R.?"

"Sorry, no. I have a client coming in shortly who has paid an exorbitant amount of money for me to do all sorts of unholy things to him. So, I need to get back into character."

"No, no. Thank you for your help," I said.

Finn and I rose to leave when she whispered.

"Ballet."

"Ballet?" Finn asked.

"I did ballet as a girl. It's why I could move so quietly behind him," Zelda paused, "I like you both. I can tell. Please. Run, don't walk from this. I feel awful for what happened to your girl, but I can feel power, and these ones walked on water."

Your girl.

Helen was ours now. Finn regarded her warning. Moved to slightly adjust his sport coat before responding.

"You don't understand. I don't walk softly."

She looked at Finn the same way I did now. The way you would look at shelter in a storm. Finally, she stood with all assuming confidence returning and let her coat fall back onto her chair. She stood in a black leather corset and fishnet tights. Sex and control on display. Zelda, the dominatrix, had returned and set out to stake a claim.

---- ---- ----

"Daphne," I whispered.

"I know," Finn replied, "It's just all the other details were a bust." He seemed to be chewing on something as we sat in the car. I chewed on the memories of a party in an old factory that felt cold with a draft. Still, I did not mention the Guild.

"You're right. All these pebbles we find don't do anything when flung against the wall. We need boulders."

"It'll come together. No pressure."

"Finn..."

"I keep thinking of Helen. Where she came from. How she could have been one of Bill's daughters. I keep thinking of her mom. I can't go back to that table telling her I failed. I will not. I'm done going to kitchen tables empty-handed." His tone chilled. A hard man had become harder.

"You should let me drive."

It was the most absurd request I could muster, and it worked. When you want to lower the temperature, you change course fast to a proposition you know you will lose. He looked at me like I had just asked to stop to skin a cat. I told Finn I had to step out for a bit. An easier request to swallow. I would be back.

— ———— ————

I could see my mother in the way people sat sometimes. Watch strangers lean in as the other person excitedly talked. The way it allowed validation for the one talking. It was a small thing, but it mattered. Mama always made people feel like they were on to something; the whole world just needed them to say a little more. It required warmth.

The doorman at Owen's residential tower was doing it now. An elderly woman, maybe widowed or perhaps never married, was telling him about an artist she had read about. She had brushed up a serious amount of knowledge on a 19th-century Spaniard, and the doorman not only allowed her to talk but engaged and leaned in with excitement at the appropriate times. It was cute. I waited on the sidewalk for Owen. He had wanted to meet upstairs, but I didn't trust myself still. He had called with an ask for a walk and lunch. He knew I would not say no. Women would chase the man for his looks and then kill him on command when they saw where he lived. I was not them, though, and he knew it. The looks did not hurt, but I had to do more than stare at the man. The sidewalk hustle continued all around me, and out he came, resplendent as ever.

As he stepped out onto the sidewalk, I reminded myself to breathe. I admired him for the moment before he saw me. He smiled big and bold, the genuine kind. He approached me, and we kept eye contact the entire way.

"Well, aren't you dapper today? Just one time, I would like to find you in a wrinkled shirt and jeans."

"Unfortunate byproduct of a corrupted youth."

"I still have a bit of corrupting to do to you." I was in a mood. I had to remind myself we were on a sidewalk. Far from his door. Far from his hallway. Far from his oversized bed. Far from his headboard.

For his part, he flashed a grin and let his eyes consume me from head on down for a moment.

"Where to for lunch?" I asked.

"Somewhere public to keep our graces good. Luckily, I know just the place."

—— ——— —————————

After a short cab ride punctuated by physical tension, we arrived at the bistro. A place that appeared to be popular with business types who looked to break the rules a bit. Squares with wobbly lines. I had to change my mindset. I had to enjoy the company and the additional chances I'd been given. Appreciate the now, for it can be taken away. I sat at the table with the sculpture entirely focused on me. Yet I was self-aware. A constant battle of the mind to justify my belonging. My entry.

We ordered and kept the topics light. The naturalness of conversation returned quickly and comfort set in. The warming of a heart that I used to confuse with being content. This was not being content and docile. This was recognition of comfort and belonging. To know how well you fit into another. To yearn to be nestled against his chest with only music playing in a dark room. No needing. No wanting. Being happy where you were was not being content. Then the surface of the water started to break.

"How did you ever come to be the police anyhow?"

"A lucky misunderstanding. A pull for experience." Why spoil the moment with a story of attempted rape and my own personal longing for death? The bread here was baked and served fresh. It would be difficult to enjoy it then.

"Tell me the truth, Winona. In a thousand lifetimes, I bet this is the only one you are the police."

"Prefer to see me locked in an office? Climbing a ladder to the top in a corporate free-for-all? A lifetime preparing a coffin with a luggage rack. I prefer to be stabbed head-on, personally."

"Not an office, maybe a creative fiel—"

"Artists and writers? Do I really strike you as someone who sits around treating life as some sort of lazy river? In days gone by, perhaps they knew adventure, but not now. Now the world has been made so safe for the space to create that atrophy has set into the entire scene. Take your Guild events. Monolithic thought. There is no danger in art anymore." The truth unsaid was that a girl was not likely to be killed at an art gallery or behind a desk.

"To court danger then? That's why you took after a badge?"

"To court adventure, my dear."

"You could have traveled the world instead."

Oh, sweet Owen, who never had a bill to pay.

"Travel is a poor substitute for adventure."

"I beg to differ. I have been fortunate to travel extensively and felt the thrill."

"The thrill of what, Owen? A new meal? A building to look at? Tell me a story that moved your blood, and don't recount how seeing the Taj Mahal took your breath away. The greeting card business has monopolized the cheap emotion of viewing."

"Well, I was on safari in South Africa—"

"With a guide carrying a large gun?"

"Well, yes—"

"He can tell the story. You cannot. Place your protection in another's hands, and you bend a knee."

Owen let out a laugh that seemed to break the stale air in the place. Genuine emotion had not gone extinct after all.

"I am unsure how I can win with you, Winona."

"You can't. I always have an ace up my sleeve." I could not help but smile and look at him as I tore warm bread apart. "Well, there it is."

"There what is?"

"Why I became the police."

"I am still lost."

"I wanted to be the guide on your safari. Not just a passenger. Life is too short not to experience truly, and in a world that has been fully charted, the only place left was the south side of Chicago to experience danger and be paid for it. I have bills to pay, after all."

"Bills are such a mundane topic, don't you think?" Her voice burst the comforting isolation Owen and I had come to enjoy over lunch. "I saw you across the room and had to stop by."

This bitch. Gabrielle Jardin.

"Gabrielle, please sit down." Owen politely extended an open hand to a seat at our table as I tried not to recoil. She took the seat effortlessly without acknowledging that anyone except for Owen was present.

"My companions won't miss me for a few minutes."

"They might," I said what I had been thinking.

She laughed politely and finally turned to me as though she intended to dismiss me. She held the gaze and let indifference settle in after glancing down to note how I had manhandled the bread before me.

"Anyhow, it feels like it's been ages since I have seen you two." She finally took her attention from my manners.

"It feels like an ice age," I could not stop the smirk as I said it.

She settled her gaze back on Owen. He was blissfully unaware of the contest being played before him. I felt the reoccurring stab of desire for him to lust after her again. A desire for competition that first surfaced within at my introduction to the Guild. She cast easy on my eyes after all, and when he thought I wasn't looking, his gaze should want to wander. I leaned forward and took grains of salt in my hand. They were conversing now. Throw salt over the left shoulder to ward evil spirits away. Silly superstitions.

"Winona?" Owen kindly cut in.

"Yes?"

"Are you alright?"

"Yes." And with a quick motion, I threw the salt over my left shoulder.

Owen smiled as he looked at me while Gabrielle just stared. I met her eyes.

"Didn't work."

"Trying to melt the ice age?" Owen asked. I realized Gabrielle and I had both turned with a quiet laugh to him in some apparent surprise for the clever inquiry.

"I'm surprised to find you here, Gabrielle." Back to the game at hand.

"Guy has been talking about this place for months, and I was finally worn down."

"Who is the lucky guy I can thank for bringing you here?" I had nearly chomped the words.

"Guy...You know, Guillaume. My brother. He is over at the table." I turned to regard and saw her brother awkwardly taking up space in a clear struggle to maintain a satisfactory level of entertainment for the other two guests at the table. "I am actually surprised to find you two here. I assumed Owen was far too stiff for this place, and well, I thought Bridgeport was a different scene entirely."

"I don't recall telling you I was from Bridgeport." A subtle alarm had gone off in my head. An instinct to protect that which I was associated with.

"You are not the only one with detective skills, my darling." She laughed as she said it. "To be honest, I found you fascinating from when we first met, and I sent out a few inquiries."

"A surprise anyone even told you anything. The neighborhood does not like outsiders. It's a working-class thing."

"People always talk, as I'm sure you know."

"They do have a habit of hanging themselves with their own words. Owen was just telling me how he imagined me as an artist in another life." She struck me as the type to be jealous of talent. Real or not.

"An artist? I could see you in the abstract field. The project a spilled gallon of paint on a canvas. A twenty-minute soliloquy by the artist. Do not look offended! The Guild promotes all mediums and forms of art. It is the mission to be inclusive of an entire spectrum of talent."

I turned and let my gaze rest on Owen's chiseled, albeit uncomfortable, face. "Abstract? No, I work with classic beauties. Couldn't you tell?" I smiled to drive the nail in.

"Oh, don't go throwing yourself a parade after one victory," she said.

"I just might later. I was always fond of parades. Fireworks too. A family thing."

"Me too. Our family rides on the float, though."

"Memento mori." I had let it slip out and found myself blushing.

"What was that, darling?" Owen asked and leaned in on the table.

"Memento mori," I repeated clearly. "Remember your death." I whispered it to myself every morning I woke up angry to have seen another rise.

"Morbid for lunch," Gabrielle quipped.

"Roman commanders were celebrated with triumphs, parades, and they would position a slave behind them to whisper 'Memento mori' to remind them at the height of their glory of the inevitable." I had regained my ground and found comfort in assertion. "It might be useful to bring back the tradition to c-suites and board rooms, don't you think?"

"A regular bank of knowledge."

"Understanding the past helps you understand people. None of us are as original as we think we are."

"You give me slaves, and I'll let them whisper."

In the ensuing tension of a stare, neither of us realized Owen had stood up. Only when his outstretched hand broke our field of vision did we both dethaw. I looked up from my seat to find him beaming down on me as his hand hovered before me.

"Take my hand," he said. "Dance with me." I felt struck by the audacity of the move. The place was crowded and full of chatter, with a slight playing of music apparent.

"Now? Here?"

"Yes, Winona. Now and here. Excuse us, Gabrielle."

I stood without realizing I had. He pulled me in close. Our hands clasped together, and I couldn't bring myself to make immediate eye contact as I dodged the breaking of a dam by taking in the books that lined the shelves set against the brick on the wall. The floor had fallen out, and I was free-falling. He caught me, and the world fell away. We danced in a room full of strangers. A few stared. A few smiled. He led me to a song we could not quite hear, but it didn't matter. Nothing else mattered. Everything in me began to crumble. Walls fell, and my heart opened.

"I'm in love with you," I said for the first time to anyone.

"I've been in love with you since our first date."

The dance ended, and I do not think my feet touched the floor on the entire walk back to the table. A blissfully empty table.

--- ---- -----

"Well, I'm fucked."

Finn choked on his sip of coffee before he quickly readjusted behind the steering wheel.

"Anyway, how about Niamh? Need my ice cream recommendation to not look like a fool?"

"No," he grunted.

"Pleasant today."

"I'm sorry, Winona. Tired. I think of Helen day and night. I remind myself we have to help the Professor to help her. It tears me up to give a fuck about him. I even went to mass the other morning. To appease the anger about it all. It actually felt good. Felt like my folks looked down on me and smiled. I haven't felt a part of something in a long time. Hell, outside of the job, last time I was a part of anything was The Himalayans."

"Himalayans? You climbed the Himalayans?"

Finn let out a deep laugh. An honest laugh that did not seem to end. I watched him attempt to compose himself and fail for minutes. Finally, he wiped the tears from his eyes and settled down.

"I'm dying to know what just happened," I followed up my question.

"The Himalayans was a club I founded with a few friends as a kid entering high school. The whole neighborhood wanted to be firefighters or the police. I wanted to be a cartographer. I was too young to know the world had already been mapped. In the neighborhood, though, a few other kids thought the same way. One wanted to be an archaeologist. One wanted to be a librarian. We wanted to hide in plain sight. The Himalayans were born. A play on a place far away from what confined us but led to dime store novel dreams of danger. It sowed just enough confusion to keep from schoolyard beatings. We felt in it together. The closest we came to climbing the mountains, though, was the steps of school. The thought of us climbing anything more than a slight incline killed me."

"That is oddly sweet. I had figured you to be a much different student. I can barely fathom you in a pew now too."

"When's the last time you went to church? I don't mean to step out of bounds, but there was a component that helped the anger."

"Closest I have come to church is the 914 N Orleans St payphone. St. Luke's was right th—"

"What?" he replied.

"The payphones. The first was 121 N LaSalle St. The second was 4442 N Western Ave…."

"Yea, I know. Keys missing."

"No, Finn. The keys themselves. The locations themselves." I could not doubt it anymore. I could not hold it from him anymore. My chest tightened. "The two key. A-B-C. The four key. G-H-I. Then it would be the seven key. P-Q-R-S. Finally, the five key. J-K-L. C-G-S-L. The Chicago Guild of Saint Luke."

"We know that. The wife mentioned his club."

"The addresses. City Hall. Chicago. Across the street, a Guild Hall for the school. Still etched into the stone. Guild. Finally, the Church of Saint Luke. They double-traced the route for us. The keys and addresses. Whoever made the phone call made it obvious." My hands were on the dashboard.

"Winona, tell me what has you so white."

The sky had fallen on me. I needed fresh air. I stepped out of the car and looked for grass to stand in. I needed earth beneath me. My mind was in disarray, and I needed roots. Finn had stepped out and looked on silently as I stared forward. My hands on my hips in an attempt to exert control.

"What is it?"

"The Guild? It's a collective of people with too much money and time. They fund various art projects and the social causes of the day. It's…it's…"

"It's power," Finn reached the finish line first.

"Calcified power. The absolute kind that requires bloodlines and money. Even then, you can't join. You have to be invited in. The kind where you jockey for position with what money cannot buy."

"Winona, how do you know this all?"

"On the social scene I circuit, there were whispers. It is seen as the social Everest….and I've been."

"Jesus Christ."

"No, no, no." I can't be taken off the case. "This isn't a conflict. It's an advantage."

"A fucking advantage? You know the people. Even if they are tangentially connected."

"We don't know anything yet. We have phone calls placed, the keys removed, and a loose connection that might be complete bullshit to CGSL. People I passed at an event as an unlisted guest. I can explain it. I know these kinds of people. I've spent my adult life running from what I was to their social graces. I know how to talk to them, disarm them, read them. When you're a pretender, you have to master it. That is under the assumption it's an internal conflict. What if it is from the outside? An attack on their institution? What better way to mock it than the game with the phones."

He heard me. Yet he did not speak for a time. Instead, simply regarded me. Regarded the crossroads we stood at.

"You should have been in sales."

"What greater power existed than to be able to take another life? A hunt. A game. Document it with pictures. A trophy. Or a bargaining chip to use against. How better to keep people in line than let a life sentence swing over their heads? Take a girl from a small town. Tease a lifestyle…." I stopped myself cold. Thinking of Helen and her chase for a different life, I wanted to collapse. In my own right, I had not been different, just left breathing. "Finn, we still don't know. Possibly a misdirection. The message in the letter still hangs in the wind."

"Maybe not a misdirection. Money left behind. A lot. Only people who don't care about money are the ones who have too much of it. A hunt, you say."

"Could be. Could not. I don't know. I'm only musing." More than death, I wanted to be wrong. Not a fingerprint to have brushed anyone associated. Finn had remained in a moment of concentration. Did he hear my words of doubt? I had released a balloon of thought, was all.

"Here's the thing. I'm hunting now."

No. He had not.

— —————— ——————

He awoke every day to November 5th. He awoke to destroy keys. He awoke every day to November 5th. He awoke to destroy keys. He awoke every day to November 5th. He awoke to destroy keys.

I stared at my ceiling and repeated the words. There was comfort in repetition. The ceiling provided a stop to the path that I wore into the floorboards. A pacing loop. November 5th. The gunpowder plot. A bold and overt act of treason or revolution. An attempt to swing a wrecking ball at history. Was the Guild the crown here? The money left behind to imply the reason Finn had thought. The phone locations and keys a clear arrow.

Or am I too close? Terrified to be amongst her killer, do I project doubt? Deny the chance of internal politics of their stratosphere? A boring game for control of the fiefdom. A game with Helen being nothing more than a captured piece. If that was the case, then the killing of the Professor had been a flip of the board.

I needed the letter. The people among the ranks of the Guild loved power, but they loved thinking of themselves as unique more. Gabrielle had taught me that already. When money was of no consequence, the void had to be filled. Uniqueness was the currency. Solve the letter. Pull back the curtain. You look inside to the conversation that flipped the board.

I needed sleep.

CHAPTER THIRTEEN

The library was as uncharacteristically uninviting as before. Ms. Eberhart ushered Finn and me in with minimal greeting for our appointment. Where she was cold, the students at the tables we passed were hot. Hatred masked as passion showed in the eyes that tracked our walk. I winked at the plump blonde who sneered. Blew a kiss at the boy next to the girl sitting like a gargoyle. Opportunities were opportunities, after all. Whoever laughs wins.

We reached the librarian's office and took a pair of seats. Items alighted tightly on her desk with an exactness rarely seen outside a ruler. A small quote was the only memento signifying a living person used the desk. It laid outside the prison of precision that ensnared the rest of it all. I leaned in and read, "Without libraries, what do we have? We have no past and no future." Quoted, but not attributed. Odd omission for a display from her. She took notice of my attention and adjusted it slightly to align it in the proper orbit.

"It was a gift," she responded in a premeditated stifle of the expected inquiry to soften the conversation and make it more personable. My plan was muted before it started. Onward then.

"Ms. Eberhart, I wanted to follow up with you regarding the Professor's reading habits."

This had been my idea. The Professor conceivably solved the cipher. Even if books were moved in and out, a clue might be hidden in his habits.

"We already went on the Guy Fawkes expedition, Detective."

"I remember. It was quite the date. I wanted to know if anything else had come to mind. Any late nights he had here or unusual things you can think of."

The tight librarian tightened up more. Her cardigan stretched with her grip. She pulled it in as she sat. Her face betrayed nothing, but a slight clenching of her fists holding the garment appeared as an involuntary tremor. Maybe it was my remark, though. The woman probably has not been on a date in a decade. Even if she dreamt of one.

"What Professor Hickey did with his nights, I do not care to know. Regarding his reading, I have told you about his obsession with the Gunpowder Plot."

"Yes, but was it newly onset?"

"It was only in the weeks before his…death that he came here looking for the subject matter."

"Before that?"

"Nothing, really. I'm afraid a library is not the ideal place for pamphlets."

"Pamphlets?"

"Political material. History is not as political as some would like it to be. We cannot truly judge our time; to think we can is a fool's errand."

"The Gunpowder Plot was the Professor's first extended time here then?"

"Yes," she said succinctly.

"Curious as you seem to have developed a deep-rooted opinion of the man. I'm not sure what it is, but it seems to be final."

Ms. Eberhart exhaled for what seemed like the first time. She had been caught off guard. A crack in her logic she had not anticipated. People talked. Cracks formed.

"I do not have to have had dinner with a person to have developed thoughts about them. I can meet someone and have minimal contact before I decide I do not like them."

She punctuated the end. I liked her a little more.

"Is there anything else, Detective? Is your man here going to ask me for a book recommendation?"

"No, ma'am. I'm just here on account of my looks." Finn's voice sounded foreign in a way a man does when entering a space that had been exclusively occupied by women.

With that, we all stood and made our way back to the halls of the library. Ms. Eberhart asked if we were competent enough to find our way out. Humor in the strangest places. That is, if she had meant it as a joke.

"What do you think of her, Finn?"

"I'm ten, maybe fifteen years her senior, and she still made me feel like a child. I haven't dealt with someone that emotionally removed since the nuns. You?"

"I think she needs to get laid, but I do know she hates the Professor. It's easy to imagine in this cloistered kingdom that word travels. I'm sure our dearly departed professor's more vanilla escapades were known. Eberhart probably took it as a moral affront."

I stopped talking. A third presence came into our peripheral at the doors of the library. It was the girl who had been sitting like a gargoyle. Maybe my kiss had landed. Finn and I both turned. Took her in. She shrank a bit. I didn't feel like hearing a lecture from a possessive coed. Finn seemed to sense my irritation and exuded calm.

"How can we help you?" he asked.

"Just call my friend. Please. She might be able to help you," the girl said as she proffered a folded piece of paper. Finn took it from her, and we watched her scurry away in a hurry back to her boy, still blushing. Finn opened the paper and handed it to me without a word or expression.

"Angelina. 273-968-3733," I read it aloud. A look back into the great hall of books and I caught the last vestige of Eberhart's glare. Possessive this one.

---- -------- ----

Dragons. Mama loved dragons. Since she was a girl, she told us. With a bloodline from the West of Wales, it came naturally. Her love of the fantastic started with the playful fairytales she had been told as a young girl. Y Ddraig Goch. The red dragon of Wales. Ever present in protection. "Unforgettable tales from a forgotten totem for a forgotten people," Mama was fond of repeating. The corners of the talk tinged with a sadness for the ghosts of Wales that came before her. People needed to be remembered. Individually and en masse.

Her blood tied into the great civilizational veins the world had known, though. The dragon had appeared across continents. Across great cultures that had no meaningful contact or connection with one another. Mama knew that. She did not understand the how or why but took her enjoyment in belief. A trust in the faith that people had lost in our civilized age. Included in the loss, a lack of appreciation for timing.

--- ---- -------

Back on the detective floor, it was time to put our timing to the test. The phone rang three times for Angelina. Then, on the fourth, the phone answered. A young woman's voice on the line.

"Hello?"

"Angelina?" I asked. More nervous than I should be.

"Yes, this is she."

"This is Detective Winthrop of the Chicago Police Department."

"Oh. Hi." The girl was nervous. It felt like the nerves of anticipation. Finn stood next to me. His palms were flat on the desk. He was intent on listening to half the conversation.

"Did I catch you at a bad time, or were you expecting our call?" You had to fish sometimes.

"I was expecting it. Rebecca told me what she did. I honestly don't know why she did it. It wasn't a big deal, and it's over now, anyhow."

"Bear with me, Angelina. Rebecca was light on details, so I may need you to hold my hand here a bit as we talk."

"Oh, that would make sense. I'm sorry. I just felt like you would've known, but how would you have? It's hard when things happen to you. You assume everyone knows what happened."

"That's okay. Let's start with why Rebecca gave us your number. Why do you think she did that?"

"Because of the murder of Professor Hickey, right? You are the detectives investigating the Professor's murder?"

"We are, and you know something about that?"

"Well, no...not exactly." Her voice faltered in a way that made me imagine her eyes were welling with tears. "Not his murder, but what they did to me."

I leaned forward into the phone and kept the line tight between my fingers. "What happened, Angelina?" Finn heard and tightened his grip on the corner of the desk. The girl started to sob on the other end of the phone.

"His friend...Professor Hickey's friend. He made me do it after."

"What was his friend's name, Angelina? What did he do?" I knew I had to slow my line of inquiry. I did not want to scare her away from her revelation. I knew I had to, but it was difficult.

"He made me get an abortion." The girl was barely audible over her tears. "They were so kind before. They wanted me to come to the party. I'm sorry, Detective."

"Please, Angelina, take your time. Who was his friend?"

"I only know him as Thomas. He wore a mask when we met, but it came off after. I—"

"Angelina, did you say a mask?" My voice came across sharper than I had intended.

"Yes, yes I did." She was still speaking between gasps of air and tears.

"Angelina, I would like to come talk to you in person. Would that be okay?"

"Yes, Detective. I would like that."

"Are you still near campus?"

"Yes, yes, I am."

Do you know the coffee shop a couple blocks west of campus on 52nd St?"

"Yes."

"I'll be there in twenty minutes. Come whenever you are ready. I can wait for you, Angelina."

--   ---   ----

Finn acknowledged without incident that this line should be completely mine to reel. I sat at a table farthest from the windows to the sidewalk. My handheld police radio sat deliberately in front of me on the table. A light tower to Angelina. Finn sat near the entrance. To be unnoticed. That was our hope, at least. The radio zone for the second district was more active than I had anticipated. I took in the shop more. Tried to gauge if the radio was a nuisance. The rest of the coffee shop acted as a full-time hangout for the University students. Meek conversation filled the air. Voices buzzed at the periphery of my hearing. I couldn't reach into any of the dynamics between people. It irritated me. To be so close to fuel for the imagination, but to be denied. Reading body language would not do. Language was far more invigorating to feast on. I turned the radio down.

"Detective?"

I looked up to find a slender brunette with large eyes and prominent teeth standing before me. She was dressed comfortably but carried invisible weight in her movements. Cute and fresh but not in an overpowering way. Young too. She looked so young. A natural instinct in me wanted to wrap my arms around her and tell her it would be all alright. I answered with an affirmative nod.

"Hi, Angelina. Please join me."

Her smile was only a fraction. She sat down across from me.

"The radio give me away?" I asked.

"No, Rebecca said you looked like an elf."

Momentarily stunned, I realized my mouth was open and closed it.

"Not the workshop kind, but Elves from Middle Earth. Tolkien, you know?" My features had to have reflected the flip to compliment as she continued, "You're familiar with the series, Detective?"

"Intimately. You can just call me Winona, by the way."

"Okay." She had brought her left knee up under her chin and wrapped her arms around her shin. It made her seem more juvenile than before. Or maybe due to the lingering instinct for protection I wanted to provide.

"Thank you for talking to me earlier, and thank you for coming here today. It can't be easy."

"There was no force. I want you to know that."

Right into the deep end, then.

"There are other ways people can hurt you, Angelina. Other ways we can be preyed upon."

"I know Detec—Winona. I just wanted you to know that there was a reason I did not make a police report. It had been consensual. Legal too. I read the state statutes, but that doesn't mean it wasn't wrong. Just everything that happened after and then Professor Hickey's murder. I've been restless. Maybe the murder was the result of something similar? I don't know. All these scenarios and thoughts have played out on repeat."

"Let's start at the beginning of your story, Angelina. Take your time and remember how little I know. Feel free to channel Tolkien in detail."

She cracked a genuine smile and looked down, beginning to chew on the edge of her sleeve. Listen and let them be their own hero.

"Okay. It is not as complicated now that I am mapping it out in my head. I had been in Professor Hickey's lecture. He engaged with us all. Challenged and forced students to defend positions. I had never felt an intellectual passion like that. It was like I traveled without ever leaving. I'm from a small town just over the border in Wisconsin. I never really left until I came here. People there never concerned themselves with international affairs, let alone rigorously debating them. I'll admit I mostly sat silent for them. It intimidated me a bit."

"Their concerns were closer to home." Again, I had said what I meant to think. I read the confusion on her face. "Your hometown. People must conquer their necessities before they can free themselves to worry about the world. I did not mean to interrupt, though."

"That makes sense, but I found myself free to do just that. I was not comfortable, though. I wanted to be. I think that is why I ended up going." She came to a halting stop and bit harder on her sleeve.

"Where did you go, Angelina?"

A hesitation. Her eyes cast down to the table before an answer. "His office hours. I went to show him I did have opinions and thoughts. Notions and ideas to be tested. I wanted to refine the way I think and challenge myself, so I went to him as a crucible." Her voice strengthened as she spoke. "He was more rigid than I expected. He did not like his view to be pressed. He wanted to silence the absurd, as he would say."

"Sounds like the same character I've heard about." I leaned into her. "Not to speak ill of my victim, though." Her eyes momentarily brightened as she sensed an ally. An armed ally. I continued, "Help me understand where it all went from the office hours."

"After a few weeks of office hours, he began to invite me to gatherings. They were innocuous at the start. Gatherings at quiet bars where the conversation would be free and open. Club meetings on campus for political causes. Apartheid, indigenous rights across the Americas, real evil to fight. Then one day, after a meeting on campus, he asked me if I had ever been to a ball. It sounded so regal. I allowed myself to dream a bit. He said I had the 'look that required a gown.' We had been wrapped up lately in the labor movements, so it didn't surprise me he wanted to take me to an event." Red returned to her cheeks as she recalled the compliment.

"Did you have a dress in mind immediately? There is something to be said about looking right leading to feeling right."

"Exactly. I know it was immature, but I still was excited. We really should be beyond such fairytale notions, but I guess we still have work to do on it."

"Men need to be adored. Women need to be desired. I do not think we will ever change that dynamic."

She sighed in agreement and continued, "The ball is where I met him. I hadn't been told it was a masquerade ball. I was not the only one, though, as some other girls were not wearing masks either. It all was a whirlwind of people attending to our every need. In the middle of it all, I was approached by a man wearing a mask that covered his nose up. He walked over to me and lifted the mask before saying hello. Thomas. He had been particular about that. Not Tom, but Thomas. I thought it sounded more mature too. He was older. From the Northeast based on his accent. Beyond charming. Different from home and the boys on campus. He was dignified and came across with a warmth that the other guests did not have. I felt drawn into him. He even asked me to dance. It felt as if I was moving between clouds."

"The mask, was it just across his eyes, or did it cover more? Was there anything unique about it?"

"Not particularly. Your common masquerade mask, but it stood out the moment he lifted it. It felt like a reveal of sorts."

"Nothing related to animals?"

"No, not his."

"Not his?"

"No, but I remember very ornate masks. They took my attention away from appraising the other dresses. I had been so nervous about being up to par. A man wore a wolf mask and carried a replica in his hand. The Professor wore a coyote mask. It'd been white."

"A man wore a wolf mask? Do you remember anything about him?"

"I don't, to be honest. I just remember passing them and laughing to myself that it took Romulus and Remus themselves to stop comparing myself to the other girls. My minor involves a heavy study of the foundation of the Roman Empire. It felt like a sign to breathe easier."

Romulus and Remus. Another R.R. I strained to keep a leveled feel for the conversation. I took a moment under the guise of letting her compose herself to center myself from another haunting reminder of the notes.

"What happened next, Angelina?"

"We moved closer and fell into a rabbit hole. We danced. We laughed. We held eye contact. I wanted him. The night ended, and he invited me to his condo in the Gold Coast. The next thing I knew, I woke up next to him, and he told me he wanted to see me again."

"But he did not?"

She turned away, and I saw her eyes well with tears. Her cheek rested on the knee she'd pulled up. I wanted to wrap her in a blanket.

"No. He didn't….and then I was late." The girl's emotional wall held. Near breaking but intact. I found myself proud of her.

"Did you go to him?"

"First, I went to Professor Hickey, who brushed it off as a minor inconvenience to his day. Barely worth registering. A foregone conclusion to what I should and must do. I asked him for Thomas' number, and he refused. He became irate when I pressed the issue. He told me these were not the type of people you pushed on. He told me they push back."

Helen. Angelina. They were pawns. Peasant girls from a forgotten place to be used and discarded. I had compartmentalized the hate I felt for the Professor with the rationale that I could help Helen. This was tearing down my own walls. His throat was slit, and Hell gained an occupant. No. No. There was another. The man in the wolf mask. The wolf in that mask killed Helen. Went after a sheep. He still walked. He had to be put in prison. A waiting room for Hell.

I held my hand back from reaching out to her. "Where did you go from that point?"

"Day after day, I went to his condo building and waited in the lobby for him. Finally, on the fourth day, I saw him coming out and went to talk to him." She continued to hold strong, but the wall began to crack as she wiped the welling tears from her eyes.

"How were you received?"

She let out a sigh of exasperation before responding, "He accused me of an ambush. He said it could be anyone's kid, that I was a college girl who probably slept with multiple guys a week. He became irate when I told him no and that there was only one possibility. He grabbed me by the arm and shoved me into a recessed part of the wall. He told me he had a family, and this would not be allowed to happen. He told me I should just go back to Wisconsin and live out my life in the trailer I came from. He calmed down, but like Professor Hickey, he told me that the people involved were powerful and that they would not stop with me. That they would go after my scholarship at the University. That they would crush my family. Go after their jobs. My dad is a mechanic. He gets by supporting my mom and little brother. The scholarship here is my lifeline."

I sat silently and came up blank in any words of condolence for the girl before me. She lived, and that would be the best I could tell her. She continued telling me how Thomas had pulled a cab and driven her to the clinic. Sat at her side less as a companion but more as a guard holding her at gunpoint to keep the direction true. She broke down and cried into her crossed arms.

"Where did he live?" I asked colder than I would have liked. I regretted not having Finn's emotional intelligence here. He would have made her feel protected with warmth.

"181 W Ontario St, Unit 3204. One of the doormen had been nice enough to slip me his unit number after I first started showing up."

"Are you up for a few more questions?"

"Yes, Detective." She used the cuff of her sleeve to wipe her face.

"You mentioned the ball was for a labor event?"

"I thought so. Professor Hickey said it was for a union or something. So, I figured it was a labor event."

"A union?"

"Not a union…he called it a…Guild! That's it. A 'Guild event'. It is why I was so taken aback that it would be a ball and even more stunned when we showed up."

I hid the storms that had come over the horizon in my head. Maybe it was a good thing Finn sat tables away.

"Did he say anything else about the Guild? Any other name a part of conversation?"

"I don't think so. I became wrapped up in the event so quickly.

It's dumb of me, but I had never been to an event like it."

I wanted more. I wanted to dig in and have her rake her mind for additional details, but it would not have been worth the cost. She believed I was there for her at this moment, and it meant something. Push harder, and she becomes painfully aware that I am here for something else.

"Angelina, why do you think Rebecca gave me your phone number?"

"Probably so you would understand why she wanted to know who killed the Professor. So she could thank them."

Fair play Rebecca, but you may like them even less. We wrapped up the conversation with her not having a single recognition of a fox, a Daphne, or a cipher. I thanked her and stood to walk her to the door.

She stopped me with a gentle tug of the arm.

"Also, Detective…He didn't know I was from Wisconsin. I never told him that. I was too embarrassed at the ball and wanted to fit in. It is part of what terrified me when he mentioned my family."

"You have a knack for detail. If you ever tire of Rome, you should look into this line of work. Lord knows I need the company."

She smiled, and life seemed to return to her features. We walked past Finn, and I watched her set her course on the sidewalk. When she was a block away, Finn walked up beside me.

"Looked rough," he remarked.

"She was still fragile and needed to be questioned with care."

Finn simply nodded in agreement. I filled him in on the details. I could hear his jaw tighten.

CHAPTER FOURTEEN

"Thomas Oliver. 181 W Ontario St, Unit 3204. She was right."

Finn walked up and placed the copy on my desk. He was surprisingly adept at bureaucratic tasks. He had reverse-engineered the address with a visit to the County Assessor's office. Anyone with sense wanted to color inside the lines with the taxman. Especially if you were on bullshit.

"I looked into the name then. He lists his primary residence in Hinsdale. Must be the family home. The condo a weekend getaway," Finn continued. "Let's go for a drive and have a talk with him."

"We don't have anything on him, and as much as it pains me to say it, he did not commit any crime that we know of."

"Legally? No, but I'm not suggesting we arrest him. We have plenty on him to talk. We can shake the tree to see if an apple or two falls. You need more time on the street to understand leverage, Winona."

"Alright." The last jab stung. An out of character insult. Knowing what happened to Angelina appeared to carry a dark sadness within him. With this case, he struggled to separate work from life, and it came through the cracks.

It was Saturday and getting late in the afternoon. We surmised the condo to be the place. Maybe he told the wife and kids he would be working late or had business to attend to. Convenient path to complete freedom. We parked right in front of the building. Skyscrapers still awed the little girl from Indiana in me. In the good and bad. To imagine the sheer amount of people who took residence here. To pay a fortune to live here. No grass. No green. Strangers on the other side of your walls. I did it, though. It was convenient to manage. Everyone wanted to be convenient, and now we were the Jetsons. Humanity was taking the path of least resistance. Including me. Not as different from the rest of them as I would like to be.

---   --------

The front desk attendant was kind from the start and even kinder after our introduction with credentials. He asked us about problem makers on the block and if we could shove off the hypes who took refuge in the alley by the dumpsters. We let him know we would tell patrol and even make a call to plain clothes units. It seemed to satisfy the man. Smoke and mirrors went a long way, even in our line of work.

"How do you want to handle this?" I asked Finn as the elevator opened to the 32nd floor.

"You had the coffee shop. I have here."

"Okay." I grew a little worried on the steps down the hallway toward 3204. I found I naturally fell into his shadow. Tracking behind him. Each step light but purposeful.

He knocked hard on the door with a closed fist. A heavy thud. The door creaked open, and an unassuming, middle-aged man stood before us. I knew better than to imagine a monster, but still, how he checked the box of ordinary in every category surprised me. Height, weight, appearance. He looked like a character from the background. Perfectly forgettable.

"Tom Oliver?" Finn asked the man who stood regarding us with a look of curiosity. His eyes had drifted to our gun and stars on the belt.

"Yes, who are yo—" He began to inquire before Finn cut him off.

"Detective Hansen of the Chicago Police Department, and this is Detective Winthrop." Tom's expression looked as curious as ever, but his eyes passed over Finn to me and held for a second that made my bones creak.

"How can I help you?"

"We want to talk to you about business from Wisconsin."

"Wisconsin? I do not have any business in Wisconsin. You may have me mixed up. All my work is based here in the city."

"All the same, we should talk."

"I'm terribly sorry, but I have company over, and it just is not the best time. Leave your card, and we can schedule another, more convenient time."

"Not another time. We will just make our way to Hinsdale and talk the business from Wisconsin there."

After Finn's words, synapses finally started firing in the hollow man's head. It amused me to watch in real time. First came the recognition, followed by an immediate bout of fear, then a collection of senses to manufacture strength. I enjoyed the onset of panic.

"No, no, no. That is not necessary. We can talk, Detective, but I do have company here that makes it beneficial to talk elsewhere."

"Look at that. We are already on the same page," Finn said with a smile that caught the man off guard. "We can give you a ride for a quick talk. Tell your girl you will be back soon. Although I hope she does not charge by the hour."

The man turned to retreat into the unit when Finn stopped the closing of the door with an outstretched hand.

"Sorry, habits," Tom Oliver said as he walked away from view.

"You believe he actually has company in there or stalling?" I asked Finn.

"The Gucci handbag there," Finn said as he nodded toward the entrance table. There sat a flamboyant clutch purse. "And the perfume. It's not a subtle scent. Makes me believe she's expensive. Plus, he's willing to leave her here alone, so he probably has dealt with her before."

I found myself flat-footed. I had been tuned into Tom Oliver to a degree that I had lost the scene. My mind had declared my hatred of the man paramount, and I had fixated. The embarrassment even worse that the signs were a purse and perfume. Sorry, Susan B. Anthony.

The whispers of light conversation wafted from within the unit before Tom returned with a light coat draped over his arm.

"I like to be prepared," he said as he must have taken notice of my puzzlement at the coat.

We silently made our way to the elevator and down to the lobby. The front desk attendant waved goodbye before we reached our unmarked cruiser. Finn made his way to the driver's side, leaving me to motion Tom to the backseat, which he took to awkwardly as the door creaked and moaned, giving the impression the entire door might fall off at any moment.

"Only the finest for Chicago's finest," I said as we settled into the car. Tom laughed lightly, while Finn did not even acknowledge the comment. We pulled off in haste.

The closest police district station, the 18th, stood barely over a mile north and west. Our detective area was due northwest five miles. Instead, we drove south and west. I did not ask. I did not convey any movement out of the ordinary. I sat silent. Tom lightly hummed to himself in an apparent nervous tick as we continued our travels.

"You were not wrong, you know. My company for the night.

Thankfully not hourly at this rate." Tom had broken the silence with an apparent attempt at humor. Maybe to remind us we were costing him money.

"We will be there in a minute. Then we can start," Finn's only response.

Where "there" was, I still had not a clue. Downtown and the high rises faded behind us. Then residential three-flat apartment buildings gave way to more open space. We were nearing the industrial section of the city. A place where the concrete to feed downtown construction was poured from. Where scrap yards bought scavenged metals. Afterthoughts in the Chicago ecosystem, but of utmost importance. Balance was key.

"It's been years since I've been back here," Finn remarked as he steered onto loose gravel, and we entered what would appear to be a vacant industrial lot if not for the nightman manning the booth at the entrance. Finn exchanged pleasantries with the nightman, and we were promptly waved through. The humming from the backseat had stopped. Just the crinkle of the bench seat now. Tom moved back and forth as if he was pacing a floor. I caught Finn's eyes watching him through the rearview mirror as he continued to drive into a remote section that was closed off on three sides by the sides of brick walls. No windows on those walls. No openings at all. No light but dusk. Finn parked the car and sat.

"Where are we? What is this about?" Tom's voice had risen. Not quite a tone of outright panic yet, but approaching it.

"All sorts of people don't like to talk. Doesn't matter where you come from. I used to bring Polacks here. Mexicans too. It's funny. Different continents, but all I heard was "NO ENGLISH! NO ENGLISH!" but the harder I hit them, the more English they knew."

"Clever game, Detective, but you're dealing in a different stratosphere now." Tom Oliver had regained his composure and apparently his balls.

"You're right. You have farther to fall." Finn stepped out of the car. Moved to the rear and opened the back door.

Tom Oliver scurried to the other side with a flurry of kicks. "You have any idea what you are about to do?"

Finn had grabbed an ankle and ripped him forward. Took him by the lapels then and tossed him clear out of the backseat to the gravel lot. I raced out and rounded the front hood to see Tom Oliver on all fours coughing in the dust kicked up by gravel.

"What was her name?" Finn barked.

"Wh—" Tom Oliver managed before the heavy right boot of Finn connected with his ribs, causing him to gasp and flip to his side.

"Wrong answer. What was her name?"

"Ang…Angelina," he confessed between groans of pain and a slight coughing fit. He had regained position on his knees with one hand grabbing at his ribs.

"Good. Remember her. Now let's talk about business. How did you meet her?" Finn grabbed him by the collar and pulled him to his feet.

"At a bar—"

Finn's fist connected with the midsection. The man doubled over. He was not allowed to fall as Finn held him up by the same fabric. He connected again with the midsection with a heavy fist.

"I thought the rules were clear. Think of me as God. All-knowing and here to test you." Tom Oliver stayed bent over, gasping for air. Finn held him like a wayward child but continued, "I'm a fair god too. Get your fists up. Let's give you a chance."

Tom Oliver looked up in bewilderment at Finn for a moment before he launched himself into a feeble counterattack. Finn was a maestro. Every movement was precise, and every oncoming fist weaved out with brutal consequences. Tom Oliver would have better odds in London in 1349. Finn did not stop. Even as Tom Oliver crumpled to the ground. The connection of body blows continued.

"Finn…Finn…FINN!" I finally screamed.

The butcher paused and looked over and, between heavy breaths, said, "You have a problem with how I do my job?"

Tom Oliver lay shaking and whimpering but now looked up at me through the hands covering his face as if I was bringing water to the desert. Finn caught it too.

"Don't look at her. She can't help you. No one can stop me. I stop me. That's it."

"Finn, I want to make sure he can answer questions, is all. Alright?"

"Fair point," he grunted. "I'll ask again, where did you meet Angelina?"

"A..a…a…a party. I swear it. You have to believe me."

"What kind of party? How did you get there?"

"A masquerade ball. Through a friend. He's a professor. I mean, he was. He was killed," Tom Oliver said, shaking between each syllable as he lay in the gravel.

"We know. Went out brutally. What do you know about that?" Finn closed the gap with Tom Oliver as he spoke. Moved down and crouched next to him. For his part, Tom Oliver attempted to shrink back out of the instinct contained in any wounded animal when confronted.

"I'll tell you everything. I swear—"

"I bet you will. I have the credit card transaction log for the abortion," I said, cutting into the dynamic. "Tonight's episode is much cheaper than a delivery to Hinsdale would cost you."

The look of physical trauma on his face gave way to true terror now. Physical wounds could heal, but your own home caving in on you with full knowledge to family and friends would be too much to bear for most people. Finn smiled up at me and directed him to keep talking with a roll of his fingers.

"Hickey invited me. The girls were always free at the Guild. The

Chicago Guild of Saint Luke, he called it. I had been to a few events, and he was always right. They were young, pretty, and impressionable. You flash brightly to them, and they would be eating out of your hand. Not like the calloused whore back at my place."

I sensed Finn restrain himself as he leaned in closer. I saw Tom Oliver shudder in anticipation.

Tom Oliver realized talk of the Chicago Guild of Saint Luke drew our interest, and he clung to it for salvation. He spoke of extravagant events he attended via association with our dearly departed Professor. He spoke of his surprise in the background of attendees. Tiers of people. Socialites with generational wealth and Ivy League-educated bureaucrats to members of the press and the political class. People who had their hands on the levers of society. He begged us to believe he was merely an associate. A small moon in the orbit of it all. I believed him. He was a pawn on a board. Not the hand moving the pieces.

"Does the name Daphne mean anything to you?" Finn asked.

"Daphne? No. No, I don't think so."

"And any contact with the Professor in the lead up to his untimely passing?"

"Yes. Yes. He had been all worked up in a mad craze, making no sense. So, he came to me to help him move money around. I'm his money manager, after all."

"Bagman," Finn cut in and spit on the ground beside him.

"In a way, yes. He wanted to liquefy assets that would fly under the radar, and he needed it right away. So, I helped him get it. It was just that when he got it, he made an offhand remark when I joked about spending it wisely. It was just a joust, but he didn't come back at me like usual. He just said, 'The pictures this money is for are priceless. I could murder the queen and get off with them.' I didn't think anything of it until he wound up dead."

Finn stood and looked down in disgust at Tom Oliver. "When the pain wears off, and you regain your confidence, you might have second thoughts. You might come up with a plan to tell your wife. The other option is to drag you to Homan and Walnut and feed you a jab of heroin myself. I'll fucking make sure you're addicted or dead. Everyone will think the stress of it all got to you. You money guys don't jump from buildings anymore, anyhow. Now get gone. A restaurant is open twenty-four hours about seven blocks north of the gate we came through. It draws cabbies at all hours of the day."

Tom Oliver did not hesitate. He made his way to his feet and sprinted like a wounded gazelle. We watched him fade into the night.

"I meant what I asked." Finn had turned to me. "Do you have a problem with how I do my job?"

My mind raced back to the night in the alley. To the night the same intervention had saved me.

"No," I whispered without gathering the strength to look at him, "But I worry about the nightman."

"Don't. He's a neighborhood kid. I grew up with his old man. He would sooner slit his own wrists than talk."

"And the hooker when she sees his injuries?"

"She can play nurse," he laughed at his own joke. "But her I worry about even less. She will know the game better than we do. The more invisible she is to the world, the better she likes it, I would take. Plus, no face."

"No face?" I asked.

"Old habit. Never go for the face. You can't hide it in booking photographs no matter what you do," he said proudly. He paused before continuing, "Remember the photographs. When you doubt what is done, remember that little girl they took because they could. Remember Helen. I'm keeping my word."

I nodded alongside him, and the images played like a slideshow for me. Helen was still in the photographs, but I felt like I had observed her life. The loving parents who built a modest but loving life for their one and only. The classroom portraits and birthday photographs that adorned her childhood home's walls. The onset of rebellion and desire for more. The trek out to the city. The loneliness of being adrift in a foreign place that led her to somewhere she thought safe. The end came brutally and surprisingly. Done because they could.

"Nice bluff with the credit card logs too," he remarked, breaking my internal immersion into Helen's life.

I nodded again at the man who carried me, and my mind drifted to the man who avenged me when I was my weakest. We made our way back to the car.

----   ----   ----

I walked through the door into my condo. Everything was still the same. Nothing disturbed since I'd left. The air felt the same. No one to be mad at for having left milk out. No used dishes in the sink. Still the pristine image made for a catalog. The positive lay in that my lemonade remained untouched in the fridge. I sat down at my excuse for a kitchen table and thought of calling Owen but gave that to tomorrow's to-do list. A reason to wake up and not be disappointed to see another day.

The minutes slipped and slipped until I realized it was past midnight. As a little girl, I would try so hard to stay up to catch the Brownies. Mama would warn us how shy they were and that they disliked being seen or visited. She would recount how they appeared every night to help with the chores and tidy the home while we all slept. On nights Dakota and I crept down terribly late, she would allow us to help put out the offering for the Brownie to get us back to bed. The requisite payment being a bowl of cream or potentially buttered bread. It was only fair to look after them as they looked after us. Harmony between the mystical and the physical.

That was until one night, he came home after three days in the dark of night. We were being led up the stairs when the bowl was knocked over, followed by a string of expletives broken only by the shattering of the bowl against a cabinet. The heavy footsteps fell towards us as we were ushered upstairs and told to close the door behind us. We should have listened to her directions. We should have gone to our room. But, instead, we listened to him.

"Fuck your fairies. They're not real, but money fucking is. Stop filling the girls' heads with nonsense and stop wasting what we have. Am I the only fucking person in this house with any sense?"

Mama stood her ground without a word. I see now she knew how to let the fuel burn off. Let him tire himself out. Stand but don't engage. Let him breathe fire until he saw it futile and retreated. I had been so locked into their conversation that I had let Dakota slip by me. Before I knew it, she was climbing down the stairs with tears streaming.

She had trekked and shouted, "They're real! They're real! They help Mama every night! Not like you!"

I heard him first. "What did you say?" came drifting up as if it had been voiced out of a cavern. Then I saw him move. He squared around and advanced on the staircase with a terror so fierce my memory made his eyes glow amber in the dark. It was out of character. He had come home too early. The cold, distant father I knew had been replaced by a monster with blood on fire.

Before he could repeat himself, Mama made to block the first steps he sought with her small bones. She sensed it too. Dakota behind her and the strange man in front of her.

It was only a whisper, but I heard it: "Try. Try, and I will get you when you sleep." Mama's message had been a well-placed thrust. He threw his hands up, snorted, and growled about a lack of worth. The door slammed his goodbye, and he would not be seen for a few more nights. Dakota was scooped up and carried up the stairs. My outstretched hand taken as we were led to bed.

The buzz of the refrigerator returned me to the here and now. The lemonade sat next to an empty glass. Being haunted had its health benefits. I took it back to the fridge. No butter for bread, but plenty of milk. I filled a bowl and left it out in front of the oven. I led myself to a stiff bed with one question on my mind:

Some dragons need to be slain, right, Mama?

CHAPTER FIFTEEN

The morning came with the usual daily disappointment. In sudden ar-
rhythmic death syndrome, a girl can dream of an answer. The lottery
tickets didn't hit either. The milk was undisturbed. Owen had answered, though. He was on his way over. I spent an inordinate amount
of time getting ready for a daytime rendezvous. Black leather pants
and a white blouse that flowed freely. Aggressive, but appropriate. Our
last rendezvous had shattered the wall between us. It had been different from sex. The time we spent together transcended the physical.
We had felt connected on a spiritual plane. I needed to wrap my legs
around him, with eye contact that could not be broken. Nothing to
exist outside of us. Mhm.

I answered the knock on my door and worked hard to keep my hands
to myself, but my lips were his to kiss. I felt a little dazed after he had
obliged my want without a word. We made it out the door with clothes
on. I felt as proud as a Puritan.

"You were vague on the phone. What do you have planned today,

Winona?" he asked, bringing me back to earth as we waited for the elevator.

"Just an idea I have that might make us laugh. You'll see."

I held his hand through the building exit and onto the street. His blood had truly warmed to public affection, after all. I alternated between admiration for him and a lurking desire to ask questions. I watched him without worry, though. People flowed around us. The city was alive with the streets for veins. The first floors of buildings we passed were busy with customers for urban necessities. Dry cleaners, snack shops, and bistros. People moved about their day as was expected of them, but here I walked in love. I wouldn't let work crash into us.

I let us walk three sidewalk panes past our destination before I yanked him back. "The River Styx" read the window in heavy black and gray shaded letters. Curtains closed the view. Tarot card reading. Communication with the dead. The door mentioned no other services. You had to reward a business for being clever. Show just enough to spark curiosity. Too many establishments hung cheap beads in the window accented by a neon sign more fit for a sports bar. They embarrassed themselves. Here they presented an invitation to mystery. A dark mystery.

"Taking me to a haunted house? You should know I scare easy," Owen turned and asked. We both stood and let our view take it all in. People still flowed around us.

"Not quite. We will let the cards fall," I whispered. A trick to bring him close. "I'm curious to hear how the spirits speak of you."

"You're being serious?"

"Of course not." I slapped his chest for good measure with a manufactured laugh. "These are fun, though. When I was first promoted to detective, I used to come to shops like this. It gave me the opportunity to listen to people lie to me. They're professional liars. It helped sharpen me. They want you to believe them the same way a lying of-fender wants you to believe their story."

"That's a clever trick, Winona."

I blushed at the compliment. Dakota had always been the clever one. An imagination to rival Tolkien, Mama used to say. I was the strong one. Not strong enough to admit the truth, though. I wanted a reading of Owen. I would not sabotage my love, but I wanted a read-ing.

"My sister, Dakota, has a place like this too. In Missoula. Mon-tana."

"I remember you mentioned that. You do not speak much of her."

"She is the pretty one…and the creative one. She doesn't like to speak to me much. It's rooted in family."

"Montana, though. I hear it is beautiful. I have always wanted to explore your American West."

His stiff upper lip had returned. I shouldn't be disappointed that he hadn't wanted me to open up on a Chicago sidewalk about my fail-ure in protecting her. How it had driven her to the edges of the wil-derness. To an enclave of a town where she had put down a stake. The spirits and fairies she so loved were easier for her. Her own walls of fantasy. Chicago need not breach it.

"I haven't been. One day though, I'll head West." With the subject appearing closed, I leaned in to open the door for us. We entered near darkness.

The motif of the exterior continued to the interior. Flames lit the setting. No electrical light of any kind. Heavy, dark fabric wrapped the rods that held tapestries on the walls. I waited for a raven to flutter by but instead was met by a middle-aged woman dressed in all black with a laced shawl wrapped tightly around her shoulders. She emerged from a hallway but did not greet or engage us. Framing the entrance to the hall were two stone figurines. Statues half a person high. The woman stood and stared at the pair of us as if we were a delivery.

"Hi, I'm Winona. We were hoping for a reading today."

"That'll do." The woman's voice was so common it came across as odd after all the effort henceforth. She moved towards us with still no regard. Mystical realm or not, capitalism still ruled the day. I understood the act she put on, but you needed customers to feel comfortable enough to follow you. I bet the register had cobwebs, but here we were being treated as inconvenient. I reached out and let my fingers intertwine with Owen's. He gave my hand a slight squeeze and smiled like a child. Men were allowed to be more comfortable with the unknown. Physical safety less of a concern. Still, the smile of anticipation was cute. I cannot imagine that boarding school education covered tarot, after all.

"Esmeralda is my name," she finally spoke again.

"Not Sharon?"

I hadn't been able to stop myself. Anger or disdain did not flicker across her face, but instead, I caught a slight trickle of amusement. She took hold of a candle, turned about, and returned down the hall. After four steps, she waved for us to partake in the procession. We dutifully followed as I found myself needling Owen's ribs and making abject spooky sounds.

The hallway ended abruptly after only a few more steps, and we were let into a remarkable room in its nakedness. Bare walls held within them a singular circular table with three mismatched chairs. Nowhere to be found were tasseled drapes, hawked relics, or arcane notations etched about like I had come accustomed to. The great Esmeralda took her seat, and we followed suit. I watched as she removed a pack of cards bound by a single leather strap from the interior of her robes.

"Let's begin with you," she said as she locked eyes with me.

Tie rocks to me and throw me in a fucking lake. This witch.

"I'll let Zelda have her way with me before I fucking go in there again," I exasperated as we emerged onto the sidewalk.

"Come now. I found it rather ace. She truly had mastered the character, and whose Zelda?"

She had deliberately read me first. Not the man all the women walking by couldn't help but sneak a glimpse of. No, the lonely, forgotten witch laid the deck for me. The tower had been laid before me. A single card, and she refused to move another. "Destruction forthcoming to those who believed." She regarded me and pivoted to Owen. A full reading there with explanation and gentle guidance. The ace of wands to guide him. "Opportunity" at his grasp. I was left to wallow. She had known that I grasped the cards as they appeared.

Dakota would be proud I had remembered. Nights spent watching her when there was no one else. Letting her practice on me, again and again, to keep her mind occupied. Her novice excitement in explaining each and every card that had been drawn for me. Always done near a window so we could see the moon. Unsure if the night would bring his return or not.

"Let's move to the other side of the street," I opined.

"Honestly?" Owen asked with a laugh. "You feel that shortchanged about the reading? She did a masterful job of working you. I have waited long to see a man or woman get the best of you. So, Esmeralda, take a bow."

Esmeralda. I'll curse the name.

"I saw it. That is the problem. Let's just get to lunch."

Saw it, and it still hit. She gave me an idea, though.

— —— ——

"Any progress with Guy Fawkes?" Owen asked from across the booth and over the clatter of the commotion at the corner of Polk St and Carpenter St. Divination to a deli.

He awakes every day to November 5th. He awoke to destroy keys.

"Huh?" I said through a mouthful of bread, turkey, lettuce, giardiniera, and mayo.

"Guy Fawkes. You asked me about him just the other week. It stuck with me that you came to me for the question."

The cipher had still been on the back of my mind but never floated out of sight. Finn relied on me to take care of the secret message. Finn fixated on the second masked man.

"It has been a dead end. It bothers me that I haven't been able to connect the dots for it. It strings together something larger."

"You're quick. I have no doubt it will come to you."

A few more hundred years in the library, and maybe I'll find a worthwhile scrap.

"There is another component I wanted to talk to you about, Owen." I had put this off too long. Owen's reading had put me at ease to ask: "What do you know of the bones of the Chicago Guild of Saint Luke?"

"Do you want to go to another event? I have to say we have a hit-and-miss record. The first one we attended was not our best night if you recall."

My face flushed red. The abandonment. The stranger. Actions that triggered immense guilt. I wanted to abandon course. I wanted to reach across the table, playfully steal a potato chip from his bag, and keep the conversation light. I wanted a lot of things, some I could still get. Helen could get nothing, though. Her wants and desires had been snuffed out. Her own parents too. Left behind as hollow vessels to walk their days through to the end. Fuck my guilt.

"No, Owen. I mean more conceptually. Esmeralda is an artist in her own way, and it caused the Guild to come to mind. What do you know of them? I need a bridge to Dakota and have an idea that may work."

Lies. Necessary lies, so I told myself. Finn risked himself physically to work towards a justice that looked as though it would end more as vengeance. I could risk as well. Weave a small lie to ensnare more detail. Better than outright asking him. To potentially drive a wedge between us. The small crumb could be the one to start the right path. Owen would understand if he saw the pictures. If he'd met Helen's parents. The plan worked. I felt awful.

"Ah, well, what do you want to know?" A curious expression swept across his face. Not his genuine smile. Not the admiration his eyes conveyed when his heart was open. Rather like a bright pupil who had been issued a challenge.

"Art is characters, but it all seemed so predictable when you took me to the event. What had previously shocked the system had been incorporated into the system. Art that was Wall Street financed, law firm approved, and pushed to packaging to be peddled by the favored journalists. I love the endeavor. I love the spotlight being shown on it. I only hesitated at the execution. How can you rebel against the system when you are the system?"

He chewed over what I said. I could tell I'd struck a point, which was the key. Present an open door they may have already started to walk through. It provides the individual immediate comfort and to feel intelligent for having apparently found it first.

"I understand, Winona. Even the most outlandish exhibits or attempts at shock can become stale. How do we crack the jaded surface?"

"How does a cartographer do the task?" I asked.

"In poverty now, I would assume. The world is already mapped."

"The physical world. The plane we exist on. The art supported by the Guild is stale because it is of the physical realm. The pillars of society have consumed all, and art was no exception. A cartographer maps new worlds."

"New worlds?"

"Yes, Owen. You believed Esmeralda played a character. Esmeralda believes. Dakota believes it in her bones. Realms, spirits, fairies, the whole set of cards. What you attended today was theater of the spiritual plane. And theater is art. A type of art that connects us to ancestral feelings that have existed in every culture."

"The tarot card reading today felt like religion," he said with a softening in reception of the path I spoke.

Saint Luke. Religion indeed.

"Religion. Sorcery. Call it whatever you want. It is poison to the people of the Guild. People in love with themselves. People far evolved from such relics as religion. People who have conquered the physical realm. Move their emotion with gypsy magic! To be told your riches and victories mean nothing on another plane. Imagine an exhibit similar to what you just experienced. An exhibit to be guided through, complete with history, cross-cultural references, and consequences told face-to-face. The lords and ladies can sneer but watch and count how many partake. How many consults with a Dakota or Esmeralda, how many even schedule further consultation? How many react when confronted by a woman who does not wish to accumulate? Does not wish to be a pawn or a queen. Trust me, handed poison, they will drink. The Tsar did."

An intense focus came to his eyes when I spoke the last line. An add-in that may be too dramatic, but now was not the time to hold back. Theater was art, after all. I could gather what I needed while saving what we had.

"Rasputin had Moscow. Dakota would have Chicago," he said quietly. "The entire lot can be insufferable. The introduction of this could surmise to be the act of art itself. Guerrilla art. Winona, there are layers upon layers here." He smiled genuinely.

That took an unexpected turn. He had never given himself enough credit for his own creativity. The man hooked me with blackout poetry, after all. He had taken my idea of rough stone and, in one breath, crafted a sculpture. I wanted the plan to be real. I wanted to work side by side with him to introduce the magic. The two of us pulling a clever caper over the eyes of Chicago's self-loving top caste. This was not about me, though. This was about a girl who believed in their promises. A girl who thought she found the magic to change her own lower middle-class life through these people. A way to bring the secrets to me.

"The mission of the Guild is admirable, but isolation leads to rot. This will be great fun, Owen. Plus, Dakota is the pretty one in the family. She takes after my mother. She'll put them in a trance without speaking," I finished and raised my glass of water for a toast.

Dakota, my Trojan horse. The Guild to burn as Troy did.

-- --- ---------

"An undercover situation?"

My sell to Finn had not gone well so far. He hated the idea of me working undercover. Working without a clear blessing from the chain of command. "Where you know your gatekeeper…rather well," he continued, returning to one of his original objections.

"Let's not pretend I would be the first undercover to have fucked someone."

"Related to a murder investigation, maybe," he retorted while reaching for additional sugar packets to drown his coffee with. I wanted to throw the entire cache of packets at him.

"You always remember your first." The humor had fallen flat. His lack of amusement immediately apparent. "I could be department history." The second attempt worse than the first. We sat in mutual silence as I regarded him. He was more intent on the door and the other patrons. A dark storm seemed to perpetually sit on his horizon as of late. A storm he embraced.

Finally, he spoke, "I want this unwrapped. I want this torn open,

Winona, but your plan exposes you. Without Hartes knowing, we can't get the support units. We can't get the wire."

"I would have you, Finn. You saved me once before. I would only need you in the vicinity of any meet I have. You could get to me."

I did not play a game with Finn. I did not tell him what he wanted to hear. I told him the truth. I knew he would tear through the gates. The realm of the Guild produced men who hit hookers, intimidated coeds, and killed the unsuspecting. All while finely dressed. Finn was different. Finn's formative years were spent in the jungle. He honed himself as the working police of Chicago. He was a man. One of the last. He would be upon them like a true wolf on sheep if need be.

"Aye," he deflated. Resigned himself to his coffee and accepted the facts of what would occur.

"Aye? I wonder who we have been spending time with?"

"Alright…alright…we are already in the quagmire of your own love life. So let's not bring in mine." A small smile crept in. "But I do have one question. How do you control it when we go to trial?"

He assumed we'd have success. He had faith in the plan and my ability to execute it. He thought I knew how to handle my job. The rapid realization shot across my mind, and I couldn't help but feel proud. I shouldn't have cared. Affirmation had gone away when Mama passed, but here I was, beaming.

"Once a jury sees those pictures, they will not care how long I sat on the devil's lap." The unacknowledged truth that we would both be suspect to career suicide was not even worth a discussion. It had been accepted. Finn kept at his coffee, and I ordered dessert for a meal.

--- ---- -----

No sandman came tonight. I stared at my bedroom ceiling, wishing I'd painted constellations there instead of dismissing the idea months ago. Stars to trace. Stars to sleep beneath. I evaded the truth of why I was up. I did not need a big sky. Doubt had cracked my wall of confidence. I'd thought if I could convince Finn then my own mind would follow suit. Instead, I'd placed the burden on myself. The investigation had stalled. We had no money to truly follow as it was not taken. No physical evidence to shortcut. We had followed clever guideposts to the Chicago Guild of Saint Luke, but they appeared to be part of an internal game.

Pulling back the curtain of the Guild was necessary, but was I the right one to do it? My mind played against itself. To know that if I failed...I would let Helen fade into oblivion. Her name forgotten. Her parents left to fight the lie all alone. Here I lay under a blanket, worried about being accepted into high society. A burden to crush.

I needed to lean on history to gain perspective. To put events and actions in a proper place. Remind myself what we were capable of. Steel myself with the real-life stories of others.

Not fantasy, but men and women who breathed air and touched soil. Men had gone over the top and climbed over trenches into a hellscape that was certain death at the sound of a whistle. As *In Flanders Field* held their memory, the investigation would be Helen's poetry. Her name would not be whispered about. She would not be an afterthought. Not another small town suicide. She did not die. She was murdered. Her name would set fire to the polished floors. Her memory would be corrected.

Falling asleep, I imagined myself on the western front. Maybe my self-conceit was fit for the Guild, and I would not have to pretend. No, imagination was not just for the mystical. I was my mother's daughter, after all. Just a slightly different version. I let it run amok beneath my plain bedroom ceiling.

CHAPTER SIXTEEN

"Frost wedging."

"What?" Finn replied while reclining in the chair. I stood with my palms flat down on his desk in a manner that prompted him to lean back.

"In frost wedging, water finds its way into a rock through a crack. The water freezes in the open space, expanding, causing the crack to enlarge. Eventually, the rock is broken apart."

"I missed that day in rock class."

"It's what we are going to do, Finn. I am going to break them," I said with a too-happy smile.

Sergeant Hartes called us in from the office doorframe. Dockers. A button-up from Marshalls. Tie from a bygone Father's Day.

The meeting came and went. The line of questions was soft. Nothing to penetrate too deep. He was keen enough to know there was movement below the water but kept his head above it. He served as our barrier for the investigation. He had absorbed the questions from above and outside. Left us to do our jobs. We fed him what we could.

He did not want more. People were not beating down the front door, but rather "watching from the front bushes" is how he had put it. No one wanted their fingerprints to be too clearly pressed here. They'd still watch, though. It should've unsettled him more. It should've terrified him more than if the mayor himself called for an update. He was not rattled, though. Stayed casual. I appreciated it from him. The rest of the conversation fell by the wayside. Finn and I made our exit.

Finn took a drink of coffee and resumed his unblinking stare at the floor. The rest of the detectives on the floor moved around us. A conversation about work. A conversation about family. Conversations that sounded scripted. At least they moved, though. We sat here and did nothing. A pile of scrap to think on. Stagnation did not fit Finn well. I felt the tension between the two of us. Helen was the source of it.

"Winona, when will you and Owen pitch your idea to the Guild?"

"Soon. Tomorrow."

"Good. I have someone we are going to meet for lunch. I wanted this meet to occur before you knock."

"Who?"

"Better you wait and see. You aren't the only one who rubs elbows."

— ———————— ——————

Lunch off Rush St. I would have expected the setting for Owen or his contemporaries, but not Finn. I knew the area. Any young woman who ventured here had to know they would be fending off older men. It was a known hunting ground for the man who bought and the woman who wanted to be bought. Not prostitutes, no. No, Oak and Fire patrons practiced a civilized trade. A trade with a name. "Gold diggers paradise" it had been first called to me. I'd been once and playing lapdog to wrinkles wasn't for me. All this contributed to my confusion as to why Finn brought me here. Surely he didn't think I needed etiquette lessons on behaving in high society from a dusty corpse he knew.

We waited patiently after being led to our table. We were the cheapest dressed people in the establishment, and that included the staff. The slight hesitation by the maître d on our entry had been amusing. Finn's slight and deliberate adjustment of his sport coat to display the revolver and tin had smoothed the process. Working class, but still somebody.

Finn continued to tap the table but otherwise exhibited no sign of annoyance. The rest of the place was a far different scene with the sun up. Business conducted all around. The suits were obvious, but the inter-generational family seated at a table headed by the octogenarian was sure to be business too. Unfortunately, the tables were spaced just far enough apart to inhibit my ability to eavesdrop.

Finn grunted before I heard the chair at our table move back. My focus was brought back to the unknown matter at hand. A man sat. Roughly the age of Finn. He had taken the seat without hesitation. He was modest but well dressed. He was handsome in a dignified way. For women a decade older than me, he would be ideal. He was not tense. He was not rigid. He also was not relaxed. He gave off an aura of control. Yes, he would be the type to gravitate toward in a decade.

"Finn, we are overdue," the stranger started with nary a concern or glance for me.

"If you say so, Patrick."

"I do. We are two of the only relics left from the neighborhood. It should be a more regular occurrence."

"You still know my weakness for nostalgia. You haven't withered as I expected."

"Withered? Big word. Must be your company. Count me as sharp as ever. Me being here as your proof." The man extended his wrists forward to show them bare and gave a slight shake. He continued after he amused himself, "I have to say I'm surprised by your choice of dining. Developed a little with age."

"Decent food here. I could not get us a reservation at Wells and Schiller." Finn tracked Patrick's eyes as they finally acknowledged my presence. "This is Winona. My partner."

Patrick's eyes held on me, but I did not sense lust. They were distant. An assessment. I was being put on a set of scales. I held firm in silence. I had no other sense of how to react.

"Patrick Rivers," the man said, extending his hand across the table.

Ah, Patrick Rivers. A story went he owned a gas station in Lincoln Park. Amid the tax problems, big oil came for his license. Big oil is a bully. They get what they want. They said some mean things in a courtroom. The problem was that this particular big oil company's Midwest headman lived just outside the city. He lived where the ballplayers lived in the Northshore. Thought he was a somebody. A different somebody knocked on this executive's front door. Two to the chest and one to the head. Patrick Rivers still owns that gas station, and a bully was dead. So they said.

He did not make his money in gasoline, though. Instead, waste management. Rivers Brothers' Waste Management. A conduit between the Sicilians of the Outfit and legitimate businesses. Said to be as close to made men as one could be without the blood. They had found an angle everyone needed. An angle no one wanted and put their hands deep in it. The Rivers brothers were alchemists. Backed by the Outfit, they had taken near complete control of the city's waste management. Construction sites, high-rise condos, industrial sites. Businesses were keen to sign up. Pay a tax for your trash, and you avoid getting into a debt no man could pay. They were smart in not asking too much. Just enough from everybody sufficed and kept the tremors below the surface.

"I'll have a lemon water," Patrick said to the waitress who appeared.

"Same," I said more confidently than I meant to. Finn hadn't wanted me to learn manners. He wanted me to be in the presence of a killer. To sit across the table from a detached soul and still have to ask for the specials.

"Where are you from, Winona?" he asked levelly.

"Bridgeport."

"Really? What's your family name. I have deep-rooted connections to Bridgeport."

"Bridgeport by way of Indiana. I doubt you know the Winthrops of Sangamon St."

"Can't say I do. Beautiful neighborhood, though. I like a place that holds to the old ways. A place that acknowledges its own need to self-protect. Would hate to be thought of as an outsider there."

"Adapt or die."

Patrick Rivers let out a laugh at my response. He turned to Finn. "I like her. Personality, it's a dying trait. Winona here has it in spades."

Finn didn't flinch at the interaction and continued to tap the table unamused. Did he not see a killer but the neighborhood boy? The memories of throwing rocks present when he was being scolded by his mother. For her to see the cunning man whose currency is violence that little boy had become. Finn held no fear for this man. Because he saw the boy or because he knew himself? Either way, I sensed it was refreshing to Patrick Rivers to sit for a meal and be dismissed.

"What else is new, Finn?" Patrick had re-centered his attention.

"Still the same problems as the last time we broke bread. Work has become more interesting, though."

"Ah, Finn, we don't talk work. Neither of us. It is what makes the meal a thing to look forward to."

"I am still not interested in your work. Let the accountants care for that game. How many sisters do you have again?"

"Six. You know that. The Rivers family—famous for having six angels and two devils to balance. What is this about, Finn?"

"I've been thinking about the neighborhood, is all. The people that made it up. How they will be forgotten to history. You and I remember the struggle day to day. A forgotten people."

I sat back in my chair. Listened. Finn started to use my words, but this was not a conversation for the uninitiated. Patrick took a sip of lemon water and casually adjusted the silverware before him before he spoke, "You are playing on my nostalgia now. They were good, honest people. The world did them no favors, though."

"No, it did not. Especially for our mothers."

A flash across the eyes faltered the sense of control Patrick had exhibited. It lasted a fraction of a second if it even happened at all. Flooded with memories, I wondered how my own eyes looked. He sat up straighter, and his hand hovered closer to the knife laid out before him.

"My mother…"

"—was a saint, Patrick. The whole neighborhood would take up arms to defend her. Don't think I don't remember how kind she was to all of us. Your father, on the other hand—"

He let out another laugh. "Now that was a hard son of a bitch. Dear lord. He tried to keep Mike and me in line. Failed in the end, but I'm happy he didn't live to see it. It would've broken him in a way worse than death ever could." He raised his glass and tilted it towards Finn. The gesture was matched.

"Toast with water, and it's death by drowning for you," I said out loud and blushed immediately. "According to the Greeks." I talked when I thought. "Bad luck is all," I murmured.

"Honey, if it's water that gets me, I'll consider myself one lucky son of a bitch."

Finn laughed at the take, and I continued to sit like a child. Another self-inflicted wound. Would anything outside of a muzzle solve my problem? The waitress interrupted to gently take our orders like my personal savior.

"Your sisters did balance Mike and you out, Patrick. They were the light of your father's eye. I don't think there was one guy in the neighborhood who had the stones to ask them out."

"Must be why they are scattered all over the damn country now. All married to men who are nothing like us. Thank God. Kids too. All of them. Caroline says we need a secretary just to keep the birthday card distribution straight."

"I believe it. I'm happy they are not like us too. The neighborhood needed people like us, but at a distance. To keep the wolves out. That's the work I wanted to talk to you about. I am hunting a wolf, Patrick."

"Is that so?"

"A girl was taken by a wolf. She was not much different than your sisters. Humble origins but a strong character. Good family with a mother who watched over her and a father who protected her the best he could. The kind of girl that when she was taken, it sent a ripple that destroyed lives."

"And are you going to find this wolf?"

"Depends. These people cast large and legitimate shadows. Off any record, I wanted to ask you what you have heard about the Chicago Guild of Saint Luke."

"I don't know anything about socialites, Finn. I deal in trash—"

"They killed her, Patrick. For sport. The same kind of fucking people who stepped all over our people. They went and took a girl who could've been from the neighborhood and murdered her. We both know blood on our hands, but I'll be damned if you know this is not different."

"—But I do know about power. Is that what you are asking me about?"

"I'm asking you about the Chicago Guild of Saint Luke. You do deal in trash, Patrick. Not just waste but trash. People's trash. The power lies in knowing what people discard. It may start in high class, but the whispers travel all the way down to the sewers."

They regarded each other as two lions on a plane might. Equal breadth in power with control slipping.

"A poor girl was killed? Working class girl?"

"Throat slit. From a small town south of the city. A forgotten person to history. Her memory forever scarred," Finn retorted without breaking eye contact.

"And you think it has to do with the creams at the Guild? Half are too doped up to know where they're at."

"Maybe. What do you know?"

"I know the devil can wear a suit and tie. I hear their parties are good for other's business. Girls. Drugs. Money of no consequence."

"Ever been?"

"Are you really asking me that? I like reality, to be honest. I don't play dress-up. Heard whispers down in the sewer, is all."

"Didn't think you would have enjoyed yourself, anyhow."

"Power they are born into. The whole lot. When you're given power, as opposed to having earned it, you are prone to want to wield it. Justify your possession of it. Our betters, Finn. They want to remind us of that. They probably killed your girl out of the same notion."

"Perhaps." Finn drew into himself in thought about what Patrick said.

"A lifetime of victory. That is what we are up against, then," I cut into the conversation headfirst again and sounded as dejected as I felt.

"Victory defeats," Patrick replied as he broke a roll and reached for butter, finally able to retrieve the knife before him.

"Come again?" Nothing made you feel more like a child than not following in a conversation.

"Victory defeats. What greatness is achieved without struggle? It is not a romanticized look back. It is the damn truth. On a small level, think of your favorite band. When was their best work? I don't even know who you've picked out in your head, and I can nearly guarantee it would be their early work. When they were living in a storage unit and had to make it. When choice is eliminated, the human spirit is engaged. You are hardwired to survive. To want to survive. On all levels. Your internal fight is activated, and you produce. Music, mayhem, whatever it may be. But you produce." He was now pointing the knife blade down at me as he talked. "When the door is opened for you, when you've driven in your own vehicle, the need has disappeared. The class of people you are talking about I know of. That's it. I see up to the tower, but I will always live on the ground. You stop looking over your shoulder when you no longer fear someone being there. I see them, though. The people you talk about are born into it. Blind. They are blind." He continued to wave the knife about. He was only interrupted by the delivery of our food, where he almost nicked the waitress' leg.

"Alea Iacta Est," I murmured.

"My turn for clarification, honey." Patrick looked hungry for an answer. No one likes being lost.

"Nothing. Never mind."

"That's why we make such a good pair, Patrick. Her thoughts and my looks. We just need to justify you. Are you going to tell me anything else, or are we to move on to our meals like the rest of the people here?" Finn had been hungry as well, apparently.

"I'll tell you happy hunting, Finn….and let you know if anything floats my way. You should be careful with these lunches of ours. The only thing the Feds hate more than monsters are cops, you know. Either of our pelts is the highlight of their career. Fucking accountants with guns."

I settled in as a ghost for the rest of the meal. The two men bartered memory for memory and left me as an outsider. Finn had exposed me to more than just danger. He had exposed me to himself. A man set in motion to not turn around. Conquistadors arrived in the New World, and their commander, Hernan Cortes, ordered them to burn the ships after landing. Eliminate the way back, and you could only move forward. Finn had become Cortes reborn.

Taking me to meet a mob associate. To sharpen me, yes. To make me comfortable with a killer in front of a plate. At the cost of what, though? I did not see a boy from the neighborhood. I saw the family of the oil executive. I saw the mourning and loss a man like Patrick dispensed. He can lie to himself.

"You don't think you told him too much?" I finally broke the silence on the way back from the meal.

"No. You don't understand. It would be like turning on family to him. I served with his brother in Vietnam. Got him out of a bad situation over there. He'll never forget. Sees it as a debt he cannot pay."

"A man who killed a family man and left his body on his Northshore doorstep does not have a moral compass we should be leaning on."

"That story is almost true."

"You talked too much, Finn."

"Like your bartender friend? You don't think he would sell you out for a rock when the craving hits?"

"That is different. He does not murder people."

"He just helps peddle poison."

I rolled down the window. Let the wind drown out anymore he would have to say. I was done. Johnny Bones had a problem. He was not the problem. Patrick was no Penitent Thief. The car made more noise than usual. I wanted to be a ghost.

---- -------- ----

I wanted to be in a bed of grass. Not my bed.

November 5th. Guy Fawkes. Daphne. Romulus and Remus. None of it would be sorted now, and it wasn't what kept me up. The meeting tomorrow did. When we spoke after work, I selected the location. It felt appropriate.

Dakota kept me up. It'd been over six years since we spoke. Great promise, Winona.

CHAPTER SEVENTEEN

The cemetery was framed by a shoulder-high brick wall regaled with wrought iron piping. Mausoleums and sculptures intermixed with more modest headstones. Dates from the late 19th century to the middle of this century. It had been a mistake to pay attention to the dates. So many children. We took survival for granted in the present. Owen stood next to me with the wind circling about and driving his hair in every which way. Outside of the dates, the walking tour was quite pleasant. Finn played the part of dutiful mourner. A stranger in a graveyard paid his respects, but there had been minimal company outside of him. Until there was.

"Owen. Winona." Gabrielle had dressed for the setting. A deep black coat wrapped around black jeans and a tight black shirt. Guillaume stood off to the side with a new woman clinging to his arm. His apparent disinterest did not seem to bother her. It did not lessen her grip. I needed to be let into the Guild to break this open.

"Who chose here?" the unknown woman spoke.

"I'm guessing you, Winona," Gabrielle said with even less regard for the woman than she had given me.

"Guilty," I acknowledged. "You'll understand soon enough." I wanted to bait them. As irritated of a front as they put on, I could sense curiosity. They owned downtown, but a graveyard was out of their clutch. It put them on uneven ground, and I wanted to entice them into liking it. It was different than seducing a man but built on the same foundation. Show them a taste, and the hook is set. People were not calculus.

In the silence that followed, both women began to look around. Gabrielle was taking note of the detail. No doubt she was jealous of the level of craftsmanship involved in the stone. The woman probably wanted a pyramid for her burial, complete with the scores of dead slaves to accompany it. Or a pyre on a piece of private beach. A rival to Achilles' own.

"And here I thought you would plead the Fifth, Winona," Gabrielle said with a slight drip of a smile. "Beautiful, are they not? Even in the permanent presence of death, the beauty holds."

"Death can be beautiful. The final chapter to a captivating existence. The nightcap, if you will." I realized Owen and Guillaume were having a much lighter conversation with zero recognition of what was being said around them. Both smiled, and the mystery woman slacked her grip on Guillaume as Owen came into her orbit. I returned to the manner at hand. "Tell me, Gabrielle, have you ever conversed with death?"

"Are you asking me if I have spoken to ghosts?"

"Ghosts, spirits, the afterlife. The people who have moved on."

Gabrielle became more focused in on my presence. Her dismissive posture replaced by a defensive scowl. A debate raged within her. Did I mock her or not?

"No, I cannot say I have." She gave little and held tight. The smart play. It did not expose her position, and with no follow-up inquiry, the onus was squarely on me to advance the conversation.

"Would you like to?"

She did not answer. Not since her first appraisal of my body had I felt her stare upon me as much. Yet, it was an opportunity. Her rapt attention was my opening. Curiosity the drug. I had to exploit the opening.

"That feeling, Gabrielle. The pause. The contemplation. The possibility. Didn't the questions themselves move you? Owen and I asked you here for that purpose. I have long admired the Chicago Guild of Saint Luke's work in the arts. Provoke thought and allow people to feel. The living world can be far too predictable and mundane. People shuffle about, and it is the Guild that brings a spark to them. The work you have done to advance that cause is noble. But does it not feel stale? As the wider culture has become more nihilistic and self-absorbed, have you not felt a dulling of the knife in the projects you promote? And yet, with few questions in a cemetery, I was able to give you pause."

"This is most unexpected from you, Winona." She softened as she understood she still had power. "I must admit we are flirting with the truth of art."

We. She forgets she does not create. Merely finances. Rides coattails and mingles. A crown was not enough for this bitch. She needed to be able to tell people she forged it.

"I knew we were more similar in our taste than we thought. An exhibition. Necromancy and magic. The history across cultures, the artifacts, and the ability for guests to interact. A form of art that spans thousands of years but is shunned in our modern times," I continued in my advance.

"Interact?" she asked.

"Yes. Gypsy magic, darling. Have mediums present. Allow guests the ability to sit before them. Feel the pull of a mystic. Fortune reading, speaking to the dead, dream interpretation. All performance art that would provide the crescendo of the exhibit. Feel your own draw. Your own pause from questions for me. Now replace me in your memory with an aged woman clad in black named Esmeralda. Or a younger witch we know from Montana. No crystal balls or velvet drapes. Not the infomercial store-bought hustle. Rather dark magic in a dark room before a dark soul. Ask Owen. She shook his soul."

"Is this true, Owen?" She turned her attention to him and bit her lower lip in waiting. My fists were squeezed.

"Winona speaks the truth. We visited her, and I was ever skeptical, but Esmeralda...." He let his eyes drift to the rows of gravestones as the words died on a vine. Drama must have been a heavy part of the curriculum at Harrow. Gabrielle seemed to be entranced by the performance. Maybe more than that.

"Art of the next world. Well done, you two. Guillaume, imagine the tremors the Adfields would have when confronted by such? They always feel as though they are at the cutting edge of culture and trends. What a blunting stop it would be to their arrogance to be usurped by a traditional exposé of semi-religious norms. The cultures we could promote—"

"From Romani traveler to Haitian Voodoo," I finished her thought and was met with a glare before she softened again.

"—Yes. We would continue the Guild's mission. Promote a diverse cross-section of culture and individual artists. The artists different than what you would expect. The setting would be key. It would have to set a serious tone to eviscerate any notion of infomercial fortune-tellers. Guests would have to walk on hallowed ground. The ground that by instinct demands you obey." Her tone was steady. Direct. Reflective of boardroom leadership.

I spread my arms out. Gestured to the small stone chapel on the cemetery's northwest corner, nestled between a bevy of elm trees. "Voila, my dear."

It was a short walk to the chapel through the rows of headstones. A chilling endeavor, regardless of the company. Gabrielle betrayed that notion. The woman had warmed considerably. She made physical contact with me on the walk. I served as the reassuring handrail as she sought to balance herself on uneven ground. The talk was small but not contentious. Owen and Guillaume engaged in a spirited but lighthearted conversation, also at odds with where we were. Mere steps behind, and I could not make out any of their exchange with the battering of the wind. Apparently content with just being present, the unintroduced woman didn't make a sound.

The chapel bricks were weathered. Nothing aged as well as brick. The pitched roof showed its lack of attention via missing shingles. Stained glass windows survived undamaged, though. With the light of the sun, they shone like a beacon. With inspection, we found the dedication in the foundation corner listed 1896 AD. Four stone steps led to two large wooden doors. The iron handles were shaped to be the side profile of angels. Each was set to face the other towards the opening of the door. We all stood at the base of the stone. I had missed all these details when first taken here.

"Not quite the Parthenon," Guillaume quipped to us. His tone was devoid of scorn. Not a comment to mock. Simply an observation.

"We need Saint Luke, not Athena." I met him with a smile and gestured for him to take my hand. He awkwardly obliged. We started up the stairs. Gabrielle led herself on our heels while I caught the other woman catch Owen before he had taken half a step with an outstretched hand for assistance. Ever the gentlemen, he assisted. The doors creaked open, and we made our way in. Spiderwebs connected the wood crossbeams. Dust covered the dozen or so pews. Disturbed in various spots. A few votive candles remained in the stand that stood to hold dozens. The place had not changed since I was last taken here by a man I flipped a coin for. Rays filtered through the stained glass windows. Colors danced as I produced a lighter. A short walk to light the candles.

"Open doors?" Guillaume said as he paced the walls and stood before a stained glass window portraying a struggle between a man and beast.

"I arranged it," I bluffed.

"And she can plan. Winona, you continue to unfold in unexpected ways," Gabrielle said as she sidled next to me before the candles. The candlelight flickered across her beauty. Even the light favored her. Her brother had become enamored by another stained glass window. I sensed a begrudging fascination blooming within both of them. The visualization had commenced. The seeds sprouted.

"You wanted hallowed ground. I give you consecrated floors." I turned to face Gabrielle.

"Yes, Winona. Yes." The beautiful woman now spun about in place. Her eyes darted around, and the wheels turned. "We could move the pews and create an open theme. Your gypsy recessed at the altar for interactions. We could move a confessional in for privacy. There looks to be a rear chamber behind the altar." Her attention had ended with a note of the long, thin hallway that led to darkness. With the train on the tracks, the woman made her way to the hallway at the side of the altar. While the main chapel had been in relatively good condition, the hallway begot room after room in disarray. One contained a card catalog in ruins with drawers open and cards strewn. Other rooms filled with empty beer bottles. Graffiti covered most of the walls. Teenagers, most likely. Wild enough to cause a little havoc but tame enough to mind the main chapel. Probably decent kids. No gang affiliations. No "CPDK." The hallway ended in a single, larger room. Barren of furniture with the only note being red spray-painted letters of "NWBTCW!"

"No War but the Class War." Guillaume stopped at my shoulder as he spoke. It was just the two of us in the room now. The others had found other nooks to explore.

"Excuse me?"

"NWBTCW. It stands for 'No War but the Class War'. Our friend in common taught me that. He had a fondness for acronyms. To simplify a message for the masses. He felt like they conveyed a wittiness that attracted the curious. Like it has done to you now."

"Our friend?"

"The Professor. He was heavily involved with the Guild, after all."

Acronyms. Involvement in the Guild. I caught my own breath. A trick to stop my questions. Make survival the top interest of the body. Shift away from the inquiries that burned within. Breathe in. Air returned. I was grateful for it. Shift the conversation now.

"I wonder what he would think of CPDK." I waited for him to respond. Nothing came but a lack of recognition and the underlying unease we all felt. "Stands for 'Chicago Police Department Killers'. Venture to the south or west sides, and it's the only acronym you will see." We stood in mutual silence. We lingered a moment in silence and contemplation. I thought of Bill Yenot. The savior I would never be able to thank. Guillaume had the emotional intelligence to quietly bow his head. He surprised me. We bound back down the hallway to the main chapel, back to the others.

"Find treasure?" Gabrielle asked. We descended from the dais, each waiting for the other to respond.

"No gold, only knowledge," I said as we took the last step. Out of the corner of my eye, I sensed an exhale and a slight smile from Guillaume. The door had been opened to the Guild. For the autopsy, the fake endeavor would be paramount. Guillaume looked over in a moment of illuminated thought at me. It appeared as if he had seen me for the first time.

"Winona, this place. This place works on so many levels. The Guild does charitable work beyond the art shows. Restorations of antique buildings in underserved communities. People can feel pride in their neighborhood. The chapel here would be a prime candidate for renovation and restoration. We could use your gypsy magic exhibit as a launch. Do you know who has control of the chapel?"

Must need deductions for tax season.

"Beautiful idea, Gabrielle. It is not run by the Archdiocese. I'll have to dig a bit. The cemetery is maintained by a local historical non-profit. I can't imagine they would turn down such a generous hand."

"Call me Gabi."

Don't call me Winnie.

Gabrielle looked over as everyone nodded along and smiled at the kindness. She basked in the acknowledgment of what had been extended. I watched, and she was led by her brother and the woman not named to a stained glass window to admire. A discussion on detail, possibly. Owen had a smile so cute and knowing I wanted to slap him. I knew what he thought.

"What am I to make of the both of you without blood drawn? Gabi and you—"

"Shut up."

"If I did not know better, I would be concerned."

"Shut. Up. What was her name anyhow?"

"Who?"

"The little vixen on Guillaume's arm who keeps her eyes on you. I might hand her a drool cup."

"Maybe you still aren't playing nice. Her name is Thalia. I think she is an actress."

"Puppets."

"Pardon?"

"Actors. Actresses. They're puppets." Maybe I was being a bit territorial. A woman's right to be, though. Thalia was fresh in the way of youth. Men often failed to see the ambition cloaked in innocence that could define a younger woman. I knew. I lived it.

"Ah. How did you find this place anyhow?"

My turn to scramble. "A friend took me here many moons ago. Thought I would like it." Flimsy but honest. Just enough truth. Don't drill, Owen. Please.

Instead, he leaned in close, and his hand reached the side of my neck with his fingers gently placing the hair behind my ear. "You did well today, Winona. Gabi and Guy softened to you. The side benefit of this place being restored too. Good to come from our grand trick."

My eyes met his, and the chapel faded away. I wanted to kiss him. I wanted our bodies intertwined. He leaned in, but I turned away. His hand stayed. A more disappointed smile appeared.

"Not here. Not on holy ground," I whispered with downcast eyes.

"I had forgotten how respectful you were of venues."

"Not here," I said more firmly. I saw the confusion. The man deserved an explanation, "...My Mama used to take Dakota and me to holy places. She would tell us all about the faith. The history of the adherents. How the religion and tenets had lasted through centuries or a millennium. Carried and preserved through the spoken tradition and books passed down. What was held to for refuge. The suffering the people had triumphed over. The pain and scorn they survived to carry on. She ensured we understood that. I took to history. Dakota took to the spiritual. We both learned to walk lightly in their house. To be respectful. That's why I turned, baby."

Owen held my eyes, and a sense of warmth emanated from him to me. I had never spoken so openly of family to him. He understood, and it meant the world to me.

Did you see, Mama? I was good. I was respectful. Please, Mama, tell me you saw.

CHAPTER EIGHTEEN

The Ossuary stood still. The bar empty. Barely dusk. Johnny Bones was stocking bottles when I walked in. Finn already occupied a stool at the bar. Our rendezvous point. A place cops did not go. A place that socialites did not know about. A place for strangers. The same reasons I had sought it out many nights ago. Finn disapproved of the call. After the graveyard, Owen accepted my need for a few hours to run errands. The plan was to head to him for dinner after. Our tour to continue. I wanted to dream about him sitting beside me on a couch instead. His arm around me. The conversations, all of them. None of them work.

"Do you need a map?" Finn barked as I sat down. A couple fingers of whiskey set down. A slight smile cooled me off.

"I'm not from here. Remember?" I reached for the glass of water Johnny Bones had placed before me. He only winked at me with a quarter grin tonight. Professional senses had no doubt let him know a meeting not to be interrupted was beginning. Or maybe it had been Finn. He tracked Johnny Bones' movement. Finn saw an addict.

Nothing more. Johnny Bones was more, though. He was a kind soul and worked steadily. Finn would not see it. The job exposed you to so much it could blind you.

"You are not wrong. How did it go?" He began to rub his leg a tad. "I'm going to have to bring flowers next time. I could only pray on one knee for so long. Make-believe was never for me."

"You would make a terrible puppet." I pivoted ninety degrees on the stool to regard his profile. He did not react to the increased personal attention. Faced forward like a sentry.

"Kill me if you ever think I would be a good actor."

"Deal." I smiled and raised my glass, and he met mine.

"Sláinte. I'll circle back with Hartes about our progress. Feed him some lines. Keep the Guild on the outside. Don't want anything memorialized on paper."

"Agree to agree." I hesitated, then continued, "You know the kind of people who come here and work here are not just addicts and bust-outs, right?" I had had enough of Finn's tracking. "He paints, you know. They are pretty damn good too. The people who traffic in and out of here can be rough, but they can also be creative. You would be surprised by the conversations I've had here. Men and women. They work, but it does not define them as it does us. The curators, collectors, the damn Guild...they don't have a monopoly on the town. Plenty of talent drifts around. Johnny Bones is one of 'em."

"I don't doubt it. Talent can be found in the most unusual of places. Your house of bones qualifies." He seemed to have exhaled, and the ever-present alert toned down a notch. Johnny Bones became just another bartender. A background character. "Copper first. Copper last. Nothing in between. That is how they see us."

"Who?" I did not follow.

"Everyone. Anyway, what is your take on how it went?" Finn had moved right past me.

"It went well. The Jardins bit on the idea. From what Owen told me, the Guild is a fairly loose affiliation. Operates not much different from most major charities. A coalition at the top that drives the purpose and mission. It's the zenith of gentry in the city. They were watering the seeds I planted right away. It seems to be a game of cultivation of talent. Whoever can bring the artist or exhibit forward gains more social credit within the group. We offered them a chance to be the artist themselves essentially. We present the idea and they can take the credit. It opened the door for me. More people. More meetings. More slip-ups."

"Who was the girl?"

"The little thing is Thalia. Don't know much else about her. Seems to be the brother's flavor of the week. Know a family by the name of the Adfields?"

"No. Doubt they are steerage class. A coalition, eh? Bound to be rivalries. Bitter blood flowing within. Hickey's murder was brutal. You don't use a knife unless you can embrace hate. It's one thing to shoot a man, but to slice him? That takes a bit more. Happy they did, but still not a thing most men can carry out. Don't forget that, Winona. Don't ever forget that when you're walking."

I nodded. Took a drink. "Talked acronyms too. In the back of the chapel, vandals had spray-painted a large acronym on a wall. Guillaume let out that Hickey was fond of them. Went on how he thought they were a brilliant form of communication in politics."

"Tells us R.R. taunted more than us. Taunted him. Personal."

"Tells us the Jardins knew the Professor more than passingly too."

"You look like you want to spit on the ground whenever you say her name. She that bad?"

"Yes. Yes, she is."

"Too bad she did not wear a wolf mask."

"Trust me. I've wished upon a star. Fucking bitch." I realized I'd tilted back in the sideways stool. It surprised me Finn didn't comment on the woman's other characteristics. Any other man would. So I thought.

"Helen. Helen, what were you doing around these vultures?" Finn said more into his glass than to me.

I could never explain to a man of Finn's age how a young woman could feel trapped. The roads in town are a path out. Wait too long, though, and they become walls. Maybe she wanted to try the world outside. Cast her die. Go for broke. A brave move. To be the one who got away from the hometown. To come back victorious. Finn the boy had never left home, but he had dreamed of the Himalayas. Maybe he could relate more than I gave him credit for.

"I haven't forgotten her, Finn. Don't worry. I know why we are here."

He finally turned to face me. A small crack in the façade as he let out a quiet sigh. "I'm proud of you for being able to come back here so freely. Clearly it's a semi-regular occurrence."

"I'm not the one with scars from here."

"You're a tough one."

"I mean it. The man had to have scars after that."

Finn seemed to brighten at the memory. "He really drew the wrong card with Bill. That son of a bitch never had worse luck." A somber smile crept across his face as he stood from the stool. Finn raised his glass to an empty bar, sans Johnny Bones and me. Johnny Bones had stopped washing the glasses. Tuned in now. Finn turned to the bar room. Looked upon it as if it had overflowed with loved ones and colleagues. He bellowed, "A toast. A toast to Bill Yenot. Rest easy, brother, and stand beside Saint Michael. We have the watch from here."

I followed the words with a drink. Caught a last glimpse of Johnny Bones. He finished off a quick pour he'd made.

"You would've liked him. He wrote. Stanzas, letters, even songs," Finn said barely above a whisper. He sat as quickly as he had stood. "Remember him for that. Not just what he did for you."

This, too, was holy ground now. Consecrated floorboards.

--- ---- --------

Were we less lonely in death if we were remembered? Did the memories of the living touch through? No answer. I had wanted to pause in the cemetery. Stand before a grave and ask. With Owen beside me, I'd been too embarrassed. It was an absurd thought, anyway. Mama had not contacted me. Why would a stranger? Because I stood on their doorstep? My grave a secondary concern to me. Desperate for an answer, I had given little thought to rest. Cemetery. Cremation. It had not mattered to me. But maybe it should. I would want flowers. That was not too much to ask.

-- --- ----

I waited for Owen to finish getting dressed and sat on his countertop with my legs crossed. My legs swayed out and in in a constant timed motion with death on my mind. Finally, he emerged into the kitchen, and I could not help a catcall. He smiled. Closed the gap. Forced me to unhook my legs as he took the kiss he wanted. I leaned my head back and could not help but exhale.

"Will you get me flowers?" I asked like a brat.

"Tulips."

"Please." I smiled as he remembered.

"Not quite a bouquet, but I do have this for you."

Between his fingers was a small brown envelope. It looked no larger than a business card. He proffered the envelope to me. I took it quicker than I meant to. He smiled. I looked it over before turning it around and tore at the edges like a child with a Christmas present. But careful not to damage the contents. Inside was the folded page of a book. I slid it out and saw the vast majority of the page had been redacted via black ink. Each word boxed out to be imprisoned. I scanned the page, strung together the remaining words, and read along in my head:

"Are you my beautiful treasure? Chemicals and electricity. An intelligent figure looking my way."

I wanted to swoon but held myself to clutching the page to my chest. A treasure itself. I opened my eyes again and met his. He eliminated the remaining space between us as my legs wrapped around him. My arms draped around his neck, and his hands were set upon me. I felt powerless against him in the best way. I wanted him to take.

"Control me," I whispered into his ear, accompanied by a gentle bite. My body was pulled closer to his, and his hands gripped my butt even harder. He pulled me from the counter in a single motion and without a word. With a firm grip of my hip, he turned me around. I threw my hands out onto the outer counter to balance myself. Staring forward and breathing hard, I felt him behind me. I felt my dress be taken up roughly. I felt him now. I felt him in control.

I found myself nestled against his chest and under his sheets. There is a certain attachment that follows sex. To be physically one with a man, know each other intimately, intertwine like vines and climb to ecstasy. I looked up at him and tilted his head down for another kiss. A soft kiss. We now enjoyed the warmth of a fire after having plunged recklessly into the flame.

"How different a king is in his own castle," I said as I traced his jaw with my finger. His arm wrapped around me, keeping our bodies pressed to one another.

"Venues. It is said a venue means so much," he said with an innocent smile.

I couldn't help but laugh and lay my head back on his chest before speaking, "Well, in the name of Eros, feel free to tear these floor-boards up and bring them wherever we walk."

His turn to laugh. The small moments bore so much in life. The interactions of love that occurred every hour that wouldn't be captured by a scholar. Wouldn't be documented in history. But they were the defending aspect of humanity. Small tokens and gestures that made living worth it. History had no care for these things. History remembered names. History remembered events. History did not remember the people as they were. At best, we were left with a two-dimensional view of who we studied. Forgetting the life they led beyond their big, defining moments.

"We're going to be late," Owen noted as he nary reacted to the traces I made on his hand. My head rose and fell with his breathing. A rock for a pillow worked sometimes.

"Let us be."

"Gabi caught wind of our plans with the Adfields tonight." My hand stopped tracing. "She invited us all to her place after. I politely declined."

Her place. Apparently, he did not need clarification. It took a moment before I realized he waited patiently for my affirmation. Focus, Winona. This was good. Exactly what we wanted. The Guild already fought over us. We were moving between Sparta and Athens. I smiled for real and felt awful. The deception. Helen. Helen is why I lied. Why did I let it happen like this?

"You're right, though. Let's get moving." I watched him get dressed. Took a picture in my mind. I wanted a Polaroid. A token to hold onto.

--- --------

18th St and Allport Ave. The Adfields had interesting taste. Pilsen drew its neighborhood name from the Bohemian settlers who carved out their own space here a century or more ago. Long since gone. Almost exclusively Hispanic now. The bones the same. The flesh different.

"Didn't I say it's the best carne asada in the city?" Nicholas Adfield exclaimed across the table.

A table off-balance. A slight movement when anyone readjusted. A wire basket of tortilla chips to be shared. Salsa in red or green. The comment brought me back from a gaze through the window. A slight rain had started. First, I overdressed for dinner. Now I dressed wrong for the weather. Man and nature against me.

"47th and Ashland. Back of a grocery store. Then we can talk. I'll admit, though. This here is good." I shook the taco in my hand as I spoke. Best to be honest when we can be. Especially in the game I played now. I hadn't been able to pin an assessment on Nicholas or Anna. They'd been refreshing in conversation throughout dinner. Early on, Nicholas had gently asked about our pending event, but Anna had silenced him before the inquiry finished. Word spread fast. The Jardins were still our ticket, though.

"I like the sound of that. Shopping and eating," Anna spoke with a smile.

She had been most kind all night. No undercurrent of competition. They had asked genuine questions. Been open to mine. Even when I asked about the Roman School. A downplay of the successes. A deflection of praise to others who worked alongside. Capable, sharp edges underneath, no doubt. Still, I found myself at ease. We spoke with one another as if it were a small-town conversation. Neighbors in a quiet town meeting for the first time. The casual attire should have been my first clue. Conversations continued. A dinner with food picked up at a counter moved quickly.

We ventured across the street now. A bar with a lime green neon sign. All classes gathered at bars. Why did it always have to be drinking?

----   ----   ----

I'd been eighteen. I tasted vodka and lemonade on a summer day. I attempted to run with the boys, and it caught up to me. Limitations were such abstract thoughts when you were young. Every cliff was an edge, a chance to fly. Never time to think of the fall. Of the doom. I had fallen into the front door. Dakota helped me to the couch. My knee highs flaunted my legs. Dakota was worried. Her worry pierced my haze, and the need to reassure her flooded through me. I told her not to worry. I wasn't going anywhere. Dakota held me tightly. Murmured to me that no one ever truly left. That the spirit stayed present. Even sober, I wouldn't have had an answer for her. I knew what she wanted but didn't know a truth to tell her.

"She isn't anywhere but the ground." A deep voice.

He'd been standing in the hallway the entire time. We both were struck by the words he delivered. Detached language as if it'd been read from a recounting of a long lost scroll. Not from the man who we were a part of. Not the man who had pledged his life to Mama in ceremony.

"Your sister can drink to escape. It will not change that fact." He hadn't looked at me. Only Dakota. Drove the knife deep into the layered fabric that bound us as family. "At least your mother hid in stories. The fantasy she would drivel on was repetitive, but at least she took to her imagination." Now he had looked at me. "I'm happy she is not alive to see you now. So willing to dull your own mind. She would be embarrassed to watch you."

The fabric had been severed.

-     ----   ----

"You okay, Winona?" Finn asked with his face aglow by the bright, soft green tones of the colored lights from the dashboard. I had run down to the car from Owen's place upon our return. Owen had believed my friend in patrol worked this beat tonight and I ran out to say hello. A block west and there Finn had been. He'd waited for my call.

"Sorry. Thinking on my drink order. Thinking on chance."

His silence let me know he had initially not understood. "Chance?" Finn finally admitted defeat from the driver's seat.

"I can't separate them, Finn. The Adfields were kind. I found myself comfortable, but that gave me pause. The kind of comfort that would allow me to follow a man. We could use a little chance." I leaned forward, tapping my fingers on the passenger dashboard. I accompanied it with a halfhearted smile. "Go home...or a place more Irish."

I looked over at Finn. Imagined the young Griffin Hansen, who studied maps. Plotted adventure with his Himalayans. Vietnam most likely killed the boy in him. A taste for worldly adventure numbed by blood.

I returned upstairs and nestled into Owen's lap. He'd been seated on the couch. His place felt like a cathedral in comparison to mine. I admired the high ceilings, and he told me about the legend of Saint George. In a moment of bliss, I realized a storyteller could dig deep into my being. Mama's imprint.

Do you see Mama? Do you know I want to do just like you did?

He broke into my blissful dream.

"Have you called your sister yet?"

"I haven't been able to get her on the phone." It wasn't a lie. The game I'd sold was yet to be caught. I dreaded the call. I delayed the call. But I hadn't lied. Dakota would be difficult. To bring her to talk to me. To bring her back. When she fled West, she had called the city "spiritually dead." The magic had been ground down by a machine of man's competing ambitions. The Dakota dream took her far. Land to be found that a thousand different footprints had already soiled. Like all things, she framed it as if she had no choice. To stay would be to suffocate, and how could you say no to that? Life with one option cut people's ability to negotiate or persuade. Her shield to my reason.

"I can reach out to Esmeralda," he responded without a trace of disappointment in my lack of action.

"No. I'll do that too. I don't want her gypsy magic to ensnare you."

"I just had assumed based on how you left…."

"You may be a gorger, but you're still a man. Men are oblivious to the subtleties of communication. You all need a road sign for everything. A gypsy woman would steal your deed and titles. Can't risk your heart either."

"Oblivious to the communication, are we?"

"Tha—"

He closed the gap and leaned forward while still seated. He kissed me without hesitation, and I melted further into his lap without a thought of resistance.

I lay awake in his bed. My back against his headboard. Looking over at him. Fast asleep next to me. Not a care or thought in the world. A mind extinguished with the victory of spilling. I was satisfied as well. He had made sure. I admired the ceiling further. That was not why I was awake, though. A line danced in my mind. A line haunted me.

He awoke every day to November 5th. He awoke to destroy keys. I walked within the Guild, but pins were in my eyes.

He awoke every day to November 5th. He awoke to destroy keys. Fuck Guy Fawkes. All I had. I looked over and reminded myself I had more. Still, I had to be haunted by a Catholic revolutionary with a penchant for gunpowder. Guy Fawkes.

I hope that life persists after death. So Mr. Fawkes can know he haunts one more soul. More to contribute to the world than his name being a euphemism for men everywhere. If he was where the good people went, I hope he and Helen could laugh at how the threads tied them to each other. Find a tiny bit of amusement in it all. In what way did a small-town girl from Illinois and a 17th-century plotter intersect? Love bound people across time. Did the revolutionary love? Understand the dance of romance four hundred years after his time? That the mother or father did not even know the man who courted their daughter. That she had not even told them his name. Did he recognize the small-town girl with a mother who barely had a handle on her love life?

I nearly fell out of bed. Guy. Helen's mom said she spoke of seeing a "guy." Not a guy, but a *Guy*. She had not understood what Helen had told her. The dragon had a name.

CHAPTER NINETEEN

"Guillaume."

Finn looked across his desk at me. Phones continued to ring. Papers shuffled. Typewriters clicked and clacked. But Finn did not flinch.

"Guillaume," I repeated myself. Still not a move of acknowledgment that I had spoken. "Guy. Guy is short for Guillaume. Gabrielle uses it as a hypocorism." Finn leaned back. He registered me talking. "Not much, but the note is all we have. The note belonged with the photographs. The photographs show two men. The clue in the note connected to a Guy. I—"

"The other note," Finn spoke quietly but with a firm tone that carried the words to me, "The other note that accompanied the cipher in the mail. The other note said what?"

"The card with the quip? "R.R.?"

"No. What else?"

"Solve today or wither away."

"Solve today or wither away. Solve today or wither away," Finn repeated back to me.

"'Make haste' was the message to the Professor, I figured." A flash of slight embarrassment that it had drifted from my thoughts.

"Wither, Winona. Guillaume Jardin. Jardin. Jardin is French for garden. Wither away."

"Fuck. How had we been so blind?" I couldn't believe I hadn't drawn the constellation together when the stars were so clearly visible.

"We're still leaping. I'm not discounting any aspect here, but we are taking long steps to arrive nowhere. Officially, that is. None of this matters for charging or court." Finn brought me back to the ground.

"But we have one eye open now," I said to cement the development.

"Aye, I still cannot make sense of the logic, though."

"Why's that?"

"The cipher. The letter. They were sent to the Professor. They ostensibly were a ransom note for the photographs. Without knowing what the cipher reveals, it's hard to say for sure. But clearly, it put the Professor into motion. It prompted him to withdraw the money and meet his killer at the University. The killer left the money—"

"Another strike for Guillaume. Money to him is nothing. He wouldn't think it worth the burden of carrying," I said what I knew. I knew this more than anything.

"Then why ask for it?" Finn counterpunched still.

"To provide cover. To lure the Professor into thinking he was off to meet someone else."

"Fair. Even still, why would Guillaume hint to himself with the quip and clue?"

"Arrogance, Finn. I told you. These people play subtle games with each other." Guillaume had seemed different. Aloof. His blood, though.

"Right. The Professor solves the cipher and deduces it to be a ransom note. Meets his end. Why?"

"Why?" I asked.

"Why kill the Professor?"

"Secret is only safe between two people when one is dead. Guillaume had been Helen's guy. At least, she thought of him as such. As for the Professor...maybe he'd been a past participant. Maybe he preferred to watch Guillaume and Helen. Groomed her to be comfortable around them both."

"Why kill Helen?" Finn continued as a detective should.

"Because they could." The notion bone cold. "An exercise of power. Currency moves beyond money in their circle. Power and prestige are exercised in one's acts. I've seen the light in their charity work. Now I see the dark. You should see them at the advent of a new idea. I brought an event idea and a new space, and it chummed the waters. To kill is a primal exercise of power. They would do it because they could. Guillaume is a wolf in sheep's clothing."

"I track halfway. We have one eye open. Guillaume the wolf, but signed by a fox stamp?"

"More misdirection? Guillaume would make a game of it. Maybe it's all an inside joke." I felt like a boulder that had been nudged downhill.

"We need to go to her parents again."

Finn was right to temper. Question it all, but my dragon had a face. I could not help feeling a surge of hope. Pieces clicked into place.

-- --- ---------

We drove by the McDonald's still adorned in purple and white for the high school. Wilmington would hold them tighter now. Teenagers were seated atop and around a picnic table in front. The large home improvement store that shared the parking lot buzzed with pickup truck professionals and everyday folk doing their own work. A monolithic town. One class resided here. They fixed and repaired for others but also for themselves. Life had continued unabated for the rest of the town. But we were parked at the home where it had not. Helen's childhood home. A structure now. Not a home. Robbed of peace. I tasted bile when I thought of my bubbly excitement at our advancement in the investigation last night. Worse when I realized I had made the current moment about myself.

"You ready?" Finn asked with a calm and soft delivery. "You look like you're trapped inside yourself."

"Just introspective thought. I don't recommend it."

"You're learning. Let's go."

We exited the car and walked up the driveway, carefully respecting the manicured lawn. The front porch was still well-kept. An American flag still hung from a pole attached to a support beam. It would be a truly welcoming home if I didn't project such dark clouds overhead. Finn made to knock and stood respectfully with his hands clasped. He stood as if he were the somber messenger himself. I could not help but wonder if he'd taken a similar position when he had to notify his partner's family. Or if he had returned home from Vietnam and visited the childhood homes of friends made overseas who had not come home with him. His life had been defined by loss, but he still stood straight. Even now. The dread emanated from him, but his shoulders took the burden. He had come prepared.

The heavy hands I had watched work a man over in a gravel lot now deftly knocked on the Waterloo's front door. After a few minutes, the fall of steps approached. The door creaked open. Helen's mother stood and registered us. No words. No emotion. There was no hope of good news on her face. Nor was there disgust with us. We might as well have been a package. After a moment, she stirred back and motioned us inside, still without a word. The house frozen in time from our last visit. The pictures hung in the same place. They would not need to make room for more. That realization nearly caused me to drown. We returned to the kitchen table and heard the back door open and close. No one joined us. We declined her offer of coffee or tea. We sat in mutual silence for seconds that felt like an eternity. In that span, I looked out over the kitchen sink and through a window to the backyard. I saw Helen's father at work. He left when we arrived. I was grateful he had. A deep wound in a good man was nearly unbearable to gaze on.

"Thank you for keeping us informed, Detective." Her eyes synched with Finn's. "Even without information, it helps to know people still walk who are looking after Helen." Her voice had nearly given way when she spoke her daughter's name. The finely constructed walls almost collapsed with simply her name. A mother's loss was nature inverted.

"Of course, Leda. Sorry, Mrs. Waterloo."

Finn caught my slight surprise at the exchange and gave me a sleight of hand across the table. She hadn't noticed our exchange. I didn't know Finn had taken communication of the case beyond Hartes.

"I'm done guessing. I'm done guessing why you are here. I've run through more scenarios than you can imagine since I saw your car pull up. I've tried to settle myself. I failed. Why are you here, Detectives?"

"We wanted to touch base with you on Helen's romantic life again," Finn replied with his eyes now downcast. He was to take point here.

"We talked about this, Detective. Helen was always pursued. Boys liked her."

"I remember. You had mentioned a guy. Would you mind revisiting that with us?"

"No. It's fine. I just don't know how much help I will be. Helen was so tight-lipped recently. She used to laugh and bask a little bit in the attention she would get. We would go to the store, and she would point a boy out to me and give me a rundown of the drama. Just usual teenager stuff."

"And more recently?"

"She was just different. Honestly, I took it as a sign of her growing up. I would tease her and ask, but she always kept her answers vague. Would just say it was different in the city than back home. She wouldn't say much more. I remember feeling selfish for wanting my little girl to be less of a woman. For wanting her to share more with me. I pried. I'll admit that, but she gave me so little. Like I said, she just said she found a guy."

Finn leaned in on the table. "Mrs. Waterloo, do you remember exactly what she said about finding a guy."

"Not exactly, but she would just say variations of 'Don't worry, Mama. I found someone. He is a good guy' or 'I found a guy, Mama. Maybe you can come up and meet him one day soon.' Just a little trace of teasing to me."

Her eyes had dampened with the emotion. Candles could melt amber. Glaciers returned to rivers. And unmarked memories hidden pretty would return to the grieving mind. In her crack of vulnerability, I could feel Finn pause to press the answers we needed.

"Leda, she said 'guy' when talking about her current relationship?" I asked her with all the sincerity and kindness I could call upon. "You remember that word specifically?" She met my eyes with more distance than she had Finn's. I had not been the one calling her. I had not been the one she knew to walk beside her daughter's memory. But I did every day.

"That I do. I remember laughing to myself as I had taken it as a sign of maturity. She was not out leading boys on but had found a guy. Found a man. I liked to tell myself she understood the difference."

She did. Helen knew the difference in her choice of words. She told her mom in a way she probably was playing as a long game joke. "Here he is, the guy, Mom!" "His name is Guy." I imagined her expectations for the meeting. How she would want him introduced. How she worried about the way her father's calloused hands would judge the manicure that walked his daughter through the door.

"I don't follow. Am I helping? I'm just confused on it is all. Please tell me how I can help. I do not know anymore. I torture myself with questions. You don't know what I would do to have known more. I would have begged her."

"Mrs. Waterloo, you are helping. You are a tremendous help. It's like I said before when I called. I can't get too much into the details but know we are on it. We are working, and what you told us has helped in your daughter's investigation." Finn had been quick to read the need for reassurance. I was grateful for the deft handling. His message seemed to have done enough.

They conversed more, and Finn continued to shepherd the poor woman. I found myself staring out the window again. Her father hadn't stopped working. He'd been moving steadily without pause. In a moment between carrying the mulch, I caught him wiping each eye with the back of his hand.

"He doesn't like to sit still anymore. So mostly he does what you see now, or he walks through the neighborhood," Leda said as she noticed me watching her husband. I could not help but blush and pray that she hadn't misunderstood what had transpired.

We excused ourselves shortly thereafter and made our way to the front door with her offered guidance. As the front door closed behind us, I heard the back door open and close again. A deep wound indeed.

---   ----   -----

As we drove back, the entire town of Wilmington had taken refuge in my thoughts. Not just the home off Route 102. Main St was a single block dominated by a series of two-story brick buildings at least a century old. An antique shop neighbor to a gunsmith. The gunsmith neighbor to a bar that reserved the street in front for Harley Davidsons. Appropriate that the zenith of the working man's luxury would be death on two wheels. They worked hard without a safety net. If they lost their employment, they did not eat. If they failed, they died. Living in that reality redefined all aspects of life. Even your hobbies or what you do for enjoyment. Throughout the entire drive, I didn't see one head hung low. American flags flew from mounts. Business windows supported the community and the children who made it up. The girls of the town had apparently won the state championship in basketball two years ago. The newspaper cutouts and team celebration photographs still taped up. No patriarchy here, as the University of Hyde Park would teach. No backward living for the denizens of Chicago to use as the butt of a joke. The Guild wouldn't believe anyone lived here by choice.

They did, though. A forgotten people, and they probably preferred it that way. Even if the people they voted to represent them hated them. Even if the musicians they paid to see were frauds, who played a character. They knew they had no choice in the matter but continued on. It was bravery not defined by a single moment or defining act. Instead, bravery in the face of a lifetime of endurance, knowing you had no champion. Half of the rich defended themselves. The other half simply played foil and masqueraded as champions of the downtrodden who were more likely able bodies but chose not to work. Those who worked and scratched out a living to defend what little they had? No. No champion for them. No champion for Wilmington. Just daughters taken with promises. Daughters murdered.

A daughter Wilmington had not fully claimed in her death. There had not been a note or whisper to us from anyone. Not a stop to express hopes we could help. The town thought she had quit. That was the cardinal sin here. A beautiful girl runaway with the world at her fingertips killed herself because of heartbreak. Because work had not panned out. Because…who knows why. I am sure each corner of the town had a different variation of the same story. The part that would be consistent would be her choice. They thought she chose to end her

God-given gift. They needed to know the truth even if it would break their hearts.

— ———————— ——————

We were nearly back. Cornfields long gone. All concrete and asphalt now.

"Do you know about the pharaohs, Finn?"

He looked over from the steering wheel with a hint of disbelief at my first words in over an hour. He had mirrored my silence.

"I've heard of 'em."

"They believed the afterlife to be similar to the living world. A continuation, if you will. It's why they buried themselves with their belongings and treasure. So convenient for the powerful, don't you think?"

"Hard to fathom losing power when it's all you have known."

"Right, but to think you can bring your treasure with you? To believe in an afterlife with your treasure means an afterlife of slavery for slaves. No respite for the forgotten masses. There is a certain brutality to it."

"Didn't know you to be an acolyte of Ra, Winona."

"Didn't know you knew who Ra was."

"Himalayans. We traveled far and wide in our knowledge."

"Ah. Yes. How could I doubt the adventures of young Griffin?"

"From Himalayan to hound, unfortunately. Time is brutal."

We parked and made our exits for the night. Finn's words were another layer of string wound around my mind. A hound who would not relent.

———— ———————— ————

Once home, I realized I didn't own a single object I would carry with me in death. Not one item with enough value to carry on a journey. Maybe I wanted death to be the end. Not a journey. No concerns. A vast emptiness I wouldn't even be aware of. Consciousness stolen by nature. My blood dried out. Blood. Mama was my blood. Maybe I wouldn't have to carry any trinkets with me. Just my memories, so I remembered her if we were to meet.

Please, Mama, remember me. Tell me you remember my voice. Can hear my thoughts.

Silence.

Helen's family might perform the same rituals. They might reach. Maybe a parent can reach. Their pain is deeper. Their reach deeper. I should count myself fortunate to have Dakota.

Fuck. Dakota. I had to get her buy-in still. I needed more time behind the curtain to observe Guillaume for Helen's sake.

She was to be called "Rasputin of Chicago." We declared for her a moniker before even ensuring her involvement. I had stripped her of her name for her own sake. Dakota was only known when I let her name resonate. It rattled my bones like an echo in a canyon.

I sat at the kitchen table and stared at the postcard. It had laid dormant in a drawer for years. Layered over by takeout menus. Out of sight, out of mind. The name turned down. The picture turned up. A scenic view of a sunset over Missoula, Montana. "Greetings from the STILL Wild West" emblazoned across the top. Her message read:

"I write.

A bird takes flight.

Will you call me even when I am out of sight?"

Underneath her signature was a phone number. I never called. I had not the courage to face up to my own transgressions. Now I was left to hope she hadn't moved in the time that passed. I needed my blood.

I reached for the phone. My unsteady hand dialed softly. The phone rang three times before it was answered.

Silence.

The nerves in my hand would not settle. My breathing far too laborious for a phone call. I twisted the phone cord in my hand to stay occupied in the seconds that seemed like lifetimes.

"Twilight?" Dakota's voice came through the line. I'd expected a chill. I'd expected to have to journey to her through a battlefield of words and memories. Instead, she came to me in an instant.

Twilight. The name traversed time. I wanted to cry. I wanted to cry tears of joy for a change. The name she would call me when we were playful. Born from my contrasting loves. History, the daylight. The known, visible, and documented. Clear to any willing scholar to study and learn. Magic, the dark night. My secret fascination with the mystical, the next world, and all that was arcane. Her world. Dakota witnessed it all. To her, I was paused in the sliver of time between night and day. Her Twilight.

"Dakota." I felt the rush of warm energy as if the damn had broken. I still needed to learn how to communicate it, though.

"Is he dead?" she asked in an almost hopeful tone.

"Unfortunately, not. Hopefully soon. Then we can celebrate."

"If only you fully believed in what waited for him. I won't be cutting him down. He wastes our words. You though, long time no talk. Tell me everything. Are you married? Living in Glenn Ellyn with a couple beautiful ones who pull on your apron string?"

"Still working through all that, but I have hope."

"Hope is as beautiful."

"Et tu, Dakota?"

"Me? I'm trying to find a cowboy who wants a witch for a wife. I've come close, but it hasn't been in the cards yet. Us Winthrop women have a history to avoid, after all."

"We do...I have missed you all these years. Your voice. Your memories. Your spirit. I should have reached out. I should have visited. I should have called."

"I knew you would. It kept me afloat, Twilight. I knew the time would come for us, and it has."

I used the back of my sleeve to wipe the tears that formed in the corner of my eyes. I had family. I had good family. True blood without a wound. How had I been so ungrateful?

"Dakota…"

"I'll come." Her declaration stunned me.

"How—"

"Don't worry how. I'll come to wipe those tears, and whatever else it is you need me for. We can stand in the grass. Now tell me about this hope, and I'll tell you about these cowboys."

I could not help but laugh through the tears. My blood. She knew. And her hand did not hesitate to extend. We continued on as sisters do. I regaled her with tales of a beautiful English gentleman with an impeccable upbringing. The one I had worked so hard to corrupt. It all ended up paling in comparison to the rodeo of romance she had ensnared herself in. Destined from the day she was born and named for wild country. It didn't hurt that wild men weren't fearful of what they didn't understand. I learned long ago no one would be able to paint her picture fully.

We talked beyond late. Sleep came fast.

The city woke me in the night to steal my sleep. To steal my dreams. I went to the balcony and attempted to look upon the stars. The city stole them too. I hope the stars in Big Sky balanced my view.

CHAPTER TWENTY

Finn stood in the back doorway vestibule of the detective area. He patiently waited for me to come down. Eager to work. Catching a scent had deepened his focus. No doubt Wilmington contributed too.

My morning had been a blur. Lack of sleep would hamstring me today. Survive with movement. My appearance was akin to an unkept monster. Oversized sunglasses hid the worst of it. The detective floor would inevitably whisper about another long night for Winthrop. By lunch, a tale of a reverse metamorphosis. At least I would have a starring role. Even if it was a cautionary tale.

"Are you coming?" Finn's bark had snapped me back to reality from my distant glare to the clusters of detectives. "No one cares how you look. Most of all men here." If his bark hadn't caught my attention, his too-accurate reading of my internal monologue had been the verbal equivalent of pulling me around by my hair.

"Well, we are in a good mood today. For the record, I think you look splendid."

"A burden I bear." He smiled and motioned me to our car. He had been receptive to the quick turnaround for more interviews. We needed more on Guy. We needed handholds. What we held to now barely allowed for our fingertips.

The now familiar drive to the University repeated itself. The brick, the stone, the trees. The gothic beauty endured. Now the true tenants visible under a shadow. A cathedral of celebration to themselves. Cloistered monks of academia. Functionally useless in the real world, but arrogant in a realm built and maintained by others. They would never visit a small town but would pass judgment on it. Academic papers or policy debates cite the small town as an obstacle to progress. The shameful secret persisted, though—they needed the servants of Wilmington. The people here could not change a flat tire. I hope it haunted the cathedral.

We parked and made our way through the lawns and sidewalks of campus. Finn barely registered any motion around us. A couple decades ago, the students' predecessors spat on men like Finn. They sat in their safety and vilified the boys who returned from Vietnam. The boys who did not have a choice in going. I shouldn't have been surprised that Finn moved through it as smoothly as any sidewalk.

We returned to the building of the crime. Walked by what had been Professor Hickey's office door. How naïve I had been. How I had hoped the photographs were purely theatrical. We continued past. Beyond my walking memory in the hallway, the building to this point held no memory of the Professor. No memorial. No flowers. Not even a handwritten sign. Another community that didn't want to remember one of its own. What I will show will leave a black mark on their souls.

The end of the hall brought us to our destination. The door was slightly ajar. I nudged it open. A waft of citrus and ammonia. Seated at the makeshift desk sat the janitor, Halfpenny. He placed down a small, well-worn book upon our entry.

"Detectives? Do you need me to let you in to talk to Ms. Eberhart? She locks the door inadvertently from time to time."

After the way she had looked at you, Halfpenny, I hope she locks you in with her, I thought. Based on the book, I hadn't been wrong. It made me happy to think about. Maybe good could grow here.

"Actually, no, we are here to talk to you," I said with focus. A glimpse into strangers' lives and I already saw white for them. I needed to temper myself.

"Sure, Detectives. How can I help?" He had risen from the desk and invited us into his workspace. Half closet, half office. He grimaced at our pause. Three adults could not fit into the space. We parted in the doorway to allow his exit to the corridor. The man's embarrassment at his station and my inability to anticipate the interaction almost made me blush. It wasn't just aristocrats who overlooked the conditions of the working class.

Now in the corridor, the century-old building's vaulted ceiling carried the noise from the footsteps hitting the tile around us. We traded a den for a cavern, and neither would work.

"Any chance we could find somewhere a bit quieter?" I asked. The man had already begun motioning to an empty classroom across the hall. Well adept at anticipating the needs of others, it seemed. We followed his lead as he produced an enormous set of keys and clicked us through the lock to the empty room. The desks were arrayed linearly, with a slight stadium raise for each level to loom over the one in front. The result created a gladiatorial feel for the Professor or lecturer who stood in front. He moved deep inside the room and remained standing. Finn opted to sit on the lip of the desk. Not wanting to self-relegate myself to a desk and cement my status, I opted to stand too.

The two men were veterans of the same war. No doubt that produced an unspoken bond. Finn and I had acknowledged it on the ride over. Finn's suggestion that I take the lead had surprised me. Halfpenny would expect to talk to Finn as before. We needed honest answers about powerful people. Best to surprise him a bit from the beginning. Something might shake out.

We all stood in silence briefly while Halfpenny idly scuffed at the ground with his shoe for a previously missed spot. Have to admire a man's dedication.

I ended the moment. "I can't remember. Do you often work nights or days in this building?" He continued to work at the ground with the sole of his boot.

"Nights. I pick up day shifts when I can, though. Eases the bills, you know?"

"Intimately. I know we talked about it before, but again refresh me. Did your duties cover Professor Hickey's office and the surrounding areas?"

"Nightly, ma'am."

"'Ma'am' still isn't necessary. It makes me never want to look in a mirror." He smiled at the statement. "Back to the Professor's office. Not necessarily the night of the incident but more in general, do you remember any regular company? People who would move in and around the office?"

"With all due respect, Detective Winthrop, he was a professor. He held office hours. Students would be in and out of his office constantly."

"Yes. I imagine they were." I completed a semi-circle around his stake on the floor. Halfpenny moved to stay square with me. A bit of a dance. I was accustomed to men letting their movements stay behind a split second of mine in order to hide wandering eyes. It almost unnerved me that he mirrored my timing instead. War or prison could leave such scars. When death marched on you every day. "But what about at odd hours or odd people? Things you would not expect to see."

"Yes to both. Odd hours and odd people. They would leave quite a mess in the office. It would be my final stop most nights."

"The people that came by, do you remember them? Men? Women? Anything distinctive?"

"They dressed well. I remember that."

"Would you remember them again if we showed you photographs?"

"I don't think so. It would be late, and I just wanted to stay out of the way. I learned to be a ghost a long time ago. I can't afford to lose this job. Draw attention from the faculty and their guests, and I would be in the breadline."

"Fair. Just remember the clothing, then."

"Expensive. The stuff you would see a star wear on television. The kind of things people who look through you wear."

We continued on about the habits and movements of these unknown people. Once it had been established that he would not be able to identify anyone, he moved to the background. A ghost indeed. It was more out of politeness than anything that kept me asking questions. People could feel important when we asked them questions.

We had only whisperings. Barely strings to tie together. We needed chains to bind Guy.

We started to wrap up when the door opened. The librarian, Ms. Eberhart, made a sudden appearance. A full stop upon recognition of the company her beau was with.

"Ms. Eberhart." The greeting came out cooler than I had meant. Her features deepened. Still stone.

"Detectives."

"We were just finishing up here talking to the good man," Finn said, straightening from the reclined perch on the desk. The librarian remained silent. Stood still with her arms crossed regarding us as if we had shown up to haul him away from her. A touch of first-time love, especially when it strikes in adulthood, comes with a protective fear. A raw jealousy. Imagined threats against your days and nights.

Funny, I should immediately see it in others but miss my own behavior when it came to Owen. My claws came out in an instant. Good for you, Eberhart. Defend the man as if his heart were a rare book.

The four of us now stood in silence. It had tipped to the point of awkwardness. Finally, Finn broke the standoff and headed for the door. Eberhart stepped aside. We had just reached the doorframe when the janitor's voice stopped us.

"I'm sorry I was not more help with the strange case of—" He started but did not finish the thought as Ms. Eberhart cleared her throat forcefully. Halfpenny looked over and smiled at her broadly. "People can be terrors when hungry."

--- ---- -------

The V8 turned over and sent a startle by the passing students. American muscle frightened the fragile student body in more than one way. The unmarked squad car was the new banner of American imperialism, apparently. I wonder how they will tell the story.

"What did you think?" Finn said as he still smiled in delight at the roar of the engine.

"He won't lose sleep over the dead Professor, but he would over losing his job. Losing his ability to be near Eberhart. He can feel the pulse of the place, after all."

"Survival instinct never leaves a Marine."

Finn drove. I thought about survival. An instinct, yes. There stood a man who made it through war and dragged himself to work each day. Worked to clean trash and discard it. All while invisible. No, not invisible. It was wrong to view him as no more than an animal bent on survival of self. He came every day for her. The way they watched each other, even briefly, signaled a love only survivors could understand. We knew each other with only a glance. After all, a mountain broke to pebbles. A forest turned to ashes. A storm cast a shadow in life, but flowers would grow vast on the ground where they walked together. In the chaos of life, he would protect her. He came not just to see her but to protect her. A woman's dream. My dream. To be protected, but to protect in turn. To bring him into an embrace and allow disarmament.

Helen. Helen had no protector. Helen had no one who stepped in at her moment of need. Alone and terrified as she was. The knowledge that slowly killed her father.

My own life crashed into my thoughts. Owen had never needed to survive. His life had been defined by want, never need. Only heights, never depths. Could he look at me in the same way? Could he walk the storm with me to let the flowers and grass grow beneath us? I whispered an incantation for it to be, and Finn kept driving.

-- --- ----

Our next stop proved to be the same dance, just more lust, and less love. Zelda still had interest in putting handcuffs on me but no interest in my work. In identifying Guy or assisting the case, she could not. Her business danced in a legal grey zone in definitions of what would constitute prostitution. She did not have sex, but she evoked physical pleasure through pain. Her instincts were sharp, and she knew the people in play would be able to bring her trouble. She knew that an identification would bring her into the lights of a courtroom. Information drawn out. No, she did what she had to. I could not expect the woman to drop the drawbridge of a castle she had built stone by stone and let the world in, no matter the suffering that stood at her walls.

Sympathy only went so far. Survival went the whole way when you were alone.

The workday ended with no more solid grips than we had started with. Tonight might be different. Yet the failure of the day lingered as much. I looked out a cathedral window. It proffered an expansive view of Lake Michigan from the high-rise rooftop. The enclosed space had been chosen by Gabrielle for our dinner. The Association of Chicago Athletes specialized in obscure sporting interests of the rich and bored. A meal. A drink. A never-ending stream of social gossip. The sweater still wrapped around the neck. Ready as a noose. WASP paradise. Gabrielle was already seated when I arrived. Her pleasant nature in greeting still unnerved me. Suspicion lingered, and if her goal was to keep me afoot, she succeeded. Even now, as we awaited our light snacks, I had caught my own sense of guard being lowered by the trivial nature of the conversation.

"Guy just returned to France. He hasn't been since the beginning of August."

"A family home?" I asked but was not interested. They were French by birth. They were wealthy by birth. The occupants here assuredly discussed international travel as I would discuss the grocery store.

"Yes, near Provence. We have a cottage there."

"We might have different definitions of a cottage." Humor that knelt. I deflected and stroked her ego of pedigree.

"Owen has been. I'm sure he could take you next time you cross the pond." At another time, I would've held back from a desire to claw her eyes out at such a suggestive statement. Owen can tell me more later.

"And your brother hasn't been since August?"

"No, but this visit is much shorter. In August, he spent the entire month. Arrived on the first and would not leave until the 31st. Lunar cycle nonsense. His full moons require picking up after."

"Full moons?"

"Do not be lulled to sleep by his meekness. Our mother always said he was a werewolf at heart. I would venture she would've chosen differently if she knew how deeply he would incorporate it."

"What monster did she assign you?" I was more ready this time.

"Dr. Frankenstein, I was. Beautiful nickname for your daughter, don't you think? She did not mean it to be harsh. Rather a nod to orchestrate and assemble."

"My Mama loved the stories rooted in monsters and myths too."

"To surviving the wasted times of our mothers, then!" She raised her glass. I met her glass and faked a smile. *It was nothing wasted, Mama. Please. Hear me. Please.*

"Plan on speaking to him soon?" Her eyes held to me like a blacksmith in a forge. "The two of you are our primary benefactors for the soirée of séances. He will want input."

"Soirée of séances? Clever." Gabrielle drew the compliment from her own mouth reluctantly.

"Thought of it just now. I treat events like a garden. Know what you plant, but how it grows will evolve."

"Not me. I'm meticulous in planning. Before the first step, the last one is known."

"Orchestrate. Just like your mother said then."

"Just like my mother said." She chewed on the words. Family secrets were not just for the poor and working-class, after all. No matter how well you trained yourself, the memories would burrow to the surface. Our blood was the Achilles heel of us all.

The conversation stalled. The tables around us continued in idle conversation while we each sat and further retreated into ourselves. Both apparently drowning in our thoughts when the waiter's hand stretched forward with the interruption that was the delivery of our snacks. Goat cheese spread on fine Parisian bread.

"For the event, I wanted to ask you a few questions. I want to avoid any redundancy with past Guild events. I wanted to lean on your experience here. For food and drinks, you could take creative?"

She tilted her head slightly as she mulled over my extension of responsibility. Even I stared.

"I can handle that, Winona. We have connections. People always banging on the Guild door to be featured. It should not be a problem."

I tipped my water forward in appreciation. "I hoped to avoid other repetitions. Ideas came to me today even. To risk being honest, there was a moment we both hid behind masks." I dipped my head and looked out the window. A feint of vulnerability. "If we two had such a moment, do you doubt everyone is familiar with it? The desire to hide. To conceal. How free are we to explore, then. We are bringing people to the spiritual realm. Maybe it would be appreciated if there was a level of anonymity with the subject matter. Even a theatrical step could put people at ease. Owen had mentioned the use of masquerade attire at previous Guild events."

"Did he?" Gabrielle sat back in her chair and continued to regard me with only those few words. My own heart quickened in pace. Had I overplayed a hand? Exposed too much? Her silence left me with one foot off the gallows. The next to follow if I was to stumble myself to failure.

"He did." Jab for jab.

"I did not know Owen to venture to the masquerade balls. Lord knows I avoided them. They were more the realm of Guy and the Professor."

"The Professor?" Feet back on the wooden planks. No swinging today.

"Oh, yes. I was sure you had come across that by now. He was insatiable for social events."

"Girls. He liked girls. We know that. We know he watched."

"Watched?" The word had struck Gabrielle. Her turn to lean forward. Her jaw cinched slightly. Her eyes narrowed. No flash of anger. No gentle curiosity. Rather the blacksmith's eyes looked over the forge in deliberation. To strike the hammer again or not.

"Yes. He liked to watch. Maybe from behind a mask?"

"Is there something you wish to ask me, Detective?"

"I shouldn't talk about work, but we have been at an impasse in the investigation. The frustration can rise to the surface." I had dipped my chin and avoided eye contact now. Weakness personified. Take the bait.

"We all want to know what happened to him. The whole saga hangs like a cloud. It stripped away a sense of protection we had."

"Alright, Gabrielle. We've heard rumblings that the Professor had a proclivity for girls who fit his students' age brackets. That he was less than faithful to his wife."

"Ah, yes. His wife. The mysterious woman. We swear he made her up. She never came around. Your other assertions, though…well, we saw with our own eyes. The women, more girls, as you said, were young and impressionable. They were wide-eyed and eager to please. Weak men prefer pliable women. Never kept them masked, though."

Here I thought she did not attend masquerade events. She hadn't caught her own slip. Gabrielle exhaled with the talk of sex and strangers. A comfortable topic, apparently. A stark reaction to the previous moment's. "Watched" had rippled the pond.

"No mask for you then?"

"Oh, Winona, plenty of masks, but I would never cover my face. I will not deprive the world." The smile that accompanied was effortless. She stood to bathe in the truth of her statement.

Distracted. I had to push. I needed to provoke. "November 5th."

"What of it? The soirée must occur before Halloween, or the entire feel will be lost."

"Does the date carry any significance for you? Or anyone in the Guild that you have heard of? Perhaps the Professor?"

"I don't know the man's life. A birthday? An anniversary? Maybe you should ask his widow?" She dismissed it succinctly without hesitation. An attachment of confusion without a hint of curiosity.

"Maybe I'll consult the lunar cycle," I quipped over my glass. Her glass stopped halfway up before continuing.

CHAPTER TWENTY-ONE

What would it take for the proper maintenance of our building? The windows were rectangular and drafty. A quarter of the blinds didn't work but simply hung at a slant. It was a far cry from the cathedral windows. I'd told Finn of it all from seat to seat. Gabrielle had been unnerved. Nothing but hunches and feelings, but it had solidified that we were right. Dots were being connected. Planets were aligning. My synapses were firing.

It all came to a pause with the overhead page. Hartes needed me in his office. The page hadn't been for Finn and me both. Just me. The walk to the office was the same as usual. The ties were still bad. The shirts still wrinkled. The greetings grumbled. A working file of notes in my hand and the sergeant's door beckoned. Ammunition ready for needed answers. There was a time to shoot from the hip, and this was not it.

Hartes raised his head and motioned me in. Seated back in his chair, he looked at me softly as I took a seat. He dressed the same as the others. It was a sharp contrast to the company I had recently kept.

A dumb detail to notice. I did not judge. I repeated the thought to myself. Hartes stayed seated, but his hand had taken to his tie. He looked down to examine it like a crime scene. No blood. Not even a stain.

"Winona, I got a call from the 11th District."

The 11th District. West side heroin, working police, and nonsense. The hellscape was a problem for the detectives of Area 4. The mere notion that I had been pulled into their orbit gave me pause. They practiced a bare-knuckled style of investigations. No cooperation. No witnesses. Cases were cleared, though. Murderers were convicted.

"Beat 1113, to be more specific," he went on. He continued to examine the tie.

"Yea, what about it? Do they have anything for me?"

"They have someone for you."

--- --------

He died at the Clover Motel. A cheap place frequented by addicts and street-level hookers. Hung himself from a cross beam in a room. The management had made entry after his prepay stay ran out. Once the door opened, they found him. The beat cops found the commerce of the neighborhood on the nightstand. The Area 4 death investigation detective had been contrite in meeting me in the parking lot. He did not know the man. He did not know the story. The confusion at my relief with the revelation was understandable. I hadn't been able to hide the smile at the unexpected manner of death. He had the good grace to die with his feet off the ground. He died alone. Disconnected from the world. A deliberate choice? Doubtful. It was our escape with Mama. We knew when to run outside to the grass. She would be right behind us, she told us.

He died separated from the earth. I would make sure he would not return to it either. The body would be burned. Left with the county, and the ashes disposed of in a plastic bag. Taken out with the other unclaimed and unwanted. Left out. Where? I did not care. My final judgment on the man.

"And the note?" Detective Boyd from Area 4 asked. We stood in the parking lot after we surveyed the scene. The evidence technician snapped his photos, and Boyd marked down his notes. Clear and easy to write up for Boyd, but still had to follow protocol.

"Inventory it. Burn it. I don't care. Just don't list me as a recipient of it. I don't want to be associated."

He had the gall to leave a note addressed to me folded on the nightstand. The outside read "Winnie." I didn't read what was inside. His words would disappear with him. I made my sentiments clear once more with Boyd. He accepted it without another question.

The parking lot blacktop cracked. Sealed in spots, but weeds burst through. The painted lines denoting spaces were barely visible, yet the address here would forever be beautiful to me. The living nightmare finally over. I needed to tell Dakota tonight.

I'm not going to cut him down.

Dakota's words carried back to me. A coincidence?

I needed food. Then a bit of work. Mama always loved a cheese-burger.

----   ----   ----

Esmeralda's building stood still. The gothic nature of the stone stamped out the passing of time. My hand hesitated at the door. I needed the woman. I didn't believe. I told myself again. She ran a busi-ness. I was not here to partake. Only here to pay. It should be smooth.

The door opened with a light touch. No waiting for her as she already stood near the front. Had she been watching me through the window? Witches. Inadvertently tensed muscles sent a message of physical aggression. I moved to relax and rolled my shoulders back with a smile, but the perception of a threat had produced a smile from her. The physical world posed no danger to her. Or so she thought. Beliefs easier held to before you were hit. Or shot.

The witch maintained her silence in black. Her body appeared almost withered beneath the shawl that wrapped around her shoulders. I stood and caught myself reaching for nothing on my shoulder. My hands fell for the pant pockets, and I leaned sideways to the door. The silence stayed, as did Esmeralda's amusement. She caved first.

"Back already?"

"You didn't see me coming?"

"But I did, blackbird. I waited. I wondered why you."

I could not help but let out an air of frustration. "Owen was busy. You get just me today."

"No, blackbird. Not your walking temptation. Why you?"

I knocked myself from the lean to stand on two feet. I felt lost at the juncture of conversation. Esmeralda didn't move.

"Because I am here for business, Esmeralda."

"But the business has been settled. Your prettier friend finalized the details just an hour or so past."

"Prettier friend?" My breath quickened. My hand involuntarily had taken ahold of my pants. The dark color had given the illusion of the room being smaller than it was, but the walls seemed to move in.

"The blonde who could own a man's soul. The one who does not believe but wishes to play. She came to me to be generous for my services. Explained she had an event catered to the services I offer and wanted my commitment. She said she heard about me through you and your man. If she wishes to alter the terms of the commitment, you can tell her I only deal directly. No proxies."

The walls were within an arm's span.

"When? When did she want your services?" I clawed in my mind for a rational explanation. I clawed for calm.

"Within the fortnight. Very in tune with the movement of the moon that one is."

My hand reached out for the wall, and I kept myself stable. I told myself I was overreacting. Gabrielle simply had more experience in the requirements and commitments of event planning. It made sense for her to take the initiative. I myself had floated the idea that she handles food and drink. A reasonable thought. Well, reasonable if she was a reasonable woman. Had I been outmaneuvered? Isolated?

"Are you okay, blackbird?" Esmeralda's tone sincere. The walls pushed back into place.

"Yes. Yes. I'm fine. The arrangement is fine. I came by to ensure Gabrielle treated you with the proper respect."

"You must have the blood of the stars to concern yourself with such things. Very kind." She bowed her head in deference. The slight movement of acknowledgment could be interpreted as a deep bow by such a proud woman.

I needed air. I needed the grass. I made haste to the exit and was assaulted by the sounds of the city immediately. My thoughts suffocated with every step. No salvation in the driver's seat. I wanted to sink into the seat but needed to know up from down. What had happened needed to be sorted. An overreading of the situation based on a conversation with a witch in the 20th century? Had Gabrielle done a menial task of arrangement for me? Doubtful.

The lines of intrigue spread through my mind. Scenarios rose and fell. A city of thought was built and destroyed in a moment. I burned through it all. Instinct left me with two plausible readings. The first: Gabrielle had made the move to book Esmeralda as part of a scheme to solidify control of the event and allow her to crown herself with the accolades. Juvenile and disrespectful but harmless in my grand ambition of nailing Helen to them.

The second. The second scared me. I thought back to the lunch conversation and dwelled on if I had tossed a lit match unsuspectingly.

Had I been too forward? Had Gabrielle understood the line of questioning and knew much more than I had anticipated? Was Esmerelda just a slight nudge of the first domino that ran directly into the shadow investigation? I wanted to find her. To beat answers out of her. I wanted to be Finn. I wanted blood. Then answers.

Out of the car now. The payphone at the corner had been occupied. A slightly overweight woman spoke and finished upon realizing I had been waiting. I dialed Owen's number while repeating a mantra of calm to myself. You never looked as bad as you thought. Never as frantic as you felt. Tattoo it to my fucking forearm.

Ring.

Ring.

Ring.

Finally, Owen's secretary picked up. What a relief it had been to discover she was a round middle-aged mother of three. Owen's sweater for Christmas already selected. Minnesota nice traveled with her across state lines. What a relief it was now to have her pick up and tell me about her latest adventures on field trips. Owen would be with me in a minute. How I hated time.

"Hello, Winona?"

"Owen. Did you talk to Gabrielle recently?"

"She called me today. Wanted to know details about the event. Wanted to kn—"

"Did Gabrielle ask about Esmeralda?"

"Actually, yes. She wanted to know more about her. I think she was going to speak with her."

I bent over at the waist and heard Owen continue to talk through the phone. The voice carried from another realm now. The street noise dulled. The people passed were out of focus.

"I'll call you later," I said before the phone unceremoniously hung back on the receiver. Around me, the world continued unabated. Men and women moved about, eager to cross another day off the calendar. Eager to move one step forward without a question on their mind. They came back into focus. The panhandler's grin and the smell of urine from the alley were back too. I thought I'd been careful. I'd thought wrong. It was not Owen's fault. I blamed him, nonetheless. To be so easily fooled by her. To willingly give information before he consulted me.

Remember our last meeting. I had given information without prompt. In my desperation, I had turned to her. Turned hard to her. A door opened, and I walked right in. I still had to know more. How far had I walked in?

— ————   ————

Finn was at his desk when I arrived. Niamh was standing over him. Seconds passed before they took note of me. Niamh and I exchanged pleasantries before she made an excuse to leave. Finn and I only now. Niamh had read me clearly. Finn looked puzzled. I stood and chewed on thoughts. Waited to be asked, but he was content with the silence lingering between us. He rearranged the desk, and I waited. I realized he must know about my dad's demise. Perhaps he was not being intentionally irritating in action but did not know what to say. He had gleaned enough from me to understand that the situation was complex.

"We might have a problem," I finally spoke. I kept my hands from my face with a concerted effort. Deep breaths drawn to ease the internal tension. Never as frantic as you felt. I would not be the woman on the floor who appears overwhelmed. Niamh would bear the burden if I did.

"Does it have anything to do with why Hartes wants to talk to us?"

Finn listened. He sat back. He understood. He saw what I drew.

How deep? We needed to know, but now the minutes melted. The meeting with Sergeant Hartes loomed. Hopefully, he would be having a good day. Family at home. Provided for and protected. I took to mirror Finn. Sat back with a blank mind on the meeting beyond the musings of the conceptual. My lean back became obnoxious. A juvenile stunt to annoy. Play the caricature they drew for me. I would have to fuck a quarter of the city with the rumors. A Messalina challenge.

Tick tock.

Tick tock.

Tick tock.

Time moved through wet sand. I needed the meeting. Needed the distraction. The move by Gabrielle had taken seed in the fertile soil. My mind could dance on the ground, but the roots grew and disturbed. Finn stayed seated, deep in his own thoughts. Eyes occasionally moved to Niamh. I dared not wonder about the thoughts that accompanied the looks.

The PA came to life. It cracked at first. Held a moment of unintentional silence before a whispered curse. It had to be Hartes. After years, he still could not manage the system to page. The man acted like he was dropped from the Flintstones to the Jetsons. Finally, he realized he had the line open and summoned Finn and me.

Purgatory would be an office with a PA. A bureaucratic quagmire of desks, graphs, and overhead summons. Perhaps I already had died. Here in purgatory with my answer. A case to slip through my grasp. It would explain why I had failed to have died or been killed, despite my best efforts.

Finn started the walk to the office. I trailed in his wake. The door opened. Finn took the seat to the right. Hartes asked that I close the door. I did and took the seat to the left. Hartes did not play with his tie. His eyes were not downcast. Finn and I had his focus. He didn't fully have ours, though. I found item after item on his desk to ponder over in silence. I wanted to turn the picture frames and ask questions.

The set of his jaw stopped me. Finn had kept him informed. I did not understand the sudden tension.

"You're both off of the Hickey murder. The call came down today."

Hartes' words had been physical. I was struck in the chest.

"The fuck are you talking about? You were in agreement with every step!" Finn's voice started low but built into a roar that pierced the fog of my mind.

"It is out of my hands, Finn. It was taken out of my hands. Downtown told the Captain. The Captain told me. I told you. That's how it goes here," Hartes spoke concretely. Finn's hand thrust forward and took hold of the desk. For a brief moment, I watched as the desk moved a fraction of an inch. The scene of a desk flipped by Finn played in my head. The physical power, aided by a maelstrom of anger, delivered dramatic retribution to the news. In Hollywood, he would've flipped the desk, but not here. His hand pulled back as fast as it had gone forward. He straightened himself out of the chair and walked out. I exhaled.

Finn read the situation correctly. The decision had been made rungs above the good sergeant's head, who sat before us as no more than a messenger. You did not attack the postman if you received bad news in the mail. Neither should we blame Hartes. I started to leave but turned at the door. He looked exhausted at his desk.

"Do you know why? We kept you updated. They didn't like the direction?"

"You did, and they did not. 'Nothing concrete' was the party line. I went to bat for you. The people who made the decision were never detectives. They don't understand it. We don't paint by numbers here, but they fucking can't understand that. They only understand a finish line."

"I see." I did not need to know more. I know what happened. I had walked right in when invited. The mirage of being the one in control had been eviscerated. I didn't know if I wanted to stand or slump in the chair. This was not purgatory. This was Hell.

"Winona, I told them what was on the record. I only burned the book you had written. No other notes off the record." With that, he returned to the paperwork that made a mess of his desk.

The rage found a compass. I had been a living nightmare for minutes before I realized I had even started. The betrayal fuel. The hatred kindling. Hartes' response the match. I screamed. I swore. I insulted. I did not stop till the well was dry. Hartes took it all in stride, which only made it worse.

The exit reminded me that the world existed on the other side of the door. A few looked over, but most did not. Even those who did were not interested beyond a glance. I had expected the obvious. I had expected commentary. The woman who could not handle her emotion. The woman who lost it.

Niamh's hand closed on my wrist. She had been seated on Finn's desk when I walked out. She looked at me. I wasn't able to meet her eyes. Afraid to see how far I had set us back. Her grip relinquished as I turned to finally meet her. Fear. Shame. Disappointment. It was Russian roulette of despair.

"They see you now," she spoke first. She spoke softly. Her eyes did not waver. They did not judge either. I caught myself staring. Tucked the hair behind my ear to buy a moment.

"Who?" All I could muster. I was dumb and emotional.

"The floor. You aren't a woman playing detective to them now. You're a detective fighting for your case. That is how they see you now."

I managed a nod. She continued on her way.

Finn kept the same composure he had walked out with. I found myself lost. Kind words in the dark to placate my sensibilities were paper armor to the Polaroids of Helen. Had she watched over the meeting? For the first time, I hoped for nothing to accompany death. The thought of Helen knowing what happened would break me. Disposable in life. Disposable in death. It was my fault.

"We didn't even ask who it was going to be assigned to now," I said.

"Doesn't matter." The retort from Finn came swiftly.

"Doesn't matter?! We've been kneecapped, and you're still walking for a reason I don't fucking know. I thought you cared about Helen. Her mom. Her dad. Her li—"

Finn stood with an abrupt quickness and closed the gap between us. I had been around the man when he struck with a righteous fury that radiated. An internal furnace that burned with purpose, but not now. Now all that emanated was a still-cold wind.

"Are you old enough to know Tet?" His words were soft. He took a step back and leaned to sit on a desk edge.

"I remember hearing about it. The North Vietnamese and Vietcong offensive that overwhelmed our defenses. A brutal surprise." A boy down the block had been killed in it. I didn't want to tell Finn his name. I didn't want to remember myself. The shrieks from his mother when the news had been delivered could be heard on the entire block.

"That is what everyone remembers. They forgot the NVA failed. Charlie failed. We beat them back. It was a surprise, but we countered and ground them down. Welcome to your own personal Tet. They surprised us damn well here. I don't know how, but they did. We need to regroup. Make sure your sister magician is still coming into town to start."

Dakota. I had to call her. Dad was dead. She had a right to know. I had nothing else to deliver.

Finn continued, "A hand has been played here. They made a move against you with maximum efficiency. You can take away a couple things from that. First, that they can. They apparently have a deep reach even here. Second, that you scared them. Which one did you scare, Winona?"

"The sister. Gabrielle. We had lunch. I pressed hard about her brother."

"Gabrielle. Sinister bitch that one. I could tell just from her walk."

"Protective of her brother. She caught my scent on the trail." The entire conversation condensed and replayed through my mind. It took mere moments to remember every line. To remember every hint. To review all her body language. The missed cues and gestures. How I had failed. An honest accounting. History an autopsy. Without emotion. I failed there too. I longed to feel. The review had shot out the streetlights on an already dark night.

"That it?" Finn's voice echoed as if from a distance, but the man was mere steps away. "Crushed you because you were asking questions about her brother? Made her scared for her brother, did you?"

I acknowledged the assessment with a nod. No trust in my own ability to speak. I wouldn't hold together for much longer.

"Did you ever ask yourself who took the photographs, Winona?"

CHAPTER TWENTY-TWO

Dakota took the news. I heard her spit on the ground through the phone. She would respond in the spiritual realm later. He deserved no less than the curse of denial. With death, his memory would be denied. His trace disappeared from the earth. No one would record the man. Forgotten forevermore. People truly died longer after death. When they ceased to be thought of. No descendant will walk by a frame and ask who the man was.

Dakota's joy had been interrupted, though. No longer needed in Chicago. I tried to explain. I'd made the decision myself, Esmerelda would do. I'd have to tell Finn later. Give context that I myself was barely needed now. She didn't listen. She ran back to her woods.

With the call behind me, I sat alone at my kitchen table. Turned to the ghosts I imagined. What you could wish for one day. A full table. Your desire to hear of all the other's days, no matter how trivial. Not here, though. Here the setting only necessary for one. More a residence than a home.

The murder of Helen had given a bolt of purpose. The brutality of the crime. The stymy of justice. A worthwhile banner to carry in life. To have sat at her parent's kitchen table. To have felt a truly empty chair. Not my self-pity.

My notes were before me. General progress reports scattered on my table. I had taken Hartes' tipoff and packed up all that had not been officially filed. Anything logged would be given to whoever took over the case, who was anointed to carry the company line by either incompetence or intention. I rotated pages. Read what I had written neatly. Read what I had written in the margins. The musings of a motivated detective. I should add Finn's question about the photographer.

I took a page hidden beneath a few others. A copy of the cipher. My thoughts scribbled over it.

He awoke every day to November 5th. He awoke to destroy keys.

The piece had focused me then. It focused me now. The xerox copy was heavier than it should be. Would it have been the words we needed? Guy's own arrogance coming back to hang him?

No.

No.

NO!

The papers were on the floor now. It did not matter. My body gave way. The cabinets hard against my back. The floor an unforgiving seat. No one but me walked on these floors anyway. This was not my case anymore. I'm sorry, Helen. I failed. You were terrified then. You needed a defender, and no one came. You may have even called out for one, yet still, no one came. The damsel killed by the monsters. Not like in the books we read. The detective unable to bring vengeance via justice.

I sat amongst the notes and wept. I could not stop. I let the tears fall and stain the pages. No divine intervention had guided me. Mama had not come to help me avenge Helen. Nothing. That is what waited for us. Nothingness. For if the soul persisted, I would've been guided. I would've been able to help Helen.

Mama, show me. Show me now. Show me something. I don't care about answers. I don't care about the question. Show me. Show me a way to help Helen. Please, Mama.

Silence.

The papers had not fallen into a particular pattern. No light clicked. No magic to connect points I had missed. My tears had not struck a point overlooked. No architect. No blueprint. Life waited for death.

-- --- ---------

The sun had risen on schedule. The morning was orderly. Dishes done. Chairs neatly tucked under the table. My plant on the counter leaned towards the window to catch more sun. Four minutes past eight and the greeting to Rick, today's doorman, quick and superficially pleasant. The sidewalk stayed still, but the people moved. I would not encounter a stranger on a path to destiny today. The axes of life would not be tilted through a small encounter. Destiny. Fate. Fairytales told to adults to cushion the blow of reality. The inconsequential maze we existed to struggle through. You had to entice the runner to attempt to complete the pathway. Only at the finish line would they encounter the dead end. Then it was too late. We had the small pleasantries of this world to buy and consume, though.

Two minutes till nine, and the coffee had lost its taste. The young man playing guitar on the sidewalk had written a song for a lost love. The deep end of emotion drowned him. He had thought they were meant to be. I wanted to tell him he had found comfort. Nothing more.

Seventeen minutes past ten, and I darkened Owen's doorstep.

"The day starting, alright?" The eyes of the man followed his words to look over me. He had expectations.

"I bought a coffee. Deconstructed gods." My voice was a flat note. No pulse.

Twenty-five minutes till eleven, and we were still at his table. Polite conversation from a short distance. Had this been the experience of my father throughout his life? Trapped by responsibility and desperate to escape for moments from the forced conversation. People treated you as a well they could come to draw water out of at any time.

"Do you know why I don't drink, Owen?" His mug stopped mid-rise. My abrupt entrance into the coliseum of conversation containing substance had been a verbal snap of the fingers.

"No. No, I do not. I had always hoped you would be comfortable enough with me to tell me, though."

Comfort. The word struck again. All we could hope to achieve in this life.

"Many moons ago, I'd been out. Invited to a gala. I abandoned my date. Lusting for anonymity and authenticity, I ventured to a bone yard bar. I stood out. I didn't like it, so I drank deeply." I cast him a look from the side. "I didn't have the tolerance. Throughout the night, I stepped outside to gain my composure. To regroup."

"A night like that one—"

"Then a man attacked me. He pinned me to the alley asphalt. Pried my legs open. Ripped through my clothing. Already at a disadvantage, the alcohol further tilted the scales against me. The man's breath hovered over my face." I didn't look away from Owen. He reached for me, but I didn't embrace it. "The anticipation he had. The helplessness I felt. Throw in childhood memories, and I became the patron saint of water."

"Winona…"

"Don't worry. He didn't succeed. A man named Bill Yenot stopped the man cold. He was a police officer. His partner wrapped me up. Carried me to safety," I spoke coldly. I spoke of it as if I was testifying to a set of facts on the stand. "Bill did the Lord's work. The partner took me to the hospital. Told me that the man who attacked me had lived. Told me, 'Even God didn't want him.'"

Owen reached over to grab my hand again. I was still. I had lived with the memory and believed it to be a catalyst. The first stone cast to put a series of events into motion. It led me to the police department. The path that clicked into place with the discovery of Helen.

I had been wrong, though. A chance encounter by two patrolmen. Not a brutal tilling of the soil to allow a flower to grow. Simple. Two patrolmen had come across a citizen and were willing to do what was right. Everything that followed scattered occurrences.

"I wish—"

"What would bother your friends at the Guild more, Owen? That I had been beaten, pinned down, groped, and nearly raped in a dark alley or that a policeman defended me so?"

"Winona, you know—"

"I know the answer." With that, I pulled my hand back. Noted the time to be thirty-seven minutes past eleven.

"The Guild." My voice did not even register with disgust. "Talk to Gabrielle lately?"

--- ---- -----

Fifteen minutes past two. My condo empty sans my shadow. A stillness that permeated in contrast to the hours at Owen's place. He told me "The Nights of Séances", presented by the Chicago Guild of Saint Luke, would be held in three days. I felt betrayed when he told me. A woman was taught to guard her heart. Watch out for the knife.

It was rumored to be a grievous wound to experience infidelity in a partner. A woman was not taught how to protect her creativity. My idea had been stolen, and Owen had not seen the depth of the problem. To him, it was merely a scheduling of events that Gabrielle had taken over. A rational step due to her experience and connections. The expedited timeline necessary to trump a move from a social adversary in the Guild. I didn't understand the complex social web, apparently. The prestige of presentation to the members.

Eighteen minutes past two. My petulant anger had been stunted with the onset of memory. Owen had been placed in the dark by not just Gabrielle. The exposition was our inside joke, not a link in the chain to ensnare suspects closer in a murder investigation that traced from the webs of political power to a forgotten town. A girl now forgotten. Remembered momentarily as a cautionary tale. Then cast aside.

Twenty-two minutes till three. A potent mix of apathy realized. The question Finn posed about the photographer should have lit a great fire, but it had only been a flicker of spark. The plant needed water. I needed blood to flow.

The afternoon passed into the night without much movement. I canceled plans with Owen. I canceled plans with the TV. I lay on the couch. Face to the cushions. In my bones, I knew the absence of an answer had been the answer. The events investigated had proven it. We were limited to the physical world.

Seven minutes past seven. Night had descended. A borrowed bottle of wine from a neighbor was my only company now. An elderly woman who had always been kind in our interactions. I told her I would repay her shortly. I would not.

Fourteen minutes past eight. The glass stayed filled before me. Still a coward.

Nine minutes till ten. I hadn't moved. Nature should cocoon me. Wall me off from the world. Walls strong enough to withstand failure. A slingshot of it all around my head. This wasn't a story. This was my life. I had failed in the role of hero. More, I had the eternal hope snuffed out. A brutal combination of reality.

Eleven minutes past ten. The air was crisp as I stepped out on the balcony. The clouds were thin and wispy across the city. No secrets held within. No angels dancing. Or trumpets playing. The iron of the rail was less challenging than the stones of a mountain. The Greeks should've climbed Mount Olympus. They would've discovered the truth.

The wine glass still full. A drink to ease the glass. To ease the task. One leg over the rail. The other followed. A light frame had an advantage. Eleven stories straight down. A man three balconies over lit a cigarette and paid no heed to me. Maybe I would be a brief eclipse of the moon to the residents below me.

Thirteen minutes past ten. Evelyn McHale needed competition. One foot forward.

Fourteen minutes past ten. A firework from the street exploded. Growing up, the only rule had been no fireworks in the library. No care that we didn't have a library. Mama told us one day we would, and we wouldn't want to hold a bonfire in the library. Mama did not like people who burned books.

Burn books.

He awoke every day to November 5th. He awoke to destroy keys.

Destroy Keys.

The key to the cipher a book.

Destroy books.

November 5th. Guy Fawkes Day. A celebration of fireworks. A celebration in fire.

He awoke to fire.

He burned books.

Synapses fired.

Guy Fawkes.

The protagonist burned books. The protagonist named Guy.

Guy Montag.

Fahrenheit 451.

The key.

My hand grips on the rail strengthened.

The balcony lip underneath supported both bare feet now. A quick clamor back into what had been my cage. I wanted to wrap my arms around the concrete balcony. The balcony was the same as all the other units in the building, but this one was mine. This one was life. I lay and breathed in the night air deep.

I exhaled. *Fahrenheit 451*.

Thank you, Mama.

A sword had been placed in my hand. A sword to slay dragons. I rose.

I had a library to visit. I did not care for the time.

CHAPTER TWENTY-THREE

I drove fast. I had no one to notify first. The exterior doors to the wing holding the University library were locked. The vital piece here had always been to know a man with keys. I stalked the exterior windows. I peered through the old glass. Flashlight in my hand. My confidence dimmed. I had been greedy to expect two miracles in a night.

Yet through a bush, I saw a shadow sway back and forth. The figure had stopped with the illumination. The janitor had turned to regard me. A faint smile to my wave. I motioned to the door, and he nodded. We came face-to-face when it opened.

"Evening, Detective."

"Halfpenny, I need access to the library." The words rushed out of my mouth. I doubt the words had even been clearly understood.

"Please. Come in." He opened the door and waved me inside. The absurdity of the situation dawned on me. The man didn't have the knowledge I did. He had been mopping a floor and was now confronted by the police at a side door unexpectedly.

"Sorry about the light. I didn't want to use a siren to get your attention." I softly smiled the way I knew men always appreciated. He returned a polite smile and nodded, not for my smile but for my memory. The man had indicated a reluctance to the police that took Finn's bond to overcome. Here I stood alone. Guided but alone.

"That's alright, Detective. You spooked me a bit, but better you than a burglar. Well maybe. I don't know you well enough."

My own small laugh surprised me. Men who could make a woman laugh were always dangerous. Every girl learned that.

"Don't worry. My intentions are solely for the library."

"I don't have the key, Detective. The librarian treats the place as her fiefdom. Even the cleaning is done under supervision. We were told she was given the blessing of the trustees here due to the preservation requirements of documents she keeps."

"Where is Ms. Eberhart then?"

"Guinevere is not here, Detective. You've come in the middle of the night, after all."

"Do you have a protocol for when you need access?"

"Yes. She has a number she can be reached at in case of emergency. Her availability was the bargain for control of the library. It's posted in our office."

The janitor led the way as if he did not know her number by heart. My mind instantly romanticized the genesis of Halfpenny and Eberhart. A late-night call for access. Two lonely souls in an empty building. A spark born in the dark. The fiction I hoped to be true.

He went through the motions to look at the number and dial from the phone on the desk. A brief conversation ensued concerning my presence and need.

"She'll be here in ten minutes."

"Does she live that close?"

"Barely off campus." He blushed after his response. Men in love varied in expression.

We waited nine minutes before I heard the click of shoes that I knew well. The steps of another small-framed woman.

"Hello, Detective." Her greeting in the night was as cool as the one in the day. Halfpenny made himself scarce with the talk of a need to work. I caught the lover's glimpses between the two before the departure.

"I need you to open the library."

"Did you forget something? Is that why I was woken up?"

"No. I need a book, and the University hours just wouldn't cut it."

"I can't seem to understand—"

"I can't seem to understand how a university professor reading a book that is a staple in high school literature did not raise a flag to you, Ms. Eberhart. Or another man. You don't strike me as allowing much to happen in this library without being aware of it. Especially actions out of the ordinary. How much did they donate to keep you silent?"

"You've lost me, Detective. But let's see if I find you. Follow me."

The woman moved slowly. Consequences were for one's actions and lack of actions. They could settle on you like chains. Slow her to a crawl. I followed her steps, keeping her half an arm's length in front. Best not to be surprised. The walk gave me time. Time to review the woman. It did not add up. She had directed a student to come to me with her experience. It was a vague hand, but I knew hers to be the one guiding Angelina. Maybe she was not bought but threatened. They could've moved to take her books from her. They could've shuffled her to retirement. Stolen her purpose in life. With each step behind the woman, the belief grew. I wanted to be right. Her cooperation so far a bulwark to my belief.

Step.

Step.

Step.

We passed windows. We passed tapestries. We passed paintings. Guinevere Eberhart did not regard any of it. Her eyes kept straight.

Her back straight. Her steps consistent. Even the first fight of the cold to come with October did not register to her.

Step.

"Ms. Eberhart, who is the quote on your desk from?"

Stop.

Her head turned a quarter of the way. Her breathing became a slight bit heavier.

"Ray Bradbury."

Steps continued.

Click.

She produced, and the library lock was defeated. I paused before the cornucopia of knowledge before me, but she kept on at the same pace. She was consistent and precise. Not an ounce of movement wasted. Still slow, though.

"Hand me the book."

I saw that her hands betrayed my assessment. They shook with the reach from the shelf that contained first editions of American classics. The focus fractured. Her eyes began to well. Her hand paused a finger length from the book.

"He told me if you came not to impede."

"How kind of him. How kind of you."

The arrogance. He had chosen a book with his name as the central character. He had taunted the Professor. He had directed this woman. Why? Because he could. The same reason he murdered Helen. He could be touched, though. He exposed himself with the murder of the Professor. A roundabout path to justice for Helen.

The key was in my hands. Ms. Eberhart stood as still as a statue that could weep. The cover fell open, and I could weep myself. Stamped on the interior cover was a fox. The signature fox walked, and my hands shook. A firework display in the library. The cipher unfolded and lay before me:

C.F. Forest

---- -------- ---- ---...

---- ------- -- --- ---- --- -------- ---- ---- ----.

- ---- ---- -- --- --------- --- ---- -----.

- ---------- ------.

1) pg 47 line 11 word 7
2) pg 127 line 30 word 9
3) pg 61 line 5 word 4
4) pg 6 line 11 word 7
5) pg 5 line 4 word 9
6) pg 126 line 30 word 10
7) pg 1 line 1 word 5
8) pg 4 line 20 word 4
9) pg 6 line 2 word 5
10) pg 99 line 1 word 2
11) pg 27 line 8 word 2
12) pg 41 line 5 word 2
13) pg 61 line 5 word 4
14) pg 39 line 2 word 3
15) pg 5 line 27 word 5
16) pg 42 line 11 word 5
17) pg 3 line 20 word 7
18) pg 2 line 6 word 9
19) pg 140 line 1 word 4
20) pg 7 line 30 word 8
21) pg 17 line 4 word 9
22) pg 80 line 14 word 2
23) pg 30 line 3 word 1

24) pg 145 line 2 word 12
25) pg 34 line 8 word 5
26) pg 45 line 13 word 5

Clue: He awoke every day to November 5th. He awoke to destroy keys.

I began to work as I stood. The librarian stood still with her hands clasped in front of her and tears falling. Guilt strikes hard.

Page. Line. Word. Decipher. Pages flipped and my counts tracked. I wrote each word out disconnected from the previous. Finally, I looked down upon my Rosetta Stone.

Your pleasure cost you…
Your mistake to not burn the pictures will cost more.
I wait half in the moonlight for your coins.
A janitorial shadow.

The chair caught my fall. My mind fractured. My mind raced. I met the librarian's eyes, and she nodded through tears. She anticipated my thoughts. Anticipated my questions.

"He could—," she choked out, "he could be her vengeance."

"How?" Was all I managed through the fog of disbelief.

"He found the pictures one night while cleaning. He then found the poor girl's story with patience. Pieced it together stone by stone. He listened to the calls. They never saw him. He was beneath notice. Then, Gavin waited. With the pictures gone, they panicked. The twins from the garden visited the Professor nearly every night. They schemed. They plotted. They just never saw the man who came to clean." The librarian appeared to be on the verge of collapse, but she persevered. "Don't you see? They're monsters! They butchered that poor girl!" The librarian trailed off to a whisper. "And he came for them. He came for them."

I stood fast, and my hand took to the grip of my gun.

"Don't worry, Detective. He is gone now. He wanted you to know. He wanted you to know why. He wanted you to tell her family. He wanted you to know. That is why I was not to intercede."

Nothing the woman said stopped me from scanning the room. An enclosed building with limited visibility and a killer near. A killer with government-funded experience and training. The totality of her words finally sunk in.

"Them? What else did he want me to know?"

The librarian steeled herself. "That he is not done." She had adopted a coldness in the mission from Halfpenny, no doubt. The delivery of the message assured it. I began to right myself. Plot to survive an exit. My hand did not waver with the gun braced against my thigh. A slink to the exit through the jungle of books. Eberhart was cemented in place. Still, she regarded me.

"A champion for her." Her chin lifted as she finished.

"Excuse me?"

"That's who he is." She had felt a need to explain. Thought now of why her love had done it. Why he had taken up the banner for a girl no one cared for. For a brief moment, she did not worry about what would come to the man she loved. She simply admired him. I wanted to correct her. Tell her no. He was much more than Helen's champion. Tell her he was a Patron of the Defenseless.

The librarian had not lied. I stalked the halls. Cleared the office. The entire wing was empty except for her and me. A flash message had been put over the radio for an unarmed white male, possibly in a custodial uniform. The jeers on the radio from other units had been expected. Carnage gripped the surrounding neighborhoods. Officers on the beat responded to calls of gunfire, domestic abuse, robbery, and the other components that make the cocktail of urban living so appealing. A detective coming over the radio zone requesting resources to pursue an unarmed man? Pound sand.

The midnight watch commander at Area 3 said the same when I returned with the car keys. He had a triple homicide with a known offender. The genesis being an argument in a bar that hosted one victim's birthday. My fairytale connections had to wait. And wait.

Left alone, I returned home. I waited for sleep to come. In view through the window, the moon was my only companion. Steady. Predictable. Traits to admire in a companion for life. Beautiful all nights, especially revealing its full self tonight. My predicament revealed itself.

Am I still to hunt the wolf or the man who hunts the wolf? Everything connected in my head did not exist on paper. A history unrecorded. A decision for the morning. Let Guy howl tonight. Let him not know for one more night. For Helen's vengeance hunted.

Goodnight moon.

— —————— ——————

Finn sat in a state of acceptance. He took the revelation well by a measure of his outfacing emotion. The cipher was solved. Halfpenny a killer motivated by vengeance. The cipher an invitation to the Professor's curiosity. It arrived around the time the photographs went missing from his possession and panic induced. The forgotten man watched who the Professor scurried off to in fear. He listened to who the Professor called. The Professor thought he could buy the working man off. The librarian's loquaciousness built it out.

"Patron of the Defenseless? I knew I liked him. Never doubt a Marine," Finn said. He wore a slight grin to accompany the chain store shirt and tie combination.

"Noted." I gave him a look intending to signal agreement. But my face was bereft of color from the lack of sleep. The moral conflict had not abided within. One of Helen's killers had met his fate. The others seemingly still to be targeted. Was that not justice? No. No. Violent retribution had occurred. An intoxicating notion as it may be, it warred with the pillars of society. It brought me joy to learn the Professor had been hunted and cornered. That he knew prolonged terror for his actions. It satisfied blood lust.

Helen. Her parents. Halfpenny did what society refused to do. They controlled the city. They would never have faced the consequences.

No. Not for justice. Not for textbook ideals. For memory. The Jardin's deeds forever attached to their name. Staked to them. A murder in the dark deprived the city and a small town of the truth. The result to be a shroud of victimhood to conceal the Jardins. While the memory of Helen from a small town was one of suicide. One of choice. One of quitting. Her parents left to drown in an attempt to convince neighbors of the truth. A public prosecution to solidify the truth into memory. The memory of Helen restored, and the memory of the Jardin name tarnished. History must be documented.

Finn had initially been content. He had seen Halfpenny act as the hand of God. A walking Old Testament. It had been the notion of the memory of Helen by those who knew her that brought him to me. The notion of her parent's closure. The rightful wrapping of Wilmington's collective arms around a lost daughter. Not for her name to be whispered as a cautionary tale of a wayward soul, but as a stolen daughter. The distinction mattered to Finn. It mattered to me.

"Do you want to break it to Hartes, or should I?"

I contemplated the question posed. I had done the work. I had crossed Hartes' orders.

"No, your reputation is to remain intact. I'm already the outcast here. My actions. When this rolls up and makes it to the Jardins, let them know it was me. It would be expected. We can still keep you in the dark."

I stopped his protestations. The memory of the previous fight with Hartes had legitimized my title, and I was in no mood to allow a backslide. By the time we were four steps from the office doorway, he resigned himself to the fact that this was not to be his fight.

At the entry to the door, I turned back to Finn.

"Alea Iacta Est."

CHAPTER TWENTY-FOUR

Even liquid poison had not dulled it. Delicious but destructive. A can of Coke sat half drank next to the driver's seat. Round two of a dopamine reward. I told myself it would help. Hartes had not even cracked the door for my return to the investigation. It was to be handled by Danes and Visoliv. Danes was a fine detective, but with less than twelve months until retirement. Men in that situation did not risk a pension at the finish line. Visoliv was the son of the Chief of Patrol. Nepotism was a time-honored department tradition.

Hartes hadn't battled my logic. My solve. I had been too close to it all. That was his assessment. He requested a progress report. He would alert the command staff. Answer the questions. Ensure the appropriate people, including targets, were notified. Additional patrol visibility in their residential vicinity. His response was sterile. Fluorescent lighting to my raw lightning. The keystone identified, and I was to sit back. Take a couple days off, he said. I thanked my patience that I hadn't spit on the ground.

The glow from the gas station sign continued to flicker and cast an annoying light over the car. The lottery advertisement in the window was inviting, but my luck was out. I sat. I waited with my thoughts. We agreed to meet here. Another drink of Coke, perhaps.

A knock on the car window. It brought my attention to the gun in the cupholder in front of the Coke. My iron grip on the handle.

"Take the scenic route?" I asked.

"Forgot how lovely a gas station off 290 is," Finn remarked. There was a lot to admire. The locals milled. Broken bottles littered the cracked pavement. Weeds that belonged to a jungle burst through the openings.

"Decent selection inside. Free."

"Nothing is free, kid. Nothing." He could not help but laugh at his own line. Every neighborhood ghetto had this gas station. Indistinguishable from the others, but cops could come in for a few free items. The unspoken trade being the response from those same cops. When the station needed help, which they always did, guys showed up. Cleared it without question.

"Looks like we're free. Hartes even gave me the next two days off. Plenty of time to get ready for the ball."

"Are you back in the good graces of Owen yet?"

"Tonight. I made plans to meet him."

"Don't oversell. We need a slow reintegration, and the soirée will be the perfect first step back in."

"I know how." The truth slipped to Finn. A lifetime of takes had made the manipulation the novice step. I felt guilty for the manipulation of Owen. I had dared not tell my love the truth.

"Rest of our discussion remained unchanged?"

"Yes. No point in hiding in the shadows. We carry a torch to them. The Jardins will have expected us to slink away. They should already be unnerved by the prospect of being hunted. We will exploit illicit missteps. I intend to haunt Gabrielle and Guy. Let it start tomorrow night. We will get what we need to drag the whole fucking thing into the light. Tomorrow I light a fire in their bones."

"Tend to the bonfire in your soul, Winona. It can consume."

"Et tu?"

"I'm already ashes." He looked away while regarding a local. "Winona. You have to be careful. Keep your eyes open with regards to Halfpenny too."

"I don't think he will be our problem. He could've made a move on me at the University. I wouldn't've stood a chance. He's a killer, but with a purpose. That's my read."

"Aye. That he is. The question is, what will happen if something gets in the way of that purpose. It's been gnawing at me how I missed it. I've run through our interactions over and over. I could barely sleep. Niamh nearly lost it with me over the pacing. Do you remember when we met him?"

"I remember being thankful for you being there. Your shared experiences...." I still was not comfortable talking to the man of war. I was afraid to kick a stone. To trigger an avalanche.

"War. Yes. We shared the war. We shared combat. We shared the Marine Corps. You can tell pretty quickly when you're talking to another man who went if they lived 12 months inside with running water or if they were walking in the jungle. Rotated taking point. I knew which he was. He knew I was like him. An instant recognition. It is difficult to explain." He slightly raised his hand to forestall me. He continued, "I knew he had killed. No doubt in my mind. I wore a groove into the floor over what I missed, though. It finally hit me. It wasn't who he was while a Marine. It was what he said he did after the war. Well, where he said he went. Halfpenny said he went to Phoenix, we thought the city. Then to Chicago. Everyone had different motivations when they got out. I didn't think much of it. But Phoenix. The Phoenix Program. Congress held hearings. Maybe you read about it in school. It was the CIA's weapon to counter the Vietcong. Rip out their structural roots. Kidnapping, heavy interrogation, and assassination.

He told us who he was, and we didn't see him. We looked right past him too."

A cold draft followed Finn's words into the cabin of the car. A killer. A clever killer.

My closet had been open for hours. Goldilocks the mood. Clothes had fallen to the floor or been thrown out of the way. The red cocktail dress was too slutty and too obvious. Countless women had no doubt thrown themselves at Owen in such a manner. They had one card to play. The dark blue gown was too conservative. I still wanted him to see a woman with a desire to be wanted. I had caught him with mystery. I should lean in on that sentiment.

As I worked the closet, the guilt was building brick by brick. My frame too small to be a hod carrier underneath the weight of it. I had to about-face with Owen and have him take me to the soirée. It was the only reasonable path with the Jardins. My name to be "plus one." No trace on a guest list. Deniability. The twins projecting out of fear. The final flourish of fate was that it was set to be a masquerade ball. In truth, I wanted to see the fear in the Jardin's eyes through the slits.

Scene after scene played out. Interactions imagined. Words said. Power dynamics shifted. I could taste the precipitous exposure. Their entire lives, they'd never known true fear. I couldn't be visceral vengeance, but I could let them know it stalked them. A trained killer possessed by purpose pursued.

Their pursuer. It dawned on me that Halfpenny had been nary a concern to me. His justice wouldn't do.

My dress hung over the chair in the corner of his bedroom. Exhaustion set in after the level of physical exertion. I'd worn it for only a few minutes. Half asleep, Owen pulled me in. His solid arms held me against him with tender strength. His hand gently grazed me. The same arms had held me across his knee not too long ago. The handprint he marked me with still evident from behind. A balance I needed. His slut and maybe his wife.

I needed everything else he'd done tonight too. He had no hesitation in extending the plus one. Confirmed by the receipt of his gift to me. I'd overthought the entire process. To Owen, it had been our joke still. No matter who sent out an invitation. It had fortified his love of the prank. He'd been muffed by my initial anger. They'd taken the bait so deeply that they were now presenting the event themselves. Not just sneaking away for a fortune-telling and gypsy curse, but they had taken ownership. Arrogance, petty games, and an unending desire for control blinded them. Or so Owen thought.

He fell asleep. I slipped out of his arms. My naked silhouette cast to the wall with the moonlight that peeked through the windows. A few steps and a look back through the French doors to his bedroom. Owen hadn't stirred. Still naked. Still beautiful. Still asleep. Again, I wanted to snap a Polaroid of the moment.

The table was the same as we'd left it. His gift to me lay in the box still. The ribbons strewn open. I admired it again. A thoughtful man he was. I picked up the invitation. It'd been encased in a gothic frame. The summons inside simple. A plain white business card. A call to converse with the dead. It'd been written on a typewriter. The title of the gala written first. "Hell is Empty…"

"…and all the devils are here," I whispered to myself the rest. Shakespeare's words. Clever, Gabrielle.

-- --- ----

I felt good. I looked better. The dress cut deep in the chest and high up the thigh. Tight enough to accentuate what I had and to improve what I lacked. A deep black to devour the light. A shawl draped across my shoulders. Heels red-bottomed. They'd been one of Owen's first gifts. The latest in my hand. Masks were best suited to be worn after you were inside the premise. Our driver gave a doubletake when we told him where to take us. I reassured him we were not grave robbers.

The entrance gates to the cemetery were open and flanked by two men. The brick wall that marked the ground's boundary blocked any view in, but a slight mist of light was visible. Now we saw why. Candelabras sat atop gravestones. Nature bent the knee and cooperated perfectly. A gloomy affair to set the mood.

The man on the right quickly inspected our invitation and gestured for us to enter. The first step to the gravel pathway emitted a chill. Owen mistook my pause. I now knew I walked amongst the spirits who felt tethered to their bones. Those who had refused to wander away. He wouldn't have understood. The path to the chapel was framed by couplings of smaller candles. Gabrielle had done a marvelous job. The mood struck a level of authenticity and sincerity that would strip any notion a guest had of the cartoonish buffoonery of late-night advertisements for fortune-telling. The chapel was framed in the distance, with the light from inside projecting out through the stained glass windows. A kaleidoscope of color on the thin vapor of fog that rode the gloomy night.

"Do you like it?" Owen's voice cut through the brisk air. I turned to take him in. Still, my breath caught at the way a tuxedo fit him. Effortless from the first day. I loved him from the same day.

"The scene?"

"The mask, Winona. I know it is a bit foolish, but we should play the game along with everyone else." A slight embarrassment settled into me. He'd put thought into it, and I still held it in my hand like yesterday's paper. A classic masquerade mask, it flared wide and covered the top of my face but gave my eyes enough to see.

"I love it!" I adjusted my purse carefully. The weight of my revolver inside made me feel like I was dragging a cinder block on a string. I was careful to position myself. My mask slid on, and I smiled as he tucked my hair behind my ears and gently straightened the mask. My heart beat wildly as we felt so alone.

"I'm in love with you, Winona Winthrop. Know you hold my heart in your hands."

"…Promise?"

"I promise." His voice was firm. Not a waver. Not a trace of doubt. His hands remained steady as they cupped my face.

The worst cage locks from the inside, but his hand was the invitation for me to walk out to free my heart. I wanted to tell him just that. I desired to match his beauty of words, but my own shame cowered my voice. Still, I whispered, "I'll be in love with you forever." Let all who wandered witness my proclamation and pass judgment. They could do no worse than I have done to myself in the past.

He kissed me softly. His own mask slid into place. Hand in hand, we continued our candlelit walk to the sound of voices ahead. I wanted to pause to take it all in. The way he looked at me. An innocent love. A pure love. Not tainted by misdirection or lies.

"Is that a tear, Winona?" He looked over and wiped the tear that escaped past the mask.

"Just a happy tear. Let's go." Off we went.

An unassuming chapel. Walls that still held secrets. Our entrance did not cause a ripple, but I felt like a boulder dropped into a pond. A wide array of guests was scattered about in evening wear and masks. Faces concealed beneath every color and decoration. From feathers to sequins. Even the serving staff wore fabric masks. Tray after tray proffered to the attendees in the maelstrom of the beginning.

A scan around the chapel revealed changes. Black lace wrapped the banisters. Chandeliers resplendent with candles hung. The pews had been removed to allow for unrestricted movement. The walls were not even left to their own device. Tarot cards half a man's size hung between the stained glass windows like tapestries. Display stands were everywhere. Tokens of death and the afterlife were on display. Items that appeared to span time and continents. The corresponding story neatly displayed alongside. I glanced over and confirmed that Owen was in the same state of intake. The dingy chapel no more. A museum to death and the afterlife now.

The floorboards emanated a dark power to even the most secular guest. The patrons talked amongst themselves, but you caught signs of unease when you looked closely. The slight movement of eyes to ensure it was seen where walls met. The sound of careful steps. The women, even the fiercely independent, held a little tighter to their men. We were all trespassers here, after all.

The sweeping hand of a serving girl returned my focus. I hadn't even noticed the girl before us. In truth, she might not have even noticed me by the track of her eyes. The last button undone to provide a plunging view mere moments before the approach would be my guess. I moved past her breasts and realized she did not offer drink nor sustenance. Rather a Ouija board and an invitation. I politely declined for both of us.

"Not one for games tonight?" Owen asked.

"There'll be games, baby, but not yet." I directed him to look to the altar. Dominated by two empty chairs on the dais with a stark bare wood table between them. The ornamentation and theatrics of the decorations came to die at the steps that rose. Esmeralda would've allowed only so much. The event was Gabrielle's, but the true séance belonged to Esmeralda. We continued in silence. Gravitationally pulled to a display of Aztec tools used for the sacrifice of humans. Difficult not to wince at the barbarity entwined in the story of the weapon.

Our funeral silence was broken by Nicholas of House Adfield. The gate broke open at that point. They all came through to pay their respects. The judge and her lover. Wave after wave of Guild royalty. All worthy of judgment, but none who I wanted before me. None of who I wanted to instill the new fear in. To tell ever so casually that they were now the prey. A capable predator with the potential to follow them day or night. No easy nights on thousand thread count sheets. I imagined the delivery. I imagined the planting of the information. I imagined the spawn of fear.

"Still with me?" Owen's hand on the small of my back registered first. Then the words he spoke.

"Sorry—"

"Don't be. I'm rather fond of your episodes of daydreaming. It's a sign of creativity. It's endearing." A smile graced his face. The genuine one that was all mine.

He reassured me without even knowing he had. My heart settled into a consistent rhythm to match my steps. We took in the knowledge around us. The fears and celebrations of people who came long before us. It made me wish Dakota were here. Her eyes wouldn't gloss over at the mention of history. I would've been her shepherd.

Still no sign of a garden. No Jardin had made an appearance yet. I was stuck instead with the banal conversations of the well-off. None of them insulting enough to be damning. None joyous enough to be a salvation. Caught in conversational purgatory again and again. People were still on edge. They kept things close to the chest on this night. These people were terrified. Weak followers who hid behind bloodline and money. Barely capable of tying their own shoes, let alone striving to cement their own personal power with murder. That is until a quiet murmur spread across the chapel. It rose enough to force Noah, the banker, to stop the dry assault of a recitation of favored holidays that trapped Owen and me. The source of the commotion was apparent.

Esmeralda had taken her seat. She hadn't commanded the attention, but it came to her anyhow. The anticipation was responsible for the reaction. She sat, and we all watched in silence. We stood like devotees to a deity. The witch did not acknowledge. Nor did she invite anyone to come forward. Paralysis was the result.

Then death brushed by my shoulder. They stepped into our field of vision. I had looked for a dress to help me. Gabrielle had no such concerns. Clothing could impede her at best. I expected the men would soon be able to find Esmeralda less of a draw.

Guy stood awkwardly. But now I knew the monster that lay within. A baring of his teeth at the sight of me. His mask more decorative than a representative totem. No wolf mask. He did not wish to reveal too much to me. He no doubt thought the law was his primary concern. How wrong.

"Hello, Owen. Winona." No crack in her confidence. A slight smile. More subdued than Guy's preposterous grin.

"I never knew a Jardin to make such a quiet entrance," Owen said. The odd man out. Ignorant to the game.

"Tonight is about the dead, Owen. Not the living. We're a respectful family." Her lips pursed when she finished. Her eyes affixed to him.

My gaze fell on the obnoxious presentation of her breasts. "I believe traditions with the dead may vary."

"By culture and by class," Gabrielle retorted.

I knew what I wanted. I wanted to call out down the street. To the car where Finn patiently sat. My own hand caressed my purse. Felt the handle of my revolver. Violent fantasy to violent fantasy. Reel after reel played in my head in mere moments. The allure of instant vengeance was an intoxicating notion. I had no doubt why it'd set Halfpenny in motion. Even now, bloodlust ran wild. Memory, though. The memory of Helen being the girl Wilmington would try and forget. The girl whispered about and then forgotten. Not a victim, but forever a quitter. No. The Jardins would be brought to the excruciating light. The proper path had been laid, but they would know true fear first.

"It truly is a shame your talents were taken away from the Professor's case, Winona." Guillaume broke the grin to speak. A direct and to-the-point personality apparently ran in the genetics. Still, it caught me off guard to be addressed in the open.

"The department works in mysterious ways, Guy." I caught the slight hesitation at my emphasis of the hypocorism.

"I didn't know that, Winona. How did you two know?" Owen came across as genuinely befuddled at the development. His eyes came to rest on me. A slight tense in his body came along with being left out.

"The Professor was a dear friend of ours, Owen. We have been in regular contact with members of the command staff at the police department. For the best interest of us all."

"Information a couple notches away, even up, can be filtered. Did it ever worry you, Guy, that what you'd been told had been selective? The people you know may believe they are telling you everything, but what if they have not? Your trust in other's obedience and reliance in their forthcoming truth has an uncontrolled variable in this case."

"True, Winona, but we've found the requisite information can be drawn out with the right pressure…or massaging. The people we hear from are in their position for a reason. They would not be much use to us or anyone else if they did not prove reliable."

Guy made a fair point, and he knew it. He hadn't taken a step back. The aloof and strange boy who tagged along with his twin was gone. Mental acuity ran in the genetics as well. The fact that Gabrielle's eyes stayed on Owen didn't fool me. Her ears were devoutly dedicated to this conversation. Violent reels replayed.

"Trust is a beautiful component of human interaction. The trust they place in you. The trust to deliver your end of the bargain. Or the trust to follow you. To know they are safe even when they are vulnerable. We women do it on every first date and many times after. Just praying we will not be unceremoniously dumped in the woods," I regaled. He'd struck. It had been my turn. Not a slip. A deliberate show of strength to regain the high ground.

"I agree." Gabrielle's two words caused her brother and me to abruptly stop. The thunder sapped. I turned to her to catch her smile expanding. "Women do have to be so careful with who they jaunt. Strangers carry an inherent danger when biology tilts the scales. I've always been rather selective for that reason. How about you, Winona? Does it factor into your wide decisions on partners?"

This bitch.

"I have my man, Gabrielle. If you hadn't noticed." An instinctual hand placed on Owen's arm. He didn't recoil from me but didn't lean into the gesture, either. To him just another tiff in the cold war between Gabrielle and me. I could read on his face how he tired of such roes. He had no layered context to what he witnessed. The double disadvantage of being uninformed and being a man blinded him to the severity of the conversation. I wanted to point a finger at them both and explain it all to him. Expose with blunt force trauma the truth. Of Helen. Of the cover-up. Of the power exercised by the Guild. Tell him I was not being a juvenile, jealous girlfriend. Well, not just that. Instead, I let the silence linger. I would be able to tell him once it all unraveled. I would need his forgiveness.

"Well, NOW you do. Tell me, Owen, did Winona ever tell you how she found this place?"

A palpitation of the heart. A blanking of thoughts. I stood as still as stone. Gabrielle, a gorgon.

"I do not think I have heard that tale." Owen turned to me. An innocent smile. Anticipation in what he expected to be a sweet story. My chest caved in.

"Shall you, Winona, or can I have the pleasure? It was the night we first met, was it not?"

Owen left. I'd been unable to voice a single word. No repudiation. He saw the tears in my eyes. The pain that emanated outward from him had been of a spiritual nature. A deep wound delivered by my own hands. Still, I stood shattering in place.

Finally, I whispered, "How?"

"I told you, Winona, people talk. Identify what they want, and they share. Identify what they need, and they spill. The question of who to ask can be difficult. You were close to no one, well, that partner of yours. Griffin? Him, we did not even try. Guy knew the type and said it would only tip our hand. Lovely how he kept so close. A couple blocks and a night spent alone in a car while you partook in the fine dining. That is dedication. Is he close now? Doesn't matter, I suppose. With your lone-hand status, it turned to 'Where did Winona Winthrop frequent?' The spots where the desperate travel to carve out a place in higher society? Yes, obviously. Where were you territorial, though? Where did you not take Owen? Disgusting place. What was the name of it?"

"The Ossuary," Guy injected. Smooth and calm.

"Yes. The Queen of Bones you were. Your vault of secrets behind rolled steel bars on the window. Thankfully, we had the combination. That bartender broke so easily when Guy laid out his reward. Do forgive him soon. Heroin can be a kiss of death."

They both laughed. Then they walked away. I still hadn't moved.

CHAPTER TWENTY-FIVE

I stood as a boulder in the river current of patrons and guests moving through the venue. The slow trickle of tears lost to the passing. Owen's departure noted. Still, I hadn't moved. Even the cast of an eye from Esmeralda from the dais hadn't inclined me to move. Through blurred vision, I watched the society that had gathered sneak away from their pack to speak with Esmeralda. Waiters and waitresses were the only ones who approached. A decline through a wave of the hand. Content to die in place.

No.

I'd lost Owen, but I hadn't been here for Owen. I would not let my mistakes shatter glass. The Jardins had made a move to destroy my love. They could have my career next. Let them put me to the stake. Helen Waterloo's memory would be amended. Helen Waterloo would ascend to the patron saint of Wilmington. A martyr for the working class. The forgotten. The defenseless.

I dried my tears with a napkin offered by the waitress who passed by. The girl was young, and her face sympathetic. One button higher than our first encounter. She did not know my plight, but her concern dwarfed that of any of the countless people in the room I'd come to know. We knew our own.

I moved through the chapel. My tears dried. My mascara ran but was hidden by the mask. The people continued to part. A small smile cracked Esmeralda's expression as I walked by. Her eyes maintained on the reading before her but undeniably read me too. We knew our own.

Gabrielle and Guy were nowhere in sight. I didn't know how much time had passed or where they'd gone. I didn't know how you celebrated the destruction of life. No toast had been made. No appointment with black magic. They'd simply vanished. They wouldn't have left. They killed for sport. They were far too proud of their cruelty. They would want to watch the carcass decompose. They had taken photographs, after all. I needed a better vantage point. No way for a surprise walkup from behind. The brick wall next to the entry doors would suffice. A view of everything in front. A view of who came and went.

The river flowed clear without a boulder. The dark arts resumed. Curiosity took hold. Slowly the tension faded from their shoulders as they grew comfortable trespassing on the dead. No relief came to me. My hand still tapped the handle in my purse with rhythm. I still held the message to be delivered. The seven trumpets for Gabrielle and Guillaume Jardin.

The door swung outward quickly, and the clink of glass followed. Nothing. Not Owen. Not Guillaume. Not Gabrielle. Nothing. A waiter exited. Drink flutes deftly managed on a tray. I must've surprised him to be standing in the shadow of the door. He hadn't been the first to walk by and not take notice. The shadows danced tonight. He half-turned and inclined me for a drink. I politely declined. The man should've been less shy in engagement. I wanted to share the tip.

Instead, I waved him off like royalty. Let him proceed out. He'd seen my jewels and judged me, no doubt. I was not one of the others. I wanted him to know. I wanted all the staff to know. I didn't see them as a monolithic serving block. Dressed the same. Masked the same. They were individuals. Even he accented himself with a lapel pin. A—

The pin.

Where had he gone? The door held wide open to the dark night. My eyes searched frantically through the grounds. Fine suits and dresses. Waiters. Waitresses. Guests gathered outside and were attended to. I couldn't distinguish in the light of the chapel, let alone in the dark.

The pin.

I had only blinked. He had offered a drink. I had declined. A moment's thought on the interaction. He had disappeared in that minuscule frame of time.

I peeked at the interior of the chapel with a wish for Owen.

The pin. The lapel pin was a fox. Halfpenny.

Under a waning gibbous moon, I moved through the clustered ignorance.

Slow is smooth. Smooth is fast.

I had been on countless raids. Worked through buildings with armed offenders after a pursuit. The hunt was the same here. I told myself that. The difference was the people. The handle of a .38 special in my hand. Concealed by the purse.

I couldn't induce panic among the rows of graves. Waiter after waiter. Man after man. I worked through each. Nothing seen.

The door of the chapel opened behind me, and out walked Charlotte. Hidden beneath an ornate forest green feathered mask to match her dress. She zeroed in and began to close in.

"How are you, dear? I—"

"Guillaume and Gabrielle?! Charlotte, have you seen them?"

I would not fail. I would not allow them to become martyrs. I needed to see their names nailed to the mantle of the victim. Then, their obituary would be written correctly. Nailed to the deed they did. Helen's memory corrected.

"Dear, I heard what happened. I was late, you see. Owen will—"

"I don't give a fuck about Owen right now. Do you know where Guillaume and Gabrielle are?!" The pause from an active search for conversation had been detrimental. The space to think had allowed a rabid mentality to take hold. Poor Charlotte's face confirmed it.

Slow is smooth. Smooth is fast.

My own eyes continued to search through our exchange of words.

"Are you okay, Winona?"

Play the game. Even here. Even now.

"Yes. Sorry, Charlotte. A pressing matter has arisen, and I need to speak with the Jardins."

"Well, I just saw Gabrielle. She is inside entertaining."

Inside. Lights. A crowd.

"…and Guillaume?"

"He came out here about two drinks ago." The constant state of surveillance amongst the core tenets of the Guild had come to use. I regained an even keel. Information to register gave way to build out the task.

"Thank you, Charlotte. I need your help." I noted the slight hesitation on her face. No doubt, a desire to avoid stepping into a relationship quagmire. "For work, Charlotte. I need your help for work, and I need it now." The hesitation traded for curiosity.

"Tell me, Winona."

Charlotte set off down the long drive and three blocks to unleash a hound. Finn would be here soon. One Jardin stood safe in the chapel. The other unaccounted for. I traveled deep into the cemetery. Deep in the night, the light from a half-hidden moon was the only guide.

Headstones ranged from traditional upright to full-on monuments.

Slow is smooth. Smooth is fast.

Row after row, I looked for signs. A disturbance. A struggle. Grass bent. Blood droplets. Nothing after the bare steps. My heels had been discarded. The commotion of the chapel acted as a distant marker. The systematic search balanced against caution. The knowledge that a killer with a purpose made me pursue. How far would he go to ensure his vengeance?

Smoke.

A cigarette had been burnt here recently. A tripwire to the explosion of memory. A smell synonymous with my father. It stabbed at my senses. It'd been a mark for distance as a child. Where to tread lightly in a small house. Here it'd been put out more than moments ago. The faint trace indicated nearly half an hour since it'd been snuffed out. My father would've been deep in sleep at that point.

I canvassed north. There. A carved stone slab sat atop a granite pedestal. A half-smoked filtered stick lay on the corner. The .38 took point. I rounded to find death stacked. Death below ground. Death above it. Guillaume lay before the grave marker. A rictus grin. His throat slit. The tongue pulled through. An empty champagne flute next to the man. A scrap of paper inside where the golden liquid should've been.

"Follow the waiter to the key."

Typed on a typewriter. An ink stamp of a fox walked over the words. Vengeance had won over memory. I had one chance.

– – – – –   – – – –

The ground was hell on my feet. Outside the chapel, they drew more attention than the weapon in hand. The newly minted congregants of the dark arts thought theatrics were in effect. No sign of Finn. No sign of Charlotte. No one had seen her return yet. The Adfields were jealous. They believed Charlotte played a role in the game at hand too. Their senses were too dull to see the true panic in me. I had to keep Gabrielle Jardin alive. To drag her into the light. She had to breathe before the exposition of shame suffocated her. Halfpenny had gone to find her. Finn would find me. Into the chapel I went.

Guest after guest passed. Waiter after waiter. Still, I found neither. The symmetry of uniform worked against me. Gabrielle would be a blinding light in any room. Only candles here. The chapel floor continued as it had the entire night.

Where? I had to suppress the wave of shame. The memories of the man from a night of flight flooded over me. The moment we'd known in the sacristy. How we'd moved through the mini labyrinth in back. Between rooms, each stop a different stage in the pursuit of pleasure. It was a quiet place. Tight confines. Poorly lit. Gabrielle would have made it her place of recluse. An entrance to the side of the reredos. The elaborate décor ended at the back entrance. Down the hall, light shone behind a closed door.

Slow is smooth. Smooth is fast.

The .38 led point again. Eight open doors to clear to reach the ninth. I moved horizontally, but it felt like a descent.

Clear. Clear. Clear. Clear. Clear. Clear. Clear. Clear.

Nary a sound from behind the door cracked open. Framed by the light from inside. I nudged it open. I made entry.

Clear.

Except for Gabrielle. Bent forward at the waist from an opulent couch of velvet. Her hair concealed the face that rested on a small table. A step closer, and she shot upright. A trace of the white powder from the table still stained her nose.

"The couch was not here before," I remarked.

She sat momentarily stunned and motionless. Silent for once.

"Your gun seems a bit of an excessive response for recreational drug use. But maybe it's for sharing the truth with Owen."

My blood turned to fire. A moment and the barrel was pointed at Gabrielle. Her face kept composure. Her veins betrayed her. Her neck pulsed like a raging river. The left hand clenched into a tight fist. White from being deprived of circulation. The right hand the only movement. She reached for a pillow. She would need more than that. The barrel returned to the ground. I took three more steps. Gabrielle Jardin exhaled in response.

"Now that we are civilized again. Take a seat, Win—"

"Shut up, bitch," I spoke, calmer than anticipated. "I'm here be—"

"I know exactly why you are here, Winona Winthrop. The poor girl who came to the city. Came from a wretched little town that clings to a river refusing to sweep it away."

I felt the barrel rise a quarter but steadied my desire. She registered it. She reached again for her pillow but stopped and continued, "Don't you understand? We know. Guy and I have been updated from before you came on to investigate the murder of Hickey. What a convenience that was. We still haven't figured out who to thank for that. Who was trying to curry favor with us? We will pay that debt. Anyhow, that girl from the backwoods. Pretty in a lowborn way. Guy discovered her after the Professor invited her to our event. First, Guy wanted to play. Hickey wanted to watch from afar. The usual. The girl, though. I saw how she looked at Guy. Her eyes adored him like the others. They were greedy for what he stood to stand on. Like the others too. The problem was her spirit. I could see the implosion at the end. We would not be able to buy this one off. Not after she said she was pregnant. Guy could be a slave to his desires, but even he knew when to be rational. The perfect time to act on our dreams. The perfect convergence of need and want. The theatrics were the only way to fool her. The girl was clever, after all."

Pregnant. Helen. My chest wanted to cave in. My own body conflicted as the tears of sorrow also shed.

"You are being hunt—"

"Hush, Winona. We both know power is the way of the world. It's why I am telling you now. Absolute power we have. You could chisel what I said into stone, and it would go nowhere. The words of a scorned ex after the philanthropist lover of her former man. Yes, Winona. Owen will be mine too. Everyone saw what happened tonight. I would not even have to coach a statement. Checkmate, darling."

It wasn't the creak of a door but rather the scuff of a shoe on the floor that alerted me. Gabrielle took her eyes from me to the left.

"Excuse me! All staff was given clear directions to stay clear of here."

My gaze traveled to the right, and I saw what Gabrielle had missed. The single mark ka-bar held in Halfpenny's hand. Positioned at his side. The handle black. Blade black. No reflection. He regarded me.

"Aglaope." A slight bow of the head to me. The killer, dressed as a waiter, turned to the heiress with square shoulders and a strong walk of purpose.

"Hello, Dauphine." Halfpenny had extinguished any warmth in the room with two words. I caught a glimpse of Gabrielle. Fear etched into her face as she sat stone still. Finally, she caught what she had missed.

Halfpenny spoke slowly but moved quickly. Moved quickly for Gabrielle.

I blinked and stared down the barrel of the .38. He led with the knife. I fired twice. Hit twice. Chest and arm. He lay in place. The man's chest rose and fell still. I made my way with the barrel at point. His eyes closed, yet he drew breath. I whispered, "I'm sorry." I did not know if he registered the words. I would tell him I had to do—

Thunder cracked. Lightning struck. Rain ran down my decolletage. Yet no thunder clouds overhead. A wood plank ceiling is all I saw. The pain brought reality. Not rain, but blood. The ruffle of a dress. Gabrielle rose with a .45 caliber 1911. I gasped with the pain. I gasped at the realization.

"Well, how convenient of a night." Shoulders back. Heel to toe, she came for me. My .38 was nowhere. My hand frantically searched. I felt weak and getting weaker. The rain worsened. Blood in a cough. Gabrielle kept her pace calm and steady. Only to pause and lean down. She re-emerged into view with my .38. Eyes closed, I braced for the answer I had always sought but now did not want.

Mama, I don't want to die.

No shot rang out. Only the click of heels reverberated. Eyes back open. Gabrielle had gone to the door. A check of the hall. A soft close of the door. Thorough, even now. She turned her attention back, but her heels did not set in my direction.

"NO!" I intended a bang but produced only a whimper. Still, I crawled.

I saw the .38 in her hand. Now I saw the intent plain. The pain thumped with each movement of a crawl. The shot that now rang out. Gabrielle stood over Halfpenny. An execution pointblank. I only made it to the tips of Halfpenny's fingers. Face down, I wanted to weep.

"How convenient indeed. I worried when you didn't take my bait earlier but thank the gods, you didn't. I had the self-defense case set, but this is clean beyond reason. Know you killed this man. Know he killed you. You can die a hero, Winona. I'll give the eulogy of how you gave your life to save mine. Consider it my gift. Guy is going to revel in the fortunate turn of events. Luck forever on our side."

"Gabrielle…"

"Last words, darling? I do not take confession."

"…hell isn't empty, bitch. Guy already waits for you."

I would never see a star collapse into itself, but I turned and saw Gabrielle Jardin register my words. A moment of pause, then a supernova. The energy was mine, though. I was to my knees in one motion. I took the ka-bar from the tip of Halfpenny's fingers to my hand. Her dress slit served as my guide. The knife plunged into her inner thigh. I rotated the blade. The woman's cry pierced the dead air. I fell back. Faded to an empty black.

CHAPTER TWENTY-SIX

The light bright. The voice familiar.

"Winona?" My name carried differently on an English accent.

I nudged a hand to the side. Cold metal. Not the bars to a cell but the guardrails of a hospital bed. My hands instinctively raised. There was not a cuff on either wrist. I blinked away the fluorescent light, and Owen came into focus.

"Hi." A simple greeting was all that came to mind. No need to complicate it. I knew too little and wanted the cocoon still. He looked down and smiled. Brushed my hair behind my ear. The beeps and drips of the room swept into my senses now. Time passed differently from a hospital bed. I didn't know if we sat in silence for minutes or hours. No intrusion to the serenity till I broke it.

"Finn? Where is Finn? Is he—" I sat up with the proclamation. How had I been so callously selfish to bask in my own romantic love without answers? Stupid girl. Owen's hand steadied me with a light touch of the arm that propped me up.

"He's safe, Winona. He's safe. In fact, I already told him we owe him the name of our firstborn. He found you, Winona. Cut through the party like a Winged Hussar at Vienna. He found you. He called in an officer down over the radio. He carried you into the ambulance himself. Patrol cars blocked intersections your entire way to the hospital. I…I had just returned. I saw the lights, but the policemen stopped me at the entrance. I could have been the Queen, and they would not have cared. They knew you were hurt, and not a soul was coming in…or out." He paused to let me speak, but I motioned him to continue. "Finn found me. Demanded a bloke to take me to the hospital. He stayed behind, Winona."

"Where…Where is he now?"

"The hallway. He has been your guardian. Well, more of a rabid dog. I dare a man to attempt entry without an invitation. I think one of your uniformed superiors soiled himself coming across Finn. I do not think he has slept, Winona."

"Call him in." I sat up and felt the strike of pain even through the numbness of painkillers. For the first time, I looked around the room and realized the pleasant aroma had been from a bouquet of flowers next to my bed. The card indicated they came from The Bridgeport Flower Company. We did not forget our own. My own bedside clock was next to them.

Owen went to the hall, and now the door creaked back open. With downcast eyes, Finn slowly closed it behind himself. He stayed near the door. He looked awful. Sleep-deprived and worn down from a heightened sense of alert. Yet still, he stood straight.

"Am I contagious?"

I saw a smile break from beneath.

"I'm so sorry, Wi—"

"Shut up, Finn. You saved my life."

"You shouldn't have been alone. I shouldn't have left you exposed."

"Do you remember you told me you wanted to be a cartographer when you were young? Do you remember what I wanted to be?"

"You never told me."

"Dead, Finn. I wanted to be dead. But I don't want that anymore. You showed me."

He continued to grumble and gravel as if he had failed. Every attempt I made to shush him just brought more protest. How could I have been so lucky in a sentinel sent to me?

"Griffin, what of it all?" I needed to know. He could tell me the answers I sought without any more questions.

"Guy is dead. Found with a Cuban necktie near a grave. Gabrielle bled out from your slice of her femoral artery. Dead by the time I arrived." He read my reaction and answered the unsaid, "When I called in the 10-1, the cavalry came. Understand it's different when it's a woman, Winona. I don't want to hear anything from you. I've heard enough from Niamh. It just is. The guys saw me carrying you. They wanted blood. It took my charm to keep them from starting to get answers from the guests. The street deputy who came to take control of the scene saw too. He listened and concluded the same sequence of events took place as I did. It took a full damn night and the next day to piece the rest of it together for them. It's memorialized. The whole thing. The county cover-up. The parties. The Professor and Jardin connection. The cipher. Halfpenny's vengeance. Helen. All of it. Whoever the Jardins had on the payroll can't touch it now. Their power only invited the weak, anyhow. Even the papers have begun to write it up. The structure collapsed in on itself."

"…Halfpenny?' My voice was weak in reluctance to be heard.

"Dead, Winona." Finn looked away from me for the first time. No doubt he lusted for the deed done by Halfpenny. I knew the Valkyries had come to the chapel. Carried him to Valhalla, where he was waiting to do battle again. Or waiting for his love.

Ms. Eberhart. Forever a Ms. now.

My turn to look away.

"The Waterloos?" I asked a question I didn't know the answer to now.

"I'm going to go today. The Chief of Detectives is going to accompany me. To extend his apologies and condolences. It will all be set straight, Winona. Helen's memory restored. They are going to talk to Wilmington stakeholders."

A blessed sense of relief set over me. It was as if I felt Helen's soul take rest. Finally free. Yet I knew I had one more obligation.

"Finn. Helen was pregnant. Her parents deserve to know."

Finn nearly cracked. A blow I hadn't wished to deliver but knew I must. A weight now shared. Finn accompanied me in silence for a while. Eventually, he continued to answer my nuanced questions. I dug deep at any potential weakness. Everything had been uncovered. Brought to the light. He let himself out and vowed he would be back from Wilmington soon.

Owen returned and took his seat beside me. I smiled at the knowledge I'd been told. I smiled at the company I had now.

Owen placed a hand against my cheek and spoke, "When I went to your place for a few items to make you comfortable, I saw a number written down. I called. Roundabout phone calls later, and I connected with her. Dakota was already on her way. She will be here soon."

Of course, she had read the stars.

Fox Hunt

To:
From:

asked

1) pg 98 line 6 word 9
2) pg 78 line 20 word 8
3) pg 100 line 28 word 6
4) pg 100 line 6 word 5
5) X
6) pg 24 line 8 word 6
7) pg 223 line 7 word 7
8) pg 257 line 5 word 12
9) pg 147 line 8 word 7
10) pg 190 line 15 word 9
11) pg 134 line 5 word 3
12) pg 81 line 11 word 4
13) pg 81 line 11 word 5
14) pg 153 line 13 word 10
15) pg 294 line 25 word 4
16) pg 166 line 5 word 9
17) pg 118 line 29 word 11
18) pg 207 line 1 word 11
19) pg 17 line 1 word 8
20) pg 2 66 line 16 word 3
21) pg 13 line 1 word 3
22) pg 98 line 24 word 3

Clue: You here the key and think it can carry an end
      to it's end, yet it cannot carry.

Cipher Notes

C.F. Forest

Cipher Notes

Cipher Notes

C.F. Forest

Cipher Notes

Fox Hunt

Cipher Notes

ABOUT THE AUTHOR

A resident of Chicago, Illinois.

Fox Hunt

Made in the USA
Monee, IL
16 July 2023

39413405R00187